Praise for *In a* [Fix]

"Bright, fizzy, sexy, and amusing—th[e] [perfect] tack of postsummer blues."

"A fast-paced, sexy romp with characters as original as its intriguing premise!" —Diana Gabaldon, #1 *New York Times* bestselling author of *Outlander*

"In this sparkling series opener, Ciel Halligan is not a shapeshifter, but she does have a genetic quirk that allows her to look like someone else by changing her aura. A wisecracking, whirlwind romp of a romantic urban fantasy adventure."
—*Publishers Weekly*

"Seamlessly blending humor and action, Grimes thoroughly impresses with her debut novel. *In a Fix* features a hilarious heroine with an unusual ability and a penchant for getting into trouble, making for a refreshing read. Add in two yummy alpha male love interests, both of whom the heroine cleverly holds her own against, and the reader is sure to be fully entertained. This deliciously sexy and fun-filled romp simply is a must-read."
—*RT Book Reviews* (4 ½ stars, Top Pick!)

"Fresh, fun, and sexy." —Vicki Pettersson, *New York Times* bestselling author of the Sign of the Zodiac series

"Urban fantasy and paranormal novels crowd the shelves these days, so this reviewer is impressed by debut author Grimes's fresh take on the genre. Fans of both hard and soft fantasy and crime drama will love her protagonist's spunky, irreverent attitude as well as Grimes's character-building skills and unusual story line." —*Library Journal* (starred review)

Tor Books by Linda Grimes

In a Fix

Quick Fix

QUICK FIX

Linda Grimes

A TOM DOHERTY ASSOCIATES BOOK

NEW YORK

QUICK FIX

Copyright © 2013 by Linda Grimes

A Tor Book
Published by Tom Doherty Associates, LLC
175 Fifth Avenue
New York, NY 10010

www.tor-forge.com

Tor® is a registered trademark of Tom Doherty Associates, LLC.

The Library of Congress Cataloging-in-Publication Data is available upon request.

ISBN 978-0-7653-3181-6 (trade paperback)
ISBN 978-1-4299-5645-1 (e-book)

Tor books may be purchased for educational, business, or promotional use. For information on bulk purchases, please contact Macmillan Corporate and Premium Sales Department at 1-800-221-7945 extension 5442 or write specialmarkets @macmillan.com.

First Edition: August 2013

Printed in the United States of America

0 9 8 7 6 5 4 3 2 1

For my whole wacky, wise, and wonderful family—
family is everything.

QUICK FIX

Chapter 1

Decapitation, I thought the second time the hand landed on my butt. Perhaps evisceration. Or I could just stick with a classic— dip him in honey and stake him out over a giant fire-ant pile.

I gritted my teeth and smiled at the man beside me, all the while glaring my murderous intent over his shoulder at Billy Doyle, who was *supposed* to be recording the incident, not passing the time of day with every female from eight to eighty who stopped to flirt with him. (Granted, that part wasn't entirely his fault. His field of charm worked like gravity—once it caught you, it was hard to escape.)

Damn it. I knew I should have pushed him into the tiger habitat when I had the chance.

Billy, several yards away, widened his gorgeous eyes at me in the picture-of-innocence look he'd probably mastered in utero, and cocked his head toward his little sister, Molly. She was a miniature female version of Billy with dark, wavy hair (in her case contained by a thick braid that hung halfway down her back), inky blue eyes, and eyelashes lush enough that she'd never need mascara. She even had the Doyle dimples.

Molly had just pointed her brother's high-end cell phone my way and, judging by her gleeful expression, was capturing my posterior for posterity. Trust Billy to foist his one chore off on the nearest willing relative. Why do something yourself when you had an adoring sibling within reach?

But I couldn't stake this entire job on a ten-year-old's aim with a phone.

The hand squeezed. I jumped.

"Sorry, Thelma. Did I startle you?" the owner of the offending appendage said, the ogle in his voice matching the one in his eyes.

Biting back the retort that came naturally to my tongue, I said instead, "Oh, not at all, Mr. Brown—"

"Leo," he interrupted.

"Yes, um, Leo . . . I must have backed into you by mistake."

I even managed not to choke on the last part. I was getting better at staying in character.

The real Thelma Parker was a mousy thing whose overwhelming desire in life was to get herself appointed to the Friends of the National Zoo—aka FONZ—board of directors without having to form a love connection with Mr. Grabby here. I'd developed a certain reputation for dealing . . . efficiently, shall we say? . . . with matters of *l'amour,* so here I was, dealing. Granted, I had more experience making than breaking said connections, but still. How tough could turning off a guy be?

Mr. Brown patted my sixtyish (but apparently still alluring) derriere, breathing like it was his first time in a Zumba class, making me glad I'd worn one of Thelma's industrial-strength body shapers. At least there was *that* extra layer between me and Sir Pantsalot. Geez, the things I do for my clients.

Sometimes I question the wisdom of my career choice. Just because I *can* slip into somebody else's life, does that mean I *should*?

Philosophy aside, at least I get to help people. Not everyone is adept at getting around life's roadblocks. Take Thelma, for instance. She'd be traumatized by this jerk. If I could spare her that by the simple act of assuming her appearance, and arm her delicate sensibilities against further assault, didn't I have a moral obligation to do it?

Especially when it paid so well. (Hey, a girl has to eat.)

Besides, I—Ciel Halligan, aura adaptor extraordinaire—happen to be pretty good at maneuvering past roadblocks. Well, as long as they aren't my personal roadblocks. Those I tend to suck at.

My job is made possible by a tiny genetic quirk. It's all about altering energy on a biomolecular level, and if you happen to be born with the trait for it . . . well, let's just say interesting career opportunities abound for enterprising adaptors.

I glanced back at Billy, who'd moved on to making a big show of pointing at some sort of marmoset (a golden lion tamarin, according to a nearby sign) and saying to Molly loudly enough for me to hear plainly, "That one reminds me of Ciel—tiny and fierce, and likely to fling poo if provoked."

I managed to keep from rolling my eyes. Barely. Billy, my best friend and honorary cousin (my mother and Billy's stepmother were sorority sisters—cute, huh?), had a habit of showing up at my job sites and lingering in the background to annoy me. Why had I thought it would be different just because this time he was supposedly assisting me?

I refocused on Mr. Brown. Beads of sweat glistened beneath the few strands of gray hair stretched across his pink head. Normally D.C. was cooler in September, but summer apparently hadn't gotten the memo that it was time to leave. He dabbed his forehead with a handkerchief, giving my rear end a temporary reprieve.

"Why don't we get out of this sauna?" he said. (Huff-puff-wheeze.) "My office is air-conditioned, and I keep it cold enough to make you shiver." He winked, reaching out again.

I sidestepped him nimbly, pretending to sneeze. (I perfected fake sneezing at an early age. It beat the heck out of fake stomachaches for playing hooky because you could eat ice cream without making your mom suspicious.) Undeterred by the possibility of germs, Mr. Brown readjusted his aim, following through to his target.

Gawd. If anyone ever tells you a job is easy money, run the other way.

Thelma was a referral from a nonadaptor buddy of mine. Actually, Monica was more Billy's friend than mine—he's the one who'd had a gargantuan crush on her back in high school. But I'd had a soft spot in my heart for her ever since she'd failed to get sucked into his gravitational field, so I'd agreed to take the job on short notice. Quick fix, collect my not unsubstantial fee, *sayonara.*

It went against my grain to take a job without a thorough investigation of the client. I pride myself on being completely familiar with all aspects of a client's life before going in to fix whatever the problem happens to be, but since this job didn't entail dealing with anyone who knew Thelma well, I figured it would be okay.

I removed Mr. Brown's hand from my backside and wagged a finger at him. Not the finger I *wanted* to wag, but since Thelma wasn't the type to flip off any man, much less the one who was dangling the FONZ board membership over her head, I held back. Restraint is an essential part of the job.

"Ah-ah-ah, you naughty boy," I said. Which he somehow mistook for encouragement and came at me again, this time with both hands.

I blocked him with my own, giggling nervously, just as Thelma would have—*the paycheck, Ciel, think of the paycheck!*—engaging in what amounted to an absurd game of patty-cake. Geez. Bashful clients were the worst. If I could get through this interview without whacking Romeo upside the head, I would have earned every freaking penny Thelma was paying me.

Feeling the impulse for violence grow, I threw a panicked look at Billy and Molly, who were apparently so entranced with the diminutive golden-red primates hopping freely through the trees that they didn't notice me. They wore radio collars so the zookeepers could keep track of them. (The marmosets, I mean, not Billy and Molly. Though, honestly, that might be something to consider in the future.) I leveled the glare at them (Billy and Molly, not the marmosets) that I wished I could direct toward the dipwad I was doing the deranged keep-your-hands-off-my-ass dance with. Molly caught on to my dilemma and tugged on her brother's sleeve.

Billy *finally* focused the telephoto lens of his outrageously expensive camera on me and Mr. Brown, grinning in a way that suggested he was enjoying my situation a little too much.

The ants, I decided. *The honey and the fire ants.*

But not until after he gave me the evidence I was going to need to convince Mr. Brown to recommend Thelma for her board position sans any hanky-panky. (No, blackmail isn't, strictly speaking, an attractive behavior—or, you know, legal— but where the welfare of my clients is concerned, I am not above it. Besides, think of the favor I was doing poor *Mrs.* Brown.)

"Come on, Thelma. Just one little kiss. Stop being coy." The hands were getting busier.

At last Billy gave me a thumbs-up, indicating his photographic efforts had been fruitful, and sent Molly scampering my way. She shoved herself between me and the human octopus, hugging me around my waist.

"Aunt Thelma, it's so great to see you," she said.

Billy joined us at a more leisurely pace. "Yes, Aunt Thelma. Thanks for inviting us."

I smoothed my short, faded-brown hair and, once Molly had unlatched herself from me, tucked my tailored shirt more tightly into my sensible, knee-length skirt.

"It's great to see you, too, sweetie," I said. "Both of you. Mr. Brown, may I introduce my niece Molly and my nephew Billy? They're visiting from out of town and thought it would be fun to see the zoo together after my meeting with you." The last part was true, anyway.

Molly sneezed into her hand (not fake—she was getting over a mild cold), wiped it on the seat of her shorts, and extended it toward Mr. Brown enthusiastically. Polite, if not precisely hygienic.

"Pleased to meet you," Mr. Brown said, not sounding—or looking—pleased in the slightest. He ignored Molly's hand.

"Nice to meet you, too," Billy said. "I see you've been sizing up Aunt Thelma."

Mr. Brown's left eye twitched.

"For the board position?" Billy added disingenuously. "I got some great shots of the interview. You know, for Aunt Thelma's scrapbook. I'm sure she'll want a reminder of the day she got fondled—I mean, FONZed."

More twitching. "Yes, uh, well, I'll do whatever I can to convince the other board members, of course."

Did he look paler? Yeah, definitely chalkier than he was before. Sweatier, too, but that could have just been the heat.

Billy clapped his shoulder heartily. "I have the utmost confidence in your powers of persuasion. Maybe you could even get your wife to help. Rumor has it she's a real pit bull when she sets her mind to something."

Mr. Brown's huffing and puffing amped up to an alarming extent. Boy, his wife must be something else if the mere mention of her elicited this kind of reaction.

"Mr. Brown? Are you all right?" I asked, not having to pretend to be flustered this time. If this guy croaked how was I going to explain it to Thelma?

He looked at me, his mouth opening and closing like a beached bass. The hand that had recently groped my ass now clutched at my shoulder.

"Tiiim-berr," Billy said under his breath.

Sure enough, Leo came crashing down—onto me, his face landing square in the middle of Thelma's matronly bosom.

"Damn it, Billy," I said, reeling under the weight, "how in the hell am I supposed to finish the job now?"

Chapter 2

I watched out of the corner of my eye as Billy's mouth sculpted a large mound of raspberry sherbet into a smaller mound, his tongue flicking over the frozen pink confection, lapping at drips along the side of the cone as necessary.

Damn. I swallowed hard.

"Ciel?" I felt a yank on my sleeve. "Hey, are you listening?"

Looking to my other side, I was pulled back to reality by Molly's eager face.

I was myself again, all external traces of my client safely stowed in the large handbag beside me on the bench. Lascivious Leo had been dispatched by ambulance to the nearest hospital after the EMTs assured us it was likely only heat exhaustion and not a heart attack. I'd call later to make sure he was okay—and that he followed through with the board offer for Thelma. I was pretty sure he'd expedite the matter.

"Um, sure thing, Moll. Only I didn't quite get that last part." I glanced back at Billy, who was plowing a groove through the center of what was left of his scoop, transforming it into something that looked disturbingly like a—

Molly tugged my sleeve again. "Ciel!" she said, and sneezed. Her cold hadn't affected her energy at all.

I ripped my eyes away from Billy's lips, back to safer ground, to find Molly staring at me as if I were a somewhat slow two-year-old. "I *said* your ice cream is melting all over your hand."

Crap. It was. I dug a wad of napkins out of my pocket. Before I could wipe off the sticky mess, Billy grabbed my cone-holding hand and licked the chocolate runnels from my fingers, the innocent shine back in his eyes. A shiver ran up my spine and down my . . . never mind. He knew, damn him.

"Shame to let it go to waste," he said, and something told me he wasn't talking about the ice cream. "What's the matter? Aren't you hungry? Maybe you should've tried the raspberry. It's my new favorite." *Bingo.*

My nipples contracted and I hunched my shoulders to hide the obvious. I knew exactly which raspberries he was referring to and the allusion was . . . unsettling. Yanking my hand away, I stumbled through the first excuse I could think of. "Uh, no, it's not that. Brain freeze, that's all. I'm better now." I jammed the cone into my mouth and took a huge bite, wincing as I turned my little lie into a big truth. Ouch.

Billy laughed, but Molly dropped her adult demeanor in a flash of sympathy. "I hate it when that happens. How can something so good blast you with that kind of pain? It's not fair, is it? It's downright treacherous is what I think!"

"It's treacherous, all right," I said, giving her brother a dirty look.

Billy had brought his baby sister down from New York

ostensibly to visit me but really to get her out of our mothers' collective hair. Auntie Mo and my mother (aka Auntie Ro to Billy and his sisters, short for Aurora) were BFFs as well as sorority sisters—Tri Delts—and considered themselves honorary aunts to each other's offspring. They were deep into preparations for this year's annual Come As You Aren't masquerade party, and believe me, no one wanted to be anywhere near ground zero right now. When they were in full-on party mode for the adaptor event of the season—one of the few big social gatherings each year where adaptors could relax and let it all hang out—they steamrolled over anything and anybody in their way. Smart relations learned early on it was get lost or get squashed.

Molly was always a bubbly little thing, but her joy at escaping the forced labor of party prep had her even more effervescent than usual. You could practically see the energy fizzing out of her ears. Granted, the cotton candy, popcorn, chocolate chip cookies, and ice cream I'd seen Billy feeding her with abandon all morning while they were following me around probably hadn't helped.

"Did Billy tell you what I can do yet?" she whispered, barely containing herself, like a bubble on the edge of bursting.

Billy shot her a warning look. "Sis, maybe this should wait until we're back at Ciel's."

My antennae sprang to life. Wait? Ha. That would entail patience, not exactly my strong suit.

"Noooo, Moll—what can you do?" I said, ignoring her brother's threatening brow. "Hey, he's not teaching you to drive his car, is he?" I added, just to watch him blanch. Billy's cherry red '57 Chevy Bel Air was the love of his life, and the thought of anybody else behind the wheel usually gave him the heebie-jeebies.

"Let's not give the munchkin any ideas, Ciel," he said, glancing warily at his sibling.

Molly laughed out loud at her brother's discomfort. "No way. He won't even let me *ride* in it without plastic bags and paper towels." She was long since resigned to her tendency to get motion sick and determined to make the best of it. "But, anyway, watch—"

She grabbed my hand (the one not holding the increasingly sticky ice-cream cone) and looked intently into my eyes.

"Molly—no," Billy said. Too late. Her eyes shifted from their deep blue into a light spring green—the same color as mine. *Exactly* the same.

My jaw dropped, which I realized only after Billy reached over and shut it for me. I batted his hand away. "Molly! This is so great. When did you start? Aren't you a little young?"

She hopped up and down and giggled, a sound so infectious I couldn't help adding my own to it. (Okay, I might have hopped a little, too. But at least I didn't squeal. I draw the line at squealing.)

"Yeah. I'm precocious! Isn't it cool?"

Billy stood and blocked her from the view of a group of passing tourists. "That's enough, Moll. Change them back—and no more showing off in public places. Remember our talk?"

She closed her eyes demurely, and when she opened them they were blue again. "Sorry," she said, looking anything but.

"She says she only noticed after we were down here, but I have my doubts."

"You *know* Mom wouldn't have let me come if she knew. She'd make me stay inside, and I'd never get to see my friends or go anyplace or do anything! It's going to be awful enough when I have to tell her. I just wanted one little vacation before my prison sentence starts." Molly looked so glum you'd have thought she was headed off to solitary confinement for a year.

"Cry me a river, Paris Hilton." Billy laid the sarcasm on with a trowel, but I could tell he was proud of her. Whether for her accomplishment or for bending the rules so she wouldn't get her trip yanked out from under her was harder to say. He wasn't much of one for following rules.

"Come on, Molls," I said. "It's not that bad. In a few months you'll have enough control, and your mom will let you off the leash. We all go through it."

"I can control it now," she said, determination molding her features.

Just like her brother, I thought. Poor Auntie Mo was in for it.

"Come on—let's go to the Think Tank. I want to be a primatologist," she said, grabbing her brother's hand and pulling. The Think Tank was an open laboratory at the zoo where the public was invited to watch dedicated professionals teach primates language symbols to test their higher reasoning skills.

Billy held her back. "You can control it, huh? Is that why you're sprouting a five o'clock shadow?" He kept his voice low enough that only Molly and I could hear him.

Her hands flew to her chin, which *was* suddenly looking a bit bristly. "Huh? How'd that happen?"

Alarmed, I took the spot on the other side of her, helping Billy block her from the meandering public.

"Concentrate, sis." He paused while Molly squinted. "There, that's right. It's gone." He rubbed his chin and grinned. "Guess I should've shaved this morning. Just to be on the safe side, maybe you better not touch anyone until we're back at Ciel's, okay?"

Molly's wholehearted pride in her new ability was shaken,

and she looked like she could use a hug. I didn't dare give her one, though. No telling which of my features she might randomly project. If my strawberry blond hair appeared abruptly on her head, folks might notice.

"Maybe we better head back to my place," I suggested, and watched her face fall into gloomy resignation. I hated to disappoint her, but it wasn't worth the risk of discovery. Besides, it was sweltering, and it was a long trudge to the apes.

Billy put the kibosh on that right away. "Forget it. She'll be fine. Right, kiddo?"

Molly's eyes lit up. "Thanks, Billy. You're the best," she said, and took off at a clip altogether too fast for the heat.

I slugged Billy's arm as I scrambled to keep up. "Yeah, Billy. You're the best."

Laughing, he took my gooshy cone and tossed it into a nearby trash can. "Buck up, cuz. If you get too hot, I'm sure I can figure out some way to cool you off. Maybe we can take a cold shower when we get back to your place."

"We?"

"Always willing to lend a helping hand. I keep telling you, I'm wonderful with a loofah."

Chapter 3

Orangutans have the sweetest eyes. Only not so much when you see them peering at you from the face of a ten-year-old girl.

"Molly," I whispered beneath a cough, widening my own eyes, trying to convey the message to her without attracting unwelcome attention.

She cocked her head and her nose flattened. I grabbed her arm and pulled her away from the baby orang she'd just handed a grape to, brushing its gingery fur with her hand in passing. Billy caught wind of what was happening when he glanced indulgently at his baby sister. He'd been charming the pleasantly plump, totally smitten research assistant so Molly and I could sneak closer to the apes (a total no-no, but since when had that ever stopped a Doyle?). The look of alarm that came over his face was almost, but not quite, worth the panic I was feeling.

Pushing Molly ahead of me, and keeping my body between her and the others, I called back over my shoulder, "Um, Molly is feeling a bit queasy—must've been all that popcorn and soda. We'll just run to the ladies' room."

Behind me, I heard Billy assuring the assistant that his sister would be quite all right, and then distracting her with some inane question about the mating habits of primates. As the door to the Think Tank shut behind me, Molly shrank and sprouted coppery hair all over her body.

And that wasn't supposed to be possible.

I picked her up and ran, my mind somersaulting through how-the-hells and WTFs. The first restroom we came to was blessedly free of occupants. The entrance was made of glass, though, so I took cover in the nearest stall, latching the door behind me. I sat on the toilet and turned Molly to face me. Rich, dark-chocolate eyes full of the ancient wisdom of the forest stared up at me. She drew back her lips, showing me nubbly little baby teeth.

"Molly?" I said, keeping my voice low. "You have to change back. Now would be good."

She whimpered.

"Seriously, Molly. Right now."

She raised both hands and shrugged.

"Oh, my God. You can't, can you? Can you even understand me?"

"Ciel? Are you in there?" Billy's voice was followed by a pounding on the door.

"Yeah, we're here," I hollered back.

The door opened. "Are you alone?"

"I think so. For the time being." I stood, moving Molly to my hip, and peeked out from the stall.

Billy quickly searched the other stalls before taking Molly from me. He held her away from him, examining her from top to bottom, and looked at me, eyebrows propping up his hairline.

"Don't ask me. *I* don't know how it happened—she barely touched the thing."

"But we can't . . . no one's ever been able to . . . I mean, what the hell?" He gave the baby ape a small shake. "Molly, change back. Now." He spoke firmly, sounding just like his dad. When Uncle Liam used that tone of voice, nobody disobeyed.

"I already tried that. I don't think she can."

"Molly, I said *now*."

She whimpered, stretching her long arms back toward me.

"You've scared her." I took her and felt her arms go up around my neck. "It's okay, Moll. We'll figure this out. You just relax."

"Well, she better relax fast and change back into something resembling a human being, or we're going to have a hell of a time getting her out of the zoo. I imagine ape-napping is frowned upon."

A babble of feminine voices interrupted us. Billy pushed me back into the stall and followed, shutting the door just as the women entered. I fell backward onto the toilet with an *oomph,* accidentally squeezing a squeak out of Molly. The voices stopped. Billy bent over us, shielding Molly from view with his shoulders. I leaned to one side and saw an eyeball appear in the crack between the door and the stall.

The eyeball narrowed as it directed a laser beam of disapproval at me. "Ladies," the woman attached to the eye said in a voice that bounced off the restroom walls like ice cubes against a glass, "this is not a good place for a rest stop. Apparently, some people think it appropriate to conduct *business transactions* in public restrooms. Surely there's some authority nearby we can appeal to."

A whole parade of eyeballs marched by, each more scandalized than the last, as Billy looked at the ceiling and shook his head. "Stay right here," he said, and left, hot on the heels of the morals vigilantes. Huh. Like I was going anywhere with a baby orangutan dressed like a tween.

"Ladies," he said, turning on the Doyle charm full blast. "This isn't what you think. My wife had to rush in here with our little girl, who started feeling terribly ill after eating one of the hot dogs at the snack bar. Now, I'm not saying it's food poisoning. But, really, who knows for sure? More likely just too much excitement, and maybe the heat. Anyway, I couldn't just let her handle a puking child on her own, could I? *She has a sensitive stomach herself—*"

I took the cue and began making retching sounds. Molly got a little agitated and started contributing. "Ooooo! Oooo! Aa-aa-*aaa!*" I patted her back and retched some more, upping the volume.

"I know I shouldn't have come into the ladies' room, but since there was no one else here, I thought—" Billy continued, louder himself.

"Oh, you poor man!" The woman's voice thawed considerably. "Maybe I can help. I'm a retired nurse."

"No!" Billy said. "No, *I'm sure they'll be all right* in just a minute."

I stopped fake heaving. "Molly's feeling better, er, honey. I'm okay, too!"

"Well, if you're quite sure—" the ex-nurse said.

"Oh, quite," Billy said. "I'll just get them some damp paper towels. We'll be leaving soon."

I peeked as he herded the women from the room. "Can you lock that?"

"Not without the key. Do you have a pen in your bag?" He didn't wait for my answer, but dug right into the handsome leather bag I was carrying for my job. With the marker he found, and a paper towel from the dispenser by the sink, he devised an "Out of Order" sign that he stuck to the outside of the door with a hastily chewed piece of gum, also from my bag.

"My, how MacGyver of you," I said. "But what do we do when the maintenance man shows up?"

"I hope we'll be long gone by then."

"And how are we going to leave with a baby ape?"

He looked at Molly, who was blissfully playing with her toes, showing no sign of changing back to herself. He shrugged and pulled his cell phone out of his pocket. "Mark? I need a favor."

Mark Fielding, the CIA agent who had fueled my girlish fantasies, was at the door to the restroom half an hour later, looking even better than the last time I saw him. Tall, blond, and chiseled, he never failed to make my hormones do a flip-flop. I felt like one of Pavlov's dogs when he was around. If my recent inexplicable attraction to Billy surprised me, my response to Mark's presence didn't—he'd been ringing my bell since I was thirteen years old. I had hoped my lustful feelings toward Mark would tone down when they started ramping up toward Billy, but apparently that would be too simple for my life.

Mark sized up the situation with a single glance around the room, zeroing in on Molly. "How the hell did you manage to do *that*?" he said, as close to shocked as I'd ever seen him. Billy had warned him over the phone that Molly wasn't quite herself, but hadn't elaborated.

I assumed the question was directed at me. Those kind of questions usually were. "I didn't do anything, I swear. It just . . . happened."

Billy nodded his confirmation, his eyes lacking their usual teasing glint.

Mark asked no further questions. "Wait here," he said, and left.

He returned in less than a minute with a baby stroller, the folding kind equipped with a nice big sunshade. When I asked how he'd come by one so fast, he just shrugged and said there were plenty of them parked outside the Great Ape House, and that it might be a good idea if we hustled our butts. He and Billy guarded the door while I buckled Molly in and told her to keep quiet.

"Do you think she understands you?" Mark said as I adjusted the shade to provide maximum coverage. He hadn't commented much on the odd state of affairs, but I knew his brain had to be spinning. Adaptors were only able to project *human* auras. At least, that's how it was supposed to be.

I shrugged. "Beats me. I'm going to assume Molly is still Molly on the inside, just like with a regular adaption."

Billy grabbed his makeshift sign off the door and tossed it into the closest trash can. "Come on—let's get out of here. We can figure out what to do after we're back at Ciel's." He took charge of the stroller, maneuvering it through the foot traffic while Mark and I positioned ourselves on either side of him.

"Whoa, bud. Blend," Mark said. I think his lips moved a tiny bit, but I wouldn't swear to it.

Billy slowed, barely, but I still had to step double time to make my short legs keep up with their long ones. "Where are you parked?" he asked Mark.

"Veer off at the next left. There's an employee lot back there. I borrowed a spot."

Billy took the curve too fast and nearly plowed into a zoo employee. He pulled up just in time. A middle-aged woman wearing a red polo shirt with a zoo logo on it blocked our way with her hugely pregnant belly; there was no maneuvering around her. Billy stared, deer-caught-in-the-headlights fashion, while the woman leaned down to coo at Molly.

"Awww . . . a baby!"

Mark, bless him, tried to distract her with one of his rare smiles—they were killer when he chose to bestow them—but she wasn't to be deflected. I'd seen women in the grip of baby fever before, and this one obviously had nothing else on her mind. She wanted a baby fix, and no mere man, however good-looking, was going to stand in her way. Leaning down as much as her tummy allowed, she peeked under the shade and smiled beatifically.

"She's sleeping. How sweet. And look at that red hair!"

Huh? Why wasn't she freaking out? I leaned over and looked with her. Molly, brilliant little Molly, had pulled the pink flannel baby blanket up over her face. Only a few tufts of orange fur stuck out on top.

"Do you mind if I . . . ?" Ms. Zoo Employee stretched her pregnancy-puffed fingers toward the edge of the blanket.

Mark, Billy, and I all reached for her at the same time. I was the closest, and intercepted her hand before she could unwrap the surprise package. "Uh," I said. "Better not. She, um, gets sunburned so easily. You know how it is with redheads."

The woman gave me a patronizing look and squeezed my hand. "Your first? Don't worry, honey, they're tougher than you think. You don't have to treat them with kid gloves."

"I-I-uh, I know that. I just . . ." Just what? What? *Think, Ciel.*

She placed my hand on her belly and pressed down until something kicked me. I resisted the urge to yank it back as visions of that scene from *Alien* skittered through my head.

"There, honey, you feel that? That's my fourth. He'll be lucky if I remember to change his diapers and feed him, much less worry about a little sunburn. You better learn to relax if you want to survive motherhood."

I nodded weakly, my eyes darting between Mark and Billy. Mark was calm, smiling at me indulgently and shrugging, playing the part of agreeing with the woman. Billy smiled, too, but it was strained, impatience undulating beneath the surface.

"Which one of you is the proud papa?"

The guys looked at me, waiting for my cue. My mouth opened but no words came out. Why did everything have to come down to a choice between Mark and Billy? Evidently I waited too long, because they both took it upon themselves to speak for me at the exact same time: "I am."

My face flamed. Geez.

She gave me an appraising look, changing her previous assessment of me in the time it took her to purse her lips. "Like that, is it? Well, I have to say, it's quite progressive of you all to handle it so civilly." In other words, *you slut.*

"You don't understand," I hastened to explain. "I never . . . not with either of them. Really. I mean . . ." Oh, hell. What did I mean?

"She's our surrogate," Billy blurted when he saw her hand creeping back toward the blanket.

Mark's eyes gave nothing away as he caught on and entered into the distraction by putting an arm around Billy's shoulders and giving him an affectionate squeeze. "Yes, she carried our little girl for us. It's an open adoption—we want her to remain part of our child's life."

The woman dragged her eyes away from the stroller and looked from Mark to Billy, her eyes lighting with curiosity. "Oh, I see. Well, I think that's just wonderful," she said, beaming now that she knew I was a paragon of modern family values and not just sleeping with two hot guys. "Did you blend the semen before insemination so both fathers would feel equally invested?"

My mouth opened but no words came out.

"Don't look so shocked, honey. It's a common practice. Some people think it promotes better bonding with the infant. And I'm not just being nosy, either—I work at a zoo. I have a scientific interest in these things."

Ack. How do you answer that kind of question? "Um, no. No blending. I didn't blend"—*eew*—"anything. Right, guys?"

"Right," they both said, nodding in unison.

"No?" the woman said, sounding disappointed. "Then who's the bio dad? Wait, don't tell me. Let me see if I can tell which one she favors." She snatched the blanket from Molly's face.

I cringed, bracing for the inevitable.

"What the hell?" she boomed. She skewered us each in turn with a look that made me wish I were wearing adult diapers. If eyes were Tasers, we'd all be flopping on the ground. She dug into her skirt pocket—not easy, considering how tight it was—and came out with a security whistle, which she started blowing like there was no tomorrow.

Molly didn't care for the sound. Her long, nimble fingers unlatched the stroller's safety belt. In a blink she was knuckle-running off the path toward the nearest tree, oversize shorts and T-shirt flapping around her.

"Molly! No!" Billy took off after her. With an apologetic shrug at me, Mark followed, leaving me to deal with a hormonally supercharged woman twice my size. She turned to go after them but must have thought better of it. I was the easier target.

I backed away from her slowly.

"Oh, no you don't," she grunted after spitting out the whistle, and came at me, arms wide and ready to grab.

I quickened my pace, stumbling backward, afraid to take my eyes off her for the second it would take to turn around. She sped up. My heel connected with something slippery, and I went down, legs splayed in front of me.

I felt a razor-stubbled ankle connect with mine. Heard a *thwump* as she hit the ground next to me. Wondered fleetingly and, okay, inappropriately, how the heck she'd managed to reach past that belly to shave her legs . . . and then felt a little sick.

Oh God, oh God, oh God. I had just tripped a hugely pregnant woman. Not on purpose, but still. Does it get any lower than that?

Wincing, I opened one eye to assess the damage, halfway expecting to see the baby shooting out from beneath her skirt. But, no, she'd landed on her amply padded derriere and was doing her spitting-angry best to haul herself back to a standing position, so I supposed she couldn't have been too badly hurt.

I shook myself off and hightailed it after Molly and the guys, shoving the stroller ahead of me. Billy jumped off an oak with Molly wrapped around his neck as I caught up to them.

Mark was there at the base of the tree. "Is she okay?" he asked, glancing back at the zoo employee, who'd almost made it to her feet.

"Looks like it to me," I said. "Uh-oh—she has her phone out. She's calling for backup!"

Billy dumped Molly into the stroller and draped the blanket back over her, telling her to hold on tight. Mark took the lead, keeping us safely out of sight of other zoo employees until we got to his car, a Ford Shelby GT500. He changed cars like other people changed underwear, never wanting to be pinned to a particular make and model.

It was a cool car, but it didn't have much in the way of a backseat. It would have to do—Billy and Molly had come on the Metro and I'd taken a cab as my client, so we didn't really have a choice as far as transportation went. "Geez, are we all going to fit?" I asked, drumming my fingers on the car top while Billy picked up Molly and Mark shoved the stolen stroller behind a handy Dumpster.

"We'll fit. Get in the back with Molly—your legs are short enough. Billy, you're shotgun."

I might have taken umbrage at his remark about my legs, but he was right. Very few backseats are a tight squeeze for me. On the plus side, I can wear six-inch platform stilettos without intimidating men of average height. Not that I do—comfortable feet are too important to me—but I *could* if I wanted to.

Billy handed me his sister. Molly in baby orangutan form was too small for an adult seat belt, but what choice did I have? I adjusted her shoulder strap as well as I could, but she obviously wasn't comfortable with it and began squirming as soon as the car started.

"Everything okay back there?" Mark asked as he backed out of the space.

"They're fine. Let's go," Billy answered for me. Huh. Easy for him to say. He wasn't the one trying to keep his sister's busy fingers off the seat belt buckle.

"Just hurry and get us home. I don't know how long I can keep her quiet back here," I said.

"Not a problem." Mark turned out of the lot and slipped into traffic with ease, cutting from lane to lane, picking up speed with each maneuver. He seemed to have a sixth sense about when the lights were going to change and always managed to be in the right spot at the right time.

It didn't take Molly long to get out of the seat belt, in spite of my effort to keep her contained, so I decided holding her would be my best option. Only she decided *not* being held was *her* best option, and baby orangutans are remarkably slippery. She was out of my arms and climbing onto Billy before I could shout a warning.

"Hey!" Billy grabbed her and tried to pull her off. She held tight to his hair with one foot and bongoed his head with both long-fingered hands, sounds of distress spilling from her.

I tried my best to disengage her. That only agitated her more. She launched herself from Billy onto Mark, planting herself in his lap. Mark gripped the steering wheel and bore down on the accelerator, grim determination molding his features. Billy tried to pry her off him, but she grabbed the wheel.

And found the horn.

"Crap," I said. "Molly, stop that!"

"She doesn't understand you," Billy said. "Molly, cut that out!"

"Oh, and she understands you?" I blew my hair out of my face and cut him a look.

"We're almost there." How Mark stayed calm with an ape bouncing up and down on his lap as he negotiated the streets of D.C. was beyond me, but I imagine the CIA trains you to keep your cool in unexpected situations.

Molly lost interest in the horn before pissing off too many of our fellow motorists, and hopped back over to Billy. She grabbed him by the shoulders, banged her head against his chest twice, and pointed to the window.

"What? What do you want, Molly? What's the matter?" Billy sounded as close to frantic as I'd ever heard him.

Molly got very still, and I swear I saw green tinge her face. It didn't mix well with the orange. "Uh-oh," I said. "I think she might be—"

She spewed all over Billy's chest.

"—carsick," I finished lamely.

"Christ," Mark said under his breath, but kept driving.

Billy, for once, was speechless.

Chapter 4

"Molly did try to get out," I said later, once we were in my condo, shielded from the prying eyes of the world. None of us was particularly worried about the lady at the zoo. No one else had seen us with Molly before we'd gotten out of there, and they wouldn't find that a baby orangutan was missing when they followed up on her story. They'd probably write it off as pregnancy hormones and suggest she might want to go on maternity leave a little early.

"It's not like she *wanted* to barf in Mark's car," I continued.

"Screw Mark's car. What about my shirt?" Billy had showered and changed and was sitting at my kitchen table with Mark. They had helped themselves to beers from the fridge.

I was in a nearby upholstered rocker—though definitely not rocking—holding a sleeping Molly in my arms. She'd settled down considerably once her stomach was empty. We still didn't know if she understood any of what we said to her, but she looked like she did. Then again, all those orangs at the zoo had looked like they understood everything said to them, too. Who really knew?

"Your shirt won't have to be detailed," Mark said drily.

"Isn't it time for you to trade it in anyway? You've had it for at least two weeks," Billy kidded.

"You guys stop—Molly couldn't help it. We all know she's prone to motion sickness, and the stress of this"—I gestured helplessly at the hairy little bundle in my arms—"didn't help. The important thing is, what are we going to do?"

"Good question," Billy said. "I'm hoping she'll spontaneously change back. Then I'm going to suggest to my parents that they lock her in her room for the next ten years, until we can be sure she has control of herself."

I chewed my lip, my hands too occupied for me to get a fingernail to my mouth. "Should we call them, do you think? Let them know?"

"My parents? No way. Can you imagine how Mommo would react to this, especially now?"

He was right. Auntie Mo—Billy had conflated his stepmom's name to "Mommo" at an early age—could be a little melodramatic even under the best of circumstances. The closer to the party, the worse she got. It was just part of the process for her. God only knew what she would do if she found out her baby was now an ape.

Mark, who'd been thoughtfully sipping his beer, spoke. "I suggest we call James. He probably knows more about what could have possibly gone wrong with Molly than anyone else I can think of."

James is my second-oldest brother, right after Thomas, the lawyer. He's a perpetual student whose current field of study is genetic engineering. A nonadaptor himself, he's determined to isolate the gene responsible for our anomaly.

Billy nodded. "How soon can we get him here?"

I shrugged. "Thomas will know—ask him. He should be here with dinner soon."

Yes, I invited my brother for dinner and then asked him to bring it. I'd like to say it was because of our emergency, but honestly? I do it all the time. Thomas knows better than to expect me to cook.

"What's he bringing? Thai?" Billy asked. Worried about his sister he might be, but not much interfered with his appetite.

"What else?" I said. There was a lovely Thai restaurant on the bottom floor of Thomas's office building, and the owners knew him well enough that they didn't even bother to ask him what he wanted when he called them for takeout.

On cue, the front door opened. Thomas had obviously figured out my new security code. "Hope everyone's hungry—I brought double the usual," he called from the entry hall. He walked right past me with barely a wave, acknowledged Billy and Mark with a nod, and started unpacking containers of aromatic ambrosia. My salivary glands kicked in big-time when I detected the familiar scents of pad thai, drunken noodles, and green curry.

It took Thomas a moment. Mark leaned back in his chair and watched him, a bland, expectant look on his face.

"Wait for it," Billy said, observing my brother with equal interest.

Thomas's head popped up, and he contemplated the cabinet in front of him. "Why is Ciel holding an orangutan?" he said without turning. Almost like he was afraid to confirm what his eyes had told him.

Nobody said anything.

He finally looked at me. I lifted one hand in a tiny wave. His eyes swept the room.

"Where's Molly?" he asked carefully.

I cleared my throat and pointed at the small form on my lap.

"What?" He rushed to me, knelt, and stared at Molly's face. He shook his head and stood. "Good one, guys. Really good. Don't know how you got hold of the ape. Your doing, Ciel? You had a job at the zoo today, didn't you? Had me going for a second. Now, where's Molly?"

I studied my brother. "Thomas, you're looking at her."

"She started spontaneously adapting a few days ago," Billy said. "Only random features at first, not much control—didn't tell me until we were down here. Didn't want her trip to see you guys spoiled."

Thomas still looked skeptical. "Not possible. She's too young."

Mark went to the fridge and got Thomas a beer. "There have been a few previous cases of precocious adaptors. I was early my-self. It's rare, but not impossible."

Thomas twisted off the bottle cap and took a long swig. Shook his head as he finished swallowing. "But an *ape*? That *is* impossi-ble. Sorry. Nice try, but I'm not buying it." He went back to the entry hall and hollered up the stairs. "Molly! Hey, Molls! It's me, Thomas. Come on down and greet your favorite relative."

Molly stirred in my lap at the sound of her name reverberating through the condo. Mark went to explain things to Thomas; I stood and Billy took his sister, who was suddenly all squirming arms and legs. She clutched him and buried her little simian face in his chest.

"It's okay, Molls. It's only Thomas. He's here to help." Billy walked back and forth with her, patting her back.

"You're going to make a wonderful daddy someday," I said, just to be evil. I know, I know. Rotten to tease him under the circumstances. But fun.

A look of horror spread over his face. "Bite your tongue. Just looking after my sisters—and you—is enough to drive me to drink. Last thing I'll ever need is a rug rat of my own."

Thomas and Mark rejoined us. Thomas still looked skeptical. He approached Billy and laid a hesitant hand on Molly's back. "Moll? Is that really you?"

Molly grinned, baring all of her teeth, and nodded wildly. She reached for Thomas's hand, hooked the tips of his four fingers with the tips of hers, and made thumb-wrestling motions, only she couldn't reach his thumb with her itty-bitty orangutan one.

Thomas paled and plopped into the chair I had just vacated. He was the one who'd taught each younger sibling and cousin, in turn, how to thumb wrestle. "My God. It *is* Molly."

"I thought we'd established that," Mark said.

"But . . . but it's impossible. It can't happen." He shook his head as if his denial could change the situation.

I slapped his shoulder lightly with the back of my hand. "Open your eyes, counselor. The evidence is before you."

"Eyewitness testimony is notoriously unreliable. You're all having me on. You rented a monkey—"

"Orangutan," Billy said.

"Whatever. You rented it and trained it. You're getting even with me because I bailed on the party last year, aren't you? Billy?

Am I right? You're still ticked because I never paid you for filling in for me."

"No," Billy said. "Well, yes—I am still ticked about that, but no, I am not playing some elaborate practical joke on you to get even."

Molly, impatient with the turn of conversation, wiggled until she'd detached herself from Billy and scurried on all fours to my desk. We'd taken the oversize clothes off her, so she moved with no impediments. If she managed to change back into herself, there were plenty of blankets nearby to preserve her modesty.

She pulled herself onto my desk chair and carefully selected a pen from the mosaic-tile holder she'd made me for my last birthday. The rest of us watched in fascination as she took a piece of paper from a drawer, laid it on the blotter, and began to write. Her hand movements were awkward, but she finally managed to turn her initial scribbles into shaky-looking letters.

By this time we were all standing around her, staring over her shoulders.

IM MOLLY U BIG DOOF.

Thomas read it aloud, coloring a bit at the last part. Molly climbed into his arms, hugging him around the neck. Thomas really was a favorite of hers—she'd had him dancing to her tune from the time she could talk.

He hugged her back carefully. "Molly, what have you done?" he said, voice low.

* * *

Thomas stayed through dinner, holding Molly on his lap so she could reach the table easily. Her long arms came in handy for grabbing spring rolls off everyone else's plates after she'd finished her own. After the first five minutes, Billy stopped making cracks about her having the manners of an ape, and we all let her eat whatever struck her fancy.

James couldn't come until the next day, so we decided to get together again then. Thomas headed back to his office to meet with a client who couldn't come in during regular office hours, and Mark had a mysterious appointment downtown. Of course, all of his appointments were shrouded with intrigue. For all I knew he had a hot date lined up. I liked to think a certain steamy kiss we'd shared on my recent unexpected adventure in Sweden had made as big an impression on him as it had on me, but I doubted it.

When Billy took a snoozing Molly upstairs to my guest room to tuck her in, I walked Mark to the door, willing to pretend our little breach in protocol on the sailboat off the coast of Gotland had never happened, if that was the way he wanted it.

"Quite a day, huh, Howdy?" he said, reverting to the childhood nickname my grandfather had saddled me with. Yeah, yeah . . . Howdy Doody of freckle fame. I still had my share, which I'm told are becoming, mainly by people who aren't afflicted with them.

My chuckle was dry. "You could say that. Not exactly what I was expecting when I got up this morning."

"Don't worry—Molly will be fine. James will find a way to fix her." He reached out to ruffle my hair, as was his longtime habit, but for some reason pulled my head closer at the last second and kissed me, right on the mouth. It was brief and innocent—definitely not like our last one—but it still gave me goose bumps and made my breath catch. He stroked my hair and gifted me with one of his smiles. "See you later. Sleep well."

"You too," I managed to push past my stunned lips as he left. Sleep?

Chapter 5

"He knew I was watching." Billy's voice preceded him down the stairs.

Startled, I turned and looked up at him, brain still awhirl. "What?"

"When he kissed you. He heard me close the door to Molly's room." His voice remained neutral, but his eyes were narrower than usual, his black lashes shadowing their usual sparkle.

"That's silly. Besides, it was just a good-night peck. Hardly qualifies as a kiss at all." I shrugged and looked away.

"No, he was warning me off in his own inimitable style."

"Are you saying he kissed me just to make a point to you? Gee, thanks."

He paused. Sighed and ran a hand through his hair. "Not just that, no. True, he doesn't want you getting involved with big, bad me. And really, who can blame him? I suppose my reputation isn't exactly sterling—"

I snorted, and not the delicate kind.

He quirked his mouth but didn't try to defend himself. "I think he's also a little bent at the thought of losing your undivided adulation. Could be he's considering making your fondest wish come true."

"Don't be ridiculous."

"I'm not." He took my hand and pulled me to him, resting his chin on my head. "Look, cuz, if you want me to back off, give you some time to figure things out with the spook, just tell me."

I leaned into him, confused as hell. Billy drove me crazy, but he could be so understanding sometimes. He was the best friend I had. Did I want to risk losing that because of a sudden freakish attraction to him?

"Maybe that would be a good idea . . ." I started.

He pushed me away but held on to my shoulders, looking positively incredulous. "*What?* How can you say that?"

"But you said—"

"Don't be silly. I didn't *mean* it."

"Then why'd you say it?"

"I thought it would make me appear noble."

I pulled away from him, exasperated. "Only when it's sincere, you idiot."

"I can do sincere." He set his mouth in soft lines and hit me with the Doyle eyes. Yep, he had sincere down pat.

"It's not sincere just because you make your 'sincere' face. You have to honestly mean it." I tapped my foot while he considered. "Well?"

He shrugged and blasted me with the smile he used to use on his mother to get his curfew extended when we were teenagers. "Come on. Have you ever known me to give up on anything that easily?"

He reached for me again, but I evaded his arms. If I'd learned anything about myself recently, it was that I didn't think clearly when Billy was touching me.

"Is this some sort of game to you?" I said after I'd put adequate distance between us. "If you're doing this because *maybe* Mark is starting to pay attention to me—"

"Don't be stupid."

"You have to admit the timing is suspect."

His mouth twitched, and a dimple grew. "Well, it's possible the spook's sudden interest in you spurred me to move a little faster than I might have otherwise, but the underlying emotion has always been there. I want you, Ciel. It's as simple as that."

"Why?"

"Why?" He sounded confused, like the question had never occurred to him.

"Yeah—why? Seems like you have the perfect lifestyle for someone of your many—and varied—interests. Models and aspiring actresses out the wazoo. Why give that up? Unless you think you can just add me to the bunch?"

The other dimple appeared. "You'd be my favorite."

"Grrrr!" I marched to the kitchen. I needed ice cream.

Billy followed, trying not to laugh. He caught me before I could open the freezer and turned me to face him, corralling me against the fridge with his arms. "Come on. Where's your sense of humor? All I want is you." He cocked his head, and with one finger sketched a line from my earlobe down my neck, dipping lightly into the hollow of my collarbone. There was a kiss on his lips just waiting to ambush me.

"No," I said, to convince myself as much as him. "I need to think about this more."

"Okay. While you're thinking, there's another matter we can take care of."

"What?" I said, leery of the determined gleam in his eye.

"Certain damage to my car, and what you owe me for it."

I swallowed, feeling my eyes widen. "But that wasn't my fault. You were there. You know that."

"Doesn't matter. You were behind the wheel."

"That is beside the point!"

"A deal is a deal. The driver is always responsible. You know what that means."

I ducked under his arm. "A busted headlight is hardly a wreck."

He caught me and pulled me against him. "It is to me. Now," he said, his lips alarmingly close to my ear, "knickers up or knickers down? I know which I'd prefer."

I pushed against his chest. "Billy, listen to me—"

He kissed my neck. "Up or down?" he said. I thought he might be stifling a laugh, but it was hard to be sure.

Geez. I *had* made a rash statement to the effect that he could spank me if I wrecked his car. It was the only way I could get him to let me drive it when I'd tagged along on his last job with Mark—I certainly hadn't been serious.

"Oh, for Pete's sake, I was *lying*." I hated to admit it, but I had been. Bad me.

"That's even worse. Now you doubly deserve it." He nipped my earlobe.

"I still maintain it was not a wreck. Minor damage, at best," I argued after a tiny moan.

"It'll only be minor damage for you, too," he said, caressing my backside. "Tit for tat. Or . . . we could just renegotiate the terms." He placed his mouth over mine and did some things with that clever tongue of his.

I squirmed against him, trying to resist—at least, I'm pretty sure that's what I was trying to do—but my body was only too ready to open itself to negotiations. Stupid body.

A screech, followed by several whoops and a squeal, interrupted us. Billy paused for a second, then resumed kissing me, ignoring the escalating symphony from upstairs. I pulled my lips away from his—reluctantly—and cocked my head at him, lifting my brows.

He emitted a harsh sound through clenched teeth but quickly composed himself. "You're right. I'll check on her."

I stepped back, and Billy turned away from me, shook himself all over, and counted to ten slowly under his breath. The orangutan noises were getting louder.

"What are you waiting for? We need to see if she's okay."

"Just give me a second, all right?"

Oh. Well, yes, I could see his dilemma. "Um, can't you just . . . adapt?" I asked.

He gritted his teeth. "Sometimes that's easier said than done."

I patted his shoulder. "Why don't you wait here? I'll go check on her."

He waved me off, not looking at me. Part of me felt like he deserved it, after what he'd done to me at the zoo. Another part of me wanted to toss Molly a banana and tell her to shut up and go back to sleep.

The fuzzy munchkin was all over me as soon as I opened the door to her room. I patted her back and spoke softly as I paced the room with her. "It's going to be all right, Molls. Really. I promise. I know this has to be weird for you, and scary, too, but you're not alone. We're going to get you fixed. James is coming tomorrow—you know how smart he is—and I'm sure he'll have you right as rain in no time."

She settled into soft whimpers, clutching my shirt, her tiny thumb suspiciously close to her mouth. Billy joined us.

"Here, I'll take her."

Molly went willingly, hugging her brother tightly enough to squeeze a small *oof* out of him.

He looked at me with lustful regret. "I'll stay with her."

I nodded and turned to go to my room, but was stopped by a hairy, outstretched arm. "You want me to stay, too, Molly?" She nodded vigorously.

"The bed's a little small for three, Molls," Billy said. Molly shook her head and held on to both of us.

I sighed. "Come on, you two."

Hours later, Billy sat bleary-eyed at my kitchen table, a far cry from his typically cheery morning self. He'd gotten his wish—a night in my king-size bed—but a hairy little sister added to the equation tends to put a damper on romance. Molly bounced up and down on the chair next to him, sucking orange juice through a bendy straw and slurping soggy cereal straight from her bowl without benefit of a spoon.

"When is James supposed to get here?" he asked, weariness coloring his voice.

"Early afternoon. If he can get away from the lab in time to make the noon shuttle," I said. "But Mark and Thomas should be here soon."

"Did you stress the urgency of the situation to James? I

mean—Molly, get off the table!—did you tell him this is a family emergency?"

"Yes, I did. But I couldn't exactly spell out the details to him, could I? Not over the phone. If there's one thing I've learned working with you spooks, it's never trust the privacy of a phone."

He glowered at me. "I occasionally do Mark a favor. I am not a spook."

"Same as," I snapped, as testy and frustrated as he was, and started clearing away dishes.

After a minute he came up behind me, leaning down to add his bowl to the stack in the sink. "I'm sorry," he whispered.

I pressed back against him and sighed. "Me too." And I was. I'd been awake most of the night, and not just because I was anxious about Molly. Don't get me wrong—I was concerned about her, all right. But I'd mentally pushed most of that particular worry off onto James. He was the genius—he'd take care of it.

No, I'd been wrestling with myself about Billy and what I should do with him. Toward dawn I'd come to the conclusion I should just go with the flow. I knew Billy too well to think he'd back off, and, truthfully, I wasn't sure I wanted him to. Human nature being what it is, I figured the more I denied him—and, okay, myself—the more compelling the attraction would become. If we just scratched the itch . . . well then, maybe things could get back to normal between us, and I could settle into the safety of my unrequited passion for Mark. Because, deep down, I really didn't think that little good-night peck was going to change anything between Mark and me. Once he was sure Billy was out of the romantic picture and back to being his annoying, cousinly self, Mark would revert to his pseudo big-brother role.

A warm hand slid down my bare arm, pausing to play at the inside of my elbow. "Know any good monkey sitters?"

"Afraid not," I said, wondering if arms can have miniorgasms, because mine felt like it was about to. I placed a hand over his, stopping his fingers from dancing over the sensitive skin before I did something embarrassing.

"Would it be wrong to drug her juice?" he whispered.

I laughed, keeping it soft so as not to alert the primate in question. "Terribly. Though the idea is not without merit," I said, shifting my hips. He, um, noticed.

And groaned. "When I get you alone . . ."

I looked up over my shoulder at him and lifted an inquiring brow.

". . . negotiations will resume." He grinned and walked away.

Chapter 6

James stared at Molly. Molly stared at James. They were on the floor, James sitting cross-legged, Molly knees up with hands splayed beside her, gripping the carpet. It was hard to judge who was concentrating harder.

"How long has she been this way?" he said in an oddly electric voice without breaking his eye lock with her. They'd begun the unofficial stare down shortly after he'd arrived. If he thought she was going to look away first, he was seriously underestimating the Doyle competitive streak.

"Late morning yesterday. Roughly nineteen, twenty hours," I said, yawning. It was still early—he'd taken the red-eye.

"And there hasn't been any fluctuation in the aura? Not even when she's distracted or asleep?"

"Steady as an old pro," Billy said.

Molly straightened her shoulders and curled her lips, but her eyes didn't slip. I could swear she was proud. Most neophyte adaptors stumbled through their initial adaptions, wobbling in and out of new auras like special effects in a bad sci-fi movie. It took some real skill to maintain an aura this long when you were as new at it as she was.

James nodded, his head bobbing while his eyes remained steady. His strawberry blond hair caught the sunlight from the window behind him. He wore it long, longer even than my current short style. Of my three brothers, James looked the most like me—fair and slim, and not especially tall for a guy. He was four years my elder.

"So the problem is in the on/off switch. Interesting." His spring green eyes, mirrors of my own, didn't waver.

"Are you sure she *wants* to drop the aura?" he said at last.

Molly's eyes narrowed at the suggestion. She reached out with both long arms, grabbed James by the shoulders, and shook him. His gaze, if anything, intensified.

"Are you really stuck, Molly? Not just grabbing a little attention? This would be a great way to delay your trip back home."

Molly stood, shaking her head emphatically, looking first to Billy, then to me, and finally to Thomas, the staring contest tossed by the wayside in an effort to convince us wordlessly of her innocence.

I picked her up and gave my brother a dirty look. "James, how could you? Don't you think she's upset enough?"

He rose in one graceful motion and laid a hand on her head. "Sorry, Molly. I just had to be sure."

She was having none of it. She pulled away and stuck out her tongue at him.

He smiled at her—a darned engaging smile, if it's not conceited to say that about someone who looks so much like me.

"Come on, Molly. I'm a scientist. You told me you wanted to

be one, too—you know scientists have to test all theories. Now that I've scratched off 'doing it on purpose,' I can concentrate on other possibilities. Forgive me?"

"Don't ask for forgiveness too soon," Billy said. "It's a plausible theory. She wasn't thrilled when I told her we were going back early after she started projecting random aura parts."

"It would be an effective maneuver if she wanted to stay here. Something I might've thought of at her age," Thomas added. His legal mind was one to appreciate good tactics.

Molly sagged against me, her sense of betrayal evident to all.

"Piss off, all of you," I said. We girls had to stand together. "James, you should know her better. Isn't Molly at your lab every spare minute?"

He gave me a look, a mini double take. But it was gone in a flash.

When he spoke again, it sounded remote. "Relax. I told you I believe Molly."

I could see him regrouping data behind his eyes: sorting, eliminating, categorizing, prioritizing. It wasn't that he was cold or didn't care about Molly. It was just the way his brain worked. Affection had its place, and it was firmly behind solving a scientific conundrum. The fact that this one involved an aura-adapting anomaly—possibly a genetic mutation, his current field of study—was icing on the cake for him. It might provide him with the break he needed to crack the code.

Billy still looked skeptical. Thomas accepted James's verdict as gospel. I was somewhere in the middle but leaned toward giving her the benefit of the doubt.

"We have to get her back to New York so I can run some tests."

"And just how do you propose we do that, airline security being what it is these days?" I said.

"So drive."

Billy blanched. His car *was* here, since he'd been working yet another job with Mark the previous week, so technically there was no reason not to drive. He'd flown up to get Molly and bring her back as a favor to our moms. When she barfed on a plane, the flight attendant had to clean it up.

"But . . . I, uh, can't take her home until she's back to normal—Mommo would have a fit."

"I need my own lab. I've been working on an adaptor genotype, and I can't risk the data leaking out."

"Mark could probably find us something secure around here," Billy pressed.

"God, no. Government noses are the last thing we need sniffing around now. It has to be my lab."

"Where is Mark, anyway? Isn't he supposed to be here?" Thomas said.

I shrugged. "Something came up. He'll be here later."

Billy ignored us and went on talking to James. "What am I supposed to do with her there? I can't let you keep her at your lab like some sort of specimen."

"There's always your place," I said helpfully, and enjoyed the wince I'd known would follow.

"That is not a good idea. I have a"—he cut me a glance—"friend staying there right now."

"A *friend*?" I said, trying to keep my eyes from narrowing. (It's harder to do than you might imagine.)

"Friend of a friend, really. It would be tough to explain Molly in her current incarnation."

"Can't you just tell this *friend* to run along? A *friend* would understand that things come up." One of his bimbos, on the other hand, might not be so accommodating.

"I also have a job scheduled. I won't be able to ape-sit—sorry, Moll—after tomorrow."

"Oh, don't worry about that. I can help you look after Molly for a few days."

"Don't you have a client to take care of?" he said.

"Nope. I called to check on Mr. Brown—you'll be happy to know he didn't die—and he assured me Thelma will have her position. I've already relayed the news to her. She couldn't be happier. So it appears I'm all yours," I said. Sweetly, of course.

Mark showed up right after James left to catch the next available shuttle back to New York to begin his preparations. Thomas had already gone back to work. Billy and I were packing.

"How's Molly? Did James figure her out?" Mark asked first thing.

"Still orange and furry. We're heading back so he can work on her in his lab," Billy said.

"Taking your car?" Mark said with a ghost of a grin.

"Ha ha. Yes, we are. Unless you'd care to take her in yours? I'll throw in Ciel, if that'll sweeten the deal."

"Hey!" I slapped his arm with the back of my hand.

Mark laughed. "Sorry, bud, you're on your own. But I can recommend a good Manhattan car wash."

Billy gave him a sour look. "You are kindness itself. Hope you don't need me for anything—looks like I'll be busy for the next few days."

Molly joined us before Mark could respond, dragging the backpack she'd been cramming with her currently unnecessary clothing behind her. When she saw Mark, she let go of the pack and climbed into his arms, grinning big and hugging his neck.

"Hello to you, too, Molly," Mark said, patting her back. "Hope you're enjoying all this monkeying around while you can, because James is going to have you back to normal in no time."

Molly nodded enthusiastically. I was glad to see her adjusting to her situation, but hoped she didn't get *too* comfortable with her new form. The thing about projecting auras is, once you have the energy, it's always there within your reach. It could be awkward if Molly decided it would be fun to liven up future school functions with impromptu zoology lessons.

Mark put down Molly. "Billy, can I talk to you for a second?"

"Sure, come on up with me. I have a few more things to get from the guest room. Ciel, keep an eye on the munchkin?"

I nodded, curious, but I was used to the guys disappearing to plot their next job together. "Come on, Molls, let's go pack some car snacks."

Billy cut me a look. *"No junk,"* he said, his voice full of threat.

I smiled sweetly at him. "Would I do that to you?"

Mark left after his brief meeting with Billy, with only a "try to keep the girls out of trouble" for Billy and hair ruffles for Molly and me. Apparently things were back to the status quo with him. Just as well, since it appeared I was about to embark on some sort of (probably *really* ill-advised) romantic adventure with Billy.

I'd gone upstairs right after them to, um, get something I

forgot to pack, pausing at the door to the guest room. (Okay, so curiosity won. There are valid reasons for eavesdropping, and I happen to think making sure the two guys currently driving me crazy weren't discussing *me* is a damn good one.) Thirty seconds of "the Agency" this and "the Agency" that was enough to tell me it was boring old business, and I'd gone back downstairs. With my spare toothbrush. You can never pack too many toothbrushes.

I stuck to Billy like glitter on glue while we finished getting ready for the trip. No way was I going to give him an opportunity to eject his latest inamorata without me in earshot of the phone conversation. If I was going to be involved with him, I at least wanted to go in with my eyes open. Knowing Billy, he wouldn't shed his baggage before he was certain he had me in reserve. If then.

Billy came back in from loading our bags into the car. I'd watched him out the front window the whole time. He hadn't taken his cell out of his pocket once.

"All right, monkey girl, the car's packed. Do you have your Sea-Bands on?"

Molly clapped her wrists together like Wonder Woman, showing Billy she was heroically prepared to stave off an attack of motion sickness.

"I gave her some candied ginger, too," I added. I also had plenty of large, resealable plastic bags, just in case. I didn't mention that in front of Molly, though. Didn't want to undermine her confidence in the home remedies.

"All right, then. Let's hit the road. Anyone need one last pit stop before we leave?"

Molly shook her head. She'd already been to the bathroom. I, not wanting to leave Billy alone with his phone, hadn't. I looked at him sharply but decided he seemed preoccupied enough with Molly to risk a brief absence.

He was hanging up as I returned.

"Who was that?"

"Mommo. She wanted to say hi to Molly."

"What'd you do?"

"What do you think? I let her say hi to 'Molly.'"

"She bought it?"

He lifted one brow and didn't bother to answer. Silly me. Of course she bought it.

It was considered bad form to use another adaptor's primary aura without express permission, but I didn't imagine Molly much cared under the circumstances. I think being stuck in orangutan form qualifies as implied consent.

I was still a little suspicious. "So why aren't you still Molly? Since you just hung up and all?"

"Mommo wanted to talk with me again after she spoke to Molly. Any other questions, or is the interrogation over?" He winked.

I held myself tall (-ish) and brushed past him to pick up Molly. "I don't know what you mean."

"No?" He put his hands over Molly's ears on the pretext of dropping a kiss on her head, and said, "I like it when you're jealous."

He removed his hands before I could respond, so I had to make do with a dirty look.

"Did you let Molly touch you while you were her?" I said, shifting topics. "Maybe she could reabsorb her own aura somehow."

His eyes lit. "No—didn't think of it. Cuz, you *do* have a brain."

Back to projecting Molly in an instant, he took her from me, staggering a bit under the weight. Molly clutched her erstwhile aura and closed her eyes. She rubbed her hands up and down Billy's arms, bringing them to rest on his face. As her thumbs stroked his—or rather, her own, in this case—cheeks, she slowly opened her eyes.

Nothing happened.

Billy looked at me with Molly's eyes, so disconcertingly like his own. *What now?* they asked.

"Give it a minute. You know secondhand auras can take a little longer," I said.

"That's right," he agreed, though it wasn't technically so. Sure, you had to touch a secondhand aura longer to maintain it, but you ought to be able to project it instantly. Besides, it wasn't really secondhand—it was her own aura. But what are straws for if not to grasp at?

"Hey, why don't you help? Maybe a double dose would do the trick."

I obliged and added my own Molly projection to the mix, taking one of her hands and trying my best to give energy instead of take it. Unfortunately, it doesn't work that way. Assuming an aura is voluntary; it's not like you can impose it on someone, even if they are an adaptor.

Still, we waited a full minute more before we gave up, each resuming our own form. If it hadn't happened yet, it wasn't going to.

"It was worth a shot," Billy said with a too-casual shrug. "Not to worry, sis. James is the brilliant one, and we'll be at his lab in no time. Heck, he'll probably have the whole thing figured out by the time we get there."

Molly drooped against him, the saddest little ape in the whole world.

After she was safely buckled into a hastily obtained car seat in the backseat of the Chevy—an indignity she was forced to suffer because of her size—Billy walked me around to the front passenger door.

Seizing the opportunity, I said, "I am *not* jealous. Just so you know."

He pulled me to the back of the car and opened the trunk, blocking us from Molly's view.

"Did you forget to pack something? You want to run back and—"

He framed my face with his hands and kissed me, slowly. I was too surprised to protest. When he finished, he took me by one elbow and deposited me in the front seat. I couldn't fail to notice he hadn't claimed there was no reason for me to be jealous.

The thought was shoved aside by the car that pulled up alongside us and stopped, blocking our exit. I waved it along without looking, trying to indicate our parking place would soon be available. Billy slid into his seat, started the car, and gave a polite tap of the horn. The car blocking us didn't move. Finally I looked over and tried to catch the driver's eye.

Shit! "Step on it!" I yelled at Billy.

"What? Are you crazy?"

"It's the woman from the zoo! She must be after Molly. *Go!*" I said, bouncing in my seat, ready to reach a leg over and stomp on the accelerator myself.

"And where do you suggest I go?" Billy asked, looking around him. Car in front, car behind, and Zoo Lady holding steady where she was. What did she think we were going to do? Just hand Molly over?

"I don't know. Crap. Someone's getting out of her car. Two someones. *Big* someones. Hurry, before they have us surrounded!"

Billy grinned, took a deep breath, and jumped the curb. He missed the parking meter by inches. Thirty or so feet down the sidewalk (fortunately clear of pedestrians), he found a spot to squeeze through back onto the street.

Zoo Lady was slowed by waiting for her goons to get back into the car, giving Billy a chance to get ahead of her, down obscure streets. A last look behind me showed her gesticulating frantically at somebody next to her in the car.

My speculation about who it could be was cut short by Billy swerving around a corner. "Do you know where you're going?" I asked.

He gave me a quelling look I took for a yes. "Just keep an eye on Molly, okay? Make sure she doesn't barf in my backseat."

Molly looked to be on the verge of sleep, completely unimpressed by our daring escape. Candied ginger is a wonderful thing. Especially when laced with a hefty dose of Dramamine.

Chapter 7

James's lab was straight out of a sci-fi movie. He wasn't officially affiliated with Columbia, other than as a perpetual student, but they backed his research anyway. They must have really liked him, because the large work space was outfitted with more computers than an Apple showroom, and had scientific gizmos out the wazoo. I couldn't tell you what half of them were, much less what they do.

Security was tight. Even Billy had to wait for James to let us in, unusual for a guy who doesn't generally grasp the concept of "locked." Once we were inside, he gave Billy a key, so he could come and go with Molly as needed, and commandeered the freshly acquired stroller, pushing it to an alcove equipped with a sofa, several TVs, and an array of video game consoles.

"There you go, Molly. The tests might take a while, and I wouldn't want you to get bored. Have at it."

I smiled at James, a little surprised it had occurred to him to find ways of distracting Molly from her troubles. His brain usually occupied a much loftier plane. He shrugged, and helped her out of the stroller. She dove straight for the Wii, something I knew she'd been lusting after for the better part of two years. Auntie Mo thought video games rotted the brain, and persisted in shoving her offspring out into the fresh air whenever they begged to be allowed to join their peers in the twenty-first century.

Once Billy and I had eluded Pregosaurus Rex, the rest of the ride up had been uneventful. Ultimately, we'd decided it must have been a phenomenal piece of bad luck that Zoo Lady had been passing us as we were loading the car, and that pregnancy hormones, coupled with an overdeveloped sense of zoo-volunteer responsibility, had impelled her orangutan recovery attempt. That didn't fully explain why she had the goons with her, but we put it behind us anyway, certain nothing could come of it once James had Molly back to her own form.

After Molly was settled and figuring out how best to hold the controller with her simian hands, James led Billy and me to the other side of the large room. We had to wend our way around several tables crowded with experiments in various stages of completion.

"Has there been any indication yet that she might bring herself out of this?" James asked, directing his question to both of us.

"Not a flicker," Billy said.

James nodded. "All right, then. I have a few tests lined up— I'll get started right away. By the way, do needles bother Molly? I'll need to take some blood."

I spied a nearby stool and sat, hard.

Billy laid a casual hand on the back of my neck while James automatically ran a paper towel under the nearest faucet, wrung it out, and handed it to me. I dabbed my face and the insides of my wrists while they went on talking. Needles do bother *me,* just a tad.

"Not much. If you poke her while she's in front of that Wii, she probably won't even notice," Billy said.

James gave me a sideways look. "Ciel, I need you to do me a favor."

"Sure." Anything, as long as it involved me leaving before he brought out the needles.

"Mom and Auntie Mo are expecting me to show up"—he checked his watch—"in about half an hour. They're decorating—"

"Oh, no you don't! I had decoration duty last year. No way can I do that two years in a row. It's inhumane."

"Well, I can't be there, obviously. My hands are full here. You think it would be fair to make Molly wait?"

"Why can't Billy go? He's better at being you than I am. I always slip up and throw in too much of me."

"I can't," Billy interjected. "I'm meeting someone—a *colleague,*" he stressed, for my benefit, "uptown in an hour. I can't put it off. I can stay with Molly until she's comfortable here, but then I have to leave."

"*Grrr.* This is so not right."

"Sorry. No choice," James said with an angelic smile. Easy for him to be happy. Nonadaptor that he was, he never had to fill in for anybody.

"Okay," I said grudgingly. "But I'm going to do it as myself. If I have to suffer, I may as well get credit for it."

"You can't do that," James said.

Billy backed him up. "He's right. If James isn't there, our mothers will be suspicious—they know there's no way in hell any of us would do it two years running. We can't risk it."

"But . . ." I looked from one to the other. No getting around them.

"*Fuck!*" I said under my breath so little Miss Big Ears wouldn't hear.

It's a very intimate thing, wearing somebody else's aura. Lets you know everything there is to know about another person, physically at least, and there is only so much I want to know about any of my brothers. I had changed into James's clothes before switching to his aura for the express purpose of avoiding an unintentional glance at his naked body. Somehow that would seem like even more of an invasion of privacy in his case, since he was incapable of doing the same in return.

It was my parents' turn to host the infamous Come As You Aren't party, though in reality Dad had little to do with it. Mom and Auntie Mo were equally in charge every year; only the venue alternated. Dad and Uncle Liam stayed as distant from the details as any two hapless husbands could, no matter where it happened to be set. Whoever wasn't hosting the party provided a hiding place for the husband of the one who was. Right now I suspected Dad and Uncle Liam were sharing a Guinness in Uncle Liam's man cave, probably playing a friendly game of darts and commiserating over the latest economic crisis on Wall Street. Lucky bastards.

On the front porch of my parents' familiar Upper West Side brownstone, I inhaled deeply and plastered a distracted look on James's face. I thought I knew my brother well enough to pull this off, but I'd never been him in front of our mother. She had a nose like a terrier when it came to her kids hiding behind fake personas—with three of us capable of looking like anybody we wanted at any given time, she'd had to develop other ways of discerning our true identities. She claimed we all had "tells," but of course wouldn't dream of letting us know what they were.

I was banking on the fact that she had no reason to suspect I was anybody but James. First of all, she knew none of us was a willing helper, nor were any of us so altruistic we'd be likely to sub for each other. Second of all, she had no reason to suspect I would be anywhere near New York until the day before the party at the earliest.

The front door was locked. *Crap.* I patted my pockets— empty. I'd forgotten to get the key from James.

Relax. No big deal. Surely it wouldn't be the first time he'd forgotten his keys. I'd just knock—

The door swung open.

"James. You're late." My mother grabbed me, barely looking at me as she dragged me into the foyer. "I was just about to call you. You know we have a hundred things to do today. Are you okay?"

She came to a full stop and looked at me sharply. "James? What's wrong?"

I felt my eyes widen as I looked down at her. Aurora Halligan. She was my mother, but I still thought of her that way whenever I first saw her after I'd been away for a while. An imposing entity, bigger than the word "Mom"—or her diminutive size—can contain. She's me in thirty years, only with brown eyes, bigger boobs, and a much lighter sprinkling of freckles. On her they look good.

"Uh, nothing. Nothing is wrong. What makes you think

something is wrong?" Thank God James's voice didn't squeak under maternal interrogation the way mine did. That would've been a dead giveaway.

"You look pale. Are you sick?" Her hands flew to my forehead, where they paused briefly before she grabbed my chin and pulled my mouth open.

"Let me see your throat."

I came *that* close to complying before I remembered James didn't put up with Mom's nonsense. Me, I just stick my tongue out and let her look. I've found going through a quick physical is easier than balking, because she'll usually settle down once she figures out I don't have the bubonic plague.

I jerked my chin away and deflected her with a kiss on the cheek, something James was known to do in desperation. Since he wasn't normally the most demonstrative of fellows, it tended to derail Mom's obsessive concern.

"Mother, I'm fine. I just got busy at work. Now, what do you need me to do?"

She smiled up at me, her eyes the swirling light and dark brown of pecan shells, happy now that she was assured death wasn't lurking over my shoulder. Tucking her hand into the crook of my elbow, she guided me toward the living room, a cavernous space by city standards. It was furnished with good, solid pieces: oversize and overstuffed sofas and chairs upholstered in brocades and velvets. The tables (coffee, end, and occasional) were dark, heavy pieces, impervious to children. Somehow Mom had managed to marry hideously expensive with ugly as sin. But I loved it. It was home.

"You can bring down the folding tables and chairs from the

attic. Don't bother with the tablecloths—the caterer is taking care of the linens—but do see if you can find those globular oil lamps. You know the ones I mean? Good. I think they'll make splendid centerpieces, don't you? We can't use flowers this year. Your great-aunt Helen is allergic, and she claims it isn't fair that her sneezing gives her away every year, so we're trying to be accommodating. Not that it will make any difference—she can't hold an aura longer than fifteen minutes at a time anymore, poor dear. The change hit her hard. So we'll do the oil lamps surrounded by origami figures from nature—you'll find the paper in your father's study, only don't use the orange. The orange is hideous when it's backlit by the flames, and besides, it's too Halloweeny—"

"Mother, slow down. I don't do origami."

"Of course you do, dear. You made me lovely origami gifts when you were a child—remember the swan? Or was that a goose? The neck was kind of in between, but whatever it was, it was gorgeous and I loved it, such a shame the dog ate it. Anyway, you made them all the time when your brothers were out playing football. It's why I thought of using origami instead of flowers. We could go with silk flowers, of course, but that would be tacky, don't you think? If you use flowers, they should be *real* flowers, not fake flowers, though I suppose, when you think about it, fake flowers are somehow symbolic of us, aren't they? Wait—no, not really. I mean *we* are realistic fakes, not fakey fakes—"

Damn. "Mom—Mother! I've, um, forgotten how."

"Don't worry. I bought a book. Just follow the directions—it'll all come back to you."

Not likely. I'd never made an origami figure in my life. I could only hope the directions were clear and my fingers were more dexterous as James than they were as myself.

"Ciel? Is that you?" my aunt's voice piped in from the kitchen.

"Of course not, Mo. It's James. Why would Ciel be here?" Mom called back, then ran to answer the phone.

Auntie Mo made an entrance, emerald eyes flashing and auburn hair gleaming. She was named for Maureen O'Hara, and her resemblance to the actress—when the actress was in her prime, of course—was uncanny. I suspect she may fudge a little.

"Why indeed would Ciel be here?" She pierced me with a look. I swallowed hard.

Family rumor had it that Auntie Mo was visited by occasional flashes of the Sight. Billy has tried to reassure me that Mo herself was the one to start the rumors, but I'm not sure they don't contain a grain of truth.

At last she smiled and held out her arms. "James, my favorite nephew!" She said the same thing to all my brothers. "Come here and give me a squeeze."

She engulfed me in a warm embrace. I was used to Auntie Mo's exuberance and normally would have returned her affection with equal enthusiasm. Frankly, I adore her, even if she intimidates the hell out of me. But James was more aloof, so I confined myself to a few light pats on her back.

"So you're the poor bastard roped into helping us this year. You sure your sister isn't here with you? I could have sworn . . . No, I'm being silly. None of you would be here if you didn't have to be." But still she held on to me as if she could peek beneath my aura with her fingers.

"Mo, come here." Mom's voice, thank God. "The caterer is at it again. Can you handle it while I call the liquor store?"

Mo reluctantly let me go. I headed straight for the attic and started hauling out chairs. After umpteen trips up and down the narrow stairs, I started folding paper. A hundred and ten paper cranes (okay, so they looked more like airplanes; wings are wings, right?) and sixteen paper cuts later, I faked an incoming call from the university and made my escape. Even Mom and Auntie Mo couldn't argue with a command appearance before one of James's professors. Everyone in the family was getting desperate for him to actually graduate with a degree in something, so his schoolwork superseded all else.

The cab dropped me at the building that housed James's lab. I paid the driver and left without waiting for change, praying that James had come up with a solution. Cute as Molly was as an ape, I really missed her human form.

"Jimmy!" a pleasant tenor voice called out. I ignored it. Nobody called my brother Jimmy.

"Jimmy! Hey, *James,* it's me."

Crap. I turned slowly and locked eyes with the prettiest man I have ever seen. Not handsome. Pretty. Silky, platinum blond hair—looked natural, too—waving above a button-down collar, a killer tan, wide-set violet (I kid you not, Liz Taylor violet) eyes, full rosy pink lips, and an almost-but-not-quite-too-delicate nose. Body like a dancer, long and lithe. *Why* had James never brought this guy home? Would an introduction have killed him?

"Hi," I said with a neutral smile. Best to keep things middle of the road until I figured out how well James knew this guy.

His mouth curled into a pout. "Oh, come on. Is that all you can say? Haven't you missed me at all?"

Huh? "Uh, sure. How've you been?"

He stepped closer, invading my space. I tried to step back but was pulled against his chest. "Horny," he whispered. "How about you?"

Chapter 8

I pounded on the lab door, breathless from my run. "James! Where are you?"

I'd ditched Pretty Boy with some excuse about a family emergency, told him I'd call him later. He'd pulled a Sharpie out of his pocket and written a phone number on my forearm, so I wouldn't forget "this time." Geez.

"*James*. Open *up*." I kept pounding until I heard a telltale click, then pushed the door open so abruptly it almost flattened Billy's nose.

"What are you doing here? Where's James?" I said.

"I came to pick up Molly. James had an errand. What's wrong with you?"

I shoved the door closed behind us and dropped James's aura. His clothes swamped me, but I didn't care.

"James is—" I stopped short.

But Billy was too good at reading me. "Gay? Yeah. What about it?"

"What? You knew? And you never told me?"

He shrugged. "You're his sister. I assumed you knew. I mean, didn't you ever wonder why he never brought a girl home?"

"So? I never brought a guy home. I thought he was shy, like me."

Billy cracked up. I kicked off James's shoes with enough force to send them across the lab, lifted the too-long legs of his pants with both hands, and started pacing. "Shut up. I didn't know, okay? Not until about two minutes ago, when one of his boyfriends stuck his tongue down my throat."

"He's seeing someone again? Good for him. He was kind of messed up after he broke up with the last guy."

I plopped onto the nearest chair. "Jesus. Do Mom and Dad know?"

"Of course they do. He told them officially when he was sixteen, but I think they suspected long before that."

"Thomas? Brian?"

"Yup."

"Well, that's just *great*. Fucking *fantastic*."

"What are you so mad about? You have something against gay people?"

"Of course not, you idiot. It's just . . . I just . . ." I stopped, words stuck behind the tears I didn't want to let fall.

Billy squatted next to me and stroked my cheeks, loosing the stream. "What, then? What is it?"

"Why didn't he tell me? I thought we were close. Doesn't he trust me?"

"You *are* close, in all the ways that matter. Maybe he just didn't feel comfortable discussing his sex life with his baby sister. Lord knows I don't talk about mine with my sisters."

I sniffled. Loudly. "Ha. You don't have to. They can read about it in the papers." That wasn't much of an exaggeration, either, considering some of the high-profile models and actresses he'd dated in the past.

"Oh, good. You're still jealous. I plan to use that to my advantage. Just so you know." His fingers slipped to my neck and started making little circles there.

"Are you trying to distract me?"

His lips replaced his hand. "Mmm-hmm. Is it working?"

Yeah, pretty much. I leaned my head to one side to give him better access. "No, of course not."

He chuckled and nipped my earlobe. "I bought some ice cream while I was out earlier. After we put the munchkin to bed later—"

I pushed him away. "Molly! Where is she? Did James fix her?"

"No, James didn't fix her. Yet. She's napping in front of the TV set. Wore herself out with the Wii Fit. I was just waiting for you to come back so we can take her to my place for the night."

I hesitated. "About that. Maybe I'd better stay with James tonight. I need to talk to him about . . . things."

"That can wait. He won't have time for any heart-to-hearts until he figures out what to do about Molly. Besides, from what you just told me, it sounds like he might have company of his own to consider."

I pushed up a sleeve and let the number show through. "Yeah. That reminds me—don't let me forget to give him this."

Billy grinned. "Guy's not taking any chances, huh?"

"Nope. He's serious. Stunning, too. Totally drool-worthy."

"Did you catch any of his energy? If you want to pass it along to me, I'll see what I can do for you." He was teasing. Maybe.

"Don't be ridiculous. I couldn't think of him like that, not now. Not that I would consider . . . even if he weren't— Stop laughing! And why aren't you jealous, anyway? Don't you even care that I totally ogled him before I found out he was gay?"

"I probably would be jealous if I thought there was a snow-ball's chance in hell of you throwing yourself at the guy. But you're not that kind of person."

"Huh. Maybe I should find out what I've been missing."

He shrugged. "You're human. It's normal to find a little variety intriguing." He paused, a thoughtful look on his face. "Listen, Ciel, I can give you all the variety you ever want."

What? Was he offering what I thought he was offering?

Duh. This was Billy. "Is that why *you* want *me*? Because I can change into your whim of the day without you having to bother with seduction? Huh. Efficient." I should've been mad, and I was, but mostly I was insecure. I looked away from him, feeling stupid.

"Ciel, look at me. No, not at my shoulder. At me." He lifted my chin and waited until I met his eyes before he continued. "I've had enough variety to know it's not all it's cracked up to be. I want you. Only you. *As* you. You, on the other hand, haven't been sampling. I'm not naïve enough to think you wouldn't eventually wonder what else is available out there. I'm just saying there's a safe way for you to experiment, if you ever want to."

God, what an offer. "You are unbelievable, you know that? You think just because you've gorged at the great big hookup smorgasbord everybody must want to? Geez."

He cocked his head, pondering. "I wouldn't say 'gorged.' Supped until replete, maybe. But there's definitely room for dessert," he said, finishing with a wink.

I heard a noise from across the lab. Molly must have woken up and started back in on the games. "Maybe I better get a hotel room."

Back at Billy's (he having talked me out of staying at a hotel—okay, maybe not *talked*, exactly, but his tongue was involved, so close enough) I looked around surreptitiously for signs of a female presence. Near as I could tell, the only women's paraphernalia around belonged to Billy, for use with his female auras, so whoever his guest had been had done a good job covering her tracks when clearing out.

Not that I cared.

The condo was a large, open space, heavy on the black and modern. The kitchen took up one corner, separated from the rest of the room by a gray granite-topped breakfast bar. A comfortably spacious bathroom and a huge walk-in closet fit into the area under his sleeping loft. The leather and steel décor wasn't what I would've chosen, but it suited Billy.

I wasn't sure how Billy was going to handle the sleeping arrangements, so I dumped my suitcase on the couch.

"I'm taking a bath," I said as soon as I pulled out some clean clothes. I wanted to scrub that phone number off my arm so I could quit adapting it away.

"Great. Can you take care of Molly while you're at it? She could use a little freshening up herself."

"You want me to take a bath with an ape?"

"Well, I can't do it. I'm her brother. It wouldn't be seemly."

"It's not like you'd have to be naked to give her a bath. I'm sure she won't be traumatized."

"Look at her." Billy gestured broadly, his arm following his sister. Molly was running around the condo, jumping up onto every available surface, climbing the stairs to the loft, and swinging from the railing. The longer she was in orangutan form, the more apelike she was becoming. "Do you think she could take a nice, calm bath without soaking whoever is with her? At least you'll already be naked. You can dry off more easily afterward. Besides, it'll save water. Sharing baths is the green thing to do."

I set my face. No way was I sharing my bubble time with a hairy little creature, even if she was my cousin.

"Come on, cuz. Please? I'll cook dinner for us if you do." His eyes were beseeching.

"Oh, geez. You are going to owe me big-time, pal. Come on, Molly. Bath time."

"I'll make it up to you, I promise. When this is all over, I'll give *you* a bath." He flashed his dimples and headed for the kitchen.

The bath with Molly turned out to be a lot more fun than I thought it would be. We used loads of bubble bath (I did not let myself question why a full-grown man would have such a large assortment of sweet-smelling bath products on hand—I knew I probably wouldn't like the answer) and turned the jets on low to keep the froth lively. Molly decorated first herself, then me, giving us puffy white hair and beards. We squished masses of iridescence through our cupped fingers, making bubble volcanoes that shot out of the tub. I figured if Billy was going to blame the mess on Molly, we might as well make the most of it.

When we were done, I pulled two large, plush bath sheets from the linen cupboard (the ones already hanging on the heated towel bar were soaked, for some strange reason) and wrapped us in them. Molly looked adorable peeking out from between the folds, with only her wise eyes and snub nose showing. I hugged her close, rubbing her back briskly.

"What do you say, Molls—shall we go for the full treatment?"

Billy's blow-dryer had three settings: low, high, and hurricane. I did Molly first, leaving her soft and fluffy, with orange hair punked out on the top of her head. She loved the warm air blowing over her and twirled wildly with arms extended skyward, like a ballerina on crack.

I was applauding one of her more expansive pirouettes when a *bang!* interrupted playtime, making me jump. Either a car had just backfired in Billy's living room or somebody had fired a gun. I turned off the dryer and parked Molly on the toilet (lid down, of course), told her to stay put, and edged the door open.

The living room was empty. I couldn't see into the kitchen from where I was, so I crept out, gingerly shutting the door behind me. I didn't need a diminutive fur person playing Watson to my Sherlock.

Something—instinct, a sixth sense, whatever—kept me from calling out to Billy. Instead, I padded toward the kitchen, ducking to stay out of the line of sight until I was safely behind the breakfast bar. When I peeked around it, the first thing that oozed into my field of vision was blood, garnet black against the dark floor.

I stood at once and rushed into the area screaming, *"Billy!"*

But it was a woman laid out against the opposite side of the bar, one hand clinging to the handle of the cutlery drawer. She was wearing jeans and a T-shirt. Flat, leather sandals showed off her pedicure. As I stared in shocked horror, her eyelids fluttered open and her lips formed the word "help."

Galvanized, I grabbed a dish towel off the counter and pressed it to the expanding blood spot just above and to the right of her navel. There was a wound on her back, too, so I reached for another towel and covered it, applying pressure as hard as I dared. She'd been shot through and through, but I couldn't tell if it was from the front or the back. I just knew that if I didn't slow the bleeding, she'd be dead before I could find out who she was.

"Billy!" I hollered again. "Where are you? I need you. *Now*, damn it!"

No answer. I let go of the towel and disengaged the woman's hand from the drawer. I lowered her gently, counting on her body weight to keep the towel pressed firmly against the back wound, and placed her hand on the towel in front.

"You keep holding this right here," I said to her. "You hear me? Hold it tight. I have to get a phone."

A clatter on the breakfast bar above me alerted me to Molly's presence. She dropped a cordless handset on me. Smart monkey.

I was about to dial when I heard a voice coming from the phone: "Nine-one-one. What is your emergency?" Molly had already dialed for me.

"A woman has been shot. She's bleeding. Hurry!" I said, and verified Billy's address. I disconnected as soon as the dispatcher told me help was on the way, swiping the phone across my bath towel before I laid it back on the counter. My fingers were still covered in blood. I wiped them off, too. Which was silly, because they got bloody again as soon as I touched the woman.

Who was she? And, geez, what was I supposed to do with her until help came? *Think, Ciel.*

What I really wanted to do was call Mark. But I didn't dare take the time—if she didn't bleed to death, shock could still kill her. What were you supposed to do for shock? Keep her warm, right?

Okay, blankets. I ran to the living room. On the sofa was a throw cover Auntie Mo had knitted for Billy when she was stuck on bed rest with one of her pregnancies. God, she'd kill him if he got it stained. *Crap.* What the hell was I thinking? It was there. I needed something now. I grabbed it. It was as ugly as sin, anyway. A few bloodstains couldn't make it any worse.

I laid it over the woman, checking her wound as I did. It was still oozing. Oozing was better than gushing. I was afraid to lift her to check her back. The pressure from her weight on the wadded-up dish towel might be all that was keeping her from bleeding out.

"Thanks, Ciel." The words were thready, spoken so softly I couldn't be sure I'd heard my name. I stared at her face, really looking at it for the first time.

"My God . . . Laura? Is that you?"

It was. The long, auburn hair was now black and severely short, with eyebrows dyed to match. Or had the auburn been the dye job? But her forest green eyes were exactly as I remembered them. Her lips and cheeks were devoid of their usual healthy color— *duh, Ciel, no wonder*—but it was definitely Laura. She was the CIA operative who'd recently helped Mark crack a neo-Viking terrorist ring. I'd met her in Sweden when my then-client's fiancé got kidnapped by the group.

"Laura, what happened? What's going on here? Who did this to you?"

"Well, I could tell you, sugar, but then . . ." She tried for a smile, but it was replaced by a grimace as she sucked in a breath.

I was glad she still had her sense of humor, but killing was not something I wanted to contemplate, even in a punch line.

"Don't talk. Help will be here soon."

"Ciel, tell Mark . . ."

I took her free hand. "Quiet now. Save your breath." As much as I wanted to know what she had to say, I was more worried about her dying. First things first.

"Tell him he was right."

Her eyes fluttered shut again, and I felt panic grip my chest. I had to fight the urge to shake her, to yell at her to stay awake. The wail of a siren getting closer penetrated my growing bubble of fear, easing it some. *Thank God.* Maybe now my head wouldn't explode.

"Forget it," I said, babbling anything, trying to will her into consciousness. "His ego is big enough without letting him think he was actually right about something. You just hang on, and when you're better I'll help you come up with a reason he wasn't right. I'm good at reasons. Reasons are my specialty."

She didn't respond.

"Laura? *Laura?*"

I heard the door behind me open, and then Billy was there. He pushed me aside and checked under the throw, setting his mouth grimly at the bloody sight.

"Jesus," he said.

"The ambulance is almost here. Police, too, I imagine. I heard the siren," I said.

"*What?*" Billy avoided police like kids avoid brussels sprouts. His aversion was instinctive and strong.

"I had to call for help. Look at her—she could die." I whispered the last part, and hoped she couldn't hear me.

He gathered himself. "Right. You did the right thing. Let me think for a second."

His eyes went someplace far away; the sirens got louder. They were almost here.

"Billy, what's going on? Who shot Laura? Why does she look different? Is she on assignment? With you? Is she the one you had to meet?"

He ignored my questions. "Okay, here's what we're going to do. You're going to take Molly and get the hell out of here. Take her back to the lab. Or, if you can't get in there, take her to James's apartment. Come on, hurry!"

He took my elbow and lifted me away from Laura.

"But I'm wearing a towel!"

"So throw some clothes on, and do it fast. Where's Molly?"

"I don't know. She was there a second ago. Molly—where are you?"

"Never mind. I'll find her—you get dressed. Molly! Get your furry little butt over here."

Billy put Molly in the stroller while I dressed in record time. No underwear, no bra—couldn't take the time. Just jeans, T-shirt, and flip-flops. Trust me, going commando isn't as liberating as you might think. I didn't want to contemplate the places I was likely to get chafed.

I left the building just as the cops and medics were arriving. One of the officers—a young guy, maybe a rookie—held the door for me, and took a second to ask me if I'd heard any gun-fire. Fortunately, he didn't look too closely at my well-bundled baby, partially hidden by the stroller top.

"You mean a little while ago? I think I heard something, but I'm not sure it was a gunshot. I just thought it was a car backfiring. Nothing's wrong, is it?"

"Could be, ma'am. Stay alert."

"I'll do that."

I pretended to hail a taxi, but waved the driver on as soon as the police were in Billy's building. After crossing the street at the nearest corner (didn't want to risk getting picked up for jaywalking with Molly in tow), I eased into the shadows between two buildings and waited. I had to see if Laura was okay, if she was still alive when they brought her out.

The medics came out first, pushing Laura on a rolling stretcher. She had a mask on her face—oxygen, I supposed—and an IV in her arm. They loaded her efficiently, turned the siren back on, and were gone in a matter of seconds. I sagged with relief. Worried though I was, at least I knew she was now where she had the best chance at survival.

My relief was short-lived. As the ambulance neared the end of the block, two policemen walked Billy out of the building, his hands cuffed behind him.

Chapter 9

Thomas met me at the police station. After the cops drove off with Billy, I'd called him and told him everything I knew, which wasn't much. He'd caught the first shuttle out.

I'd left Molly with James—he was back at the lab, still working hard to solve her problem. He'd been shocked about the shooting, but figured it was better for him to focus on what he could fix and leave the legal maneuvering to our big brother.

Thomas and I were going to try to bail Billy out, but it wasn't going to be easy. He was being held on charges of assault with a deadly weapon and attempted murder. Thank God it was still "attempted"—Laura was hanging on. Mark—he'd been my next call, right after Thomas—was at the hospital with her and planned to stay until a CIA watchdog got there to replace him. It was just luck he happened to be in Manhattan already.

Thomas wore an understated but obviously expensive suit. His briefcase was the finest black leather, simple and sleek. Ditto his shoes. He looked every inch the prosperous lawyer he was, in

full legal shark mode, circling the familiar waters of the criminal defense system. I was sure he'd have Billy out in no time.

But I was wrong.

Tight-lipped, he led me out of the station. I'd had to wait in
the reception area while he saw Billy—apparently, honorary cous-
ins had no special right to see the accused—and Thomas wouldn't
talk until we were in the backseat of the limo he'd hired as soon
as he'd arrived.

"What's wrong? Why are they holding him? Surely they don't
think he shot Laura?"

"That's precisely what they think, and they have enough cir-
cumstantial evidence to back it up. Add to that, he refuses to
identify the female who phoned in the emergency. At least he's
keeping you out of it, but no bail tonight."

Crap. "Maybe if I told the police it was me—"

"Wouldn't do any good. It would only complicate the situation, and they'd still hold Billy for shooting Laura."

"But . . . he didn't. He couldn't have."

He looked at me sharply. "Did you see it happen?"

"Well, no. I was in the bathroom with Molly—"

"Then you don't know," he said. Pure, annoying logic.

"Of course I do. Billy wouldn't do something like that."

He looked like he was about to dig his legal heels in and say
something else (I suspect that's a reflex for him), but then made
a blinding switch from lawyer to brother, and smiled gently instead. He laid his arm over my shoulders and pulled me to him.
His aftershave was the same one Dad used. I found the scent
comforting, and buried my face in his shoulder.

"Don't worry, Ciel. We'll get him out of there tomorrow
morning at the latest."

"Doesn't Billy have any idea who did it? Why doesn't he just tell the police?" I said.

"He can't. Or won't."

I sat up straight. "What? But that's stupid."

"He wants to see Mark. Said he can't talk to anyone else before he talks to him."

"Well, then, let's go get Mark."

"That's where we're heading. So, how's Molly? Has James figured her out yet?"

"Not unless he's done it since I dropped her off at the lab. Looks like he's planning to pull an all-nighter."

"Good. Why should he get any sleep when the rest of us can't?" Ah, brotherly love.

Mark was in with Laura when we got to the hospital. Thomas and I hung out in the ICU waiting room, drinking bitter, lukewarm coffee and not talking a whole lot. Wasn't much we could say in front of the hollow-eyed occupants sitting vigil until the next brief moment they were allowed to see their loved ones.

Mark, looking grim, joined us after a few minutes—no one was allowed to stay with a patient in ICU for long. He shook Thomas's hand and gave me a perfunctory kiss on the top of my head, but I could tell his mind was still back in the room with Laura.

When I'd first met Laura on a sailboat in the Baltic, I'd jumped to the conclusion that she and Mark were involved beyond an ordinary working relationship. After getting to know her a bit, I'd decided not. But the look on Mark's face now made me wonder again.

"How is she?" I asked.

"Not good. She lost a lot of blood. But she survived

surgery—that's promising. If they can keep her stable for the next few hours . . ."

"Does she have family we should contact?" I asked, knowing I'd sure as heck want my family around me if I got shot.

"No," Thomas said shortly.

"Nobody she'd want us to," Mark said at the same time, his eyes flinting over. Guess Laura's family wasn't as warm and fuzzy as mine. But how did Thomas know that?

My mind bubbled with other questions, though, so that one got bumped down the line. "Why was she at Billy's? Were they working together on something? Who would do this to her?"

Surprisingly, Mark answered, at least partially. He didn't look pleased. "If they were working together, it wasn't official."

"Why would Billy let himself be taken?"

Mark shrugged. "Didn't have time to leave between when the paramedics got there and the police came, I expect."

"But why *as* himself? Wouldn't it have been better to use a different aura? I just don't get it."

"What good would being anyone else do him? The apartment is in his name. He's still connected, and being somebody else would just complicate matters more."

"Can you get him out of jail tonight?" I hated to think of Billy in a cell.

"Not officially. Even if he really worked for the Agency, our hands would be tied. It's a local law enforcement issue."

"Unofficially?" I pressed.

"Let's just see what Thomas can do for him tomorrow first."

At that my brother looked somber. "You better convince him to come clean about who really did it, or all my brilliant legal maneuvering won't amount to a damn thing."

Mark nodded. "I'll see what I can do," he said, and then addressed me. "You'll stay with Laura?"

"Of course I will."

"We better go," Thomas said.

Mark shook his head. "I'd prefer you to stay here with Ciel, if you don't mind. At least until Harvey gets here."

"Harvey's in town?" Thomas seemed surprised.

"Should be by now."

"Who's Harvey?" I asked.

"A colleague," Mark said. No further explanation, but then there never was when it involved the Agency.

Thomas didn't seem anxious to stick around for Harvey's arrival. "You'd have an easier time getting in to see Billy with his lawyer along."

"You have to see Harvey again eventually, you know. Besides, I have a suit your size in my car. If I need you, I'll use you. If that's okay." Mark didn't sound like he expected Thomas to refuse the use of his aura, and Thomas didn't. But he'd had to ask.

"Just don't swear at any judges. I don't practice law regularly in New York anymore, but I'd hate to lose the privilege."

Mark gave him a half-grin. "I'll restrain myself. You watch your sister. Try to keep her out of trouble."

I turned to Thomas as soon as Mark left. "So who's this Harvey, and why don't you want to see him?"

Thomas ignored my question. "Mom's left half a dozen messages on your work phone. Probably flooded your home phone, too. Haven't you given her your new cell number?"

I swallowed guiltily. "Not yet."

He hit me with the big-brother look.

"What? I'm going to give it to her." *Maybe.*

"When she can't get hold of you, who do you think she calls?"

"You could always change yours, too. It works great for at least a week." That was usually how long it took for one of my rat fink brothers to fess up to knowing my number, after which said brother folded like a bad poker hand and told her. Not that I could blame them. I ratted them out to Mom on a regular basis, too. It was impossible not to—Mom was just that good.

Thomas shook his head. "You are a piece of work, Ciel. I should call Mom right now and tell her you're in town."

"But you won't because then I'd be forced to tell her you're here, too, and neither of us wants that, now, do we?" I said with my sweetest sisterly smile.

A nurse approached us, looking professionally grave in her scrubs. "Are you relatives of Ms. Vale?" she asked, her voice as cool and smooth as a vanilla milkshake. She had the concerned-yet-detached look of someone who was used to dealing with people in high-stress situations. I imagined ICU would do that to you.

Thomas stood and stepped forward, equally calm, cool, and collected. No one was going to out-smooth him. "I'm Thomas Halligan, Ms. Vale's attorney. I have a copy of her medical power of attorney with me, if you need to see it."

I looked at him sharply. That was news to me.

"No, no. That's quite all right for now. If someone from legal demands it, I'll let you know."

We followed her back to a room filled with wires, tubes, bags of IV fluids, and beeping machinery, all connected to Laura. She was a tall woman, but in that bed, in this situation, she looked so fragile it scared me. Her cheeks had less color than the pillowcase her head rested on. I wanted badly to see her eyes, to reassure myself that their dark green depths still glowed with a humorous appreciation for life, but they remained shut. At least movement beneath her eyelids kept her from looking dead.

Thomas went at once to her side and lifted the hand that didn't have a wire attached to the finger with some sort of clothespin-like connector. He looked at her so tenderly I knew it couldn't have been his first encounter with her.

"How do you know Laura?" I asked.

He pulled his gaze away from her, but only briefly, as if to remind himself I was in the room. "We went to law school together."

"Laura's a lawyer?"

"No. She didn't finish," he said, a memory—good or bad, I couldn't really tell—distancing his eyes.

"Why not? The lure of spy-dom too much for her?"

"Something like that." His voice grew more remote, and I knew I shouldn't pursue it.

Yeah, right.

It's not that I don't recognize signals. I am, in fact, supremely adept at picking up on all sorts of subtle conversational clues. My problem is with impulse control of the mouth. "So, were you guys an item back in the day, or what?"

Thomas gave me that big-brother, stay-out-of-my-business look he's so good at. "We dated for a while," he said in a tone that didn't invite further questioning. Huh. Like that ever worked with me.

"So why'd you stop? I like Laura."

"It wasn't entirely my idea."

Oooh! Maybe he'd introduced her to Mark. Maybe she met Mark, fell in love, and followed him over to the CIA! Poor

Thomas. No wonder he hadn't presented Mom with a bride yet—he was pining for Laura.

I patted his arm.

"Stop it," he said, annoyed.

"Stop what?"

"Thinking. Whatever your little brain is concocting is not what happened, and, no, I am not going to tell you any more than that." His face slammed the door on sympathetic sisterly discussion.

I tried anyway. "You don't know what I'm thinking."

"And I'd like to keep it that way."

I couldn't tell him, either, because the same nurse led another man in, the Harvey Mark had mentioned, I figured. He was a heavy guy but carried it well. The expensively tailored suit helped, and the gray peppering his dark hair added a certain gravity to his otherwise jolly appearance.

The nurse spoke first. "Two of you are going to have to leave. Ms. Vale shouldn't have more than one visitor at a time, and then only for a few minutes." Her eyes scanned the monitors while she addressed us. Thomas and Harvey ignored her while they sized each other up.

"Halligan," Harvey said with a brisk nod, his second chin wobbling with the motion.

"Smith," Thomas responded, mouth stiff, like the name tasted bad.

Harvey seemed about to say something back to him, but instead turned to me and extended a hand. "I'm Harvey Smith, a friend of Laura's."

I thought I heard Thomas snort, but his face was blank when I stole a glance at him. I took Harvey's hand. His handshake was firm but not macho—points for him. "I'm Ciel Halligan, Thomas's sister. I met Laura in Sweden."

"Yes, I've heard about you. Laura spoke very highly of you." His smile was warm and, I thought, genuine. He seemed a jovial fellow overall. But for some reason Thomas couldn't stand him, so I kept my radar up and running.

There was a small sound from the bed as the nurse checked one of Laura's tubes. Harvey went to her. The nurse stepped aside, and I saw Laura's eyes had opened.

"Hey, kiddo. You been setting yourself up as target practice?" Harvey teased in a favorite uncle sort of way. Laura's lips curled before she opened her eyes.

"Hey, Harv. What are you doing here?" she said, her voice scratchy and painful to listen to.

"Somebody has to watch out for you. At least until you learn not to step in front of stray bullets. Who do you think you are—Supergirl?"

The merest hint of a smile lifted the corners of her mouth. Whatever Thomas felt about Harvey, it was apparent Laura liked him. "Me? Careful? Where's . . . the fun . . . in that?"

"Fun, schmun. You know the rules. You screwed up, kiddo."

The smile disappeared in a wave of what looked like shame. "I know. I'm sorry."

Thomas's face kept its stony reserve throughout their exchange, but his eyes gave him away. He cared for Laura, and it was killing him to see her like this. I cleared my throat not only to break his pained fixation, but to let Laura know we were there.

She turned, her eyes flitting past Thomas to me, and then jerking at once back to him. She swallowed, hard, and the tears that had pooled in her eyes spilled over. "Hello, Tom. Didn't expect to see you here."

"I'm here for Billy. Mark asked me to come." Voice neutral, perfectly pleasant, leaking none of the censure I saw in his eyes. Judging from the way Laura set her mouth, she saw it, too.

"Is Billy all right?"

"He's in jail," Thomas replied bluntly. "For shooting you."

"I see."

"That's it? That's all you have to say?"

She closed her eyes. "For the time being, yes."

I shoved myself in front of Thomas. "Wait a minute—Billy couldn't have done it. Laura? Who did it? *Not* Billy."

Thomas took me by both shoulders, from behind. "Calm down, Ciel."

The nurse planted herself between me and the bed. "I'm afraid you'll have to leave now. All of you."

Thomas jerked his head toward Harvey. "He stays."

"Security should be posted *outside* the room—" the nurse tried drawing herself up authoritatively. That tends to be a big waste of time with Thomas.

"No buts. I'll leave and take my sister, but Smith stays right by Laura."

Okay. Thomas might not like Harvey, but he trusted him. Harvey acknowledged him with a nod, and I was pulled from the room by my brother's very firm grip on my hand.

"Ciel . . ." Laura's thready voice stopped me, and I looked back over my shoulder. "Thanks. For helping me." Unless I was terribly mistaken, there was an apology in her eyes.

Chapter 10

Never, ever trust an ape. They'll con you every time.

I was back at the lab with Molly, having been unceremoniously dumped there by Thomas after our visit with Laura. He'd been unforthcoming about his background with Laura, and—even more unforgivable from my point of view—unwilling to discuss why everybody but me seemed to think it wasn't out of the question that Billy shot her. My stomach was twisted with worry.

Which meant I was a little distracted and not precisely paying attention when Molly locked me in James's storage closet. I rattled the knob. When that proved useless, I banged on the door.

"Molly, you get back here and open this door at once. Do you hear me? I mean *now*, young lady!" I loaded it with as much menace as I dared, hoping a good infusion of "stern parent" would jolt her into obedience.

Apparently not.

"Molly. Come on, sweetie. Open up. I've changed my mind. You can keep playing your video game." I waited, ear to the door, listening to see if my offer had any effect. Nada. So I gave in to bribe inflation and upped it. "*And* you can have some ice cream."

There was a pause in the Wii racket, followed by the sound of the fridge opening and closing. *Crap.* Chalk one up for primate intelligence—she knew better than to trust me. She got her own damn ice cream.

Shortly after I relieved James of Molly-sitting, I had decided the mature thing to do would be to limit her game playing and junk eating. So much for my misguided attempt to show respect for Auntie Mo's parenting preferences. I should've just parked myself nearby with a magazine, inserted some earplugs, and let the brat go cross-eyed and get a bellyache.

I looked at the painstakingly drawn letters on the note in my hand, a request from Molly. We were out of toilet paper, she'd written after popping in and out of the bathroom. (Well, actually she'd written "T P?" with a crooked question mark, but I'd extrapolated her meaning.) Stupid me hadn't even checked to see if she was telling the truth. Who lies about a thing like that? James kept his supplies in this—I swallowed hard—tiny room, and so here I'd come. And here I was, stuck, the treacherous *snick* of the door locking behind me my first clue that I'd been had.

Not thinking about my claustrophobia worked well for about thirty seconds. Then I pounded on the door with both fists. If I'd had any fingernails to speak of, I'd have clawed it to splinters. Since I didn't, I hyperventilated my way through a list of expletives the rational part of me hoped Molly had never had occasion to hear before, topping it off with, "*Damn it,* I'm going to blister your hairy little bottom if you don't unlock this door right now!"

The door swung open. Billy caught my wrists on a down-swing, a gleam in his eye and a wicked curve to his mouth. "Promise?" he said.

I yanked my hands free and threw myself into his arms, gulping air. He grabbed my ass and squeezed, and I was so happy to see him I didn't even slug him for it. I kissed him before he could kiss me. Not nearly as good at it as he was, I wound up hitting the corner of his mouth and squooshing my nose into his cheek.

One of his hands deserted my butt and adjusted the tilt of my head. "Looking for this?" he whispered, and then did that thing he does with his tongue. *Bingo*.

After a moment he ended the kiss and said, "Unless you want me to push you back into the closet and shut the door behind us, I believe we'd better stop this and check on the chimp."

"Orangutan," I corrected dizzily, gathering myself.

He shrugged as he turned and headed across the lab to where Molly was enjoying her last seconds of video-gaming freedom. "I know, but it wasn't alliterative."

"Wait a minute—how did you get out? Thomas said there was no chance of that until tomorrow morning."

"I know a judge who was kindly disposed to do me a favor."

"You blackmailed a judge?" I said, appalled.

"Now, why do you automatically assume the worst? Maybe she just likes me."

"Yeah, right. What do you have on her?"

"Nothing. Not one thing. She just happens to remain grateful that I'm not dating her daughter." He grinned and tugged my hair.

"What'd you do? Intimate that you'd become her offspring's prison pen pal if she didn't help you out?" I said wryly.

"I never said that."

"I'm sure you didn't have to. So, are you totally off the hook? Are they going to concentrate on finding whoever really shot Laura? Who did, anyway? Do you know? Why didn't you just tell—"

"Slow down, cuz. Allow me to ignore one question at a time."

I grabbed his elbow and turned him to face me. "Billy— what's going on?"

He opened his mouth, then shut it again, his eyes going evasive on me. "Look, I just came by to say adios to you and the monkey. There's something I have to do, and I may drop out of sight for a little while."

I inhaled deeply, ready to launch into a protest. He placed a hand over my mouth.

"A *very* little while—and I didn't want you to worry."

Twisting my head away from him, I proceeded. "But you can't do that."

He raised one eyebrow. "No? Actually, I'm pretty good at it." He pulled away and crossed the lab in long strides toward the video game noises.

I stuck to his heels by taking two steps for each of his. He gave Molly a quick hug and tickle, followed by a dire warning about what he would do to her if she ever locked me in a closet again, then handed her off to me. Words swarmed on my tongue, battering at my teeth to get out, but of course I couldn't let them escape, not with little ears right there. So I put her down and told her she could go back to playing video games (with an internal apology to Auntie Mo), all the while gripping one of Billy's arms so he couldn't leave.

Once Molly was out of earshot, I gave Billy my sternest glare. "We've already been through this. If you think you're shoving me over to the sidelines this time—"

"Wouldn't dream of it—no, *honest*. I'm going to need your help. If James were here to stay with Molly, I'd take you with me right now. But he's not. Molly's safety has to come first."

I reluctantly agreed. "Can't you just tell me where you'll be?"

He shook his head. "I'm not sure where I'll end up yet. Just take care of her for me, Ciel. I'll be in touch when I can."

It's hard to stay mad at a baby animal, especially one who curls up in your arms, puckers up her rubbery monkey lips and kisses your cheek, then promptly falls sound asleep on your shoulder. I sat with her on the battered love seat, cradling her close to my heart while my mind spun with dire possibilities. What was Billy up to? Did he even know who had shot Laura? Did Laura know? Thomas and I had learned from speaking with the surgeon before we left the hospital that the bullet had entered her from the front, so she had to have been facing the shooter. If she did know, why wasn't she saying?

Too antsy to stay still, I laid Molly on the love seat and tucked a tattered afghan around her. It was one Auntie Mo had made for James when she was in her knitting phase, a cousin to the one I had covered Laura with at Billy's place earlier. We all had at least one (some of us several, I thought, thinking guiltily of the ones I had hidden away in my linen closet at home and dragged out only for Auntie Mo's visits) made with joyous disregard for good taste by Mo's loving hands. Fortunately, that particular phase ended before she got to constructing wearables. I think the prospect of making neck holes and sleeves pushed her into her next passion, ceramics, which we all found easier to deal with, even if the various ashtrays (none of us smoke) and vases were equally hideous. At least ceramic pieces broke eventually. Sure, maybe with a little help, but nothing unjustifiable.

I roamed the lab, pulling out my cell phone half a dozen times, and putting it back in my pocket when I couldn't decide whom to call, or what to ask if I could decide. Not really expecting to connect, I gave Billy's cell number a try.

His recorded voice responded after one ring. "Hello? Hello? You'll have to speak up—I can't hear you. . . . Well, if it's important, I expect you'll call back." *Beeeeep.* Ha ha. Very funny, Billy.

I left a voice-mail message: "If you're a no-show at the party I will *kill* you. Better yet, I will tell on you and let your mother kill you. But I'll watch and offer suggestions. *Painful* suggestions. And . . . be careful, damn it."

I hung up and paced some more, winding up in front of the refrigerator, looking for something that wasn't total junk food, in case Molly woke up while I was eating. Had to set a good example.

Looked like my choice was between leftover vegan pizza and something in a casserole dish that had a piece of masking tape with "Return to Mom" written on it. I waffled. Mom's would either be wonderfully delicious or spectacularly bad. She didn't have much of a middle ground when it came to cooking. When she got creative in the kitchen, the flavors could either caress you like a long-lost lover, elevating you to gastronomic raptures, or they could blindside you, leaving you reaching for the nearest beverage with enough bite to resurface your tongue. Oddly, she couldn't seem to tell the difference herself.

It was a gamble, but since the pizza looked stale enough to shatter if I dropped it, I decided to risk the casserole. Peeked under the tinfoil. Leaned over it, into the fridge. Sniffed cautiously.

"Don't do it."

I jerked upright, banging my head on the freezer compartment's door. Spun around to find James studying me.

"Ow. Geez, don't sneak up on me like that." I rubbed my scalp vigorously, trying to dilute the pain.

His eyes smiled. "I wasn't sneaking. You were merely too preoccupied to notice my arrival."

"Huh. Well, you could at least update your fridge. Maybe get one that doesn't attack."

He shrugged. "Sorry, but I have better things to spend my grant money on. Besides, this refrigerator is perfectly adequate for my needs."

"So is this one of Mom's, um, more interesting recipes?"

"Yeah. I've been throwing it out one serving at a time, in case she comes and checks on it. She gets suspicious if the whole thing disappears too fast."

I grinned and closed the fridge. "You always were the smart one. So, did you pass Billy on your way?"

"Billy's out? When?"

"Just a little while ago. He popped in, said good-bye, and took off. Wouldn't say where he's going, only that he had to disappear for a while."

"Oh, boy. Thomas is going to—"

The door to the lab crashed open, rattling beakers and test tubes, and wrenching the resident orang from her peaceful sleep directly into a tornadic frenzy.

"Where is he?" Thomas thundered. He has a moderately deep voice normally, but when he's mad he can give Metatron a run for his money. That was him now—the Voice of God, in full wrath mode.

"Who?" I said, though I had a pretty good idea, and ducked out of his way, running after Molly. She was dragging the afghan behind her, scattering video game disks and empty soda cans as she spun her way through the alcove like the Tasmanian Devil. If she made it to the lab proper, James's temper would be a match for Thomas's, and two roaring brothers was more than I could handle.

"For God's sake, Thomas, what are you yelling about?" James said, spreading his arms to block Molly.

"*Billy.* Where is he?" Thomas ignored the three of us and stalked through the lab, looking behind every freestanding counter and in every cabinet.

I grabbed the trailing end of the afghan and yanked it, pulling Molly, who refused to release it, toward me. "Will you just calm down for a second?" I said to Thomas. I was about to execute my brilliantly improvised plan of throwing the afghan over Molly's head to catch her when something must've tipped her off. She sidestepped at the last second, clinging relentlessly to her security blanket, and circled me, cocooning my legs in hideously crafted yarn. I was on my ass in two seconds flat, eye to agitated eye with Molly, propping myself up with my hands on the floor behind me, one of them resting in a half-finished carton of Rocky Road.

"Argh!" I said. "*Stop!* Everybody just *stop*."

Miraculously, they did.

Molly blinked, yawned, and crawled onto my lap. I sighed and patted her back. Since I'm nice, I used the hand not covered with Rocky Road.

"Now then," I began. "Tell us what is going on, Thomas. Try to use your courtroom voice," I added, earning a brotherly glare.

He took a deep breath. Lawyer-like reserve washed over him in a deceptive wave of calm. "Billy left his holding cell. Unofficially."

"He told me the judge let him out," I said, seeking to calm the troubled waters. Thomas probably didn't know about the judge's daughter.

"Yeah? Well, if he said that, he lied."

"Actually, he didn't so much *say* it. It was more like he implied it," I said, thinking back to our conversation. Thomas wasn't impressed by the distinction.

"Why would he leave before he made bail?" James said. "He knows it will only add to his trouble."

"Only if someone finds out," Thomas said.

I stood, shifting Molly to my hip and picking up the ice-cream carton. "How could they not find out? Wouldn't the empty cell tip them off?"

"The cell isn't empty." The fury reignited in Thomas's eyes.

Oh. "Uh, who?" Somebody had to be filling in for Billy, somebody with adaptor capabilities. And whoever it was, Thomas wasn't pleased.

He looked from James to me. "Our brother."

I sucked in a breath. "Not *Brian*." Geez. No wonder Thomas was pissed. Brian was a lot like Billy in his propensity for getting himself into scrapes, but not nearly as successful at getting out of them.

"We have another brother I'm not aware of?" Thomas said.

I made a face at him. "But how could he? Don't they monitor those cells?"

"Billy convinced a rookie coming on shift that he hadn't had his phone call yet. He called Bri, and ever so cleverly conveyed to him that he needed to see me, his lawyer. So Bri showed up as me—and see if I don't break *his* neck for using me without permission—and made the switch with Billy while they were conferring privately. Then Billy left as me—I'll break *his* neck, too, *twice,* for thinking up this scheme and dragging Bri into it. So Bri is sitting pretty in jail as Billy, waiting for me to bail him out tomorrow. Serve him right if I left him to rot."

"You can't do that—Bri could never handle himself in prison." This from James, ever the voice of reason.

"Gee, ya think?" More sarcasm from Thomas. He seldom resorted to it so blatantly; when he did, it tended to hit you in the face, like slamming into a glass door you hadn't known was there.

Not one to throw fuel on the fire, James cocked his head to one side but didn't comment. Brian in jail was a scary thought. Billy *knew* Brian couldn't wrap his head around violence—what in the hell was he thinking to leave him in that place, alone and unprotected?

"Isn't it at least possible Billy has a good reason for doing it?" I asked, though I personally couldn't think of one. What was wrong with me? I ought to be throwing Billy under the bus. I'd never had any trouble getting angry at him before. If this is what hormones did for you, screw it. I wanted mine back under control.

Thomas looked at me with shuttered eyes. "Oh, I'm sure he does. At least in *his* mind."

"Never mind that for now. The question is, what can we do for Brian? Is there any way to get him out of jail tonight?" James said.

"Don't you think I would have already if—" Thomas stopped dead and looked at me, the shark returning to his eyes.

"What?" I said, wary.

"What was the judge's name?"

"Huh?"

"The judge Billy told you was letting him go—who was it?"

"I don't know. He didn't say her name."

He looked pleased. "Her? Well, that narrows it down. Okay, what'd he have on her?"

"What do you mean?" I stalled, not wanting to admit what I knew. No point in getting Thomas even angrier. My compulsion to protect Billy was confusing the hell out of me, but it was there.

Unfortunately, Thomas had plenty of experience reading my face. "Blackmail, Ciel. I'm going on the assumption that Billy wasn't entirely lying when he told you the judge released him. Maybe he was going to try blackmail next if he couldn't get Brian to fill in for him. Come on, what did he have up his sleeve?"

No point in arguing it. "The judge apparently doesn't want Billy dating her daughter in the future."

Thomas expelled a blast of air through his nose. "Figures. At least it gives me a pretty good idea which judge. Distasteful as it is, I think it might work." He looked at his watch. "I'll try my best, but I probably won't be able to get him out before morning."

"You're going to blackmail the judge? But, Thomas, you can't do that. Couldn't she have you disbarred or something?"

"Oh, it won't be me blackmailing her. If Billy can borrow my aura without asking, I don't suppose he'd have any objection to me returning the favor."

Chapter 11

No way was I going to let Brian stay in jail overnight. The odds of Thomas getting him released before morning weren't nearly good enough for my peace of mind, so I'd just have to take matters into my own hands. Whatever reason Billy had for getting my gentle, peace-loving brother mixed up in this, it had better be damn good.

When James was busy with Molly again, I borrowed the suit he kept at the lab for when he had to entertain university bigwigs to keep those grants flowing, and headed over to the precinct where "Billy" was still being held. The jacket was snug across the shoulders for Thomas's aura, and definitely not up to his usual impeccable standards, but it would have to do.

The young, uniformed woman at the desk remembered Thomas, and gave me a worshipful smile. "Hey there, Mr. Halligan. You back already?"

I shrugged. "Forgot to get a certain critical piece of information from my client. Do you suppose we could get the private room again? You know, privileged . . . stuff."

She seemed hesitant. I smiled big, making Thomas's teeth a half-shade brighter than they really were. Her eyes widened, the pupils getting larger. "Well, usually . . . um, sure. Sure. I'll set it up. Just be sure to stop by the desk on your way out, okay? I get off work soon. . . ."

Brian, with a big, goofy grin on Billy's aura, was handcuffed to the table when I got to the room. I waited until the door was shut behind us and then said, "What the hell, Bri?"

His eyes—those beautiful, dark blue Doyle eyes, not Brian's soft brown ones—looked perplexed. "Dude, you were just here. We've already been over this."

"Yeah, well I'm back. And this time we're switching places, just like you did with Billy."

"But why, man? I can wait until you bail me out. No sweat."

I pulled myself up to big-brotherly proportions. "Because I said so. Come on, no time to discuss. Let's go."

He shrugged philosophically, kicked off his shoes, shifted to a very tiny aura, and slipped out of his cuffs, both hand and ankle.

"Nice," I said, remembering how I'd pulled the same trick in Sweden when my last job went awry.

"I know, right? Billy gave me this aura. Said it was a handy one to have."

Yeah, trust Billy.

We finished the switcheroo, with me mostly keeping my eyes shut. I swear, if I never risked seeing another one of my brothers naked again, it would be too soon.

I made my way into the cuffs the same way Brian had—by borrowing the handy aura Billy had given him.

"So, who's going to bail you out tomorrow if you're in here?" Brian said, now thinking like a lawyer.

"Uh . . . don't worry about it. I have it covered."

The holding cell wasn't bad, as holding cells go, I supposed. There was only one other guy in there with me, and I was pretty sure I could take him if I had to, since I had access to Billy's strength. I'd feel even better if I also had access to his martial arts training. Unfortunately, some things don't convey with auras.

The guy looked Italian, maybe Greek, with buzzed black fuzz all over his head (and half his forehead). He probably shaved his scalp regularly so his skull-and-crossbones tattoo would show.

He smiled, big and evil, when he saw me glancing at him, proudly displaying a gold-capped front tooth. "We gonna play now?" he said, his voice rough, like someone had whisked an eggbeater in his throat. "You promised we'd play when you got back."

Crap. What had I done?

I clenched my fists, taking what comfort I could from the size of Billy's hands. Well, better me than Brian. At least I had no compunction about hurting other people when the need arose.

We were on our fifth hand of Five Card Draw when another officer came for me. "Looks like your lucky night, Doyle. Your lawyer's back again, this time with an order from the judge. You're free to go—for now."

Huh. Thomas must have come through after all.

"Just a sec," I said, and laid down my cards faceup—two queens and three tens. "Ha! Beat that!"

Bruno displayed his gold tooth again, looking more evil than ever before. He spread his cards on the mattress between us. Three aces and a pair of kings. "Read 'em and weep."

Yeah, Bruno had turned out to be a pretty good guy. Which is why, I supposed, Billy hadn't worried too much about leaving Brian here for a while.

And there it was again—that compulsion to make excuses for Billy.

I sighed and followed the officer out to face the music with Thomas. All in all, I thought I'd rather stay the night with Bruno.

It wasn't pretty. As soon as we were in the limo, Thomas laid into me worse than he ever had before, called me every kind of idiot there was, *yelled* at me—directly at *me,* which I couldn't remember him ever doing before, at least not this badly. Sure, I'd been around his temper before, but I was usually a spectator.

And then he washed his hands of me, threatening to evict me from my condo and my office because it was obvious I wasn't mentally competent enough to live by myself or run my own business. He further threatened to tell Mom and Dad what I'd done and let them deal with me for a change.

After that, I kind of lost track of what he was saying. I think my ears went numb.

Brian was on the other side of me. His medium-brown hair was long on top, close-cut on the sides and back, and his facial hair was kind of sketch, but it worked for him. He looked bored, like he'd heard it all before.

Which, of course, he had, when Thomas caught "himself"

walking away from the police station earlier. I could only imagine how that went over.

Once Thomas had yelled himself out, he took a deep breath and hugged me tight, muttering, "I'm going to *kill* Billy."

After a moment or two of blessed silence, I ventured to ask if the window between us and the front seat was soundproof.

"Of course. But it wouldn't matter if it weren't—the driver works for me."

Brian said, "If I'd known it was Ciel, I never would have switched places. I just wanted to say that, since you didn't give me a chance earlier."

Thomas shook his head, disgusted but calm. "Like that would have been any better."

"I would've been fine until morning," Brian said.

We were heading for Brian's bachelor pad. He shared a Williamsburg (the indie-rock/hipster culture was very important to Brian) apartment with three of his musician friends, one of whom was his current love interest. Maybe. She was the previous week, anyway. With Brian that didn't necessarily mean anything. He wasn't a player, like Billy. He was just a hopeless romantic who happened to have a very short attention span. He honestly thought he loved every girl he fell for, right up until he fell for the next one.

"Really," he continued, trying futilely to erase the skepticism from Thomas's face. "My cell mate was a nice guy—he was innocent. There was some kind of mistake, same as there was with Billy."

Not exactly the best comparison to make where Thomas was concerned. "Don't be an idiot," he said, but there was more resignation than anger in his voice. We were all used to Brian's optimistic view of human nature. He wasn't stupid, not in the low IQ sense of the word, anyway. Mom swears he tested close to genius level in those routine assessments given to all kids in school, second only to James out of the four of us. If that was truly the case, all I can say is he hides it well.

At least I could vouch for Bruno, and I did, being sure to add my opinion that Billy never would have asked Brian to trade places if he hadn't known Bruno was a safe guy. That earned me a similarly resigned look from Thomas. He had way too much experience with the legal system to trust an amateur's view of it.

"Not that I mind getting out," Brian continued. "I have a gig later, and I hate to leave the guys in the lurch. Hey, where's James?"

"He's babysitting Molly," I said. Thank goodness Auntie Mo still thought her youngest was with us back in D.C., so that was one less worry for now.

"Keeping her out of Mo's hair, huh? That's nice of him."

Thomas caught my eye and gave a tiny shake of his head. Okay, so we weren't going to explain about Molly yet.

"Something like that," I said, and proceeded to change the subject. "So, how's Jenny?"

Blank stare from Brian.

Geez. I was pretty sure that was the name of the latest. "Your girlfriend? Sandy blond hair, long legs, plays guitar, lives with you?"

He shrugged. "Oh. She moved out. But Suze is great—you're going to love her. Cute as a button. Mad organizational skills. We hired her to build us a database for our music and keep the books for us. The band needed somebody to take care of the business end of things."

Thomas looked a little put out. He had a tendency to want to watch out for all of us himself. "I could've done that for you, no sweat, no charge."

Brian flashed a smile that reminded me too much of Billy. "Yeah, but you aren't as hot as she is. And she's not charging us, either."

Jesus. Men. "Don't tell me, let me guess. Jenny didn't care much for Suze's 'skills,' and decided to leave."

"Kind of. I think it was mostly that Jenny didn't like sharing a kitchen with another woman."

"So Suze has already moved in? How convenient for you," I said.

"We're not charging her rent. We have a barter arrangement."

"Are you sleeping with her?" Thomas asked bluntly.

Brian shrugged. "Well, yeah. She asked me to. Why wouldn't I?" My brother. Just another happy-go-fucky kind of guy.

"Were you this disgusting when we were growing up?" I said.

"Hey, I did not sleep with her until after Jenny moved out."

"Huh. Big of you." My sarcasm was lost on him.

"Yeah, I thought so. It's not like I didn't have the opportunity."

"Brian, it's not right to treat women like disposable commodities." I spoke as if to a dim-witted child. That rolled right off him, too.

"Jenny's the one who left. Besides, you never really liked her anyway, so what do you care?"

True enough. She was a trashy wannabe rock star out to sleep her way into Brian's band. Still, it was the principle of the thing.

"Have you been tested for STDs lately?" Thomas asked, ever-practical.

Brian nodded, a goofy smile on his face. "Yeah. Suze made me. Seriously, you guys are gonna love her—she's the best."

* * *

Suze was at least ten years older than Brian. And she looked like a bookkeeper.

Strike that. She *dressed* like a bookkeeper. Who knew what lay hidden behind her Marian-the-Librarian glasses, her brown hair in a bun, her up-to-the-neck, down-to-the-knees dress? Perhaps the seething passion of a closet rock-and-roll groupie. Was there a tatt or two under all that starch? Why else would she be interested in my brother? Or, more precisely, he in her?

"Thomas, Ciel—this is Suze. Susan Hatcher. Suze—my brother, Thomas, and my sister, Ciel." Pretty formal intro for Brian. Usually, if he bothered to introduce a girl at all, he made do with a casual "that's so-and-so" and a wave in her general direction. My sisterly antennae rose another notch.

"Hi." Suze did the shy-Di glance-away thing, and pushed her glasses back up her nose. The lenses didn't appear to be very strong, so I suspected they were more to hide behind than for vision enhancement.

I eyed the youngest of my brothers (he was only a year older than me), wondering what in the heck he had going on this time. Brian went through a lot of girlfriends, none bashful. Or modest dressers.

Thomas didn't seem to find anything amiss. He nodded pleasantly and said, "Nice to meet you, Susan."

"Likewise," I said, and stuck out my hand. After a slight hesitation, she took it. A little on the limp side, but not to the wet-noodle extreme. Reflexively, I snatched a bit of her energy before I released her. Couldn't think of a reason I'd ever need her aura, but you never know.

"Suze is brilliant." Brian beamed at her. *That* look I was familiar with—he beamed at girls all the time. "She's already figured out a way for the band to turn a profit."

"Well, now. That *is* impressive," Thomas said, and cut me a sharp glance. He wasn't full of rapturous approval for the way I handled my business expenses, and never missed a chance to let me know it. I crossed my eyes at him really fast so Susan wouldn't notice. Not that she would, since she was too busy staring at her sensible, low-heeled pumps. Wait—was that a snake I saw tattooed around her ankle? Hmm.

"I didn't do anything special. I just drew up a few simple contracts and then made sure to collect partial payment in advance for the performances," she said, and cleared her throat.

While Thomas beamed at her along with Brian, I squatted and pretended to tie my shoe so I could get a closer look at the tatt. It *was* a snake, its mouth latched onto its tail, with the rattle on the end sticking out between its fangs. I *knew* it. More than your everyday, run-of-the-mill bookkeeper was our Ms. Hatcher. If that was the kind of body art she had on a readily visible patch of skin, no telling what she had going on where it didn't show.

As I stood, I casually checked her ears. Sure enough, alongside her conservative pearl studs were several empty holes. Might she have body jewelry in other, odder places? I shuddered. My needle phobia had prevented me from even a single piercing in each lobe. If I had to wear earrings, I adapted myself lobe holes.

So, either Suze had an interesting past she was trying to put behind her, or else she was currently playing dress-up for my brother. Not that it was any of my business. Not that not being my business has ever stopped me from being nosy. But curious as I was, this brother's love life would have to get in line behind a few other pressing issues, like Molly the ape, Billy on the lam, James's sexuality surprise, and Thomas's history with Laura. And, of course, most important: who shot Laura?

Suze excused herself after we declined her offer of refreshments. "I have to change before my night job." Huh. More bookkeeping? My, she was ambitious.

After she left the room, Thomas turned to Brian. "You haven't forgotten, have you? It's on your calendar?"

Brian's face fell. "Yeah. I'll be there," he said with a heartfelt sigh. "I just wish I could bring a date. Hey, you don't suppose—"

Thomas squashed his idea before it could get past the embryonic phase. "Don't even think about it. Mom would kill you."

Thomas was right. Nonadaptors were strictly *verboten* at the party, unless they were family members, like James. It was one of the few large social gatherings every year where our kind could relax and let their hair down without fear of being discovered. It was ingrained in all of us from birth not to jeopardize it.

"But Suze is special," Brian said. I'd seen that earnest look on his face a gazillion times before, and so had Thomas.

"You haven't told her, have you?" Thomas said, leaking a little Metatron into his words.

"God, no. Of course not!"

I believed him, and I could tell Thomas did, too.

"Good. See that you don't. And come early this year. It won't kill you to spend a little more time with the family."

Suze took that moment to reenter the room, and pretty much stopped the conversation in its tracks. Seeing Marian the Librarian turn into a flashback of Madonna's conical-metal-bra tour will do that. *This* was no bookkeeper—the cougar comes out to play—

and now I could see why Brian went for her. The transformation was so startling I had to look closely to make sure she wasn't an adaptor. Brian did not look remotely surprised to see her that way.

"What the hell happened to you?" I blurted, and then blushed. The ol' blurt-n-blush is one of my standbys, and never fails to elicit a disapproving look from Thomas.

I shrugged and gestured toward Suze. "What? Look at her!"

Suze laughed, a low, smoky sound that almost gave *me* a sexual tingle. I could only imagine the effect it had on men. Profound, judging by the looks on both my brothers' faces.

"It's for my night job. Bookkeeping doesn't pay as well as you might think." She lowered one eyelid at me, slowly. I goggled back at her.

"What's your night job? Dominatrix?" Oops. There went the ol' B & B again.

"Ciel!" Thomas glowered at me.

"Uh, sorry." I tried to look sheepish. "But seriously, isn't that look a little passé?"

Brian just laughed. Thank God one of my brothers has a sense of humor. "That's the point. It's retro-irony. Suze fronts a girl band downtown a couple nights a week. It's where we met." He gazed at her adoringly, every bit as smitten with this version of her as he was with the other.

Suze, equally smitten, gazed adoringly back at him. "Brian's band is so much better than mine—"

"No way! You draw much bigger crowds than we do."

"Only because of the way we dress. If you listen to our recordings, we suck."

Okay, so she was a modest hard rocker.

"You just haven't found the right mix yet. I told you I'd help with that—"

Thomas cleared his throat. "Brian? Can I have a word, please?" He led Brian toward the kitchen, out of earshot, leaving me and my big mouth standing there stupidly, trying not to stare at Torpedo Tits. Geez, if you hugged her, you'd be impaled.

"Well," she said.

"Well," I responded.

"Um, Brian has told me what a great family he has. It's nice to meet some of you." A bit of her earlier shyness was creeping back in. Guess the clothes could only carry you so far.

"Yeah, nice to meet you, too. Brian has said . . ." I paused, at a loss. Brian hadn't said a thing about her to any of us, as far as I knew. "Listen, can I be honest? You're kind of a surprise."

She smiled, big and wide. Was that a diamond I saw in one of her front teeth? Had that been there before? Maybe she just pasted it on for her act. "Yeah, I get that a lot."

"So, how long have you and Brian been, um, together?"

"Officially? Six and a half days. But we've known each other for almost two weeks."

Oh. Well, crack open the champagne.

"That's great," I said, easing toward the kitchen and trying to catch Thomas's attention. We needed to get back to Mark, find out where Billy went, swing by the hospital to see how Laura was doing, and get a progress report about Molly from James. Much too busy to stand around blabbing with Brian's latest. Besides, I don't like to get attached to any of his girlfriends—it's too hard to remember the names.

Thomas came out of the kitchen, leading a skeptical-looking Brian by one arm.

"Is it true?" Brian asked me.

"Is what true?"

Thomas gave him a warning look.

"That our youngest cousin is now"—he glanced quickly at Suze and then back at me—"a redhead?"

"Yeah. It's true," I said.

"Isn't she a little young to"—another glance at Suze, who was looking puzzled—"dye her hair?"

I shrugged. "Well, you know Molls. She's always been precocious."

"Mo's going to freak," he said, and burst out laughing.

Chapter 12

A big man in a black suit (must have been the CIA watchdog Harvey had been waiting for) supervised an orderly wheeling Laura's bed into the next elevator over as Thomas and I exited ours. Thirty seconds later and we would've missed them. Thomas grabbed a door as it started to close.

"Hold on—where are you taking her?" he said, using his you-*will*-tell-me voice.

The orderly stammered, "Th-the roof." The other guy looked disgusted and forcibly removed Thomas's hand so the doors could shut. Not everyone responds well to the you-*will*-tell-me voice.

From what I could see before the doors shut, Laura looked better than the last time we'd seen her. Though her eyes were closed, the massive quantities of blood poured back into her had added a little extra color to her cheeks, so at least she no longer matched her sheets.

Thomas jabbed the up button once and stood poised by the elevator we'd just left, but it was too late. It was gone. He set his jaw and waited. I pushed the button several times in rapid succession. Not that I think that makes the next elevator get there any faster, but it is a nice stress reliever. The fact that Thomas didn't stop me was telling—he was even more anxious than I was.

"Why are they taking her to the roof?" I asked, mainly just to say something. I didn't really expect an answer, but I got one.

"Because that's where the helipad is." His voice was tight. Obviously, he didn't like the idea of Laura taking a helicopter trip. I'm no medical expert, but it didn't sound like a real good idea to me, either.

"But why—"

The doors opened, and he stepped in, bumping shoulders with three surprised hospital visitors trying to get out. I shrugged and smiled apologetically, making it past the doors seconds before they shut. Thomas stood stiffly, looking as if his will alone would carry the elevator to the roof.

We got there as the orderlies were loading Laura onto a black helicopter. It didn't appear to be medical transport. Standing by, supervising the operation, was Mark. Thomas ran to him, and I followed, ducking under the spinning blades. Not that I needed to worry about decapitation at my height, but some things you do just by reflex.

"Where the hell are you taking her?" Thomas yelled, barely audible over the noise. Poor Thomas. He was having a bad day—nobody was staying put.

Mark leaned closer to his ear and said something I couldn't make out. Thomas nodded, not looking pleased, but not arguing. He pointed to me and said, if I read his lips correctly, "You take Ciel." Then he climbed into the helicopter after the stretcher.

I tried to follow him, but Mark caught my arm and pulled me back. Once we were clear, the chopper lifted off.

As soon as the din died down, I turned to Mark. His eyes were still following the helicopter's progress, his profile chiseled sharp and smooth against the night sky.

Damn. Was my heart ever going to stop speeding up at the sight of him? I should have been used to it—it wasn't really a surprise, not after all these years—but somehow it still startled me.

I gave myself a tiny shake. This would not do. I had questions, and I wanted answers. "What's going on now? Where are they taking Laura? Is it safe to move her? Why is Thomas going with her?"

He didn't reply.

"Come *on*, Mark. Just spill it. I think I have a right to know what's going on—I'm the one who found her bleeding all over Billy's floor. Besides, she's my friend, too." That was a bit of a stretch, considering we'd just met a few weeks earlier and had spent a total of maybe forty-five minutes in girlish conversation. But we'd *bonded*.

He ran a hand through his short, dirty-blond hair, looking off into the distance. "It's complicated."

"Have you noticed my life lately? I am the queen of complicated," I said wryly. "Anyway, you know it doesn't end well when you try to leave me out of the loop."

A half-smile softened the usual hard line of his mouth and sent a certain memory zinging back to the forefront of my mind. We'd been alone then, too, on a sailboat moored off a Swedish island in the Baltic. I'd been wrapped in a blanket—naked—and he'd been giving me a lesson in, um, dealing with sensations. It was a kiss I wasn't likely to forget. Speaking of complicated . . .

"Okay," he said, still not looking at me. "Laura is going to a safe house—no, I can't tell you where—because it was going to be difficult to ensure her safety here. Harvey insisted, and when it comes to stuff like that, whatever Harvey wants, Harvey gets. He is that high up the food chain. Thomas is going with her because . . . well, that's one you'll have to ask him. And if you don't stop looking at me like that, I'm going to think you're all over being mad about what happened on the boat."

Damn. The man had phenomenal peripheral vision.

"I, uh, wasn't really mad about that. I was, um, just a little surprised by the . . . I was surprised." My turn to look away. His turn to study my face.

"You were pissed as hell, and I don't blame you. I should never have—"

"That's okay. I'm all over it. Really. No problem. It was the situation. I realize that now."

"And what about Billy? Are you all over him, too?"

An image of me "all over" Billy popped into my head, along with the treacherous thought *Not yet, but soon.* Which kind of worried me. I mean, it was one thing to succumb to Billy's legendary charm while I was with him—there probably wasn't a straight woman alive immune to it—but I was standing not six inches from the man who had occupied my adolescent fantasies for years, who *still* made my heart race, and Billy was sticking his face in? That couldn't be good. What if whatever I was feeling for Billy was more than could be gotten rid of by scratching the itch?

Not that it was any of Mark's business. He wasn't the boss of me. "And what if I'm not?" I said. "What if I don't want to be over him?"

I recognized the irritated look. Mark had very little patience with people who didn't do what he thought was best for them.

"We had this talk in Sweden." As if that was that.

"You talked. I gave it careful consideration"—yeah, right—"and decided my private life is not your concern."

He narrowed his eyes, going hard-ass on me. "You decide that all by yourself? Or did your cousin help you come to it?"

"*Honorary* cousin," I said a little too quickly. It sounded defensive even to me.

"I don't give a damn if he's your twenty-seventh cousin twice removed. That's not why he's no good for you."

"That's not for you to say!"

"Isn't it?" He took my shoulders and leaned in.

I almost let him kiss me. I came *that* close. But then part of me stepped up and said, uh-uh, no way. If he wanted to kiss me, he could damn well do it when he wasn't trying to manipulate me.

I pulled back. "*Stop.* I know why you're doing that, and it won't work."

"Oh, yeah? Why am I doing it?"

"Because you know I've had a crush on you since I was thirteen years old, and you think you can use it to distract me from Billy. And it isn't very nice of you, either!"

"Is that so?"

"You know it is. You expect me to believe you're all of a sudden attracted to me after years of treating me like a kid sister? Just when Billy starts paying attention to me? Kind of a coincidence, don't you think? Well, I'm not buying it, and it's not going to work."

He didn't back away from me physically, but he pulled into himself, retiring behind eyes as gray and chilly as an arctic afternoon. When he spoke again, his voice was remote. "If that's the way you want it. Be careful, Ciel." He turned and headed for the elevator housing.

Why did I just feel like I'd stepped in it? *Damn.*

"Mark?" I said softly.

He stopped but didn't look at me. "Yeah?"

"You'll still help Billy out of this mess, won't you? I mean, you wouldn't . . . just because . . ." I trailed off, unable to think of a good way to ask if he'd sabotage a friend because of me.

His shoulders stiffened for a second before he relaxed them with a roll. "Yeah, Howdy. I'll still help Billy."

Mark saw me safely to James's lab, where Molly slept soundly on the sofa in the alcove, crazy orange tufts of hair framing her still-simian face. James listened with only half an ear while Mark gave him the rundown on Billy, Brian, Thomas, and Laura. It was plain my brother was anxious to get back to whatever experiment we'd interrupted with our arrival. I only hoped he was close to a solution.

After Mark left—without even ruffling my hair, I thought with a pang—James excused himself to get back to work. "Help yourself to whatever's in the fridge if you're hungry. There's a cot in the supply closet if you want to get some sleep. Or, if you like, you can go over to my place. I can keep one eye on Molly while I'm working."

I wasn't really hungry, and I was far from sleepy. "Can I just keep you company, or will that disturb you?"

His eyes were distracted but gentle. "You won't disturb me.

I'm at the point of making sure the proverbial pot doesn't boil over—not much to do but wait and watch."

I pulled up a high stool. "Think you'll be able to fix Molly?"

"I'd better. Can you imagine Mo if I don't?" A tiny, almost wicked smile appeared on his face, and for a second I saw the brother who used to play with me when the other boys wouldn't.

I grinned with him, sharing what I was sure was his mental image of Auntie Mo going berserk.

"So, care to explain to me how you're going about it?" I asked, more to pass the time than anything else.

His eyes lit with a happy professorial gleam. *Gaaah.* I'd done it now. Given a captive audience, he could go on for hours.

"Well, you see, gene regulation in mammals uses a mechanism of protein recognition of short DNA sequences called enhancers . . ."

He said something about hormones and chemicals that regulate gene expression. About the only word I recognized was "tetracycline," and that only because it had been prescribed for me once when I had pneumonia. Then, when he started in on some gibberish about hemoglobin and transgenic mice, and extrapolating the proper thingamajig construct into one of Molly's chromosomes . . . well, my eyes kind of glazed over.

"Have you always known?" I blurted out as soon as he stopped for breath. Didn't blush, though. This was my brother, and he was used to my ill-mannered tongue.

He froze but didn't pretend not to know what I was talking about—he knew me too well to think I'd really been listening to his genetics lesson. After a moment, he took a deep breath and said, "Yes. Always. For as long as I can remember."

I reached over and slugged him affectionately. "You could've told me, you know."

He relaxed, but not completely. His guard was still up. "Didn't think it mattered."

"It doesn't, you goof. But it might've been nice to know I wasn't the only one checking out guys while we were growing up. We could've, you know, compared notes."

"I somehow doubt we go for the same type," he said with a wry bend of his lips.

"I dunno. I met one of your friends earlier when I was you. I thought he was pretty cute."

"Really? Who?"

I pushed up my sleeve and allowed the barely faded Sharpied-on phone number to show. When they say indelible, they mean indelible. "This guy."

He actually blushed. "Ah. Well, you're in luck then. He swings both ways."

Was that a trace of bitterness I heard?

"James?" I waited until he looked me in the eye. "It doesn't make any difference to me, you know. Not a bit."

He hugged me then, both arms around me in what for him was a major display of affection. "Thanks, sis."

"As long as you don't try to borrow my clothes."

He shoved me away from him and laughed out loud. "I'm gay, you idiot, not a transvestite. Your wardrobe is safe."

Feeling confessional myself, now that we had that settled, I said, kind of offhandedly, "Hey, James—what do you think of Billy?"

He looked confused. "Our cousin?" After my nod, he shrugged. "Bit wild, but a great cousin. Why?"

I cleared my throat. In for a penny, in for a pound. "Not so much as a cousin. More as, say, a guy."

"Not my type." James grinned bigger than I'd seen him do in a while. Guess it was a relief not to have to pretend around me anymore.

"Do you think he might be my type?" I asked quietly.

Pause. Was that concern that flashed in his eyes? Then it was gone, and it was his turn to sound offhanded. "You guys got something going on?"

"No. I dunno. Maybe. I'm confused."

"Correct me if I'm wrong, but I always thought you were kind of hung up on Mark."

Geez. I coughed. "I'm a grown-up. I should be getting past childish crushes."

He studied me for a moment, then nodded, though he didn't seem convinced. "Billy . . . dates a lot of women," he said hesitantly, like maybe I wasn't aware.

I blew out a breath. "Yeah. He claims he's done with that. Is that even possible?"

He messed with some lab equipment, making minor adjustments to knobs and pushing a few buttons on Lord knew what kind of machines, all while holding his face in neutral. The classic James thinking look. I waited.

After a few minutes he reached some sort of conclusion and stopped fiddling with the test tubes and beakers. Looked at me. "Ciel, if Billy is expressing an interest in you that way, I think it must be genuine. As impulsive as he is—or was—with the opposite sex, I don't *think* he'd be reckless with your feelings. He cares too much about you to risk hurting you that way."

Something in my chest floated free. "Really? You don't think this is just another way for him to tease me? He does like to tease me."

"And, gosh, you never tease him at all."

I squirmed. "Well, I have to defend myself."

"Right. But, Ciel, one thing—are you sure he isn't more deeply involved in this"—he searched for the word—"problem with Laura than you think? Because *that* kind of trouble you don't need."

"You mean, could he have done it? God no, of course not. He couldn't have."

"But he might know more than he's letting on?" he pressed.

"Well, that's a given with Billy," I said.

"Then don't you think it might be a good idea to wait until everything has settled down before you pursue a relationship with him?"

"Well, geez, if you're gonna be all sensible about it . . ."

His lips curved, all tender big brother again. "Go to my place. Get some sleep."

"But Molly—"

"She'll be fine here with me. By the time she wakes up, I may have something that will help her. Now go."

I *was* exhausted, all of a sudden. "Call me if you fix Molly? Or if you need anything?"

"Yes. Now go on and let me work."

"Okay already." I stopped at the door and turned back to him. "What do I do if Mr. Hottie shows up?"

"Tell him I'll call him later. And keep your hands off him."

Chapter 13

James's apartment is one of my favorite places in the world. It's a two-bedroom, ground-floor apartment in Manhattan's Academic Acropolis, Morningside Heights. It looks like a stereotypical absentminded professor's place. Every inch is full of books, curios, gadgets, and gizmos, strewn about in a seemingly haphazard fashion, but that's deceptive. There's never a speck of dust anywhere, not a smudge or fingerprint to be found. It's fastidiously clean, but in a totally you're-welcome-to-put-your-feet-on-the-coffee-table way, and he does it all himself. I love it.

Since he has it fixed up with a biometric doorknob, I pulled up a partial aura of his hand for a second when I got there, and let myself in. I went at once to check on Herbert, James's pet chameleon.

I'm not overly fond of reptiles as a rule, but (naturally) I feel a certain kinship with Herbert. I think he likes me, too. It could be my imagination, but I'm pretty sure my willingness to grit my teeth and offer him mealworms from James's stash every time I come over has won Herbert's heart. The brief moment of squirming ickiness on the palm of my hand before his tongue whips out and grabs his snack is a small price to pay for the chameleon equivalent of undying affection.

Herbert's habitat took up a whole corner of the living room, floor to ceiling. It was equipped with a high-tech sunlamp, a mister to provide water droplets for him to drink, a living tree, and several crickets on death row. Herbert liked the crickets well enough, but the mealworms were his favorite. Or perhaps he was just entertained by the way I shuddered, holding them while he ogled them with his googly eyeballs, until he deigned to rid me of them. Who really knows what gives a chameleon its jollies?

Once Herbert was seen to, my own stomach sent me an SOS. The plain white fridge in my brother's sunny kitchen (fake window, with amazingly realistic artificial daylight shining through) was full of food put there by our mother. Risky, but I decided to assume James had already weeded out the more outrageous failures, and grabbed something that looked like leftover macaroni and cheese. Sniffed it. Not bad. Nuked it and took a tiny bite. Mmm . . . yummy. Tasted like it was made with some sort of mild, smoky goat cheese. Gourmet comfort food. *Way to go, Mom!*

I gobbled the rest. There was a crisp Pinot Grigio in the fridge, which I sipped while I flipped through cable channels until I found something suitably mindless on the Food Network. While I can't cook worth beans myself (I seem to have inherited the wrong half of my mother's skill in the kitchen), I am strangely fascinated by watching other people do it. And at least it might keep my brain occupied enough not to dwell on Laura.

Or on where Billy went.

Or on Mark, and whether I was being a total idiot not to try to fan his ember of interest into something more substantial. I mean, I'd been crushing on him for years. *Years.* And here I was, about to throw that opportunity away for my *cousin*?

I sighed. My really hot, not-real cousin, whom I'd loved and hated platonically since toddlerhood, who'd now walloped my stupid hormones with a two-by-four. And I couldn't even talk myself out of it on the grounds of it being pervy, since it wasn't pervy because we weren't related. Right?

Geez, the timing in my life *sucked.*

The Julia Child retrospective wasn't doing it for me. I turned off the TV and dragged my confused ass back to James's bedroom. He wouldn't be needing it tonight, and he had a supremely comfortable bed. I knew this because when I still lived with our parents, I stayed with him as often as I could. Being the considerate older brother he was, he always insisted I take his bedroom while he slept on the futon in his guest room-slash-study. When I got old enough, I realized it was probably more because he didn't want me pawing through his desk than out of concern for my comfort. As if I would have.

(Okay, I totally would have. But I would have felt guilty about it afterward. What I lack in impulse control I make up for in remorse.)

James has since acquired both a desk and a file cabinet with locks. Hard-to-pick locks. (No need to go into how I know that.) But he can't relegate me to the futon now without admitting he was only ever worried about me snooping, so I still get the good bed whenever I stay over.

And apparently so did Billy.

"What are you doing here?" I asked, feeling my eyes widen at the sight of his naked chest and legs. A creamy yellow cotton jersey sheet covered his midsection, thank goodness, or I wouldn't have been able to talk at all.

He opened his eyes halfway and looked at me from beneath ebony lashes. "Waiting for you."

My heart stopped for a second, then resumed, maybe a little faster.

"But how did you know I'd come here?"

"Why would you sleep on that god-awful futon when James will be at the lab all night?"

"Don't be obtuse. I meant here, James's *apartment,* not here, James's bedroom. And what are you doing here in the first place, not what are you doing right this second."

"Oh. Well, I *didn't* know you'd come to the apartment. I'm here trying to grab a few hours of sleep before I head out. Your showing up is a bonus. Thank goodness my luck hasn't totally deserted me—I was starting to worry." He smiled in a way that made me acutely aware we were alone, with real time on our hands, for the first time since our relationship had morphed into something beyond cousinly.

So of course I deflected. "Thomas wants to talk to you. He isn't very happy."

If anything, his grin widened. "I'll bet he's not. Did he get Brian out?"

"No, *I* got Brian out. Thomas got me out."

"*What?* You twit. What did you do?"

"I marched myself—well, Thomas's self—down to the precinct and made Brian switch with me."

He looked shocked, and maybe a little impressed. "Why the hell would you do that? Brian is a perfectly adequate me."

"I figured I was better equipped to deal with the situation than he was. What were you thinking? You know Brian can't handle jail."

"Brian can handle a lot more than the family gives him credit for. Besides, I knew he wouldn't be in for long, not with Thomas in town."

"Then why didn't you just wait for Thomas to get you out?"

"Because this way I got Thomas off my back at the same time. So, what did you think of Bruno?"

"Nice guy. Killer poker player."

"No shit. I owe him three packs of cigarettes and a box of Krispy Kremes. Now, come here."

Fine. Enough about the Brian thing for now—he could take that up with Thomas at the next family function. But I wasn't letting him off the hook entirely. "We have to talk about what happened to Laura."

"Yeah, we do." He pushed himself up to a sitting position and patted the mattress. I hesitated, but if he really meant to talk . . .

After I sat myself, cross-legged, next to him, he took my hand and rubbed it between his thumb and fingers. "But later, okay?" he said.

"Billy—"

"Laura is going to be fine, I promise. Harvey will see to it. That is *all* I know for sure right now—I'm as in the dark about the rest of it as you are. When I find out more, I'll tell you." He looked beyond me to the bedroom door. "Where's the munch-kin? I didn't hear her with you."

"She's asleep at the lab. James said he'd watch her while he worked—he might actually have something that will help her by morning." I tried to pull my hand away from his. It was starting to feel almost as good as one of his foot massages, and I didn't need a distraction like that when I was trying to get info out of him. But he held on and brought his other hand into play, gently kneading the muscle between my thumb and index finger.

"That's great," he said, his voice soft. Soothing. "If anyone can fix her, it's James."

I swallowed. Nodded. Told myself to get off the bed, but somehow didn't do it. "Yeah. He's brilliant."

Billy took my other hand, applying varying degrees of pressure from my wrist to the tips of my fingers. "You're nervous," he said after a time.

Geez, ya think? "No, I'm not."

His hands circled my wrists, thumbs pressing on the undersides. "Ciel, your pulse is going like a jackhammer. You're terrified."

"Am not." *Shit.* Were my hands trembling?

"Are too," he said with a hint of challenge.

I yanked my hands away. "Am *not.* I just wasn't expecting to see you here, is all. You surprised me."

Then, thinking a little space between us might be a good thing, I scooted to the edge of the bed.

Aaaand . . . he clucked at me. *Clucked!*

I glared murder at him. "I am *not* chicken."

He stuck his thumbs under his armpits and flapped his elbows. I grabbed the nearest pillow and took aim at his head, swinging for all I was worth. He ducked. I missed. The momentum carried me too far around, leaving me vulnerable to attack from behind. His arms circled mine, holding tight. Leaning in close to my ear, he whispered, "Fraidy cat."

Garnering my strength, I elbowed him in the gut, surprising

him into a fast release. Spun on him and shoved him backward. Climbed on top of him and pinned his arms to the bed with my knees on his biceps, the only way someone of my size can hope to hold down someone of his height and strength.

"I am not afraid of you," I ground out. "I have *never* been afraid of you, and I never *will* be afraid of you. Got that?" I punctuated it with a stiff-fingered, stubby-nailed poke to his chest.

His dimples appeared. "I am so glad to hear you say that"—he heaved himself up in spite of my knees, and I was on my back before I could suck in a breath with him hovering over me, still positioned between my legs—"because I could never take advantage of someone who was afraid of me. But since you're not . . ." His mouth came down on the side of my neck.

"Whoa! What do you think you're doing?" Damn, he had soft lips. I bit my tongue against a whimper, but I'm pretty sure he heard it anyway.

His mouth found its way to the other side of my neck. "Having my wicked way with you, just like I told you I would."

I laughed. "You're an idiot. You know that, don't you? Isn't this supposed to be romantic?"

He pushed up on his elbows and looked down at me with soft eyes. "You're not scared anymore, are you?"

"I wasn't—"

He raised one eyebrow. Damn him and his stupid understanding of what made me tick. There are disadvantages to getting involved with someone who's known you forever.

"Okay, so maybe I was a little bit nervous. Sue me."

"Ciel, you never—*never*—have to be afraid of me." He kissed each of my eyebrows so gently I had to blink back tears.

"I'm not afraid *of* you, you nitwit. I'm afraid *for* you. You're in trouble, and I don't know how to help. You won't even tell me what's going on."

"I've told you everything I'm certain about. Ciel, don't worry, okay? I've been in way hairier spots than this, and lived to tell the tale."

"Yeah, well, what if you don't this time? What if I get all attached and something happens to you?"

"Come on. You're already attached—it's true, don't deny it—so how much worse could it be? Sex will just give you a much better memory of me."

I pushed at his shoulders. "Argh! You arrogant son of a— Get off me!"

But he was laughing so hard he collapsed over me, and then I was laughing so hard with him I couldn't push him away, and then his mouth was on mine, and his tongue made me feel delicious things in places nice girls don't admit having. If he could do that just by kissing me, I would be lost once he got my clothes off. I really should . . .

Oh, hell. Who cared? I sank into the sensations and didn't wonder anything except why in the heck hadn't we done this sooner?

He shifted off me and pulled my T-shirt over my head. Reached behind my back to unhook the lacy Victoria's Secret bra I was wearing. It was supposed to enhance my curves, but could only do so much with what it had to work with, and once it was gone my hands automatically flew to cover what little there was of my chest.

"Hey, don't do that." His voice was understanding, soft. I moved my hands. It wasn't like he hadn't seen me without a top a few notable times before (both involving champagne). But now I felt more vulnerable, and steeled myself for a teasing comment.

He let out a shaky breath. "God, you are so beautiful. If you knew how weak in the knees it makes me just looking at you . . ." He took a nipple lightly between his lips, brushing it so softly with his tongue I almost jumped off the bed. My arms encircled his head, holding him to me, not sure if I'd go crazier if he kept doing what he was doing or if he stopped.

A low chuckle came from beneath the shiny cap of dark waves I couldn't seem to let go of. "Mmmm . . . raspberries for dessert," he said, and switched to the other one.

Laughter bubbled out of me as I swatted his head.

"*Ow.* What was that for? I love raspberries."

"You're not supposed to bring that up."

"I only promised I wouldn't tease you about it in front of other people."

"Yeah, well, I seem to recall a certain reference at the zoo, in front of your sister, too."

"Hey, *I* was talking about sherbet. If you chose to read something else into it, that was your dirty mind at work," he said, eyes shining with phony innocence. "Anyway, we're alone now. When we're alone I get to do anything I want."

"You do, do you?"

"Yeah, but don't worry. I promise you'll like everything I want to do."

"Huh. Confident much?"

"Have you disliked anything so far?"

He knew damn well I hadn't. "Let me think a minute . . ."

"Shall I refresh your memory?" He kissed my lips, my neck,

and both my breasts, taking his time, not moving on until he'd elicited a moan or a whimper from me at each location. "Is it coming back to you yet?"

"I'm not sure . . ."

He sat up and moved to one side of me, the sheet barely covering his, um, essentials. I blinked. "Where are you going?"

"Nowhere." He reached for my waist and started unbuttoning. "But if you can't be sure you liked what I just did, it's time for something that won't leave you in doubt."

While he was talking, he'd peeled my jeans off me in one smooth motion. I tried not to make a connection between the ease of removal and the amount of practice he must have had.

"Wait," I said, grabbing at my pants. He held them out of reach.

"What? Believe me, they'll only get in the way."

"But we can't . . . I mean, I'm not . . ."

"Spit it out."

"I . . . I use a patch." Which the doctor prescribed only to regulate my periods, but no point in boring him with the details. "I lost it during all the ruckus in Sweden. I put another on as soon as I got home, but I'm not sure if it . . . I mean, I can't be certain . . ." Geez, why is it so embarrassing discussing a simple thing like birth control?

He grinned and tossed my jeans across the room. Then he leaned in real close, and whispered, "I'll take care of it."

After that, I kind of lost my train of thought. How could a person smell so *good*? It wasn't strong. Not overly sweet or musky. It couldn't be aftershave, because he hadn't shaved. Whiskers shadowed his cheeks, long enough to be past the sandpaper phase but too short for a beard. Too dark for a five o'clock shadow—more of a midnight shadow. And as sexy as hell.

Guess I was staring, because he took my hand and brought it to his face, rubbing my palm lightly along his jaw. The bristles were as soft as a baby's brush, not scratchy at all, but a tantalizing contrast to smooth, dry lips and warm, wet tongue as he kissed my wrist.

"Want me to get rid of it?" And the beginnings of the beard were gone, adapted away in a nanosecond, leaving his face as fine as alabaster.

"No! I—" *Love it? Adore it? Geez, Ciel, get hold of yourself.* "Uh . . . it suits you."

"Okay," he said, bringing back the stubble. "But if we're going natural, stop hiding your goose bumps. They're good for my ego." He ran his hand down my waist, and I didn't cover my reaction. The sheet around his hips moved, so I guess he really didn't mind pebbly skin.

"Wait a second. Back to what I was saying. Are you sure—"

"Don't worry, I have it covered. Or, rather, I will," he said with a grin, and shifted his hand.

I would have asked why he was so prepared, only I figured I probably didn't want to know the answer. He likely hadn't been unprepared for a chance encounter since he'd hit puberty. Besides, it seemed fingers skimming up and down my inner thighs can trigger my mute button, at least where coherent language is concerned. Every upward turn of his hand brought him a little closer to the lace between him and the tiny piece of real estate he seemed to be avoiding just to torment me. But if he thought I was going to beg . . . *Gaaah!* He was right.

"Billy, please . . ."

He dropped his head to my stomach and kissed my belly button, dipping his tongue into it at the same time as he slipped his hand beneath the silk of my panties. I jerked, gripping his shoulders. His hand kept to its course while his mouth trailed kisses back to mine. He wiggled his fingers as he nipped my lower lip and groaned.

Yes! At least I wasn't the only one making noise.

"Jesus, Ciel. If you knew how long I've been thinking about getting you into bed, you'd be appalled."

"*How* long? Tell me."

"Let's just say I was advanced for my years with my lustful thoughts about you, and leave it at that."

"You mean all those times you were rotten to me when we were kids, you really wanted to get in my pants?"

His busy fingers stilled for a second. I sucked in a breath and held it until they started up again. "Guilty. I had more trouble maintaining my 'dignity' around you than our good friend Benjamin ever had with a girl. But at least I could usually adapt away my problem when necessary."

I laughed. "Boner" Benjamin was an aura Billy had inflicted on me when we had to get to Mark's sailboat incognito a few weeks prior. The poor boy came by his nickname naturally—he couldn't get within twenty yards of anything female without his tighty whities jumping to life.

"You're not adapting anything away now, I notice." Boy, did I notice.

"Doesn't always work. Sometimes I have to recite the multiplication table in my head. Got up to the elevens once—you were looking particularly fine that day."

"How about now?" I asked, running my hand lightly along his chest, enjoying my newfound womanly power over him.

"Now? I don't think even the twelves would help." He kissed me again, his tongue lingering beneath my upper lip, before pulling himself away with another groan. "God, your mouth—I get dizzy just thinking about your mouth. Do you know I had my very first wet"—he paused briefly before continuing—"spontaneous nocturnal emission while dreaming about you eating a pickle?"

I laughed again, harder, which somehow had the effect of making the things Billy was doing feel even better. "I know what a wet dream is, Billy. But a pickle?" I gasped.

"Honest to God. We were eleven or twelve—you were knobby-kneed and covered with freckles, but Lord, your mouth—" He sighed heavily, almost more of a pant. "Your mouth did not belong on a child. Mostly I could ignore it, especially since you used to run to your brothers and tell on me if I looked at you cross-eyed—"

"I did not!"

"You did. You were a total brat. You'd stick your tongue out at me from behind their backs while they threatened to pound me if I didn't leave you alone. Sometimes I hated you—until the day I saw you sucking the juice off that pickle." Another heavy sigh. "Gave me a whole new perspective on females. And pickles. After that, I never really minded when you stuck your tongue out at me. In fact, I used to try to get you to do it."

"What do you mean 'used to'? When did you stop?"

He nibbled my lower lip. "If I pull your hair, will you stick it out for me right now? Pretty please?" And then he did give a tug, a gentle one, where he already had his hand buried.

I yelped, though not from pain. But good as it felt, it occurred to me I should give something in return. I stilled his hand and tried to push him onto his back.

"What do you think you're doing?"

"I'm trying to make your boyhood dream come true. Shall I see if there's a pickle in the fridge, or can you come up with a handy substitute?"

He made a sound deep in his chest but didn't lie back for me. "Wonderful as that sounds—and you can't come close to imagining how wonderful that is—no. Not now."

"Why not? Afraid I'll bite you?" I pulled the sheet slowly across his midsection, enjoying the look of desperation that came over him, even while I was a teensy bit relieved I wouldn't have to demonstrate my inexperience with the act he was refusing. What if there was some trick to it I didn't know about? A shrunken part of my ego didn't want to compare unfavorably to all those actresses and supermodels he'd dated. I bet *they* knew all the tricks.

"Nope," he said, and had me out of my panties before I could protest. "Afraid I'll disgrace myself in two seconds flat and ruin my chances of ever getting you back into bed with me again." I got a brief glimpse of him—*yowza!*—before he pulled my legs apart and settled himself between them again. "Besides, it goes against my gentlemanly inclinations. Ladies first."

Embarrassment spread through me, heating my cheeks, but I couldn't find the wherewithal to make an adjustment. I was too busy panicking, comparing myself to the supermodels with their perfect supermodel, um, southern regions. I'm pretty sure my southern region is just an ordinary, run-of-the-mill southern region, more Myrtle Beach than, say, the French Riviera. So I

was going to have to tell Billy I wasn't ready for this level of inti-
macy, to *please* stop—

Or maybe I should wait a minute. Seemed rude to interrupt.

Okay, two minutes. Tops.

Oh, hell. This was Billy; he probably wouldn't listen anyway.
He *never* listened to me, I thought, inwardly thanking whatever
pagan god is in charge of sex. I was going to have to build an
altar to it. (I squirmed.) Light some incense. (I wiggled.) Maybe
make a small sacrifice. (I gasped.) *Gawd!*

Holy. Freaking. *Cow.* My whole body trembled. I was still
shaking when his head popped up into view. There was a gleam
in his eye, and a flash of white teeth between those indented,
midnight-shadowed cheeks.

The moment seemed to call for comment, so I said, in between gulps of air, "That was, uh, very gentlemanly of you."

"Gentlemanly? That's all you have to say after the best orgasm
of your life?"

He was right about that, but I wasn't going to admit it. His
ego was big enough. Instead I went with a dignified, "Thank
you. It was nice." His face fell, just a little. I coughed and added,
"Very."

He cracked up. When he was done laughing, he dropped his
lips to my belly and blew, doubling me over. I grabbed his head.
He pulled away and crawled forward until his face was level with
mine, kissing me until I was breathless once he got there.

"You are the most delicious thing I have ever tasted. Better
than ice cream. In fact"—he flicked his tongue between my
lips—"I believe I'll have seconds."

"Wait—isn't it your turn? I mean, I've already, you know . . ."

"Yeah, I know. I was there. But that was a puny little

girly-gasm," he said dismissively. "It takes at least three of those to equal a great big guy-gasm."

"Hey!"

"Don't worry about it. It's not your fault women can't manage the same kind of robust response men can." He shrugged. "That's just the way it is. Simple biology."

"I'll have you know my orgasm was *huge*! It was at *least* a nine on the Richter scale. You could only hope to have one like it in your *dreams*."

His smile kept getting bigger and bigger, until I realized what I'd handed him and petered out, blushing madly.

"I know," he said with an infuriating wink. And then he ducked back under the sheet.

"What are you doing? I admitted it was great. You don't have to prove—"

"Quiet, you. I'm going for a ten."

"But aren't we going to . . . you know?"

"All in good time," he said, his voice muffled.

A short while later I lay in his arms, staring into his beautiful deep blue eyes, dazed, while his hands moved gently up and down my back. I thought he'd look smug, but he didn't. He looked happy. And I felt guilty.

"I'm sorry. You used me up. I've got nothing left for you," I said with a heartfelt sigh. I hated to leave him high and dry, but I was limp.

He nodded, a smile tugging at the corner of his mouth while his hands kept moving, branching out, finding places I'd never dreamed were erogenous zones. I moaned. Maybe I could find a *little* energy.

In fact, maybe I'd just take a little trip to *his* southern region—*he* certainly wasn't limp—and see what happened. My hand surrounded him. This time *he* yelped. He rolled away from me, reached for the jeans draped across a chair by the bed, dug into a pocket and came out with a foil packet, which he held out to me. "Want to help?" he said, a wicked gleam in his eye.

Eek. "Sure." I fumbled with the packet, trying to think of what the teacher had done with the banana on birth control day in health class back in high school. Honestly? I had tried not to watch. At least I knew not to unroll it right away.

I reached for him, hesitating as I tried to figure out which side of the rolled-up disk should be faceup. My fingers trembled. (Only a little. And it was the damn condom's fault! Why did it have to look the same on both sides?)

"Problem?" he asked.

"Um . . . no. I just . . . if you could maybe . . ." *Shit!* Why hadn't I ever Googled this?

Billy took my hand, caressing the back of it gently with his thumb. "Ciel? That guy in college . . . it never happened, did it?"

My shoulders sagged. As far as Billy knew, I'd lost my virtue my junior year to a cad who'd wooed me and dumped me. That's the story I planted in my diary, and I had good reason to know he'd read it, which was embarrassing enough, but not as mortifying as still being a virgin postcollege.

"It mostly happened," I said, my voice small.

"Mostly?"

"Well, he got it on—he had his back turned, so I couldn't see how he did it—and then he started to . . . but then, before he could . . . well, he kind of let loose a little early. I think he was embarrassed. He left, and I never even saw him in class after that."

Billy took the condom from me, leaned over and gave me a light kiss, then turned away.

"Where are you going?"

"I think maybe we should give this a little more time," he said.

"No! I don't want more time!" I said, feeling panicky all of a sudden. "If you stop, I'll . . ." *What, feel like a fool? Be doomed to half-virginity for the rest of my life, because I would never have the nerve to risk half-sex again?* "Just don't stop. Please?"

"Look, Ciel, I rushed you into this. I may have been a little . . . overly persuasive. But I'm not an asshole, okay?"

I grabbed him and pulled him back to me. "Billy, listen to me. I *want* you." Then I kissed him for all I was worth, tore away from his mouth, and whispered, fiercely, "Put the damn condom on. *Now.*"

He didn't argue with me. Once he was poised and ready to follow through, he paused. "Do you want to borrow a little something from one of your nonvirgin auras? So it doesn't sting?"

"No! Then it wouldn't count. It wouldn't be *me*. Besides, I've been riding horses and bicycles practically my whole life. There shouldn't be anything left to make it sting."

He smoothed the hair back from my face and kissed my forehead. "All right, sweetheart. Okay." He started moving slowly. Kissing me deeply, he put one hand between us and settled his fingers right back on the magic spot. Amazingly resilient, that little piece of flesh. It sprang back to life in seconds, and the gentle rocking of Billy's hips pushing against his hand as he pressed farther into me sent me spinning again.

"You too," I gasped, grabbing his butt and pulling him all the way in. He tensed, and I felt his release right down to my core.

Minutes later, he rolled off me, groaning. "My God," he said. "Am I still alive?"

I snuggled against him, grinning into his chest, ridiculously happy he was as affected by it as I was. And, of course, thrilled I was no longer a half-virgin.

Chapter 14

After a few minutes of gentle caresses and quiet endearments, Billy excused himself and went to the restroom. He came back sans condom and carrying a damp washcloth.

"Okay, let's have a look," he said matter-of-factly.

Fighting a blush, I clamped my legs together under the sheet and stammered, "N-no, I'm all right."

"Let me make sure I didn't hurt you." He tugged on the cover.

"You didn't. I'm fine," I said, clinging to the yellow cotton jersey.

"Come on. It was your first time. A warm cloth is soothing."

"Fine. I can do it."

He pretended to hand me the washcloth, and snatched the sheet away when I let go to take it. Then he casually pinned down my torso, his back to me, while he pried my knees apart. "For Pete's sake, Ciel, I just had my face buried here. What do you think you're hiding from me?"

He had a point. I relaxed and allowed him to get on with it. He was very gentle.

"Doesn't look too bad," he said, glancing back over his shoulder with an impish grin. "You will live to be naughty again."

"Oh, hush. We're two consenting adults. That's hardly naughty."

He tossed the washcloth onto the floor, scooted back up to the head of the bed, and took me into his arms. "Come on, *cuz*. It's a little bit naughty. I mean, we *are* related—after all, what does blood really matter? Family is family—"

I tried to push away from him, but he held on tight.

"—and in your brother's bed to boot. Now, *that's* kind of pervy, don't you think?"

I slugged him. Hard. He kept grinning, and tightened his hold.

"Yeah," he continued. "I'd say that makes it downright unwholesome."

"You . . . you . . . I can't think of anything bad enough to call you! You said it wasn't pervy, you *said* it was okay—"

He laughed, keeping me clamped to his chest while repeating, "*Kidding*. I was only kidding. It's not perverted, I promise." Eventually, I heard him.

"Jesus, Ciel," he said when I stopped trying to kill him. "You are so easy to rile. I was afraid you might turn into a mushy little wuss after we made love. Glad I was wrong."

"Huh," I said, tucked against his shoulder but still grumpy. "It's plain to see *you* haven't changed."

He lifted my chin and looked at me, his face gone soft and serious. "Do you want me to? Because I can, if you do. And I will, for you."

I sighed and kissed him lightly, defeated once more by the Doyle eyes. "No. Don't change. Don't ever change."

The sound of clapping startled us both. I think I jumped a foot off the bed.

Standing in the doorway, leaning against the frame, was James's gorgeous friend, he of the Sharpie marker incident. A smile played a dirty little game on his lips.

"Bravo. How touching. But I didn't expect James to have houseguests—what fun! Got room in there for one more?"

I yanked the sheet up past my shoulders, shocked into speechlessness. Billy recovered faster. Leaning casually back against the headboard, he hugged me closer with one arm while he draped the other over his head. "I'm afraid you have us at a disadvantage. You would be . . . ?"

"Devon."

"Devon Spencer?" Billy asked, drawing the name from some inner file. Pretty Boy nodded. "Well, Devon Spencer, isn't that just the sort of thing that got you into trouble with James in the first place?"

Pretty Boy—Devon—shrugged, all lazy grace and androgynous charm. "But in this case I could tell him honestly his bed was the only place I played."

Anger brought back my voice. This pathetic twerp thought he could cheat on my brother? "How long have you been standing there? And how did you get in?" I said, volume low, venom high. Devon didn't notice my tone, or else he didn't care.

"James must not have changed his magic palm lock—it still works for me. And *you* must be James's sister—you look just like him. Well, with a few"—he paused for a millisecond, his eyes flitting to my chest—"minor differences." I pulled the sheet higher, pretty sure I was being mocked. "The resemblance must be why I'm finding you so tempting right now. James can hardly blame me for that. In fact, he should be flattered."

I didn't say anything, but I might have growled.

"Oh, she's a scary one, isn't she?" he said, addressing his remark to Billy. "Are you wearing a cup, friend? Might be a good idea."

Billy gave me a sideways glance, but wisely didn't mention the time I'd kicked him in the nuts when we were in fifth grade. He *had* been wearing a cup for soccer practice then, lucky for him. "Not at the moment," he said, fighting a smile he knew would get him killed if released. "Dev, you might want to wait for us in the living room."

"If you insist." He turned slowly, trying, I was sure, to show his ass off to its best advantage. (Not difficult—it was a fine ass, much as it pained me to admit it.) Looking back over his shoulder, he said, "Don't worry, little one. I didn't see everything. Only the"—another micro pause—"tail end."

How very reassuring.

Once I was dressed I felt a little less vulnerable, but I still didn't particularly want to face my brother's bisexual wannabe lover. I couldn't stay hidden in the bedroom and risk Billy flapping his elbows at me again, though, so I toughed it out. But I stuck close to Billy's side, holding his hand so Devon wouldn't get any ideas about either one of us being available.

"James doesn't know you're here," I said to Devon once we'd joined him, keeping my voice cool, like it didn't bother me a bit that, depending on how long he'd been peeking through the bedroom door, he might have seen parts of me nobody except my gynecologist, and now Billy, had seen since I was out of diapers. (Even the kid in college hadn't actually *seen* anything—it was dark during our little misadventure.)

"What makes you think that?" Devon replied, equally blasé. Only I suspected *he* didn't have to fake it.

"Because he sent me over here to get some rest, and he wouldn't have done that if he thought you'd be here. He's pretty protective of his private life." And me.

"Well, since I didn't interrupt your *rest*, where's the harm? We can all just wait together for James to come home. It'll give us a chance to get to know one another. I've been dying to meet more of his family."

Billy stepped forward then, arm extended for a handshake. "Well, any friend of James . . ." he said, gripping Devon's hand tightly enough to make him wince, and winking at me. Blast Billy. He'd just pinched some energy.

"James will be working all night," I said, hoping Devon would take the hint and leave. "No point in waiting for him. But I'll be sure to let him know you dropped by." I didn't offer my hand.

"Pity," Devon said. "It would have been—"

"Well, gotta run," Billy cut in. "Places to go, people to see. Dev, nice to meet you—"

"Wait just a darn minute!" I said. "You can't go. We haven't"—I darted a glance at Devon, then continued circumspectly—"you know, discussed that matter we were going to."

Billy took me by the elbow and led me to the front door. "About that—listen, we're going to have to put that on hold for now."

"Uh-uh. No way. If you think you can just leave me here with

Baby Face, you have another think coming," I whispered furiously.

"Sorry, cuz," he said, talking fast, keeping it low. "No time to waste. He might try to seduce you, though, so be on your guard. And remember, if you're tempted, just hold that thought and come to me later. Safety first." He tugged my hair and added, more loudly, so Devon would hear, "Good-bye, sweetheart. See you soon." He kissed the hell out of me before I could voice any more protests, and left me reeling in the doorway.

I recovered, and ran after him. Caught him before he reached the street. Grabbed his arm and tugged until he looked at me again. Then I felt stupid, and kind of pathetic for chasing him, so I said, "I saw you grab his energy. If you ever use that aura when you're with me, I'll kill you. Just so you know."

James's erstwhile boyfriend was sprawled on the sofa, his beautiful lips lingering around the rim of an imported beer. To his credit, Devon had toned down his lazy fuck-me charm by the time I returned. He hadn't turned it off completely—I suspected that wasn't possible for him—but he no longer looked at me like it was a given we'd be in bed before the visit was over. But then maybe it hadn't really been me he'd been anxious to romp with. Perhaps I'd just been a handy conduit to Billy. That rankled a teensy bit, but mostly I was just relieved.

Figuring I maybe ought to be civil, just in case he and James did get back together someday, I sat across from him in an over-stuffed wing chair and gave up a few childhood memories. Devon seemed honestly interested in my brother, and since I wasn't divulging anything confidential, I couldn't see the harm in it. I was wrapped up in another of Auntie Mo's ugly afghans (the apartment was always well chilled, no matter the season), and actually starting to feel rather comfortable in Pretty Boy's company.

"So James wasn't always the mad scientist he is now?" Devon said after I recounted a story about the Civil War reenactment James had set up in Central Park when we were kids. The whole extended family had been enlisted to either the Blue or the Gray, and my eight-year-old self had spent the afternoon fuming on the sidelines as a Union nurse. My brothers hadn't thought I was big enough, or strong enough, to participate in the battle. Billy gloated at first, but then started casting pitying looks my way, which angered me to no end. James, noticing my resentment, had finally taken me up on his horse (yes, he had even rented horses for the occasion) and trotted toward the enemy line. I brandished his amazingly realistic—for cardboard—sword, and thwacked Billy over the head with it in passing. Ah, good times.

"Funny, I had the impression James was born with a test tube in one hand and a microscope in the other." The pretty mouth wasn't so sardonic now. In fact, it looked almost tender when he thought about James as a kid.

"Not James. He's a real Renaissance man. Science is only his latest passion. History was the big thing when we were kids. He had a music period, too—did he tell you he plays concert piano? And guitar, and oboe, and violin, and a few weird medieval in-struments I can't remember the names of." I suspect James tends to overcompensate for his lack of adaptor capability, but I couldn't tell Devon that.

"No, he didn't. Where are his instruments? I haven't seen any around here."

"My parents keep them at their house. Not enough room here."

He looked around longingly. "Yeah, it's small. But there's something about it. I miss it."

"Do you miss it or my brother?"

There wasn't a trace of guile in the eyes that met mine. "I miss James. Didn't think I would, but I do."

"Do you love him?" I asked, flat out. Why be coy about it?

He drew his head back in surprise, and a puzzled look came over him. "I suppose I must. What an odd notion."

I snorted. "Well, offering to dive into bed with me and Billy is a fine way of expressing it. No wonder James kicked you out, if that's your usual modus operandi."

His smile was that of a naughty boy caught but not expecting to get into much trouble. "Old habits. If it improves your opinion of me, I knew all along you wouldn't take me up on the offer. I just couldn't resist giving you a little shock. Sorry."

"Huh. I'll reserve my opinion for now. James is the one you have to worry about."

He shrugged off my concern with a grin. "Worry gives you wrinkles."

"Look, Devon—I love my brother. A lot. I don't want to see him hurt."

He cocked his head. "Serious little thing, aren't you? So much like James. Well, tiny one, let me reassure you. I don't want to see him hurt, either. That's why I'm back—to tell him I'm willing to go for a ride on the monogamy wagon, if he's willing to give us another chance."

I tilted my head to one side, skeptical. "Can you do that? Just decide to stop playing the field and stick to one person, if it's not really your nature?" (Okay, I admit my reason for asking wasn't purely on my brother's behalf. There's nothing wrong with multitasking.)

"Honestly? I don't know. I've never tried. But I'm going to give it a hell of a shot because James is worth it."

Since I never could keep my mouth shut, I also asked, albeit gingerly, "Won't it be a little more difficult for you? Because I understand your, um, playing the field, is a little bit broader than most?" There. That was delicate, right?

He laughed outright. "What *has* James been telling you? I wonder. But, no, to answer your question, being bisexual doesn't make monogamy any more difficult, I wouldn't think. Why should it matter which gender tempts you away from your commitment, if keeping your commitment is the important thing?"

I gave him a long, level look. Decided he sounded sincere. "You know what, Dev? I believe I'm rooting for you."

Chapter 15

I was a woman on a mission: to avoid my mother for as long as possible, because once she had me, I was stuck until after the party. One of my rat fink brothers had given her my new cell number, so my voice mail was already getting overloaded with frantic messages. Where was I? When was I going to get there? Billy had called Mo, so why hadn't I called her, my mother? Didn't I care that I was worrying her into an early grave? Was I sick and afraid to tell her? Did I have a fever? Had I even *looked* at my throat? For God's sake, *call*!

Damn. When she started bringing God into it, I *had* to call. I knew from experience the police would be next.

She answered on the first ring. "Ciel! Are you all right? Where have you been? Why haven't you returned my calls? And why did you change your number?"

"Hi, Mom. I, uh, accidentally dropped my cell phone in the toilet," I mumbled, praying she'd be too bogged down with party prep to examine my excuse too closely. "It took a while to dry out."

"Again?"

Oops. Guess I'd already used that one. "Um, yeah. You'd think I'd learn, huh?"

"Why would I think that? You kids never learn, not one of you. Why, just last week Brian's phone fell out of his shirt pocket into his drink at the sordid little excuse for a bar he plays at—"

"Mom, listen, I'm in the middle of something. I just wanted to call and tell you I'll be there for the party. I'll let you know when I'm in town—" I crossed my fingers, hoping her motherly lie-detecting instincts were muffled by preparty confusion.

"*What?* You mean to tell me you're not in town yet? The party is tomorrow, Ciel. *To-mor-row!* If you don't—"

"I'll be there. Don't worry about me, I'll be staying with Billy—" Geez, I hoped she was too busy to swing by Billy's condo, because if she saw crime-scene tape, she'd go nuclear. I already knew the shooting couldn't have made the news, or else I'd be having an entirely different conversation with her. "I can help him watch Molly for Auntie Mo. Boy, she's a handful, isn't she? I know Auntie Mo must be grateful we're keeping that little monkey occupied for her. 'kay-bye-love-you."

"Ciel Colleen Halligan, don't you dare hang up on me! I need you to—"

Eek! The dreaded middle-name inclusion. If I didn't disengage pronto, I was doomed. "Sorry, Mom, gotta go. Molly needs me . . . and . . . and I'm losing the signal. I'll try back later," I said, speaking more softly as I extended my arm away from my face. I felt guilty about cutting her off, but I couldn't risk staying on the line. The longer we were connected, the more likely she'd suck the truth directly from my brain. Couldn't risk that.

Okay, mission accomplished. I should now be able to avoid Mom's calls right up until party time without her feeling compelled to call out the National Guard. Next up: James's lab. I could only hope against hope he'd gotten Molly fixed overnight and simply hadn't called to tell me yet out of some brotherly concern for my sleep.

I sipped my third cup of coffee from a travel mug as I hailed a cab outside James's place. The first two had been consumed, along with a whole wheat bagel (bleah) smothered with enough peanut butter to drown out the healthy taste, while I washed the sheets and remade James's bed. He might question why I bothered to do that this time when I never had before, but he couldn't be sure of the reason. It was at least feasible for him to assume I'd matured into a more considerate houseguest.

(Okay, maybe not feasible, but better than the alternative. I mean, I couldn't *not* wash the sheets, not without wordlessly proclaiming to my brother that I'd had sex in his bed—and believe me, that seemed a lot more sordid in the bright light of morning than it had the night before.)

Besides, I'd thought doing laundry would keep me busy enough not to think too much about whether I'd done the prudent thing buying into this relationship with Billy. He sure hadn't stuck around long enough to reassure me, had he? But busy didn't keep the bagel from congealing into a cold lump of buyer's remorse in the pit of my stomach. More than anything, I wanted to run to somebody who would give me a hug and not ask questions. Unfortunately, my usual source of unquestioning hugs was Billy.

While I was waiting for a cab, a hot little gunmetal gray convertible pulled up alongside me. "Hop in," Mark called out, his voice chipper. Well, as chipper as Mark's voice gets, which basically meant he didn't sound pissed. Which was nice but didn't stop the heat from rising in my cheeks.

What could I do? I got in, put the empty mug on the floor, and prayed the breeze would cool me off before he examined me too closely. Why did I have to see him now, so soon after I'd . . . well, done exactly what he'd warned me against? The only explanation I could come up with was that my life is a cosmic joke. Some great, omnipotent being was getting a good laugh out of setting me up.

"You okay?" he said as he eased back into traffic.

"Yeah. Sure. Of course I'm okay. Why wouldn't I be okay?" I perked up my voice as much as I could and told myself to stop thinking. I was pretty sure thinking would do no good in a situation like this.

I especially didn't want to think about how I'd always fantasized about Mark being the one who'd someday divest me of my virginity. On his sailboat. At sunset. In the summer, off the coast of one of the Keys, after dining on lobster and caviar, with a dessert of strawberries dipped first in champagne and then powdered sugar, lovingly fed to each other.

Not that I'd dwelled on it overmuch.

And not that I ever really thought it would happen. Only, now it never *could* happen, and that was kind of sad. Death of a fantasy.

Mark darted a sideways glance at me, then focused on traffic, a thoughtful look on his face. "You hear anything from Billy?"

I jerked. "What? Why would you ask that? I was at James's. But you know that—of course you know that—you're here, aren't you? You came to get me. Anyway, James sent me to his place to sleep. I slept." All technically true. I *had* slept after Devon left. Not for long, but enough.

"I just thought Billy might contact you before any of the rest of us."

Was Mark talking more slowly than usual, or did it just seem that way compared to the speed of my thoughts? I didn't want to lie, so I changed the subject. And slowed my tongue down. "James didn't call me. Is Molly better? Did he fix her?"

"Not as of half an hour ago. Thomas and Brian are already at the lab. We're going to have to decide what to do next."

"Thomas? I thought he went with Laura. How is she, anyway?"

"She's stable. There's a doctor with her, a good one. Right now she needs rest more than anything, and Thomas playing mother hen was agitating her. Harvey sent him away."

"I don't suppose you'd care to tell me the background there? What is Laura to Thomas?"

He shrugged. Not that I'd really expected an answer.

"Why does everything have to be such a big mystery? It gets old after a while, you know," I grumped. Like grumping had ever done me any good with Mark.

"It's not my story to tell, Howdy. Ask Thomas."

"I did. He won't talk about it. What'd you do? Steal her away from him? Did she break his heart?"

He smiled, a genuine one. "You have a lot of faith in my prowess. I think you're overestimating me."

"Your prowess works just fine," I said wryly.

"Not with you, apparently." He glided smoothly between lanes, moving at a good clip without ever giving the appearance of rushing.

"Oh, come on. You never wanted me. Don't pretend you were serious."

He pulled into a parking garage off a side street near the lab. Found a spot almost at once, pulled into it, and set the brake. He turned to me, caressed the back of my head, and pulled me toward him before I could think to protest. "Maybe I'm serious now."

His kiss brought every memory I had of the boat in Sweden crashing in on me. *Shit.* This was not good. This was not the kind of person I was. Granted, I hadn't had a lot of experience with men, but I was pretty sure I wasn't the type to bounce between two of them like a tennis ball at Wimbledon.

At least, I didn't want to be that type. I wasn't a cheater.

But *was* this cheating? I mean, Billy and I hadn't really defined our relationship. We hadn't declared anything openly, had we? Or was I just rationalizing?

The higher me, the superego me, the part with a conscience, said, *You weasel! You just made love to another man—fidelity should be implied.*

But the id me, the if-it-feels-good-do-it me, wasn't listening. Probably the pounding of my heart drowned the higher me out.

It was all so *confusing.*

I felt Mark's hand on my neck stroking the hollow of my throat with his thumb, dipping lower to loosen the top button of my blouse. I was going to protest, really I was, but . . . I didn't. Part of me knew I'd feel ashamed later, but honestly? I was too overwhelmed at the moment to care.

His lips trailed after his hand, and then his head lifted. I held my breath and waited. When the pause stretched to be uncomfortably long, I opened my eyes and found him staring at the tops of my breasts. Well, at one spot in particular—a love mark left there by Billy. *Crap.* Why hadn't I noticed that when I'd showered earlier? It was too late to adapt it away now.

The eyes that lifted to mine weren't as cold as I expected them to be. In fact, they were kind of understanding, which was somehow even worse. He rebuttoned my blouse while I stared at my elbow. I couldn't look at his face again. When he was done straightening my collar, he dropped a kiss on my head and got out of the car.

"Mark," I said in a small voice, once he came around to my side to open the door for me—a gentlemanly action that served to remind me in a painful way I wasn't acting like much of a lady. "I . . . I . . ." But I couldn't finish.

"It's all right. Don't worry about it."

Damn it. He was going to be nice. I can't handle nice when I feel like shit about myself.

The phrase "burst into tears" has always seemed melodramatic to me, but this time it was an apt descriptor. Huge sobs blasted from me, tears exploding from my eyes onto Mark's tailored blue shirt, splattering it with dark spots. I don't know who was more surprised, me or him.

Mortified, I tried to turn away from him, but he wrapped his arms around me and tucked me against his chest, cradling my head in one large hand. I boo-hooed for freaking *ever*, until all the dark spots on his shirt morphed into one huge, ugly blob. Great. Now I had a ruined shirt on my conscience, too.

Mark didn't say anything. He just hugged me, barely moving

in a twisty, rocking kind of motion that eventually soothed me down to the trickle I was more accustomed to when I cried.

"Bad night?" he finally said quietly. Probably afraid to trigger another outburst.

"N-no. It was an incredible night. God, I think I might love him. But then, when you kiss me, I think I still . . ." Another small squall, patted away by Mark's careful hand. "What's wrong with me?"

"Not a damn thing, Howdy."

"Then why . . . I mean, how . . . ?" I took a deep breath, looked up at him, and plunged through it. "How can I feel what I feel when you kiss me if I really love Billy? What kind of awful person *am* I?"

"Tell me something. Did you and Billy elope?" he said.

"*What?* No way!"

"Did he propose? Got a wedding planned?"

"Of course not," I said, beginning to see what he was getting at.

"Then you're not awful. And you feel what you feel because I'm a damn good kisser. I thought we'd established that in Sweden," he said with just enough humor that it didn't sound egotistical.

"You are that," I said with a short, dry laugh.

He smiled. "Or maybe it's just leftovers from that crush you were telling me about, huh? I hear tell crushes are powerful things." He was teasing now. It made me feel a little better.

"Maybe," I admitted. "And maybe it's time I grew up."

"You've grown up just fine, Ciel. Don't worry. Things will work out."

"You're not mad at Billy?"

"Sure I am. I'm tempted to punch his lights out, but not for loving you. If he drags you any further into this mess he's in the middle of, though, there isn't an aura he can hide behind that will keep me from making his life hell." He took my hand and started walking toward the exit. "Come on. The others will be waiting."

"Your shirt . . ." I could fix the ravages of my tear storm with some tissues and a simple adaption—in fact, I already had—but his shirt was still a soggy mess.

"I'll tell them I spilled a drink on myself."

"Ha. Mr. Coordinated spill something? They'll never buy it."

"Okay, I'll tell them you spilled a drink on me."

Now, that they'd believe.

"Hey, wait a second—what do you think Thomas will do when he finds out about me and Billy?" I wasn't looking forward to sharing the news with Brother Bear.

Mark laughed, full and hearty—something even rarer than one of his smiles. "Howdy, that's the best damn part of this whole situation. Thomas will be all over Billy's ass instead of mine."

Chapter 16

You can't walk into a party with an orangutan on your hip and not be the center of attention. Every adaptor or adaptor adjunct there, from "Barack Obama" to "Lady Gaga," crowded around to pay homage to Her Royal Orangeness, and Molly held court with aplomb beneath the whirling lights of the rented disco ball. It was the first time she'd been to one of these parties in something other than her own skin, and she was milking the experience for all it was worth.

Nobody even gave me, Clint Eastwood, a second glance, and I looked damn good. I mean, Clint in his *Every Which Way but Loose* days was *hot*. Not to mention the only easily recognized persona who could realistically show up with an orangutan. Lucky for me Mr. Eastwood was strong, because baby orangutans get heavy after you lug them around for a while.

Of course, I'd never had the good fortune to touch the 1970s version of the man, so my Clint was far from perfect. Mark had offered me the *Gran Torino* version he had in his repertoire of auras, but that wouldn't have worked. So I made do with what adaptors refer to as cardboard—looks okay from a distance, but pretty fakey on close examination. Since most of the adaptors present were in the same boat with their chosen famous auras, it didn't really matter.

Thomas, Brian, and Mark were going to take turns donning Molly's ten-year-old-girl aura at various times throughout the party, so Mo wouldn't freak about her missing daughter. I'd smuggled some of Molly's clothes up to my old room earlier, when I'd checked in with Mom after my "arrival" in New York. The guys would sneak off, by turn, change auras and clothes, spend a little time as the energetic Molly, then go change back to whatever persona they had adopted for the party before they were missed. Tag-team. With a little luck the confusion of the party would be cover enough for our deception.

I was left out of the Being-Molly lineup since I was officially in charge of the real thing. She was looking wild-eyed and a bit too happy for my peace of mind. Also, did I mention she was heavy? Even with Clint's added upper-body strength, if I didn't find someplace to sit down soon my arms were going to break. I could only pray Molly took to heart the lecture about proper party behavior she'd received from all of us at the meeting the day before. It was still a little tough to tell if everything we said was getting through to her—the ape aura seemed to be enmeshing itself more deeply the longer it held on.

James was itching to get back to the lab, and planned to duck out of the party as soon as possible. This would not be out of character for him since he did it every year. No one really blamed him—the party was not as much fun for the nonadaptors in attendance. They got bumped out of the competition pretty quickly. No matter how creative their costumes were, their real identities were strikingly obvious.

This year James had chosen to come as that hot Aussie doctor from *House*—the early seasons version, when the actor still had longish blond hair. The resemblance was actually pretty amazing, only James was blonder and even better-looking. Bonus for him: the costume consisted of a white lab coat and a stethoscope, things James had readily at hand. He'd already checked Molly-O's heart three times while hamming up his role. (We'd taken to referring to the real Molly as Molly-O, just to avoid confusion with the fake ones.)

Before the party, James had given her a dose of something he'd hoped would do the trick, but it was taking longer than anticipated to work, and he was a little worried about side effects, so he was keeping a close eye on her.

I also knew the chosen personas for Mark, Thomas, and Brian. We'd decided at the meeting it would be less confusing all around if we could look out for one another, and we couldn't do that if we didn't know who we all were. Mark was Julius Caesar. Easy to slip in and out of the toga for his quick changes. Thomas was Olympian swimmer Michael Phelps—ditto on the quick-change capability. Nothing but a Speedo and a lot of medals to deal with. And Brian was Madonna. He'd borrowed Suze's outfit, which I suppose was his way of bringing her to the party. Practicality has never been Bri's strong suit.

Nobody knew who Billy was, or if he was even there. He hadn't been at the meeting, nor had anyone talked to him since he'd left me in Pretty Boy's clutches at James's apartment. Once the crowd around me thinned (even the novelty of a baby ape couldn't keep them away from the bar for long) I did my damnedest to figure out which pseudo-celebrity he was. I gave up after a few fruitless minutes. If Billy didn't want to be found out, he wouldn't be.

I hadn't gotten around to mentioning my new relationship status with Billy to Thomas. No need to fog up his mind with any new concerns until after we got Molly straightened out. He was ticked enough at Billy without throwing me into the mix. Fortunately, Mark hadn't said anything, either. As frustrating as spook discretion could be, it did come in handy once in a while.

I was reaching for a stuffed mushroom from the tray of a passing member of the waitstaff when warm, dry lips connected with my neck from behind. I jumped, almost dropping Molly. As I righted myself, my eyes connected for the briefest instant with the server holding the tray before she moved quickly to the next group of partiers. She looked vaguely familiar—

"Wanna make my day, big boy?" a sultry voice whispered in my ear, distracting me. Meryl Streep, circa *The Bridges of Madison County.*

"Wrong movie, blondie," I said, pretty sure it was Billy. Who else would kiss my neck?

"But the right sentiment." Meryl tugged my hair, and tickled Molly under her chin. Yep, had to be Billy. "Why don't you pass your date over to the good doctor and come upstairs—"

I released an impatient breath and rolled my eyes, neither gesture particularly well suited to my current aura. "This is not the time or place for—"

"—to *talk,*" he said, gracefully arching Ms. Streep's left eyebrow. "I need to fill you in on a few things."

"Oh. I thought—"

He took my well-muscled Eastwood arm and hustled me toward James. "Oh, that, too, if we can squeeze it in," he said in breathy Streep whisper, lacing "squeeze it in" with enough innuendo to bring roses to my Clinty cheeks. It might even have given me a twitch in a certain male part of my anatomy, if I'd actually been projecting one. Since this aura was strictly from visuals, though, I hadn't bothered with the parts that didn't show. I might have oozed machismo on the outside, but under my clothing I was about as masculine as a Ken doll.

And, okay, I did wonder if we might manage a quickie (as ourselves, naturally), but only for a *second,* I swear. Because, seriously, I don't think I could ever have sex in my parents' house.

James was sitting on an overstuffed red velvet love seat, surrounded by a small group of nonadaptors, none of whom had put a whole lot of effort into their costumes. Who could blame them?

Meryl took Molly from me and deposited her on James's lap. "Back in a few, darling. Clint is insisting on showing me his big gun, and there's just no arguing with him when he gets all macho." Ha. Little did Meryl know, but Clint was unarmed.

James immediately put his stethoscope to Molly's chest and waved us away. "Go on, then. Have fun."

My eyes widened, but he was too busy listening intently to whatever wild rhythm Molly was beating out with her simian heart to pay attention to me. Surely he couldn't have meant what I thought.

Meryl took my hand and winked at me. We almost made it to the stairs before Don King blocked our way. "Ms. Streep, I have always been an admirer. May I have this dance?" The wild-haired boxing promoter took Billy by the hand and swung him onto the floor, spinning him twice before dropping him into a dip that left me looking at Meryl's upside-down face.

Billy smiled and wiggled Meryl's graceful fingers at me. "Later, Clint. You know where," he hollered over the music as Don pulled her up into another spin. Thank goodness Mom and Auntie Mo always paid off the neighbors ahead of time. It's amazing how a large check can muffle the noise from a raucous party.

I met one of the Mollies as I headed upstairs, whizzing past me at a clip more suitable to a greyhound chasing a rabbit. A nose ring glinted as a random beam of light ricocheted off the disco ball and hit her face. I caught her around the waist as she shot by me, swinging her up and depositing her on the step in front of me. Clint's strength was a handy thing.

"Whoa, Bri," I whispered beneath the blare of Lady Gaga's "Just Dance," and pointed to the offending piece of jewelry. "Take a better look in the mirror before you leave the room next time."

"Oops," he said with an excited Molly giggle. He turned his back to the room below, removed it, and adapted away the hole.

"Careful. If Auntie Mo had seen Molly with a pierced nostril, what do you think she'd do?"

He got serious. "You're right. Sorry. I'll be more careful."

"You do that." Then I remembered something. "Hey, is Suze here?"

"No way! Mom would kill me."

"You sure? I could have sworn . . . Nah, never mind. She already moonlights as a rock star. Why would she need a catering job?"

"That's right," he said, and skipped away toward the dining

room, where the table was laden with heavy hors d'oeuvres, shoving his nose jewelry into a pocket as he went. I hoped he'd remember not to eat anything Molly hated.

As I turned back toward the upstairs, a preset gong rang. Time for all the adaptors to drop an assumed feature and allow one of our own to show. Really cagey adaptors tended to come as people they shared common traits with, and then dropped those traits first, hoping the difference won't be noticeable. I didn't have a lot of similarities to Clint, so I went with going back to my original boobs, figuring the change wouldn't be dramatic. When life hands you lemons (so to speak), you get used to making lemonade.

My room was at the end of the hall, not visible from downstairs, so I was pretty sure no one saw me slip in. Well, except Caesar and Michael Phelps, standing over by my closet, deep in serious conversation while Caesar redressed himself in his toga. Phelps, in his Speedo, barely acknowledged me with a wave and Caesar inclined his head regally toward me as he pinned his sheet at the shoulder.

"What's going on, guys?"

"Who's Billy? Have you made contact yet?" Mark asked. Did I detect a bit of urgency in his imperial voice?

I hooked my thumbs through my belt loops and played Clint at his taciturn best. Why should I be any more forthcoming than they were?

"Come on, Ciel," Thomas said. "We need to talk to him. Now."

There wasn't much point in keeping it a secret, since Billy could show at the door anytime in his Meryl guise. Still, might as well make good use of the time I had.

"Well, boys, what do you say to a little info swap? You tell me what the big rush is, and I'll tell you where to find Billy."

Caesar looked at Phelps. Nodded.

"Laura claims Billy is the one who shot her—she won't budge on that. We think if she can talk to Billy, we might get to the bottom of things faster."

I sat on the edge of my bed, hard. "Crap. It wasn't Billy, I know it wasn't. But who could it have been? Who hates Billy enough to set him up like that?"

"That's one of the things we need to find out. So who is he?"

"Listen, have you thought of explaining to Laura about other adaptors? So she won't think it was Billy?"

"We'd like to avoid that if possible," Mark said. "The fewer people who know, the safer the entire community is."

"Hey, listen, when I found Laura—" The image of her lying in a growing pool of her own blood flew to the fore of my brain and made me catch on the words. "When I found her, she said something funny about Mark. 'Tell him he was right.' What did she mean by that?"

Caesar sighed. "I'd warned her against working with Billy on any of his side jobs. Told her she'd get hurt."

"But you didn't mean by Billy!"

"Of course not. But maybe that's the way she's reading it now, in retrospect."

"You have to tell her." I stood and turned to Thomas, ignoring the Speedo as best I could. Really, *nobody* should wear those. Even on a perfect body, they're just not decent. "You tell her. She'll believe you—I saw how she looked at you in the hospital. Show her, if you have to. Hell, *I'll* show her. Take me to her."

"Calm down, Howdy," Mark said. "We just need a little more time to figure things out. Billy can help—if you'll tell us who he is."

I sighed, at a loss for alternatives. "Meryl Streep. Last I saw, he was dancing with Don King."

They left in a rush. "Hey, guys—" I said as I went after them. No point in waiting in my room for Billy now. "Did you miss the gong earlier? Time to drop a feature." Eyeing my brother's backside, I added, under my breath, "Good luck with that, Thomas." Speedos don't offer a lot of wiggle room with an aura. As he walked off I noticed Phelps's astoundingly long, flipperlike feet shrink to Thomas's more normal appendages. As long as nobody who recognized my brother's toes looked down, he'd be safe until the next round.

Of course, Meryl was not on the dance floor when we got there. Don was dancing with Cleopatra, whose aura wobbled every time she sneezed. Poor Aunt Helen. Mom had gone with flowers after all. Guess my paper cranes hadn't measured up to party standards.

God only knew where Billy had gone. Caesar and Phelps systematically wove their separate ways through the downstairs, nodding regally or smiling Olympically at anyone who tried to engage them, but not pausing long enough to converse. I left them to it. If Billy didn't want to be found by them, he wouldn't. Instead, I went back to the living room, where I'd left Molly-O with James. He was probably ready for a break by now.

Boy, was he. Planted between simian-Molly and Brian-Molly, he appeared desperate to keep them apart. What on earth? I hurried over and took my little orange friend off his hands. "There you are," I said, laying a little extra gravel in Eastwood's voice. "Hope you're not giving the good doctor any problems."

"I wanna hold her," Brian said, hopping up and down and, in my humble opinion, overplaying Molly's youthful enthusiasm.

"*Not* a good idea right now," James said, throwing me a meaningful look. I examined Monkey-Molls more closely. Were her dark eyes shifting from brown back to dark blue? Hard to tell in the indoor light, but I thought maybe so, and her lashes definitely looked thicker. Uh-oh. Not the best timing. Still, if she was changing back, this could only be good, right?

"Hey, there, pardner," I said, possibly sounding more like John Wayne than Clint Eastwood in my urgency to get her out of there, but not really giving a flip. "Better come with me." I lifted her, praying she wouldn't start to exhibit my steely Clint stare. "Excuse me, folks. My little friend here needs to find a powder room. She's mostly housebroke, but not always reliable."

Whereupon Molly-O threw me a disgusted look and slapped my shoulder, adding a grunt of disapproval. I shrugged help-lessly at her. Nothing else I could do now—I'd apologize later for casting aspersions on her potty training.

Brian followed me. "Don't touch her," I hissed. He looked stricken, which, considering it was Molly's tender face I'd glared at, made me feel even guiltier. "Just until we're alone, okay? She might be coming back."

"Molly!" an excited voice called from across the room. *Crap*. It was Jordan, Molly's best friend, a trouble magnet if ever there was one. He looked like an absolute angel, a poster child for bira-cial beauty, with creamy caramel skin and soft, black curls fram-ing his face, but his cherubic appearance was deceptive. The kid lived for mischief. Not that he was mean; he just required an endless supply of entertainment and happened to find chaos en-tertaining.

Brian shot me a panicked look. I shrugged, tossing the ball back to his court.

"Jordy! Uh, what are you doing here?"

"Mom couldn't find a babysitter willing to stay with me this year. Cool, huh?"

Normally, parents were encouraged to leave their prepubescent children at home, since the kids would naturally know who their parents were coming as and would inevitably let the cat out of the bag. Molly, as the child of a cohost, was the exception, but she was expected to stay out of sight as much as possible, and to go to bed early.

Jordan grabbed Brian-Molly's hand. "Come on, let's go! We have to hide from your mom—which one is she, anyway? My dad said if she finds out I'm here, our whole family might get kicked out."

True enough. Auntie Mo might harbor a sneaking fondness for the boy, but it didn't extend to risking the success of the party. No one could *prove* Jordan had snuck into last year's party (no doubt with Molly's help) and somehow precipitated the fire that had upset the caterers so much, but it was suspected by all who knew him. Even if Nero (Jordan's dad last year) had officially taken the blame.

Brian shrugged his skinny little Molly shoulders at me and departed with Jordan. It would've seemed strange to anyone around us if he hadn't. No real problem for me—I'd just have to keep the real Molly out of sight if she changed back. It *was* kind of a problem for fur-Molly, though, judging by the doleful look on her face as she watched her facsimile scamper off with her best buddy. Adaptor-hood was hitting her where it hurt.

Watching the two of them go, I did wonder why Jordan hadn't

stayed home with his older sister, Monica—the friend who'd recommended my zoo client—the way he usually did. (She had been
overseas the previous year, and he had supposedly been left with
an able babysitter, but like I said, there were *doubts*.) I scanned the
room for signs she might have relented in her long-standing adaptor avoidance, and had actually come to the party.

Monica, like James, was a nonadaptor, only she had chosen to
keep herself as separate from the community as was humanly possible. It hadn't always been the case—she'd only started avoiding
us when she hit her late teens and it became apparent she hadn't
inherited the gene. There had been whispers of sour grapes among
the adaptors of our generation (she was a grade ahead of me and
Billy in school), but I assumed she was just trying to find herself.

A lot of people thought it might be a good thing if Jordan
also turned out not to carry the adapting trait, though few were
tactless enough to voice it above a whisper. The kid was a menace now; God only knew what kind of trouble he'd get into if he
could readily change forms.

I didn't catch a glimpse of Monica, and couldn't take the time
to do a full-scale search, even though I'd really been hoping to
find her so I could thank her for the client rec. Thelma Parker
had paid me very well, with the promise of a substantial bonus
for a successfully completed job. Since I'd nailed the interview I
was expecting my bank account to get a lot healthier very soon,
all thanks to Monica.

But I had to get Molly someplace private fast, in case she
started showing more of her real self. And, if I admitted it to
myself, I was a teensy bit relieved not to see Monica. She was
beyond gorgeous, carrying her brother's exotic appeal to ridiculous extremes, and her beauty had never been lost on Billy. He'd

been seriously bent out of shape when she'd rebuffed his advances back in high school.

Confession: I might have rubbed that in a bit at the time. But it was a drop in the bucket compared to the kind of teasing he'd dished out to me, so I figure, in retrospect, it really doesn't count much.

Of course, Billy hadn't let her rejection hold him back in his wholehearted effort to prove himself irresistible to every other female in our school. Or later, in college. Or later still, in all of New York City. Being so newly deflowered, I wasn't sure if I was quite secure enough to take it in stride if he were to look at her with nostalgic lust in his eyes.

Molly made a big point of visiting the en suite bathroom off my bedroom as soon as we got there, tossing me a superior look over her hairy shoulder as she closed the door behind her.

"Look, I'm sorry," I said. "It was the best I could come up with on the spur of the moment. This isn't exactly a by-the-book situation, you know."

"Oo-aa," was the only reply I got. It sounded kind of grumpy.

After I heard the toilet flush and the sound of water running in the sink, I knocked softly. "Come on, Molls. Open the door. Let me see your eyes. Are you changing back?"

Silence.

"Molly?"

Nothing.

I sighed and dug a hairpin out of my top dresser drawer. Picked the lock. (Not hard—it wasn't a great lock.) The shower curtain was closed. Peeking behind it, I saw Molly hunched over at the back of the tub, her face buried in the arms she had crossed over her knees. Still furry.

Damn. I'd really thought she was on the verge of changing back.

I climbed in and sat in front of her. "Ah, Molls. Come here, sweetie."

She crawled onto my lap and looked at me with her beautiful, black-fringed Doyle eyes. The deep blue was striking against the burnt umber of her face.

"Aw, honey. Are you stuck? Can't get any farther?"

She nodded and said, "Yesh."

I jumped, startled to hear a human voice, warped though it was. "Whoa! Molls, you can talk. Your vocal cords are back!"

A few happy, simian shrieks (most of them from Molly), and then she said, "Hoo-ay!" She didn't sound entirely like her old self yet, but it was a start.

I hugged her close. "Whatever James gave you must be working. It's only a matter of time now, sweetie. Be patient. It will come."

Chapter 17

Dad had fixed up the basement ages ago to look like an Irish pub. A little on the dim and shabby side, with the unmistakable cachet of Guinness on tap, it was as wholly welcoming as Dad himself. As I suspected, he was behind the bar, having already dropped his Moe Howard aura. He always chose one of the Three Stooges, much to my mother's dismay; truth was, he'd rather play host and bartender than try to fool anyone for long.

I perched myself on a bar stool next to JFK and said, "Manhattan. Two cherries." I didn't care how sissy Clint would look sucking the cherries off the stems. At the next gong I was going to reveal my freckles, and then somebody would be sure to guess me anyway, so it really didn't matter.

Dad grabbed a shaker, added ice, bourbon, sweet vermouth, and a hint of bitters, and did his special mix-it-up dance, rattling the drink like it was a maraca and he was Carmen Miranda. "Happiest sound in the world, isn't it, Mr. Eastwood?" he said with a wink.

"Right now I'd have to agree with you." I kept in character, in case JFK was Mom. She got really pissed off if we didn't take the game seriously, Dad excepted.

"Here you go, sweetie pie. Two cherries, with stems." He leaned over the bar and kissed my forehead. I was going to assume he'd figured out who I was.

"What gave me away?"

"Two cherries. You always specify."

The gong went off above us.

"Thank God," I said, and let my freckles loose. I threw in my eyes for good measure. Since Dad had technically outed me, I could justifiably drop the whole persona, but then my pants would fall off when I stood up, so I decided to keep playing until I was back upstairs. It wasn't like Dad would tell on me.

JFK was suddenly bald, with a recognizable constellation of sunspots on his pate.

"Hi, Uncle Joe. Gotcha," I said. Uncle Joe was Dad's fraternity brother. A lot of adaptors wind up going to the same universities—life is easier when you're not alone in your weirdness. He'd been a regular fixture at Dad's basement bar for as long as I could remember.

"Damn. Wish I could return the favor, but I'm a little hazy on which Halligan hooligan you are." He looked a little hazy, period. He'd probably been sitting there, quaffing his favorite brew, since the party started. You'd think the kiss, or even my freckles, would've given it away, but Uncle Joe knew Dad was as likely to kiss my brothers as me, and the freckles were probably a bit blurry to him at the moment.

"So, where's that hot redhead you came with? She ditch you for somebody better looking?"

"Spat me out like a dirty stream of tobacco juice. Ran off with a doctor. *Women*," I said with mock disgust.

Molly *had* left with a doctor of sorts, smuggled out the back door with James. They were on the way back to his lab, where he would work on speeding up Molly's change-back. He'd naturally been conservative in the dosage of whatever he'd given her, and he was excited to see his treatment had started working. Now he had to decide whether to up the dosage, or to wait and see if the lower dose would prove to be enough. When others had asked where my little orange buddy was, I told them I'd rented her for only a few hours, and her keeper had collected her. Mae West had given me a piercing look after my explanation; I figured she was either Mom or Auntie Mo, and had ducked downstairs as soon as I could.

I was dying to dump the Clint aura. Nothing against laconic cowboy types, but holding a cardboard aura for long was a pain in the patoot. Secondhand auras were okay. They took longer to absorb initially, but if the original adaptor had snatched the energy, it was easy to copy and hold it. Cardboard auras took more concentration, and therefore more mental energy. After the past few days, I didn't have a lot of that to spare.

I excused myself from the bar and wandered back upstairs, flaunting my freckles and twirling a cherry stem between my teeth. The gradual unveiling of the adaptors continued with predictably excruciating slowness. At least half had been identified by others and were back to being themselves, as the honor code required.

The ones still in the running had somehow managed to expose only ambiguous parts of themselves, so while they didn't look exactly like their chosen celebrities anymore, nobody else could be sure who they really were. It might continue in the same vein for one or two more reveals, but not much longer than that. Mainly because, with the amount of alcohol consumed, it became harder and harder for everyone to use their best judgment about which trait to reveal. When Marilyn Monroe sprouted chest hair, we were all pretty sure it was Mr. Henderson, who ran a specialty biker shop, but the clincher came when he chose to reveal the hula girl tattoo on his bicep. He could never resist making her dance for an audience.

Meryl was keeping herself well hidden. Not that I was looking. Much. I couldn't spot Caesar or Phelps, either. Maybe the three of them had gone off together for a powwow. Goody for them, I thought as the next gong chimed and I let fly with my strawberry blond locks. Who the hell wouldn't recognize that? Geez. How slow *were* these people?

I meandered over to the bar the caterers had set up in the living room and ordered another Manhattan while I scanned the crowd. Since I was no longer in charge of the munchkin, I didn't feel morally obligated to abstain from mood enhancers. I was just taking my first sip when Jordan and Brian-Molly came crashing through the room, giggling wildly. *Uh-oh.* This couldn't be good. Not wanting to give chase while balancing a stemmed cocktail glass, I did the only sensible thing and downed the contents in one gulp, scooping the cherries out with my tongue and spitting the stems back into the glass before handing it to the bartender, not even glancing at her. Which was probably rude, but I had to keep my eyes on the kids.

The two were headed for the kitchen, which was strictly off-limits to everyone—but *especially* Jordan—except the serving staff. Brian ought to know better. If it was still Brian, and I suspected it was, since I seriously doubted Mark or Thomas would be taking such delight in Jordan's shenanigans.

"You there—Mr. Eastwood!" a harried voice stopped me. "I don't suppose you could do me a favor and round up those two brats for me? Maybe teach them a few manners? Physical persuasion is entirely permissible. Even encouraged." Okay, this had to be Auntie Mo. Her Mae West was a little frayed around the edges since the last gong, and she didn't even try to keep up the proper sultry delivery of every line. "I have a few things I have to see to, and don't have time to clobber them myself."

"Sure thing, Aunt—um, Miss West," I said to her retreating back. When she swung around to glare at me, I shrugged my shoulders apologetically for my slip, and took off after the pair before she could lay into me. She knew I knew who she was, and I knew she now knew who I was. Didn't mean we had to get formal about it. It wasn't really cheating, since the hostesses were never in the running for the prize, anyway.

A crash and an angry, deep-throated yowl emanated from behind the swinging door that led into the kitchen. "I got it," I hollered over my shoulder to Auntie Mae-Mo, who was now being dragged into a dance by Andre the Giant (who, judging by the spectacular eyelashes revealed after one of the gongs, was a Doyle of some persuasion, maybe even Uncle Liam, from whence the eyelash genes hailed). She waved me on. Uncle Liam didn't grace the dance floor often; it wasn't something Auntie Mo was likely to pass up.

Feeling just a wee bit light-headed from the Manhattans, I followed the irate ramblings of the head caterer to the far side of the center island. There, on the floor, lay the remains of a hundred or so spun-sugar swans. Poor Mom. First my paper cranes weren't up to snuff, and now the swans had prematurely sung their song. Looked like the darkly decadent individual servings of chocolate mousse on tap for dessert would go out birdless.

One of the caterers—a tall, painfully thin, middle-aged woman with just a hint of a mustache, distantly related to Auntie Mo but not herself an adaptor—had Brian by one arm. He looked up at her with Molly eyes as big as baseballs and tried to break free. Jordan, of course, was already slipping out the back door. I took hold of Brian's other arm.

"There you are, you little scamp. Your mother is looking for you." I gave the caterer a reassuring look. "I'll take care of this. Sorry if she caused you any trouble."

The caterer didn't seem inclined to release her catch. "I can't be expected to keep things running smoothly with kids underfoot. It's not just this one"—she shook ersatz Molly a good one—"it's that other little hoodlum. He got away this time. My contract specifically states I do not work parties where children are present. If either one of them sets foot in this kitchen again tonight, I'm out of here."

"I'll take care of it." I gave her what I hoped was a reassuring smile while I pried her fingers off Brian's skinny little-girl arm. His Molly eyes got even bigger, and he backed away hurriedly. Guess my remaining Clint features didn't do reassurance all that well.

I pulled Brian out the same way Jordan had gone. "Come on, *Molly,* let's go find your buddy."

"Geez, I don't know what you expect *me* to do with him," Brian muttered in Molly's voice.

"You can try to keep him occupied in a nondestructive way," I hissed. "Take him to your old room and show him some of your 'toys'—he'll think he and Molly are getting away with something."

"I suspect he'd have more fun exploring the drawers and closets in *your* room," he said with way too much innuendo for a ten-year-old girl.

"Don't even think about it," I said. Not that I'd left anything incriminating in my parents' house. Not that I'd ever *had* anything incriminating to leave. Well, except diaries full of barely postpubescent fantasies about Mark, but knowing how snoopy most members of my family are, I'd taken care to write everything in code. Besides, I'd taken them with me when I left.

"Well, at least help me find the little bugger first," Brian said. "Molly must have a bolt hole around here, and I'm sure she's told Jordan where it is."

I gave it some thought. "Follow me. I think I might know where it is." I led the way through the dining room out to the terrace. The backyard was small, and the terrace took up most of it. At one corner, Dad had built a koi pond, and behind it a grotto, half-hidden from view by a ten-foot waterfall. In New York City you have a lot more room to build vertically than horizontally. The tiny cave was always a favorite place for us to hide out and watch our parents' parties when we were kids. I suspected the younger generation still felt the same way about it.

Sure enough, there was Jordan, standing behind an elm tree, peering intently into the cave. Huh. Why wasn't he in there himself? Did somebody beat him to it? I snuck up behind him and peeked over his shoulder, wondering what he found so fascinating that he didn't even notice Clint Eastwood's sudden appearance.

My stomach clenched around the Manhattans I had recently

downed, squeezing until I thought the cherries were destined for a return trip. Inside the mouth of the cave, standing just beyond the artificially cascading water, was Billy, completely himself again. Apparently, while Mark and Thomas had been looking for Meryl, Billy had been changing back into his own clothes. With him was Jordan's sister, Monica.

And by "with him," I do not mean they were passing the time of day like friendly ex-schoolmates. I mean she was glued to him like a bad toupee.

I froze, confused. Maybe it wasn't Billy . . . but, no. I recognized his clothes. Hell, I'd given him that T-shirt myself last Christmas. I'd had a picture of his car's hood ornament airbrushed on the back, silver on black, with a big red heart around it. It was supposed to be a joke, but he wore the shirt every chance he got.

Maybe it was Monica's doing. Maybe she'd surprised him. Caught him off guard, kissed him before he could stop her . . .

She pulled her face away from his and laughed suggestively. "I swear, Billy, if I'd known you'd turn out like this, I wouldn't have said no in high school."

Now's your chance, Billy. Push her away! Explain you're with me now!

He leaned over and kissed her.

I marched inside, Brian and Jordan in tow, and was met by the dulcet country strains of Carrie Underwood's "Before He Cheats" as we entered the house. *Ha ha,* I thought, looking heavenward. *Very funny.* Just what my life needs—a soundtrack.

Auntie Mo was herself again when I found her, having dropped the Mae West aura completely. Which reminded me to drop good ol' Clint—I wasn't in the mood to play anymore.

"I'm going upstairs to change. Molly's getting tired. I'll take her back to James's apartment with me and tuck her in there for the night so you won't have to worry about her. You'll have to find somebody else to ride herd on this one," I said, nudging Jordan toward her.

"Thank you, sweetie! It's too loud around here for her to get to sleep upstairs. You have money for a cab, yes? I appreciate it." She pulled Brian-Molly up into a huge hug. "You behave for Ciel. I'll see you both tomorrow. Not too early, mind . . ." She winked at me and grabbed Jordan by his elbow as he was trying to slip away. "Oh, no you don't, bucko. Your parents have been unveiled, and I believe they are suffering from a burning desire to spend some quality time with you."

On the way upstairs, I grabbed another Manhattan from the tray of a passing server. Downed it in one, and handed it back to the carefully unsurprised young member of the catering staff, not bothering with the cherry. I wasn't hungry.

Once I'd changed, I slipped out the front door while Auntie Mo and Mom were too busy in the kitchen to notice I didn't have Molly with me (Brian had already changed back to himself), absently grabbing my great-grandfather's walking stick from its place of honor in the umbrella stand by the front door. Great-Granddad was no longer with us, except in spirit, which the whole family was convinced now occupied the ancient, darkly gnarled cane. I felt the need of a steadying presence, both mentally and physically.

On purpose, I did *not* think about Billy and Monica. Instead, I thought about clowns.

Clowns are supposed to make you happy, but really they scare the shit out of you. Why would any grown-up subject a poor child to clowns, anyway? I thought about the first time Mom and Dad had taken me to the circus, and how I'd loved every second of it right up until they took me behind the scenes after the show and a clown had loomed over me with his grotesquely painted face. When he reached for me, I screamed and threw up all over his elongated shoes.

That's what I felt like, even *not* thinking about Billy and Monica. Like I needed to scream and throw up. My brain might have been willing to cooperate with me by ignoring what I saw, but my stomach definitely wasn't.

I stumbled down the porch steps to the sidewalk. Turned right and headed for . . . well, that was a good question. Couldn't go to Billy's place, for obvious reasons, not the least of which because it was probably still blocked by crime-scene tape. Couldn't go back to James's, because that was where—no, could *not* go back there, not now. Brian's maybe? But Suze wouldn't be expecting me. She hadn't been with Bri long enough to take kindly to unexpected drop-ins by his family members.

So where?

The second Manhattan (or was it the third? fourth? I was a little woozy on the numbers) hit my brain. I kept walking, steadying myself with Great-Granddad's stick. So what if I didn't know where I was going? I was *going;* that was what mattered.

Why? I asked myself. Why had this happened? I *finally* got rid of my annoying half-virginity, and I had to get walloped with *this*? (Yeah, I might have still been a little sensitive about the virginity thing. Sue me.)

I stumbled over an uneven patch of sidewalk, shanghaied by a new thought, gripping the stick to keep from toppling over. When we were little, Mom always said, "God punishes right away," if we got hurt while doing something we shouldn't have been. Was this punishment for letting Mark kiss me? It *was* pretty "right away" in the grand scheme of relationship things.

And it sure as hell hurt.

I started walking again. No. It couldn't be. That was a leftover-crush kiss, and besides, I'd never told Billy he was my one and only. Had I? No, definitely not.

But *he* had told *me* that. *Damn it all to fucking hell!* He *said* I was the only one he wanted. And I'd believed him.

What happened next was entirely Carrie Underwood's fault. And the bourbon's. Or maybe Mom's fault, since she had been in charge of the playlist for the evening. Possibly even Auntie Mo's . . . No, I couldn't blame her. Billy's cheating genes couldn't have come from her. And Uncle Liam had never seemed inclined to stray, that I could see anyway. Ha. Like any man would dare cheat on Auntie Mo. She'd show him. *She'd* put him in his place. *She'd* hit him where it would hurt.

Just like Carrie.

Yup, good ol' Carrie was one country singer who knew how to hit a man where it *really* hurt—right in his internal combustion engine.

But all that would never have come to my mind if I hadn't happened upon Billy's car.

There it was, on this little side street that actually had a tree, occupying Billy's favorite on-street parking place in the neighborhood. Amazing how it was almost always free when he needed it. Or, more likely, how it became free when he called ahead and informed his paid placeholder he was on his way.

Had I subconsciously walked this way, knowing it would be here? Maybe, maybe not. Maybe it was a coincidence. All I knew for sure was, I was here and it was there, and just looking at it made me ache until I felt like I had to hit something or my heart would explode.

And I had a big fucking stick in my hands.

Fighting angry tears, growling along to the strains of "Before He Cheats" still echoing in my head, I set to work on the Chevy. Pulled the key to my parents' house from my jeans pocket and dug it into the driver's side door, leaving a two-foot-long groove. Smashed the window with the head of the cane. It took three tries—car windows are tougher than you'd think—and felt a thrill when I made it through.

I switched the key for the penknife in my other pocket, careful not to cut myself when I opened it, and carved up his seat (not with my name—I was drunk, not an idiot). Sadly, it was vinyl, not leather. Still, it wouldn't be cheap to replace. Not that money was any object to my scoundrel of a fake cousin, I thought, and then carved up the passenger side for good measure.

Next, I staggered to the front of the car. I might not have had a Louisville Slugger, but Granddad's walking stick would do just fine. I gripped it tightly (imagining it was Billy's neck helped), warmed up with a few practice swings, and took out both headlights.

Feeling pretty cocky, I played out the rest of the lyrics and slashed a hole in all four tires. Okay, more stabbed than slashed. Slashing isn't quite as easy as it sounds. Vandalism takes a certain amount of strength. I was breathing hard by the time I was done but feeling pretty pleased with myself.

Ha. Imagine that. Even an interlude with Billy's *car* could leave me breathless and satisfied. I walked away, still humming. *Maybe next time he'll think before he cheats. . . .*

My sense of supreme satisfaction lasted, oh, about a block. Now that I'd vented my shock and anger, the reality of what I'd done washed over me like a cold rain down the back of my neck. No, wait—that *was* cold rain. Perfect. I ran back toward my parents' house, eager not only because it was dry there, but also figuring I better put the walking stick back where it belonged before I got caught with the evidence.

I was having a hard time remembering precisely if Billy's lips had connected to Monica's there at the end. Maybe he'd just been leaning down to tell her, quietly, that he was off the market. *Gaaah.* Maybe I had just demolished Billy's baby for no good reason.

Hold on. What was I doing? Was I turning into one of those pathetic women who make excuses for their asshole boyfriends? When had Billy's lips ever *not* connected to a willing woman? No, he deserved what I did to his car, all right. I was (almost) sure of it.

Almost.

I stopped in front of my parents' house. Stood in the middle of the sidewalk, each raindrop that pelted me driving home the message: *hypocrite.* Oh. My. God. I was a great big fucking hypocrite. If anybody had a right to be upset, it was Billy. If he'd seen me kissing Mark, would he have gone medieval on *my* beloved car? If I'd had a car, which I didn't, but that wasn't the point.

No, I really didn't think he would have.

I ducked behind a tall potted shrub as the door opened and Aunt Helen emerged, supported by Uncle Foster, who looked in need of a prop of his own. Mom and Dad said their good-byes as they walked my wobbly relatives to a waiting cab. Once my parents were back inside, I crept up onto the stoop and peeked in one of the sidelights. The hall was clear, so I slipped in and put the walking stick back in its usual spot, hoping the additional nicks and dings would go unnoticed.

From the library-slash-music room, Uncle Liam's beautiful tenor voice filled a lull in the playlist, a sharp reminder that the car I'd just trashed had been his pride and joy before he'd passed it along to Billy. My breath stopped, waylaid by the lump of shame in my throat. *Shit.* What had I been *thinking*?

I had to get out of the house. Right then. As in *immediately.*

I turned back to the front door, but more guests had emerged from the living room, blocking the way. I didn't want to get caught in the undertow, so I slipped through the dining room and continued out the French doors to the backyard. The rain was coming down harder, but I didn't care. I didn't deserve to be dry and warm. I was a stupid, jealous idiot. All I wanted to do was crawl into a cave and wallow in my shame. The grotto would be the perfect place, if it weren't likely to be occupied by the very person I was running from.

Damn it. Running? Running was the act of a coward. I might have been a stupid, jealous idiot, but I refused to add coward to the list of my shortcomings. I *would* go to the cave, and if Billy and Monica were still there, I would deal.

Stumbling down the path, past the shrub-outlined koi pond, I forced myself to the grotto, determined to tell Billy what had happened to his car. I wouldn't sugarcoat it, either. I'd flat out tell him that I . . . that I . . .

I swallowed hard, holding back the bile that filled my throat. I'd tell him I caught somebody vandalizing it as I walked by. Because, Jesus, he would *kill* me if he ever found out the truth, and remorseful or not, I had no wish to die.

Billy wasn't there.

But Monica was.

Lying on the ground, she was half-in, half-out of the grotto, her head hidden in the shadow. I knew it was her by the dress she was wearing. The lovely ivory silk dress I'd last seen pressed up against Billy now had a large bloodstain right in the middle of it.

Crap. I dropped to my knees beside her. "Monica? Monica, are you all right?" I bit my lip. *Are you all right? Jesus, Ciel, what kind of idiot are you?*

She didn't respond. Long, wavy hair the color of licorice, adorned by a single lavender orchid, lay scattered over her shoulders, encroached upon by the growing stain on her chest. An image of Laura superimposed itself over the woman in front of me. Had Monica been shot, like Laura? It sure looked like it to me, blurry though my vision was. Not surprising that no one heard a shot, with all the noise from the party.

"Ciel? Is that you?"

I jumped up and twirled. Found myself caught in Billy's strong grip, so my body stopped midspin, but my brain didn't. It kept going . . . and going . . . and going. Until I was dizzy-sick with the horror, and the booze, and the blood. I did the only logical thing I could, under the circumstances.

I hurled.

Billy jumped back a step, for all the good it did him. There's a reason they call it projectile vomiting.

To his credit, he hadn't let me go. "My God, cuz, are you all right?"

"N-n-no-o-o," I wailed. "I feel sick."

"Obviously. Drinking sick, or has somebody poisoned you? I only ask because it will have a bearing on what I do next."

"Dri-drinking. I think," I said, mentally doing a Manhattan tally. When my brain couldn't keep up, I tried counting on my fingers. But there appeared to be more of them than usual, so I gave up. "I'm pretty sure."

"Never mind. Come with me," Billy said, and hurried me down the path back toward the house. He sat me on a crescent-shaped cement bench my father had lovingly placed next to his favorite crab apple tree. "You stay right here. I have to take care of things. Got that? Right *here*."

"Okily-dokily," I said, and started to giggle, only then I re-membered Monica and grabbed Billy by his puked-spattered dress. "Oh, God. Monica is *dead*."

"Looks that way. Now, let me go so I can get help."

"But you . . . why did you . . . hey, why did you put the dress back on?" Because he was, I belatedly noticed, wearing Meryl's dress. And he most definitely had *not* been when he'd been in the lip-lock with Monica that had precipitated my ill-advised walk.

"I haven't had a chance to change yet—Ciel, I have to go." He peeled my hand from his arm and put it beside me on the bench. "You hold on right here, okay? Don't go anywhere."

I swayed. He steadied me.

"Sh-sure you have. You had on pants when you were kissing Monica in the cave. And my shirt. I mean, your shirt—"

"When I was *what*?"

"When you were kissing Monica. Are you even listening to me?"

"Ciel, I haven't taken this dress off all evening."

"But I saw you— Oh, shit!" I looked at his face. "That wasn't you?" The implications did nothing to settle my stomach. Or my conscience.

It was totally stupid to be worried about what I'd done to Billy's car—apparently for no reason at all—when Monica was in the cave. Dead. But frankly, I kinda wanted to crawl in and join her. That would be easier than explaining to Billy. God, Monica was *dead*. Why could I not focus on that?

Because if I did, I'd hurl again, and again, and never stop.

"Did you get a close look at the guy's face?" he said, speaking urgently.

I must've looked confused. God knew, I *felt* confused.

"*Think,* Ciel. His face. Did you see it clearly?"

"Yes . . . no . . . I don't know! The important thing is, I *thought* it was you. Honest."

"No, the *important* thing is, we need to know if it was some random guy who looks like me, or if it's an adaptor pretending to be me. One could be a coincidence, the other is most definitely not."

"I . . . I never saw his whole face, I don't think." How could I when it was plastered by the lips to Monica's? "But his hair . . .

his build . . . his *shirt*—they were your clothes, Billy. I was just so *sure* it was you."

"Okay, okay. We've established you thought it was me. You sit here. If it looks like anyone is heading to the grotto, stall them. I need to figure out what the hell is going on."

Chapter 18

Oh. Sweet. Jesus.

I grabbed my face, digging the heels of my hands into my eyeballs, trying to keep them from popping out of my head. It wasn't helping.

Where was I? Afraid to open both eyes at once, I lifted one hand and tentatively slit a lid. Light trickled in, thankfully dim enough not to jar my brain. The surface beneath me wobbled, sending my whole body into a one-person equivalent of the stadium wave. *The waterbed in Billy's childhood bedroom.* How the hell had I gotten here? Last thing I remembered, Billy was helping me to the bench, and then he was going to—

Shit! Before I could contemplate the particulars, my stomach decided on a little wave action of its own. I sat up quickly, hoping to make it to the bathroom before I spewed. A tin wastebasket appeared magically beneath my chin.

"Go ahead. Get rid of it," Auntie Mo said, her voice a mixture of censure and amusement. "I swear, Ciel Halligan, I can't believe you made it through college without learning your limits. How many Manhattans did you have, exactly?"

Too busy following her instructions to answer right away, I held up three fingers. Thought a second, and changed it to four. "That I can remember," I said, in the interest of honesty, when I finished.

She wiped my face with a damp washcloth and handed me a glass of water. "Here. Drink. Or if you can't abide the notion of adding anything to your stomach, just rinse and spit."

Disgusting as that last suggestion was, I did it. No way was my stomach accepting anything just yet. When Auntie Mo removed the wastebasket, I lowered my head onto my hands, my elbows resting on my knees, and gave voice to my biggest fear. "Does Mom know I'm here?"

"Not yet. She has enough to do supervising the party cleanup. I thought you and I might have a little chat and settle this ourselves. No need to worry Ro if it's only a stupid *one-time* thing." She arched a brow.

"Oh, it is definitely an aberration, Auntie Mo. I swear to God I never want to feel like this again."

I guess I sounded sincere, because she gave a satisfied nod.

"And am I right in assuming my daughter is safely with James? That you at least saw to that before you went off on your little bender?"

"Uh, that's right. Molly is with James." True enough. Which was good, because nobody could sniff out a lie like Auntie Mo, except maybe Mom. No need to elaborate on any of the petty details, like whether or not Molly was still an ape. I mean, why upset Auntie Mo when it could very well be that Molly had succeeded in morphing back to herself? That would be needlessly cruel. Not to mention masochistic in the extreme, and present condition notwithstanding, I was no masochist.

"Thank God you had that much sense. So, are you going to tell me what set you off?"

"Uh . . ."

Billy's voice cut in. "Come on, Mommo. It was the party. What other reason does she need?"

Oh, God. My eyes flew to his face. His expression was bland. Didn't he remember *anything*? How could he be so blasé?

"No, that would be you or her brothers you're thinking of. Ciel has never before used a simple family function—"

Billy snorted. "Simple? Ha."

"—as an excuse to let go of all common sense. Something must be on her mind." She skewered her son with her eyes. "And I *will* find out what."

"Really, Auntie Mo, it's nothing," I said, my voice a little thready. I cleared my throat. "I just, uh, had a little too much fun, is all."

"It's Mark, isn't it?" she said baldly.

I could feel confusion lay itself over my face. "Huh?"

"No need to pretend with me, Ciel. I know how you feel about him. It's been obvious since you were a child. Did he at least try to let you down gently, sweetheart?"

"What?"

She grabbed me into a hug, pressing my face into her ample bosom. "Oh, my poor dear. Never you mind. It's just not the same for men, especially not men like Mark. He's a wonderful person but not the type to let a woman—any woman, not just you, dear—interfere with his work. But you will get over him, I promise. Tell her, Billy. Tell her there's somebody better suited for her out there, just waiting to snatch her up."

I tried to breathe. Looked desperately at Billy, whose eyes were dancing a jig in his head.

"Mommo's right, cuz. *Mark's* not the right guy for you. Now, come on. We have to go."

"Don't be silly. Ciel needs to rest. You should know that. You've recovered from your fair share of heartbreaks right here in this bed, young man, in much the same condition as your poor cousin."

Huh? That was news to me. Billy was the designated heart-breaker, never the breakee. I screwed up my brow at him.

He shrugged it off. "We promised to help James with Molly this morning, and we can't back out now. Right, Ciel?"

"Um, that's right. Now I remember. Really, Auntie Mo, I'm feeling much better," I lied. "I'll just wash my face and brush my teeth—do you have a spare toothbrush?"

"You know I do. But—"

Billy took me by the elbow and led me to the bathroom right outside his bedroom door, fast-talking his mother the whole time. "Listen, Mommo, you know better than most how much experience I have with mornings after. Let me see to Ciel. Don't you have enough to do with party cleanup? You're not going to leave Auntie Ro to do it all by herself, are you?"

Auntie Mo looked torn. I could tell she wasn't done with me, but she really couldn't let my mother down, either. "All right then. You'll see to getting Molly home after?"

"Yeah, yeah. I'll get her back here," he said, adding "eventually" only after turning his back on his mother, who had already begun fluffing the pillows and straightening the covers on Billy's bed. Auntie Mo liked to keep her hands busy.

Billy shoved me into the immaculate bathroom. The toilet looked damned inviting, though I wasn't sure whether to sit on it or hang my head over it.

"Five minutes," he said under his breath, "or I'm coming in after you."

"Why did you have to bring me *here*? You know Auntie Mo will let it slip to Mom somehow," I said, keeping my voice as low as his. It's possible I sounded a bit whiny. The pounding in my head made it difficult for me to tell.

"This was close and I had access. Count yourself lucky you were breathing normally and had a strong pulse, or I would have taken you straight to the hospital to have your stomach pumped."

He closed the door in my face, and I heard him continuing to talk to his mother. I avoided the toilet decision and went first for the sink. Splashed handful after handful of cold water on my face, and ran damp fingers through my short, wavy hair. Brushed my teeth with the tiniest useful bit of toothpaste I could manage. Finally snuck a peek at myself in the mirror. Not too bad if I adapted away the cracked-egg eyeballs and puffy bags. If I didn't make any sudden moves, I might even get away with not having to barf again.

Billy was alone when I came back out. Not surprising. Mo was a bloodhound, but if anybody could throw her off the scent of trouble, Billy could. He'd had years of practice.

"So," I said. "What'd you do with the body?"

* * *

The epic thunderstorm didn't do my head a bit of good; I was drenched by the time Billy shoved me into the taxi, and damned lucky not to have been incinerated by a stray bolt of lightning. As soon as we got our seat belts buckled, the ceiling of the yellow van was aglow with flashing lights, and a vaguely familiar voice from the front seat said, "Hello, and welcome to the Cash Cab!"

Oh, great. The freaking game show on wheels I'd wanted to be a contestant on for, like, *ever*. I looked up, sure God could see me through the roof, and rolled my eyes. Ever heard of timing, Big Guy?

Billy unbuckled and reached for the door, ready to pull me out. I took one look at the pouring rain and yanked him back. No way was I going back out into that, even if it meant answering a few questions on the way to wherever we were going. Besides, if we won I could sure use the cash.

"Ciel, we don't have time for this," he hissed through unmoving lips as the driver gave his opening patter.

I ignored Billy, soaking in the rules to the rolling quiz show, thrilled in spite of everything when I heard "So, what do you say? Do you want to play?" from the front seat.

"Yes!" I said.

"No!" Billy overrode me, and yanked me out the door behind him.

"Spoilsport," I grumbled. Loudly, on account of the thunder.

Billy ignored me, hustling us toward a slow-moving cab. When it didn't stop (duh—rain), he slapped the hood as it passed. The driver "saluted" as he drove by.

"Where's your car?" I asked before I remembered, and choked. Recovering, I pretended I'd accidentally inhaled some of the rain.

Billy pounded my back—why do people think that helps, anyway? Seems to me it would just knock whatever you were choking on farther down your windpipe—and hurried me along to a patch of yellow three cars down, stopped at a light. He pulled open the back door and shoved me into the empty backseat.

"Hey, buddy—I'm off duty. Out."

"I'll pay you double the meter," Billy said.

"Blow me," the cabbie came back.

"Triple."

"And swallow." The cabbie lacked, shall we say, a certain level of couth.

Billy spat out an address and added, "Two hundred dollars if you get us there without opening your filthy fucking mouth in front of the lady again."

Mr. Potty Mouth smiled, tipped an imaginary hat, and put his foot to the accelerator as the light turned green.

Dripping, I leaned close to Billy and whispered, "Where the hell are we going? That sounds like near where Bri's band played last time I was in town."

"It is. We're meeting him there—he has to set up for tonight."

"Bri? But why? What does he have to do with . . ." I glanced up front. The cabbie seemed oblivious. Probably already mentally counting his money. ". . . you know what." It paid to stay nonspecific in front of strangers, even seemingly distracted ones.

"That's what we're going to find out. I saw his new girlfriend hanging around with Monica there last week. Seemed odd they would strike up a friendship. And now, with Monica missing—"

"Missing? Don't you mean"—I went subvocal for the final

word, figuring Billy would have no trouble reading my lips from this distance—"dead?"

"Maybe. She looked it, anyway. And now she's gone."

"But how can that be? I saw her. She was right there, um"—*bleeding all over*—"adding color to my parents' grotto, for Pete's sake. Hell, you *saw*."

"Yeah," Billy said very quietly. "And then *you* passed out and I had to make sure you were all right. For all I knew, someone had tried to kill you, too. When I went back to check on Monica, she was gone. So I parked you in my old room—you snore when you're drunk, by the way—and then ran back to your parents' place to search for her. Couldn't find a trace of her. What I don't know for sure is if she got out of there under her own steam or if she had help."

I ignored his remark about my snoring, having no evidence with which to refute it. "She sure looked . . . *quiet* . . . to me."

"Maybe she wanted us to *think* she was 'quiet.' Something is not right about this whole thing, and I'm going to find out what."

The cab's horn blared and I jumped six inches off the seat. The cabbie's evil eyes met mine in the rearview mirror. "Traffic. Whaddaya gonna do?" he said with a shrug. Asshole.

"God, I hate cabs," I muttered.

Billy gave me an odd look. "Sorry. My car's in the shop."

Gulp. "Engine trouble?" I asked, doing my best to maintain an innocent façade. I hoped the raindrops still trickling from my hair masked the sudden bloom of guilt I felt in my cheeks.

"No. Needs some bodywork. Vandals."

I swallowed. "Really? Gee, that's, uh, too bad. Hope the damage wasn't . . . extensive," I finished lamely.

He looked at me, hard. "Ciel . . ."

I waited. He stared.

"What?" I said finally, biting my lip against the confession that was bursting to spring forth.

"Where did you go when you left the party last night?"

"Go?"

"Yes. Where?"

"Um, I went for a walk. I, uh, needed a little air. You know, one too many of Dad's Manhattans." I attempted a laugh; it came out sounding artificial. "When will I learn?"

The cab, which had been making pretty good time during this painful interlude, pulled up in front of the club before Billy could continue grilling me. Damn good thing, too, because if he kept drilling me with those eyes I just knew I'd spill my guts, and then he'd have another body to deal with. It would be wrong to put that on him on top of all this other stuff, so really I was doing him a favor by not confessing. I can be big that way.

The cabbie turned to face us, his greedy eyes expectant. "That'll be—"

"Yeah, yeah, I know." Billy peeled two bills—hundreds—from a money clip as I got out. I was in kind of a hurry to put a little space between me and my cousin. Billy was quick, though, grabbing my elbow as he tossed the money at Mr. Smiley.

The driver gave him a suspicious look. "These real?"

"As real as that medallion," Billy said with a meaningful glance at the cab's hood.

"Ha ha. Very funny, asswipe."

Billy gave him a charming smile. "Now, now. With language like that you won't get a tip."

The driver peeled out, veering toward Billy as he left. Good thing reflexes are another Doyle trait. Not so much a Halligan trait, or I would've already been in the club. "Now, then," Billy said, the charm gone from his voice. "You were about to tell me what happened to my car."

"I was?"

"You were." His eyes were about as far from seductive as I'd ever seen them. Could this possibly be the same guy who'd finessed my half-virginity away from me so skillfully I could hardly think about it without panting?

"We-e-ll," I started, and paused to lick my lips. "Oh, look— there's the door. Come on—let's get out of this rain!" I twisted my elbow out of his grip and took off. I was soaked again by the time I reached the awning. *And* the door was locked. *Shit.*

Billy followed at a more leisurely pace, like a cat stalking its prey. Being drenched didn't faze him. "My car, cuz. Don't even try to lie—you suck at it."

My breathing sped up. My pits—one spot on me unreachable by raindrops—went damp. Not a good time for antiperspirant failure. "Shouldn't we be trying to find Bri? He's expecting us, isn't he?"

"He'll be here in a little while. Now, spit it out before you choke on it."

I gave the door one more halfhearted tug, and hit it when it didn't open. "It's your fault, you know. If you hadn't been making out with Monica the day after we . . . after we . . ." I swallowed. "I thought I meant something to you, damn it!"

"I *wasn't* making out with Monica. I told you, that wasn't me."

"How was I supposed to know that? You know you had the hots for her—"

"In *high school.* Jesus, Ciel, you could try giving me the benefit of the doubt. I told you you're the only one I want."

"I can't help it if I'm not used to you being monogamous. It's not like I've ever seen you try it before."

He glowered at me but could hardly refute it. "You could've come to me, you know. Confronted me, like any normal, overly jealous twit. Why did you have to attack my *car*?"

I shrugged. "It was there. You weren't. Granddad's walking stick was in my hand. Seemed like the thing to do."

"And if I'd been there?" he said, eyes narrowing considerably.

"Let's just say you're lucky, and leave it at that."

He clenched his teeth—and his fists—and walked very deliberately away from me, taking a deep breath as he went. "I swear to God, Ciel, when I get you alone . . ."

"I've heard that before," I muttered. Yeah, I know. Not the brightest thing to say. But it just sort of popped out.

He stopped. Turned, and walked toward me, slowly, until he was inches from me. Looming. He was a good loomer. "You don't think I'll do it?" he said in a frighteningly calm voice.

I lifted one shoulder. *You didn't before,* I thought, but of course didn't say it out loud.

And then he was sitting on the edge of a cement planter, and I was across his lap, my face half-buried in daisies that smelled a whole lot like sweaty feet and stale beer. Negotiations had apparently come to a halt.

"You know," he said, trapping my kicking legs beneath one of his, and pinning my shoulders with his forearm. "I'd hoped we'd be somewhere a bit more private if this ever happened, and a lot less clothed, but I think I might enjoy it all the same." His voice was laced with grim satisfaction.

"Wait!" I yelled as he lifted his paddling arm. I shoved my

torso up and twisted my head around so I could see his face. "You can't do this. It's not right."

"And bashing my car to pieces is?" He pushed me back down, but not before I'd seen the glint in his eyes. He was mad, all right.

"Would it help if I apologized? I feel really, really bad about what I did to your car. *Really.*"

"Good. You should. Don't worry—you'll feel better after you've atoned." He pushed me back down, lifted his arm high, and held it poised while he completed his thought. "Well, not right away, of course. But maybe in a day or two, after your ass cools off."

"Hey, Billy," Brian's nonchalant voice floated nearby. "Why are you about to hit my sister?"

I twisted toward him. Billy held me tight. "Bri—make him let me go!"

"Stand back, Brian. I am about to help your sister with her troubled conscience," Billy said.

Brian leaned one shoulder up against the building. "What'd she do?"

"She beat the shit out of my car with your grandfather's walking stick, that's what. Scratched the paint, broke the headlights. Carved up the seats. And slashed *all four* fucking tires." He leaned over to see my face better. "Did you use the pocket knife I gave you for your twelfth birthday, by any chance?"

Uh, yeah. "Of course not."

"Whoa. Sis, you did that? Not cool."

I blew the hair out of my eyes with an exasperated huff. "Extenuating circumstances, Bri."

"But there weren't, were there? Nothing extenuating at all."

Brian drifted closer. "Hey, this is kinda like that song, huh? The Carrie Underwood one?" He hummed a few bars, capturing it perfectly. Brian has a remarkable musical ability. "But that guy was cheating on her, so she had a good reason. Well, not a *good* reason, but a reason."

"I had a reason, too, damn it!"

"What reason could you possibly have for marring a man's ride like that? I know Billy teases you a lot, but hurting his Chevy—that's just low."

"She *thought* I was cheating on her."

"What? That's stupid. You and Ciel aren't even . . . *Whoa*. Dude. Wait a sec. You guys are . . . ?" He looked from my face to Billy's, disbelief brimming in his eyes until finally it spilled out, leaving an amused awareness of the truth. He burst out laughing.

"Oh, ha fucking ha ha," I said. "Would you please just tell this Neanderthal he can't *spank* me, no matter what I did to his car?"

Brian screwed up his eyebrows, considering. "Hey, does this mean it's okay for me to ask out Sinead?" he said, referring to Billy's middle sister. "If things don't work out with Suze, that is?"

Billy looked appalled. "It does not! Sinead is your—"

I twisted toward him, eyes narrowed. He stopped. "Sinead is seeing someone now. I think it's serious," he finished.

Brian shrugged. "Never mind. Suze is cool. In fact, I think she may be the one." Yeah, right. Like we hadn't all heard that before.

"Brian, can we discuss the love of your life later, please? Like after you convince the caveman to let me go?"

"I don't know. I might be nonviolent by nature, but I think even I'd be tempted to let you have it in a case like this."

"Thank you, Brian," Billy said, lifting his hand again.

"*Bri-an!*" I said, squirming.

My brother moved fast enough to catch Billy's arm as it descended. Billy glowered at him, but Brian only shrugged. "Sorry, man. Can't let anyone hit my little sister." He half raised his left eyebrow. (Halligans have remarkably communicative eyebrows.) "You understand how it is with little sisters."

Billy jerked his arm from Brian's hand, grabbed me by both shoulders, and stood me up in front of him. "Fine. I won't strike your sister. We'll just have to think of some other way for her to make amends." The look in his eyes made me think I would have been better off just letting him wallop me and getting it over with. I swallowed hard.

Inside the club, after we were as dry as we could get using paper towels from the restrooms, Brian offered us beers. I declined, fighting a wave of nausea. "Isn't it a little early for that?" I asked, trying to ignore the hops-y aroma.

"It's after two. Nothing wrong with an afternoon brew, is there?" Brian said. In addition to his band providing music for the club, he was also an unofficial assistant manager. It allowed him access to the place during the day so he could rehearse. Since his band wasn't getting paid a whole lot, the manager didn't mind if he had a few beers on the house, as long as he didn't go overboard.

"That late, huh?" I asked. Guess I'd slept longer than I'd thought. "Can I just have a club soda instead?"

Brian filled a glass with ice and squirted it full from a handheld nozzle, adding a wedge of lime before handing it to me. Billy sipped his beer with no discernible sympathy for me. "Where's Suze?" he asked Brian.

A banging on the front door interrupted.

"That her?" I asked.

"Shouldn't be. She's at home, catching up on some work for her day job," Brian said, and went to open up. He barely had the dead bolt pulled before the door shoved him aside, pushed by Thomas. On his heels was Mark. Just spiffy.

"Where the hell have you been?" Thomas said to Billy, keeping himself between Billy and the door, like he thought our cousin might bolt.

Mark placed himself on Billy's other side, blocking any chance of a rear escape. Billy smiled his charming smile and raised both hands in casual surrender. "Lower your hackles, guys. I can explain."

"Oh, can you?" Thomas said.

"Would I be here if I couldn't?" Billy's left dimple made an appearance. It was not well received by my brother, whose eyebrows strained to meet in the middle over the bridge of his nose. The dimple backed off, and seriousness fell over Billy's face. "Yes. I can. Pull up a stool. Brian, a couple more beers?"

Thomas grabbed a bar stool, noticing me for the first time. "What's wrong with you? You look terrible."

"Nothing," I said, trying to adapt away whatever post-hangover ravages had leaked through. "Maybe a touch of, um, food poisoning."

Billy quirked his mouth wryly. Thomas snorted. Mark didn't say anything but edged an empty snack bowl closer to me. His face was bland, but I could tell he knew damn well what was wrong with me. Points to him for not rubbing it in.

"Where's James?" I asked, eager to get the focus off me. "How's Molly? Did she finish changing back?"

Thomas, if anything, looked even more disgruntled.

Mark glanced at his watch. "As of about two hours ago, she was still orange and furry. Pure ape—no Molly bits to speak of."

"Well, shit. She lost ground. What's James going to do?" I asked.

"He said he had something else he wanted to try," Thomas said. "Told us to get the hell out of his way, and to leave him alone while he implemented it." He turned his attention back to Billy. "Shoot."

Billy took a breath, and looked from Thomas to Mark. "Funny you should say that. You know Monica Barrelles?"

Thomas looked puzzled. "Jordan's sister? Sure. Why wouldn't I?"

"Did you see her at the party last night? Any of you?" Billy took in everyone with a sweeping glance. Apparently, nobody had seen her except him and me. "I'm afraid she may be dead." He quickly explained what we'd found in the grotto, and how the body had disappeared.

"Is this connected to what happened to Laura?" Mark asked.

Billy ran a hand through his hair, leaving the still-wet curls in disarray. "Hell if I can figure it out." He hesitated. "You know Laura and I were working a little side project?"

Mark looked disgusted. "Yeah, she told me. Wouldn't say what it was. Said what she did on her own time was none of my business."

Billy smiled openly at that. Hell, he'd probably coached her on what to say. It sounded like a line from his playbook. "You got a problem with free will?" he said. Yeah, I know. Reckless, considering Mark didn't seem to be in a forgiving mood.

Gray eyes turned to rocks. "I have a problem with stupidity," Mark said.

Billy sobered. "Look, she came to me." He saw the skepticism in Mark's eyes. "Seriously. She approached me after Sweden. Said she knew I had interests other than just working with you, and that she wouldn't mind moonlighting a little herself. Made a crack about government work not paying all that well."

"If she needed money she could have come to me," Mark said.

"Yeah, well, I got the idea she's more the type who wants to earn it herself. Or maybe . . ." Billy stopped, shrugged.

"What?" Mark pressed.

"Maybe it wasn't about the money. Maybe she was on a fishing expedition."

"What do you mean?"

"Come on, Mark. She knows about you. She must suspect there are more like you. Maybe she was trying to figure out if I'm one of them."

Mark considered it. "Maybe. So, what did you set up with her? I assume you didn't turn down her offer."

"Of course not—I was curious to find out what she knows about me," Billy said. "We were going to meet when I got back from D.C. She was up here, supposedly setting up the job. She'd asked to stay at my place, to save a few bucks, since she wasn't on the company dime. That's what got me thinking she was digging deeper into my background."

"That it?" Mark said.

"She also set up a meeting with a friend of hers at the zoo in D.C., one of the reasons I decided to take Molly to visit Ciel. That friend never showed. Now I'm wondering if that was just to get me out of town for a few days."

"Is that why you were so distracted at the zoo when you were supposed to be helping me?" I asked.

He shrugged. "Two birds, one stone."

"And Laura was the one you had to get rid of before we brought Molly to your place," I said. At least it hadn't been a girlfriend.

"Well, I wouldn't phrase it that way," Billy said wryly. "But, yes, I had called her to ask her to clear out before we got there. I didn't think explaining Molly's situation to her was a good idea."

Mark's face remained passive. "So? I'm waiting."

"So, that's it. I never had a chance to find out more." Billy looked uncertain. "The thing is, I don't think my project with Laura has anything to do with her shooting."

"Then why was she at your apartment?"

Billy shrugged. "Not sure. Maybe she left something there and was coming back for it. Or maybe . . ."

"What?" Thomas, who'd been standing back and letting Mark do the questioning, pounced.

"Well, when Laura and I first discussed working together, she mentioned a possible stumbling block. Other than Mark."

Mark quirked his mouth but remained silent.

Billy took a deep breath, a face-the-music look coming over his face. "It's Harvey. He found out she was working on the side with me, and I don't think he liked the idea."

"He wouldn't," Mark said. "It goes against my agreement with him."

"So why was Laura working with Billy in the first place, if she wasn't supposed to?" I asked.

"Because, technically, she didn't know Billy was an adaptor, so I couldn't order her not to do it. I was counting on Billy to do the smart thing and keep his distance from her."

Billy shrugged. "I was curious. Anyway, when Harvey found out, Laura kind of freaked, called and left a message on my cell that she needed to discuss the situation. I was hoping to head her off before"—he cut me a glance—"things got needlessly complicated, but our wires got crossed. She must have showed up at my place right after I ran out to grab dinner for Ciel and Molly while they were in the tub. Somebody—possibly somebody in the guise of me—was there before Laura arrived, or maybe got there at the same time. All I know is, if she thinks it was me who shot her, she's wrong."

Mark took a sip of his beer before he spoke. "About Harvey—"

Thomas stepped on his words, "If that asshole is involved, you can bet he's on a recruiting mission." He cut Mark a look. "How many of us does he know about? He couldn't get me, not even after he lured Laura away to use as bait. He thought I'd follow her. Who's he after now?"

Aha. Well, that explained Thomas's dislike of Harvey. I grabbed a handful of popcorn from a bowl on the bar and absently munched on it, hoping my queasiness would settle if my stomach wasn't empty.

Mark shook his head, forcing patience. "Tom, Laura did what *she* wanted to do. And Harvey left you alone after I told him I'd quit if he didn't lay off you."

"Does he know about me?" Billy asked.

"Not through me, no. But he'd be an idiot if he didn't suspect, after all the jobs you've worked with me. And whatever you can say about Harvey"—Thomas snorted; Mark ignored it—"he's not an idiot."

Billy nodded once, thinking. "Okay, here's the question,

then—did Harvey send Laura to recruit me behind your back? Was that her real purpose for wanting to work with me?"

Mark looked like he didn't want to believe it. "It's possible. She's always had kind of a father complex about him—her dad was a real son of a bitch—so if he asked her . . . Yeah, she might consider it."

God, all the twisted spook intrigue. "But then who shot her? And why? And why would she say it was Billy?" I said.

"To finish the mission?" Thomas said with more than a touch of bitterness. "That's what they train you spooks to do, isn't it—always finish the mission? If she was supposed to recruit Billy, what better way than to implicate him in a crime and then let the Agency offer him a way out. Actually, it wouldn't surprise me if Smith arranged the whole thing. What's losing a regular operative compared to gaining another adaptor?"

Crap. Was it possible? My stomach gave a small heave.

Mark took a deep breath, holding it for a second before releasing it. I could almost feel him biting his tongue. Obviously, he'd gone a few rounds with Thomas on the subject of Harvey's methods before. "Harv wouldn't hurt Laura, Thomas," he said quietly.

"You've always had a giant blind spot when it comes to Harvey Smith." Thomas sounded as resigned as Mark. He probably didn't really believe what he'd accused the man of—it was likely just an old frustration cropping up.

Brian, who'd been following the conversation with about as much tension on his face as if he were watching a butterfly flit from flower to flower, topped off his beer and said, "First Laura and then Monica. So, who's next?"

My stomach rebelled completely at that thought, and I dashed for the ladies' room. Turned out stale popcorn was not the hang-over remedy I'd hoped it would be.

After its exit was complete and I'd made my final bow over the toilet bowl, I went to the sink and splashed more water on my face. A quick pat with a paper towel and I looked human enough again.

The guys were all standing when I returned, having obviously wrapped things up while I was gone.

"Here she is," Thomas said. "Everything okay, Ciel? Good. We're heading back to the lab. I want to bring James up to speed about Monica—didn't he take her under his wing when she found out she wasn't going to be an adaptor?"

Billy nodded. "Yeah, that's right. He knows what it's like, and I seem to recall him helping her through a rough patch."

"That's what I thought. Listen, you better come, too," Thomas said, having apparently forgiven Billy his transgressions. "Unless you want to wind up back in jail, we have some things to discuss about your case. Bri, you need anything, you call."

Mark took Billy casually by the elbow. "Hang back a second, okay? You two go on—we'll be right behind you."

I dug through my brain for a good excuse to stay, but Thomas herded me out the door. Brian came with us, probably just to give Mark his private time with Billy. I wasn't sure that was such a good idea. When Thomas opened the back door of the limo for me, I hesitated.

"Hold on," I said, patting my pockets. "I left something in the ladies' room. Be right back." I dashed before they asked me what I'd forgotten, so I didn't have to expand the lie.

Once inside, I crept toward the bar, careful not to make a sound. I didn't dare peek around the wall, but I could hear

Mark's voice plainly enough: ". . . isn't a game, Billy. People are getting hurt. If you—"

"Life is a game, Mark. You ought to know—you spend enough time playing superhero."

"Stop being a smart-ass. I meant what I said. You give it some careful thought before you pursue things. If she gets hurt—" *Crap.* Were they talking about me?

"Are you really worried about that? Or are you just ticked because I beat you to the punch?"

A hollow-sounding *thwak,* followed by a thud, was the answer. Yikes! I had to look. Billy's knees had hit the floor. His hand went to his jaw, and he was bleeding from the corner of his mouth. But he was smiling.

Mark was not. He looked pissed, and maybe surprised. He probably wasn't accustomed to losing control.

"If you're so worried about Ciel, you might want to turn your sights a little closer to home," Billy said. "How much do you really trust Harvey?"

Shock flickered over Mark's face. "What does Harvey have to do with this?"

"Well, I could tell you, but then he'd have to kill me," Billy said wryly.

Mark reached a hand out to Billy and helped him up in that manly, grab-each-other's-wrist way guys do. Not precisely an apology, but probably as close as most men get. When he spoke there was no longer any anger in his voice. "Could you please just cut the crap and tell me what you're talking about?"

"I'd rather wait until I have something solid to go on. Since you and Harv are such bosom buddies and all . . ." Guess Billy wasn't quite ready to forgive and forget.

Mark looked like he might flare up again, so I pulled back and made some noise. Better clip this confrontation before Billy made some other flip remark and they really went at it.

When I poked my head back in, Billy was standing, stuffing a cocktail napkin into his pocket, blood gone from his mouth and any signs of Mark's fist adapted away. Mark was leaning casually against the bar, his face bland.

"Hi, guys. I forgot my lip gloss in the ladies' room." Yeah, big fat lie. "You coming? Thomas is getting impatient."

Billy laid his hands on my shoulders, casually possessive. "There's something I need to follow up on first. You go with Tom. I'll catch up with you later."

"But—"

He kissed me, and not in a cousinly way. I tasted the residual copperiness of the blood on the inside of his lip, but that didn't stop me from melting into him, my body reacting before my brain could remind me we had an audience.

Billy pulled away first, brushing my cheeks with his thumbs, his eyes full of the soft emotion I hadn't seen since before he found out I'd vandalized his car. Had he forgiven me? Or was it just a show for Mark? I wanted to believe it was real. He touched each of my eyebrows lightly with his lips before releasing me and leaving the club without another word to either of us. Guess he'd communicated everything he'd intended. Question was, to whom?

Chapter 19

"Ciel, pick up! Pick up *now*!" Brian's voice blared at me from James's answering machine.

I rolled over and stuck my head back under the pillow. I figured I needed at least another two or three hours of oblivion before I'd feel entirely human again. Plus, sleep offered the only reliable escape from my thoughts. Part of me was still wrestling with the idea that maybe all Billy had really wanted was to "get there" ahead of Mark. He claimed Mark's interest in me was whetted by his own, but what if the reverse were also true?

That's the part I wanted to suffocate under a pillow.

After leaving the guys at the lab I'd slunk back to James's apartment to recuperate. James hadn't taken the news about Monica well, and seemed more determined than ever before to straighten out the mess that was Molly. He had assured me he'd need at least the rest of the day to set things right there, and that I'd only be in the way, so I didn't feel guilty about abandoning her.

Which was good, because frankly I had all the guilt I could handle just with the car thing.

"*Ciel!* I know you're there. Come on, sis, I need a favor. Pick up the phone."

"Go away," I hollered. Not that he could hear me. It just seemed like some sort of response was required, and that was the only one that didn't necessitate leaving the warm nest of covers.

"Okay, sis, I didn't want to have to do this, but here goes. If you don't pick up right now I'll be forced to tell Mom what you did to Billy's car. And why you did it."

Fuck. I crawled over the king-size expanse to the edge of the bed and grabbed the phone. "Seriously, Bri? You're threatening to *tell on me*? Could you be any more immature?"

"Sorry, but I'm desperate. I need you to fill in for Suze at the club tomorrow night. She was supposed to debut with us, but something came up. Only thing is, the club manager said if Suze wasn't going to be there, none of us should bother to show up—he *really* likes Suze—so I told her I'd get someone to cover for her."

"*What?* You told her about us?"

"Of course not. I told Suze I knew a singer who looked enough like her to pull off the switch with the help of stage makeup, that's all. She bought it. But, seriously, the manager is way too into Suze not to notice if it's not her. So it really needs to be her."

"So why don't you do it? I'm sure the manager won't miss *you*," I said. Yeah, I know. Rude. Sisters are allowed.

"Ciel, I'm lead guitar. I have to be there."

"Brian, are you *crazy*? Even if I could carry a tune with Suze's aura—which is highly doubtful—I sure as hell don't have time to learn to play the guitar!"

"No worries. I'll teach you three chords—that's all you really need—and we'll crank up the volume."

"Brian, I can't. I'd need more time to—"

"No, you don't. Really. You'll be great, I promise."

"No," I said. Firmly. The whole idea was preposterous.

"Who stopped Billy from hitting you?" he wheedled.

Gaaah.

"Who put ex-lax in Ryan Lockmeer's chocolate pudding after he called you 'flatso'?"

Double-gaaah. He *had* done that for me. It was my sophomore year of high school (Brian had been a junior) and I was particularly sensitive about my lack of any significant development (so to speak) on the boobage front. Even then Brian had been opposed to unnecessary violence, so he refused to beat the guy up. Didn't mean he couldn't come up with creative alternatives to exact retribution, though.

"Please, Ciel . . . I really need this gig. You know I wouldn't ask if it weren't an emergency." His voice was low-pitched, beseeching. How could I refuse?

I sighed, heavily and melodramatically. I knew I sounded just like Mom when I did that. I also knew he was too smart to comment on the similarity when he wanted something from me. "When do I have to be there?"

"You owe me big-time for this, bro."

I'd gotten up early so I could be at Brian's apartment as soon as Suze left for her day job, and I wasn't a happy camper. Didn't help that the toddler next to me on the train barfed, which apparently bothered the rest of us a lot more than her, since she promptly flung her arms wide and shouted "Ta-da!" followed by "I'm hungry!" The triple shot of espresso Brian had waved under my nose as soon as I got there was taking the edge off my grumpiness, but it was still a long haul to cheery town.

"I think next time Mom needs an adaptable body for one of her jobs, *you* are filling in for me."

Our mother, with Auntie Mo as her partner, was her own modeling agency. (Note the wording: *was,* not had.) Just a small outfit they ran out of Mom's home office, which used to be my brother Thomas's room upstairs. They worked out of my parents' house because Auntie Mo and Uncle Liam still had kids at home.

Their agency had a Web site full of the portfolios of their "models," which were all, of course, them in different auras. Though they could easily provide whatever "type" a photographer desired, they specialized in models who looked almost, but not quite, like famous supermodels. Clients paid big bucks for those bookings. Not as big as for the real deal, but close enough that money wasn't an issue for my parents, or Billy's. They tried to limit their jobs to no more than two models at a time, but occasionally an extra was required. In those instances, Mom usually called on me, and paid me the going agency rate.

The thing is, I hate all that primping and fussing (which was the same reason Dad and Uncle Liam refused to work with them anymore), and frankly most of the photographers were real assholes. Let Brian listen to "Make *love* to the camera, darling!" all day long, and see how cheerful he was then.

Brian paled at the thought of filling in for me, but didn't refuse. He didn't dare, not if he wanted me to play real-life Rock Band with him later.

"Sure," he said, barely choking on it. "I'd be happy to. Anytime."

Ha. Like hell he'd be happy to. But he'd do it, and that was enough to make whatever retro-punk-hipster-indie hell I had to live through for one evening worth it.

Maybe.

I waded through the stage clothes in Suze's closet, trying to find something it wouldn't kill me to wear, because I was *not* going to put on the torpedo tits outfit. I have my limits.

I yanked a piece of neon purple fake leather off a hanger, eyed it dubiously, and started to put it back. Brian caught my hand and said, "Hey, that would work. Suze looks great in it."

"Where's the rest of it?" Because it looked like a corset, and not a whole lot else.

"That's it." His eyes went all dreamy.

I turned a dubious eye on my brother. "Why don't you tell me which outfit is your least favorite, because no way am I doing this if you're going to be looking at me all night with Suze lust in your eyes."

He coughed and turned red. "I would never . . . I mean, ew, you're . . ." He slid hangers across the bar until he reached the end of the ugly train and shoved an outfit at me. "Here. This one bores me stupid."

I could see why. It was the only thing in the closet, aside from Suze's day-job clothes, that had even a modicum of taste. By which I mean it was neither leather nor transparent. "It'll do."

"Sound check is at seven. Don't be late," he said, heading for the door.

"Wait—aren't you forgetting something?"

He gave me the classic Brian blank stare.

"The chords, Bri. You know, the three chords I need to know to pretend I can play the frickin' guitar?"

"Oh, yeah," he said with the relaxed smile of a man who'd gotten what he wanted.

He was no longer smiling an hour later. "Jesus, sis, how many times do I have to show you?" He grabbed my hand and placed my fingers on the proper strings yet again. Held them in place, and not quite as gently as before.

I glared at him. "Hey, I'm doing my best. You *know* I'm not musical like you and James. If you don't like it, you don't have to pay me. Oh, wait . . . you're *not* paying me. This is a *favor.*"

His grip lightened and the smile returned, a tad sheepish now. "Look, you have a smart phone, right? Just check out the 'Ultimate Guitar Tabs and Tools' app. It'll all become clear to you, I promise."

"Bri-*an,* I don't have a lot of time here, you know." Plus, my phone is way smarter than I am when it comes to apps. I'm lucky I can dial the damn thing.

"Yeah, yeah. Right. Never mind. I'll tune the guitar to Drop D. All you have to do is strum. After a few drinks, nobody in the audience will know the difference anyway."

When I was on my way out the door, he grabbed a stack of paper and stuffed it in my shoulder bag. "These are the lyrics of the songs we're doing tonight. You know most of them, but there might be one or two you haven't heard before. Look them over if you get a chance."

Crap.

* * *

I was still out of sorts when I left, albeit a much perkier out of sorts. Caffeine will do that for me. I hated going into any job feeling unprepared, even impromptu favor-type jobs, but I'd muddle through. Family was family.

Speaking of which . . . I dialed James. He sounded cheerful on the Molly front. "Just give me another hour or two. I think I found a formula that will stick, but I need to test it for side effects before I give it to Molls."

"Test it? James, you're not going to—"

"Gotta go, sis. See you later. We'll have drinks with Devon—he called and told me he ran into you at my apartment. Said you were the sweetest girl ever, and I was lucky to have a sister like you." He hung up before I could quiz him further about exactly how he planned to test his new formula. Monkeys? Bunnies? Undergrads?

Oh, well. He was the scientist. Presumably he knew what he was doing. But now it looked like I had a few hours to kill. Guess I could use the time to perfect my guitar skills . . . nah. That was a lost cause, and I knew it. The lyrics? I'd look over them later. How hard could they be? Songs usually just repeated a lot, right?

Probably wouldn't hurt to study my subject a little more, though. I'd snatched some of her energy when I'd met her, of course, so I had her aura, but I didn't know much about her otherwise. Maybe I could pick up some mannerisms if I spent some time with her. This might not be a real job, but studying Suze would be good practice for when I had paying clients. Besides, I was curious about the cougarific woman who was suddenly so smitten with my brother. (Yeah, I'm nosy. Sue me.) And it sure beat obsessing about Billy and Mark, which was my other option for filling the hours.

A visit to Suze's day job by her new boyfriend's sister wouldn't be out of line, would it? A sister who just wanted to get to know the new woman in her brother's life a little better? Maybe invite her to lunch? Yeah, that would be a nice thing to do. I'm a nice person. It wouldn't seem weird.

I pulled out my phone and plugged in the name of Suze's employer, which I'd ingeniously extracted at the last minute from Brian by the simple expedient of saying, "Hey, Bri, where does Suze work? In case anyone asks tonight. Wouldn't want to give a wrong answer."

Ah. Just a few blocks away. Handy, that. Wouldn't even need a cab.

I didn't have to go in—Suze was in front of the building, wearing one of her deadly dull knee-length dresses and deep in conversation with somebody. When I got close enough to see who, I ducked behind an illegally parked delivery truck, pronto.

Zoo Lady. What the hell?

I crept closer, careful to stay hidden from their view, hoping to get close enough to hear what they were talking about.

The truck started to pull away.

Crap. Glancing from side to side to make sure I wasn't observed, I changed my aura to that of an appropriately sized former client (so my clothes would fit), one who lived out of state and had short, blond hair, enough like mine not to draw the attention of anyone who happened to be watching from a distance. Then I inched close enough to eavesdrop.

". . . they had to have taken her back here," Zoo Lady was saying, all the while absently rubbing her monstrous belly, like some ogre hungry for its next meal.

"Don't worry about that now," Suze said. "I'll see if I can

track her down through Brian. He's such a puppy—he'll let something slip if I approach him right." Bingo. She *was* involved. But in what?

Zoo Lady laughed, deep and nasty. "Just make sure you're holding his cock when you ask him. He'll tell you anything."

Suze gave her an annoyed look. "Don't tell me how to do my job. I don't work for you."

Okay, then, I thought. *Who do you work for? Let's just see where you're headed.*

I followed Suze across Broadway, down Boerum Street to Sternberg Park, taking care to stay far enough behind her not to attract attention. She stopped near the baseball diamond, pulled out her phone, and shot off a text message. Within five minutes (which I spent meticulously retying both of my shoes and pretending to rub a cramp out of my calf), she was approached by a woman walking either a long-haired Chihuahua or a Pomeranian. One of those tiny, yappy dogs, anyway. I could see the woman on the other end of the leash only from behind, but something about her seemed familiar.

I decided to risk getting a little closer, to see if I could hear what they were talking about.

The voice. I knew that voice. Hell, I'd *spoken* in that voice. Recently.

It was my client, Mrs. Thelma Parker, she who was supposedly so painfully shy she couldn't fend off the overly friendly FONZ board member. Huh. From the authoritative way she was questioning her flunky, she'd gotten over it really fast.

Something else occurred to me. Monica was the one who had recommended this client to me. And now Monica was dead. Or probably dead, I thought, tempted to cross myself even though I wasn't Catholic, and hoping like hell I'd been mistaken about what I'd seen in the grotto.

Was there a connection? *Duh, Ciel.* How could there not be?

"The other—was she taken care of?" my client asked.

Suze nodded, almost graciously. "Of course. I told you I'd see to it."

"Show me."

Suze pulled out her phone, swiped her finger over the screen a few times, tapped it, and held it up for Thelma. It was too far away for me to make out the screen, but Thelma seemed satisfied.

"And where is she now?"

"Don't worry, no one will be seeing that gorgeous face again," Suze said with an air of finality I didn't like one bit. They had to be talking about Monica.

God. Suze was a murderer. Or knew who was.

Oh, crap. What was I going to tell Brian?

Nothing, I'd finally decided. I wasn't going to tell Brian a damn thing, not before I'd talked it over with Billy and Mark. Because Suze was right about Brian—he was a puppy. A brilliant, musically gifted puppy, but tender and soft nonetheless. God, he'd be crushed when he found out. Coward that I was, I didn't want to be the one to tell him.

I'd left messages on Mark's and Billy's cell phones, telling them I'd be filling in for Suze with Brian's band—they would know what I meant by that—and that it was urgent they contact me right away. I hinted as much as I dared over the phone that Suze might be more involved with "everything" than any of us realized. Since I had no idea where they were, that was the best I could do for the moment.

I knocked again on the door to the lab, harder this time. "James? Come on, open up. It's me."

There was a click, and the door swung open slowly. Only no one was there. I peeked behind the door. No one there, either. The sound of the Wii came from the alcove, so I guessed that was where Molly was.

"James?" I said cautiously.

A throat cleared close by. Which was really odd, because there wasn't anybody there to clear it.

"I'm here," he said quietly.

I scanned the room, a full three-sixty. "Um, not so's you'd notice. James, what's going on?" This was freaking me out.

"Here. Beside you. The last formula . . . there appears to be a slight problem with it."

I grabbed at the area the voice seemed to be coming from. Hit something solid. Felt my way up arms until I reached a face. "Oh, my God! James, what happened? Why can't I see you?"

"Well . . . it's complicated. I tweaked the formula that seemed to be working to suppress the orangutan aura for Molly at the party. I would never give her anything untested, and I didn't have a test subject handy, so I took it myself." He cleared his throat again. "It appears I over-tweaked. The new formula suppresses auras, all right. Even primary ones."

Jesus. "But you're not an adaptor. How were you going to tell if it worked on secondary auras by testing it on yourself?"

"I wasn't testing for efficacy, only safety. I figured if it didn't kill me, or make me sick, or give me purple and green spots, then it would be safe enough to use on Molly."

"Geez. Is it permanent? Will we ever see you again?"

"I only gave myself a small dose—it should wear off eventually."

"*Should?*"

"*Will,*" he amended, sounding more confident. Probably trying to fend off my impending hysteria.

A thought occurred to me, and I suddenly felt myself blushing. "Um, any special reason I can't see your clothes?" Auras—or, presumably their lack—did not extend to what an adaptor was wearing.

"I had to take them off. Couldn't exactly let an empty set of clothes go wandering around the lab, could I? I didn't want to freak out Molly."

"So you're naked?"

"Well, yes. I suppose I am."

"What if you, you know, reappear suddenly?"

He was standing close enough to whisper, so I felt his exasperated sigh as much as heard it. "I don't know, Ciel. I suppose I'll grab a handy lab coat."

"Hey, I was just wondering. Wouldn't want you to traumatize Molly." Or me.

"Look, I'm glad you're here. You have to look after Molly for me until this wears off—"

"I can't do that—I have to be at Brian's club in an hour for sound check. I'm doing him a favor and filling in for Suze onstage tonight."

"You? On a stage? Singing?"

Huh. He didn't have to sound so shocked. "Yeah, *me*. Playing guitar, too. Brian showed me some chords. I'm gonna wing the rest."

I didn't have to see him to know what he was thinking. The waves of skepticism floating through the air were palpable. "Hey, it wasn't my idea. He wheedled me into it. Probably couldn't find anyone else to do it on short notice."

"Well, regardless of your commitment to show business, you're going to have to stay."

"I told you—I can't. Brian's band will lose the gig if Suze isn't there. The manager is only keeping them on because he *reeeally* liked Suze when he met her."

"Then you better find someone else to watch Molly. What about Billy? She's his sister—he should do it."

"Billy can't—he's busy." Doing God knew what. Trying to locate Monica's body, I presumed.

"Too busy to take care of Molly?"

"It's important."

"And this isn't?"

"Look, it concerns Monica, okay?"

"Oh." I could hear the pain in his voice. He'd really done his best to help Monica adjust to being a nonadaptor. To lose the friendship of someone who'd understood his own position in our world was rough, especially when the loss was so violent. "Have they located her body yet?"

"Not as far as I know," I said gently. I decided not to mention her connection to my client until I knew for sure it wasn't some awful coincidence. No point in piling it on. "Listen, where's Thomas? Molly loves him—maybe he could come take care of her for a little while."

"He went to see Laura—he won't be back until tomorrow morning."

Damn. "I guess I'll just have to take Molly with me," I said. I hated to do it—I mean, my God, how was I going to explain an orangutan?—but I couldn't see an alternative. "She can stay in the dressing room while I'm onstage, and I'll bring her back here afterward. You'll be here, right?"

"Of course. I don't want to be seen in public like this."

A giggle escaped me. Couldn't help it. It *might* have contained a touch of the hysteria he'd tried to fend off earlier.

"You know what I mean," he said. "I could start to come back at any time. If someone noticed me—"

"Yeah, yeah. I know," I said, getting hold of myself. "Hey, what about Auntie Mo? She must be getting antsy about Molly by now."

"I talked to her earlier—told her Molly was in the bathroom—and said Molly would be hanging out with me at the lab today." Molly loved James's lab, and Mo thought it was educational for her to spend time there, so that wasn't unusual. "Maybe you'd better give her a call and let her know I've handed Molly off to you, though."

"Right. I'll tell her Molly and I are having a slumber party at your place—will that give you enough time?" I usually wound up taking Molly on some sort of a "girl date" whenever I was in town, and Mo knew Molly adored James's chameleon, Herbert, so she shouldn't be suspicious.

"I'll make it work. And tell Molly not to give up hope—I'm close to a breakthrough."

"I will." But first I'd work on believing it myself.

* * *

My cell buzzed as I was leaving the lab. Mark.

"Tell Brian to make other arrangements. You won't be going to the club tonight." As usual, he got right to the point. Why waste time on the preliminaries? Since he couldn't see me, I indulged in an eye roll.

"Why, hello, Mark. So nice to hear from you. I'm fine, thanks. How are you?" I said in my perkiest voice.

"I'm serious, Ciel. If Susan Hatcher is involved in this mess, I don't want you near any of her haunts."

"Don't worry—she won't be there. That was the whole point of me helping out Brian," I explained, telling myself it was cute how authoritarian he got when he was in protective mode. Not that I actually thought it was, but getting pissed at him was rarely productive.

"Will you just listen to me—"

"Nope. I can't leave Brian in the lurch. The show must go on, yadda yadda."

"God damn it, Ciel, I don't have time—"

"What? Sorry, you're breaking up. . . . I'll call you after the show, okay?"

The string of words I heard coming from the phone as I moved it farther away from my mouth would have done a longshoreman proud.

Chapter 20

Brian was remarkably sanguine about seeing me push a baby stroller into the club. I suspect his reaction might have been different if he'd thought I was the real Suze instead of her body double for the evening.

Thinking of Suze made me wince, and not just because all the body piercings I now sported kind of ooged me out. Yeesh. I needed to warn Brian about her, but I couldn't, not before he went on. That's just not a nice thing to do to a performer. He needed to concentrate on his music—I'd tell him about Suze after the show. (There. That sounded much better in my head than "Because I'm a big fat coward.")

Auntie Mo had been thrilled I was keeping Molly overnight— she said it was good for me to keep myself busy with family while I got over "things" with Mark. Plus, anything that gave her an actual evening alone with Uncle Liam was all right by her.

I sniffed the air as Brian leaned in to kiss my cheek, and detected the aroma of a certain recreational pastime known to be popular with musicians, as well as the unmistakable odor of *eau de Cheetos*.

"Really, Bri? Before a performance?" I said, shaking my head. I knew he indulged in illicit activities occasionally but didn't think he'd do it on the job.

"It releases my creativity. Gotta free the muse." His smile was goofy, and *very* relaxed. Probably shouldn't hit him with the James-is-invisible thing yet, either. In this state, he might find it way too funny, and I didn't want to deal with a case of the pot giggles.

"Hey, you hungry?" he asked, intensely, like food was the most important thing in the world. Which it likely was for him at the moment.

"No, but Molly might want something. Help me get her to the dressing room, okay?"

"Dressing room? Yeah, I guess you could call it that," he said, and led me to a large utility closet that had been fitted out with a mirror and a folding metal chair. It smelled rather strongly of the same substance as my brother. When I waved my hand in front of my nose, Brian casually picked up a bottle of air freshener and spritzed the room liberally. It didn't help. No way could I leave Molly in there all by herself while I was onstage, even if she did deserve it, karmically speaking.

"Geez, Bri, this is where they expect performers to change?"

"Well, mostly we come already dressed to go on. This is just for touch-ups and, you know"—he shrugged—"relaxing."

"What am I going to do with Molly during the show?"

He screwed up his face, no doubt trying to squeeze a straight thought out of his head. "She can sit behind Steve, I guess. He's the drummer, and he loves animals—"

Molly objected to that with a high-pitched vocal.

"Sorry, little fur-cousin. No offense," Brian said, patting Molly on the head. She stuck her tongue out at him.

Geez. Molly onstage with us? Not a great idea by a long shot, but since locking her in the pot closet wasn't an option, it would have to do.

"Okay, okay. I'll have a talk with Molly before we go on, and make sure she knows she has to stay hidden while we perform. Now, where's Suze's wardrobe?"

His pupils suddenly got even bigger. "It's hanging on the back of the door. But I sort of couldn't go with your first choice—Suze sent it out to the cleaners with a bunch of her other stuff." He backed away. "Look, I have to go check the . . . uh, amplifiers . . . and, um, tell Steve you brought your pet—sorry, Moll! How else can I explain you? See ya in a few."

What had he done? I squeezed into the closet and peeked behind the door, cautiously, halfway expecting live snakes coming out of a hat. Medusa was a look, right?

No snakes, but nearly as bad. Resigned, I put it on while Molly stood guard. I was going to *kill* Brian.

The house was full when I went on for the first set. Must be a lot more conical-bra Madonna fans in the greater New York City area than I'd imagined. Or maybe Lady Gaga fans. Magaga fans? Whatever.

Yeah, Brian had brought *that* costume for me, the rat bastard. But I got him back for it—when Molly and I joined him for sound check, I gave him a great big hug. His eyes bulged, and his yelp was gratifying. Bet he'd have bruises on his chest for a week.

Suze's biggest fan was the house manager, who'd appeared like magic while we were making adjustments to the mics and amps. (And by "we" I mean Bri and the rest of the band. I stood where I was told and spoke a few words into the microphone when asked. Something really creative, like "testing, one, two." But I'd said it in rock-star voice.)

Joey Puccinello looked like he'd graduated high school last year. If he shaved at all, it was maybe once a week. He was skinny and on the short side—seriously, I'd been afraid to stand too close to him for fear of putting his eyes out with my armor-encased boobs. The good thing was, he was so entranced by Suze's charms he hadn't even noticed Molly peeking out from behind the bass drum.

The bad thing was, he kept hinting I should ditch Brian after the show and spend a little time with him. As if. I'd just smiled, and made no promises.

Molly was still safely stowed behind the drum set. Since the drummer was as "relaxed" as my brother, he was cool with the arrangement. Even offered to let her stomp on the bass drum pedal a few times before the place filled up, which Molly enjoyed way too much. I sensed a basement drum set in Auntie Mo's future.

Brian was at the mic, having introduced the rest of the band before I came on. I'll say one thing for Suze—the crowd loved her. Or her costume, at least. The applause was nice, but the catcalls made it doubtful the patrons were expecting much from her, music-wise. Just as well, all things considered.

I strutted across the stage (if you can call a raised platform set up at the far end of the bar a stage), employing Suze's killer curves to the best of my ability without falling off my stiletto-heel boots, grabbed the microphone from Brian, and said, in Suze's sultriest voice, "Let's get this party started!"

There was a *pop!* followed by a *thump,* and then the room went quiet.

Okay, I know I'm not the most musically talented person in the world, but I hadn't even started to sing yet. Surely this couldn't be my fault.

I peered out into the house, squinting. The guy at the sound-board stared, big-eyed and open-mouthed, at the man next to him, who was folding a knife closed and putting it back in his pocket. *What the . . . ?* Mark. And he'd just severed the cable connecting the band's equipment to the board.

He crossed the room and stepped onto the platform, sparing me a steely-eyed glance before he turned to the audience. "Sorry, folks. We appear to be having technical difficulties with the band tonight."

Raucous boos emanated from the audience, interspersed with some language I sincerely hoped Molly couldn't understand.

"The next two rounds are on me," Mark shouted to the room as he took me by my elbow and started pulling me off the stage. The boos morphed into cheers. I jerked my arm away from him, refusing to be led away like some misbehaving child.

My boobs chose that moment to go off like the Fourth of July, shooting sparks in all directions. Molly jumped out from behind the drums, climbed onto my back, and started waving one arm around while she held on to my head with the other hand.

The cheers amplified exponentially.

Mark's mouth set itself into an even harder line. "Brian, Ciel—in the back. Now."

*   *   *

"You could have warned me I was set to go all Lady Gaga on the audience," I said to Brian after I'd changed out of my costume. I'd refused to speak to either him or Mark until I'd rid myself of the conical bra. It was a fire hazard.

Mark had flashed some ID and convinced the manager to let us use his office. It wasn't much to look at, but it was a hell of a lot better than the pot closet.

"I didn't know they were loaded," Brian said, bouncing Molly on his hip like a toddler. "Honest. Suze must've reset them when I wasn't around."

"Yeah, well, you be sure to thank her for me, okay?"

"Hey, don't be mad, sis—it was so cool! Man, we've never had a reaction like that before—damn! We got a standing ovation before we even started the show!"

Molly clapped her hands obligingly in illustration. She'd snuck in a few bows as we'd walked off the stage, enjoying herself immensely. God help Auntie Mo if she'd been bitten by the rock-star bug. Scratch that. God help Brian—and me—if Auntie Mo ever found out how it happened.

"Did you stop to think people *might* have been standing up to run away from the wild animal and the woman shooting fire out of her tits?" I said, a tad disgruntled by the whole situation.

"Never mind that," Mark said, obviously impatient. "Ciel, I'm not even going to ask what possessed you to bring Molly tonight. I presume you have a good reason—"

"A really good one," I said. "Probably way better than your reason for interrupting the show. Want to hear it?"

"Two women have been shot, and you leave me a message that Susan Hatcher may be involved. You honestly think I'm going to let you set yourself up as a target?"

I glanced at my brother, whose usual happy and open face clouded over at the mention of Suze's name.

"Um," I said to Mark, "maybe we should talk about this privately."

"If it's about Suze, I want to know," Brian said, his puppy-dog eyes for once showing determination. He wasn't going anywhere.

Fuck. I took a deep breath and spilled everything, starting with how I went to her workplace and saw her meet up with Zoo Lady (I detoured briefly to fill them in on Zoo Lady and her goons chasing Billy, Molly, and me as we were leaving D.C.), how I followed Suze to Sternberg Park, where she'd met up with my erstwhile client. I skipped the part about Zoo Lady telling Suze where to hold Brian when questioning him. Couldn't think of a delicate way to put that.

The longer I talked, the colder Brian looked. I felt like I was telling a six-year-old there was no such thing as Santa Claus, and oh, by the way, the Easter Bunny and the Tooth Fairy aren't real, either. Some truths you just don't want to share.

When I brought up Monica's relation to my client, even Mark blanched. The idea of someone connected so closely to the adaptor community being a part of whatever this mess was didn't sit well with him at all.

"So Suze killed Monica. Is that what you're saying?" Brian said, his normally loose-framed body rigid.

"I got that impression, yes," I said. "Either that, or she knows who did. She seemed certain Monica is dead, is all I can say for sure."

"I'd rather not see that aura on you anymore, if you don't mind," Brian said, stiff-jawed. Because naturally I was still wearing Suze. I'd arrived as her, and adaptor caution dictated I leave as her. It was the most secure way to handle a job. Even here in the office, there was the possibility the squirrelly house manager might walk in on us.

Screw caution. I dropped the aura gladly. The Suze-size street clothes I was wearing were suddenly too large, but if that's what Brian wanted, it was okay by me. Mark—Mr. Discretion when it came to adapting in public—didn't look pleased, but he didn't say anything.

Brian was so different from the guy he'd been just minutes before that it was scary. His face was harder, his voice harsher. More like Thomas's when Thomas was in serious shark mode. My happy-go-lucky brother was gone, and I wanted to throttle that bitch for doing this to him.

But I was beginning to suspect I wouldn't get the chance, not if Brian found her first.

"Brian—" I started. His eyes stopped me. For a guy who'd never been able to wrap his mind around violence, he looked like he was ready to rip into red meat with his bare teeth. The puppy had been replaced by a Rottweiler.

"Mark," he said, "take Ciel and Molly back to the lab. I'll meet you there later. You can go out the back way—no one will see you."

Mark's eyes matched my brother's for hardness. The look wasn't nearly as jarring on him. "As long as you don't do anything stupid."

"She's using me, Mark. She played me for a fool."

"Doesn't matter now. I need her if I'm going to figure out

what the hell is going on. Maybe you better let me take care of her."

"*No*. I'll get her and bring her to you. One way or another." Brian turned to leave, not even saying good-bye to me or Molly.

"Hey, Bri," Mark said to his back.

Brian paused, then responded without taking his eyes off the exit in front of him. "What?"

"Save me something to question."

Brian's only answer was to leave, slamming the door behind him.

"Mark, what are you thinking? You can't let him go after her—that's *Brian*, for gosh sakes! He doesn't *do* confrontation."

"Relax, Howdy. He won't find her, and he needs to blow off steam. Let him."

"How can you know that?" I said.

"Call it a hunch."

"You're going to risk letting my brother mix it up with a possible killer because of a *hunch*?"

He gathered up Molly and herded me toward the door. "My hunches tend to be reliable."

"So," I said to Mark once we were in his car (a Volvo this time) and Molly was safely buckled into the built-in booster seat in back, fast asleep. "There's something else I should probably tell you before we get to the lab."

He gave me a sidelong glance. "Do I really want to know?"

"James is invisible."

His double take was strangely satisfying. It wasn't easy to surprise Mark. "Explain," he ordered as he pulled into traffic. He appeared to be weighing the likelihood of this kind of additional complication against the possibility that I'd just gone crazy.

I sighed. "It's true. He was testing some new antidote for Molly on himself before giving it to Molly—something that was supposed to make an adaptor drop a secondary aura—and I guess he took too much. Or else, since he can only project his own aura, that's the one he dropped. So now he's projecting no aura at all—he's invisible."

"Are you *sure*?"

"Geez, Mark, I saw him—or rather, *didn't* see him—with my own eyes. Yes, I'm sure."

"Permanent?"

"He doesn't think so, but who knows?"

Mark drove in silence for a while, digesting the latest bit of weirdness. When I couldn't take listening to my own thoughts any longer, I asked, "Have you heard from Billy? I left him a message, too, but . . ."

His mouth tightened the slightest bit. When he spoke, his voice was carefully neutral. "I haven't heard from Billy. I was hoping you had."

"Not a word," I said, trying to sound casual, which wasn't easy, considering how worried I was. "Maybe he's with Thomas," I suggested, not especially hopeful.

"Tom hasn't heard from him, either. He never showed up to discuss his defense strategy, which, as you might imagine, isn't sitting well with your oldest brother."

Oh, I could imagine all right. "I thought Tom went to see Laura."

"He's with her now. Said to tell Billy—if I can find him—that if he misses his court date, he'd better just retire his primary aura for good, because he was through with him."

"Thomas wouldn't do that. Hell, I'll fill in for Billy in court if he can't be there," I said.

That only made Mark's mouth go even tighter. "And possibly wind up being hauled to jail yourself? That won't be happening."

I thought about pointing out he had no say in what I would or wouldn't be doing, but decided against it. Why get all heated about it now when it might not even be necessary?

Mark parked in the same garage as he had before, the same space, in fact. If he was thinking about the kiss, though, it didn't show. My heart thumped harder as I hurried out of the car and busied myself unbuckling the sleeping Molly's seat belt.

Whoa . . . wait a second. Was it my imagination, or did Molly-O suddenly seem a little more Molly and a little less "O"? I turned on the interior light to get a better look. She was definitely less furry. Her nose was back to normal, and her eyelashes were back, too. As I watched, her own mouth appeared, followed by her hair.

"She's changing back!" I whisper-yelled, afraid waking her might somehow stall the process.

Mark was right behind me, leaning over me, pulling me out of the way. He didn't make a sound as we watched Molly waver between auras, finally settling into her own. Hastily, I slipped off my lightweight jacket and covered her. If she woke up and found herself naked she'd be mortified.

"God, I hope it sticks," I said quietly.

"You and me both, Howdy," Mark said with one of his rare

smiles. My breath caught in my throat. I was going to have to work harder at not melting every time he did that.

Fortunately, he didn't notice my reaction because he was already bending over to pick up Molly, careful to keep her well covered by the jacket. She sighed in her sleep, and reached up to put her arms around his neck, snuggling against his chest.

I was *not* jealous.

Gaaah. Okay, I was, but only a little. And it faded when I thought about Billy, whose chest was the one I really wanted to be snuggled up against. It was Billy I was missing. Billy I was so worried about I wanted to cry in frustration, or maybe hit something.

"Come on, Howdy. Let's get her in and show James the good news."

"If we can find him," I said wryly.

Chapter 21

James didn't open the door, not even after I started pounding on it.

"He can't have gone home," I said. "He knew I'd be bringing Molly back here after the show. Wait a sec. I'll call him." But his cell went directly to voice mail.

Mark shifted Molly to one arm and reached into his pocket for a set of keys. He used one, combined with a code he punched into the keypad, and pressed his thumb against a biometric pad for good measure. Nobody could accuse James of being lax on security. I wasn't surprised Mark could get in—he'd been the one to set it up.

"James!" I called out as soon as I was through the door. No answer. And the place felt . . . empty.

Mark carried Molly to the alcove and laid her on the sofa while I walked the perimeter of the lab. Nothing.

Molly's voice drew me. "I'm back. I'm me again!" Her joy was infectious, and for a minute it stopped my other worries.

"Hey there, Molly. Good to see *you* again," I said.

She jumped up and ran to me, holding the jacket around her while she hopped up and down. "Look at me, look at me!"

Yes, I hopped, too, hugging her close to me at the same time. "Oh, Molly. I'm so happy. Don't you ever scare me like that again!"

She giggled. "Hey, it wasn't my idea. Where's James? I want to show him—he worked so hard to fix me."

I met Mark's eyes over Molly's head. He shrugged and said, "He must've stepped out for a minute. I'm sure he'll be back soon. In the meantime, why don't you get dressed?"

"I left you some clothes in the supply closet, Molls. You can change in there," I said.

Her eyes twinkled at me, so much like her brother my heart contracted. "You won't lock me in, will you?"

"So, you remember everything, do you?" I laughed. "No, you're safe. I could never be that rotten to *you.*"

She flashed me the Doyle forgive-me smile (even harder to resist than the Doyle eyes) and skipped away. After she was gone, I said to Mark quietly, "Look, if James is still invisible, he could be here somewhere. Asleep, or maybe even unconscious." *Or worse,* I thought, but refused to say it out loud, as if voicing it would make it so.

Mark nodded. "You start on the other side. Make sure you step on every floor tile not covered by something solid—we should be able to feel him if he's here."

I swept a foot in front of me before each step, taking care not to step on anything I couldn't see. Mark did the same.

"Ciel, Mark—come quick!" Molly's voice rang out from inside the closet.

I was the nearest, so I got there first, but Mark was only a second behind, despite having to travel twice the distance. Molly was wearing her own shorts and T-shirt, and had one sandal on. She pointed the other toward the back corner, a look of horrified fascination on her face. "Is that . . ." she said.

"James," I finished, and ran to the corner. He was barely conscious, and kind of . . . translucent. His aura must have been reappearing, and it didn't look like the process was agreeing with him. He'd been dressing himself when he'd passed out.

Mark reached over me and placed two fingers on his neck. "His pulse is steady, but weak. We need to get him to a doctor."

"What? Like *that*?" I said.

"Not just any doctor, obviously. Dr. Frankel—do you have his number?"

"But Dr. Frankel is *ancient*," Molly said. "Older than Granddad, even. He was practically shuffling the last time Mom took me to see him. Plus, he smells funny."

I knew I should call Molly on her rudeness, but honestly? She was right. Dr. Frankel did shuffle, and he smelled like mothballs. Who kept their sweaters in mothballs anymore? But he *was* an adaptor—if his ability hadn't faded entirely with age—and so wasn't likely to be shocked by James's see-through appearance.

"He's probably asleep," I said, but got out my phone and dialed anyway. Mom checked all of our phones regularly to make sure Dr. Frankel was in our contacts, because who knew when one of us might come down with the plague unexpectedly? If we got delirious with fever and started spontaneously adapting, we needed access to a doctor who would understand.

"I'm sure he's used to emergencies," Mark said, already bending down to help James to his feet.

"What happened to him?" Molly asked, referring to James.

"A slight problem with something he was testing," I said, counting the rings. *Pick up already, Dr. Frankel. If you're still breathing* . . .

"I wonder if it was that adaptor potion I heard him talking to Monica about," Molly mused, her curiosity for the moment outweighing her concern.

I almost dropped my phone. "What? When did you hear—"

"Your phone, Ciel," Mark cut in, and when I just stared at him, he continued. "It's talking."

Crap. I brought it back up to my ear. "Dr. Frankel? Is that you? . . . Yeah, yeah, I know it's the middle of the night. . . . Yes, I'm aware of how old you are, and that you need your sleep, but this is an emergenc—what? Oh. Ciel Halligan . . . yeah, *those* Halligans."

"Why am I in the closet?" James's eyes had opened halfway, and his words were a bit mushy.

"That's what we'd like to know," Mark said as he worked to keep him steady.

I tried to focus on what the doctor was saying. "No, it's not about me. It's James. There's something wrong with him. . . . *James.* Yes, that James . . . Of course I know he's not an adaptor. I'm his sister, for Christ's sake. . . . Sorry! Yes, I *know* I shouldn't take the Lord's name in vain. . . . Yes, my mother *did* teach me better than that. Geez, I said I was sorry, now will you just listen for a second?"

Mark started walking James slowly toward the door. "Molly, grab that hat, will you? And the coat. We have to get him covered up before we go out."

"No, Dr. Frankel, I don't care if James is a nonadaptor, we

can't take him to a regular doctor. *Because,* that's why. Look, just get ready for us, okay? I'll explain when we get there!" I hung up before he could voice any more objections. "Can somebody please tell me why the whole fuck—er, flipping adaptor community only has one freaking doctor?"

Molly cocked her head. "Hey, maybe *I'll* be a doctor. If I'm not a lawyer like Thomas, or a fixer, like you, Ciel." Apparently, "primatologist" had lost its charm.

"The boy's having difficulty displaying his primary aura."

My, what an astute observation, I thought, seriously wondering if bringing James here to see Dr. Frankel was worse than doing nothing at all.

The man, well known—and more than a little feared—by everyone in the adaptor community, was leaning his large frame so heavily on his tripod cane it was a wonder the thing didn't warp beneath him. His robe looked older than me, and his lambskin slippers should have been put out to pasture decades ago.

We were at the good doctor's office, located at his home in an old Brooklyn neighborhood of detached, single-family houses. He'd converted the dining room of the large, brick bungalow into an examination room, and James was lying on the antique exam table. You could see right through his head to a wrinkle in rolled-out white paper beneath it.

"Um, yes," I said. "That's why we brought him to see you instead of a civilian doctor."

"Don't get pert with me, missy." He shook a knobby finger at me. "I brought you into this world, as well as your brother here. That little scamp, too." He pointed his arthritic digit at Molly, and then gave Mark a once-over, squinting his eyes. "Him I don't recall. Are you sure he's one of us?"

Mark lifted one corner of his mouth a fraction, and slid through a series of some of his more outlandish auras, holding each one for about a second.

"Quite sure," I said.

The good doctor harumphed, not impressed, and turned his attention back to James, who had passed out again. "Now, this . . . *this* is not natural. I've known this boy since he was born, and he has never given any indication of an aura anomaly. Unlike the rest of you hooligans."

I gave a small cough and dared to correct him. "Halligans."

"I stand by what I said. Now, tell me what he's been doing to himself. He fancies himself a scientist, doesn't he? He must have done something, because this sure as hell didn't just happen on its own." He looked back at us to make sure we were paying attention. "You might say I can see right through him." He barked a laugh that ended in a wheeze, bending him even farther over his cane.

Molly giggled. "Good one, Dr. F."

I tried to smile. Not sure if I succeeded. "Yeah, good one. Now, can you please *do* something for him?"

"Depends," the old coot said, and then just waited, staring me down.

I looked at Mark, who nodded, resigned. I started to explain things from the beginning, going back to the zoo and Molly's precocious adapting.

The doctor held up one hand, palm toward me. "Hold on there, missy." He shuffled to the hall door and called out. "Angela! Get in here, girl. You better hear this, too."

A honey-haired young woman joined us, fully dressed in

casual khaki slacks and a short-sleeved white shirt. She wore her hair in an artfully messy updo, and her clothes fit like they were tailored for her, unlike mine, which were meant for Suze's larger frame. I'd tightened the belt and rolled up the pants legs, but I still looked like a kid playing dress-up.

Oh, well. Could be worse. At least I wasn't still wearing the torpedo tits outfit. I darted a glance at Mark, gauging his reaction to her. He didn't exactly run his eyes up and down her figure, but he wasn't oblivious, either.

"This is my granddaughter," Dr. Frankel said. "She's training to be a doctor. I can't work forever, you know, no matter what you lot seem to think."

Angela smiled, nodding to each of us in turn as the doctor told her our names. "So nice to meet you all. I do hope we'll be able to help." She looked at James curiously.

Molly piped right up. "Are you an adaptor, too? I am. I just found out. I can—"

"Hold on there, Molly," Mark said, laying his hands on her shoulders and giving her a little squeeze. "Give the lady room to breathe."

Angela laughed softly. "No, Molly, I'm afraid not. We haven't had an adaptor in the family since Grampa here."

"Grampa" harumphed again. "That's what I get for marrying a normal. Damn strong genes that woman had."

James groaned. "Looks like he's coming around," Angela said.

"Get talking, missy. Make it snappy."

I started over with the zoo, for Angela's benefit, and took it up to where James told me he was testing the stronger formula on himself before giving it to Molly. "For safety, not efficacy. He already had a good idea that it would work, since Molly had shown signs of changing back at the party."

The doctor had listened raptly the whole time, sharply focused on Molly during most of it, like he was looking for signs of orange fur. Angela listened closely, too, her eyes staying mainly on James, who was starting to look more solid to me.

"And that's about it," I said. "Look, I just want to make sure James didn't poison himself with whatever he took. Obviously, the lower dose worked fine on Molly—it just took a little longer than he thought it would. He never should have given himself so much."

"Aw, Jimmy'll be fine," the old geezer said. "But I'll have my granddaughter look him over, if it'll make you feel better. Angela?"

She retrieved a stethoscope and a penlight from a black bag on the credenza and went over to James. After listening to his heartbeat, which she pronounced strong and regular, she lifted each eyelid with her thumb and shined the light on his pupils. Yup, he was definitely more solid—I couldn't see through him at all anymore.

"Looks okay to me," she said finally, after checking a few reflexes. "Whatever the side effects were, I'd say the worst is over."

"Speak for yourself," James said, pushing himself to a sitting position and groaning. "God, this is like the worst hangover ever."

"James, you're all right!" I hugged him tightly, setting off more moaning.

"Yay!" Molly crawled right up onto the exam table and squeezed in between us.

James stopped mid-moan. "Molly? Is it really you?" He let go of me and held Molly away from him, scanning her from top to toe, his joy evident.

Even Mark was smiling. So I hugged him. (What? I had to do something with all the excess happy I was feeling, and I sure couldn't hug Dr. Frankel. He smelled like mothballs.)

When I finally let go and sneaked a peek up at his face, Mark's eyes were soft. It might have been my imagination, but he also seemed reluctant to let me go. I didn't have time to speculate about it—Molly was exuberantly describing her adventures as an orangutan to Dr. Frankel and Angela, and I wanted to make sure she left out certain details, like people getting shot. Fortunately, Molly seemed to know instinctively what was and wasn't okay to talk about in front of the doctor and his granddaughter.

"And, whoa, when I saw my arms at the zoo, I almost freaked out! I mean, I've always hoped I'd be an adaptor, but that orange fur was kind of creepy, you know?" she said, all smiles and excited giggles about it now that it was over. Kind of like I feel after a roller-coaster ride. "I don't know how in the heck *that* happened."

"Yes, I wonder how that could have possibly happened," Dr. Frankel mused, with a sharp look at James, who flushed but didn't offer the doc any theories.

Angela looked thoughtful, in much the same way James did when he was trying to figure out a scientific puzzle. "Another genetic anomaly would explain it, I suppose, though the mutation has been stable for so many generations now. It would make more sense if there'd been a catalyst of some sort."

Now Mark was looking at James funny, too. What the heck was going on?

I couldn't stand to see my brother squirm, so I suggested it might be time for us to let Dr. Frankel return to bed. "Molly and James seem fine now, and we've disturbed you long enough."

"I'd feel better if we kept them under observation until morning—"

Mark jumped on the doctor's words. "Not at all necessary. If there appears to be any recurrence, we'll bring them back. But for now we need to get Molly home."

"Well, it goes against my advice, but I suspect you're going to do what you want to do no matter what I say. Jimmy, if you black out again, you get your rear to a hospital pronto, you hear me? Unless you disappear again, of course. Then you come back here." After James nodded politely, Dr. Frankel continued, directing his words to me, "And you, missy, you tell Mo I want to see Molly back here next week for a checkup."

Gulp. Guess that blew any chance we had of keeping Molly's adventure in zoology from her mother. "Um, sure thing, Dr. Frankel."

Geez. Auntie Mo was going to kill us all.

Chapter 22

Molly reached for the door to Herbert's cage as soon as we were back at James's place. Mark intercepted her hand before she touched her favorite googly-eyed creature. "Maybe you better hold off on that, Molls, at least until James gives you the go-ahead."

Molly's eyes got big. "You don't think I could project a *chameleon,* do you?"

I noogied her head lightly, looking at James. "I'm sure it's fine, right, James? But let's sleep on it first, just to be on the safe side, okay?"

"Yeah," he said. "Better safe than sorry. You can feed Herbert in the morning, before you go home." When her face fell, he added, "Tell you what, you and Ciel can take my bed tonight— how does that sound? I'll suffer on the futon, *and* I'll make you my special waffles for breakfast tomorrow."

Molly perked up. "With strawberries?"

"Yup," James said.

"And whipped cream?"

"I think that can be arranged."

"How about chocolate syrup?" I threw in, much to Molly's delight. Why not go for broke?

"Don't push your luck," James said. "Now, go on. It's late. You know where the spare toothbrushes are."

Mark leaned over and kissed the top of Molly's head. "Good night, kiddo. Ciel—you look ready to drop, too. You should go to bed." And he was looking at me like he wanted to be the one to tuck me in.

"Are you staying?" I asked, feeling myself color under his gaze. James added, "You're welcome to the couch."

"Won't be necessary," he said, breaking off eye contact with me. "I have a few questions, and then I have to go."

I looked from one to the other of them. If they thought I was toddling off to bed before I heard what they had to say, they were wrong. "Molly," I said, "why don't you go ahead and brush your teeth. I'll be along in a few minutes."

She scampered off to the bathroom, long braid bouncing on her back, visions of waffles and strawberries no doubt dancing in her head. I parked myself on the sofa.

Mark quirked his mouth in acknowledgment of my refusal to be left out of the conversation. James looked resigned, and sat down next to me. "I know what you're thinking," he said.

"Yeah? Because I'm not real sure I even know. What's going on, James?" Mark said, sitting in the wing chair across from us, leaning back and propping an ankle across his knee. I made a special effort to keep my eyes on his face. (What? Girls look, too.)

My brother leaned forward, forearms on his knees, fingers interlaced in front of him. "I've been working on a few . . . experiments . . . with regard to the adaptor genome. I'm pretty sure I've isolated the mutation responsible. The trait only exhibits when a child inherits the mutation from both parents, along with the proper catalyst."

I screwed up my brow. "But shouldn't you be an adaptor then, since both Mom and Dad are?" Biology had never been my strongest subject. Sure, I knew being an adaptor was inherited, but the specifics were cloudy.

James launched into a bunch of scientific mumbo jumbo about dominant and recessive genes, and catalysts, and the possible influence of environmental factors in the womb, and I don't know what all, until I felt the familiar glazing begin. I finally held up one hand and said, "Could you just give us the *Idiot's Guide to Genetics* version?"

He paused, thinking for a minute, probably considering just how far he had to dumb it down for me. "Okay, it's kind of like with eyes—only a lot more complex, of course, when you consider—"

"James, I get it. It's complicated. Just pretend you're talking to a ten-year-old, all right?"

He sighed. "You know how brown eyes are dominant, right? When it comes to eye color, brown eyes win over blue."

I nodded. Mark looked like he already knew all this but was patiently waiting for me to catch up.

"Basically, you inherit a gene for eye color from each parent. If you get a brown gene from one parent and a blue gene from the other, your eyes will be brown, since brown is dominant. Now, if two brown-eyed people who each have one dominant brown gene and one recessive blue gene produce a child, it's likely the child will have brown eyes. But it's *possible* the child will inherit the recessive blue gene from each parent, and thus have blue eyes. Get it?"

Strangely enough, I did. "Yeah, I'm following. So you're saying the adaptor gene is like brown eyes, and the nonadaptor gene is like blue eyes, and you lucked out with recessive nonadaptor genes from both Mom and Dad?"

"Yeah, something like that. Other than the 'luck' part. There are other factors involved, including an extra gene—a special kind of 'catalyst' gene—that's apparently necessary to activate the adaptor gene, so technically it's possible to have the adaptor gene and still not manifest—"

Mark cut in. "I don't think we need to get into all the specific permutations here. Just tell us what happened."

It was then that James started to look like a kid caught with his hand in the cookie jar. He cleared his throat. "I've been toying with a formula to activate the catalyst gene."

Mark's eyes sharpened. "You think *you* have the adaptor gene but that you don't have the catalyst gene to activate it."

James flushed. "It's possible. I thought it was a valid scientific alley to explore."

"So, what happened? And what does this have to do with Molly?" I asked.

"I'd been experimenting with different delivery systems for the formula. Attaching it to a weakened rhinovirus—the common cold—was the obvious answer, and common enough in all gene therapies. A nasal spray is the most viable way to introduce it into the body. It bypasses the digestive system and—"

"Right. Got it. Back to Molly," Mark pressed.

"Molly likes to hang out at the lab. I think she wants to be a scientist, like me, when she grows up."

Yeah, I thought. *Get in line behind doctor, lawyer, and facilitator, buster.*

"Usually Mo will check with me first, and drop her off for a few hours," James continued. "But there was one day—shortly before her visit to you, Ciel—when Mo was busy getting ready for the party that Molly came with someone else."

"Cut to the chase, James." Mark's patience was eroding.

"That someone was Monica."

Yikes.

"And just how much did Monica know about your experiments?" Mark asked. To his credit, his tone wasn't accusatory.

"Look, you know Monica and I are—God, were?—good friends. She's in the same position I am. You have no idea how tough it is to belong to a family of people who have a remarkable ability you can only dream about. It bothered Monica more than most. I thought if I offered her a little hope, things might be easier for her. So I told her what I was working on."

Mark's eyes hardened, just a bit, but his voice remained neutral. "Plus, you'd have a second test subject to verify any findings you came to by experimenting on yourself."

"No." James was adamant. "She offered, but I wouldn't allow it. In fact, we were arguing about just that when she came that day with Molly."

"Do you think Monica gave it to Molly?" I asked. Might as well get it out in the open.

"No. I don't think that at all. But I do think it's possible Molly may have gotten into some things she shouldn't have while I was arguing with Monica. We'd left her watching a video on plate tectonics in the alcove while we talked on the other side of the lab, but she was suspiciously close to my work area when Monica and I were finished. The bottle with the latest incarnation of the formula was there."

"I thought it was perfume." Molly's voice came from the hall, for once hushed and uncertain. She looked so young and vulnerable, dressed for bed in one of James's T-shirts, clutching an armful of comic books he kept for her in his study. "It looked like one of the bottles Auntie Ro has on her dresser, the ones with the bubble thing you press to make it spray. I just wanted to smell it, I didn't mean to do anything wrong." Tears welled in her eyes.

"Oh, honey," I said, hugging her. "It's okay. You're all better now, right?" I felt her nodding. "Come on, let's get you to bed."

Molly nodded off three-quarters of the way through the latest issue of Spider-Man. We both loved the red webbed-bodysuit look, and tried to squeeze in some Spidey time whenever we were together. We'd even been known to speculate on whether the original aura adaptor might have been bitten by a radioactive chameleon. Molly must have been truly exhausted to fall asleep before we got to the end.

I was tempted to lie there snuggled up with the comfortingly familiar form of my cousin, but a vibration from my pocket stirred me. I made my way out of the room before the nearly inaudible buzz turned to a ring that would wake her up, and slipped into James's study to see who the call was from before I answered it. Not likely to be Mom at this time of night, at least.

Billy. "Where the hell *are* you?" I said right off the bat.

He laughed. "Now, is that any way to greet your new boyfriend? Not even a 'hi, honey, how are you?' first?"

"God, Billy, I've been worried sick about you—"

"That's better. I love you, too."

"I did *not* say that I—"

"You didn't have to, sweetheart. I can hear it in your voice."

I growled. "*Where?*"

"Don't get your knickers in a twist. I'm close. You at James's place?"

"Yeah, but how did you know? We've only been back here for— *Oh!* Molly's back. As herself, I mean. James's magic potion worked after all—it just took a little longer than he expected."

"Yeah? Hey, that's great! How is she? No ill effects?"

"Nope. Just tired. And James isn't invisible anymore, either."

"What?"

Oh, yeah. He didn't know about that. "Never mind. Long story. Are you coming over?"

"Depends. The spook with you?"

"Uh-huh. You need to see him?"

"Nah. I'll skip that for now. Can you get away? *You* I want to see." Something in his voice made me tingle all over.

"Not until after Mark leaves and James goes to bed."

"Shove Mark out the door and start talking to James about upcoming family functions. He'll go to bed in self-defense. Then meet me at my place."

Chapter 23

Half an hour later I was at Billy's, having snuck out of James's place. Molly was fast asleep, hogging all the covers and hugging the pillow that would have been mine. Mark had left shortly after I'd rejoined the guys in the living room—he was off to make sure Brian hadn't nonviolenced Suze to death somehow before she spilled her info, I supposed. After James went to bed (Billy was right—one mention of the Halloween dinner party Mo was hosting and he was attacked by a sudden fit of the yawns), I'd left him a note explaining I'd gone to meet Billy, just in case I wasn't back before he and Molly woke up. I really hoped I would be, though, because, damn, I didn't want to miss those waffles.

The crime-scene tape was pushed off to the side of the entrance to Billy's condo, and the door wasn't latched. I pushed it the slightest bit and peeked inside.

"Billy?" I whispered.

The door opened wider. "Ignore the tape, cuz."

I did, and as soon as I was over the threshold he had me in his arms, lifting me off my feet, burying his face in my neck. "God, I missed you," he said, and kissed me.

I broke away—well, after a minute or so—and said, "Stop. Should you even be here? What if the police find us? Can't we get in big trouble for this?"

"Relax. The police are done here—they've already released the crime scene. This is the last place they would look for me." He put his lips on my neck. *Gaaah. The* spot.

"Come on," he said softly, and led me toward the spiral staircase up to the loft. The loft with the great big bed.

I pulled back. "Uh-uh. First we talk."

"Later. After."

"Nope. I'm not falling for that again." I went to the black leather couch and sat myself smack dab in the middle of it.

He grinned and sat beside me, trying to snuggle close.

"Nope," I said. "I want air between us until you tell me what's going on. Where were you, and what did you find out?"

He sighed. Tried the Doyle eyes on me, but I was ready for him and stared him down. "All right, all right," he said. "But first tell me why you're wearing those awful clothes. I can hardly find you in there."

"Didn't you get my message? I had to play Suze for Brian tonight at the club. She flaked on a gig, and it was going to get the whole band fired if she didn't show. So 'she' showed. By the way, I think she's the one who killed Monica."

"Monica's not dead."

"What? But I saw . . . hell, you saw her, too. What do you mean she's not dead?"

"I mean Monica is safe and sound and recovering from a

nasty bump on the head at the safe house with Laura, where Harvey stashed her. She's feeling well enough to complain bitterly about her dress being ruined with the fake blood."

"What the hell? Who would fake a thing like that?"

"Little Miss Monica, apparently."

"Did you find out who she was kissing in the grotto?" I hesitated to bring it up, since I didn't want to remind him of his car, but, hell, I wanted to know.

Something between amusement and exasperation flitted across his face. "No. I wasn't in a position to do more than eavesdrop, and she didn't bring it up."

Damn. "What the fuck is going on?"

"That's what I'm trying to find out. All I know is, Harvey is in it up to his eyeballs. Which is why I'm avoiding Mark—I don't want to lock horns with him over his mentor until I know what's going on. He genuinely *likes* Harvey."

"Is that the only reason you're avoiding Mark?" I asked, earning myself a sharp look.

"What do you mean by that?"

"Well, you guys seem a little, um, tense around each other. I'd hate to think it's because . . . Look, I saw him hit you at the club, okay?"

"Speaking of eavesdropping," he said with a twist of his lips. "How much did you hear before he decked me?"

"Enough."

He sighed and ran a hand over his jaw. "It was probably my fault. I jerked his chain. I know he's concerned about you—about *us*—but frankly it pisses me off that he thinks I could hurt you. He should know me better than that. Plus, he's been more zipped up than usual with me about this whole thing with Laura, and now Monica, like he doesn't trust me anymore. I'm just trying to figure out what's going on."

I acknowledged the awkwardness of his situation with a nod. "But why would somebody pretend to kill Monica?"

"I *think* it was staged for whoever was really out to kill her to see, so they'd stop trying."

"And who would that be?"

Billy shrugged. "You got me. I'm still working on that." While we were talking he'd taken my feet onto his lap, slipped off my boots, and started massaging. I'd been so shocked about Monica, I'd barely noticed. And now it felt too good to make him stop, so I pretended I still hadn't noticed. Except maybe a tiny moan or two might have given me away.

"Come here," Billy said, tugging on my feet.

"Wait—one more thing. How'd you find out about Monica?"

"I followed Thomas back to the safe house, and borrowed one of the agents watching the house for a little while so I could get close enough to hear what was going on."

"Did you see Laura? Is she okay?"

"Laura is doing remarkably well—improving by the minute. She'll be up and slapping the faces of bad guys with her feet again in no time." Laura did have a pretty impressive high kick, as we'd found out in Sweden.

"What about the agent you 'borrowed'? You didn't . . . ?"

"Of course not, you twit. He looked like he could use a nap, is all. So I gave him one." He pulled me closer, across his lap. "Enough talk for now," he whispered, and kissed me again, doing that thing he does with his tongue.

Gaaah. That thing got me every time. Hugely relieved about Laura and Monica, I gave up and gave in.

*   *   *

The sky was lightening with a predawn glow as I wandered down the spiral staircase, looking for my clothes along the way. Huh. I could've sworn they'd been dropped piecemeal on the way up to the loft earlier. Pulling the sheet up and closer to my naked torso so I wouldn't trip, I called out to Billy.

"In the kitchen, cuz. Follow your nose."

All thoughts of clothing were swept away by the aroma of French-pressed coffee and toasting strawberry Pop-Tarts. "Mmmm . . ." I said, reaching for a cup. Billy said the same thing as his lips connected with my neck from behind.

I twisted around in his arms, gazed adoringly into his beautiful eyes, and said those three little words that mean so much: "Are they frosted?"

He laughed and swatted my rear lightly, with a glint in his eye that dared me to object. The previous night had taught me I was unlikely to object to anything he did when his eyes held that particular shine, so I just smiled lazily and said, "Well? Are they?"

"They are, but if you keep smiling like that, you'll never get to them, because I'll be carrying you back upstairs again. Or maybe just clearing the counter."

I glanced at the gray granite expanse, flashing back briefly to when Laura had been lying beside it, her blood pooling on the floor. Fortunately, the building manager had been allowed to send in a biohazard cleanup crew after the police were done collecting evidence and photographing everything. Guess removing the crime-scene tape wasn't part of the crew's job description.

If Laura had died, I doubt I could have ever even walked into this kitchen again, much less looked at the counter with lascivious thoughts dancing in my head. But somewhere between me giving in on the sofa, and both of us making it all the way up the stairs, Billy had reassured me again about Laura. She was totally out of the woods—it was just a matter of her resting now. And Thomas was apparently in a *much* better mood. I suspected the two things were related.

I sighed. "Well, the Pop-Tart's faster," I said, and took a huge bite of one, fresh from the toaster. "So, where'd you put my clothes?"

"Those oversize rags you were wearing? I should have thrown them in the incinerator, but I wasn't sure if they were yours or not, so I hid them instead. It's a crime to bury your petite sexiness under that much cloth." He matched the last words with a thorough exploration of said petiteness, almost making me choke on the rest of the toaster pastry I'd hastily stuffed into my mouth while he was talking. God. Pop-Tarts and Billy—killer combination.

I swallowed hastily and pulled away before leaving became entirely impossible. "And what am I supposed to wear?"

He kissed some stray crumbs off my chin. "Take a sip of your coffee and go look in the bathroom. I found some things in my stash that should fit you better. After you shower. Right now you smell rather strongly—"

"I beg your pardon! What an ungentlemanly thing to point out," I said, my indignation waylaid by a giggle. Honestly, I was just glad he kept an extensive wardrobe for his alter-ego auras. I was tired of the rolled-up-pants look.

"Let me finish. You smell rather strongly of eau de *us*. And while I find the aroma to be the strongest aphrodisiac imaginable,

I doubt your brother and my sister would feel the same way. Now, go wash. I'll come with you to James's—I want to see Molly, too."

"Oh, goody. You can have breakfast with us. James is making waffles," I said, and hurried to the shower.

"But I just fed you breakfast!" he called after me.

"Yeah. Your point?" I said, and closed the bathroom door behind me.

Molly was still asleep when we got there, thank goodness, but James was up, sipping coffee and reading his favorite Internet news site on his laptop at the kitchen table. Guess my plan of pretending to be surprised when Billy "stopped by" this morning wasn't going to work after all.

James's only comment on our arrival together was a half-raised eyebrow and a nod toward his coffeemaker. "Help yourselves."

"I'll just check on Molly first," I said.

"I looked in on her when I woke up. She was fine—still herself—and still sound asleep," James said. "But go ahead. I'm going to start cooking soon, and she always likes to help."

Billy followed me back. Molly was just starting to stir when we walked into the room. When she caught sight of her brother through half-opened eyes, she was instantly awake, throwing off the covers and tackling him in one flying leap. "Billy! Look—I'm me again!"

Billy steadied himself. "Are you sure? That was a pretty impressive jump for a little girl. Here, let me take a better look at you."

Molly giggled as he held her away from him, his thumbs

hooked under her armpits. "Ooo-oo, aa-aa-aaah!" she said, the sounds riding on a wave of laughter.

James came running, stopping himself by grabbing the door frame, panic turning to relief as soon as he saw Molly. "For God's sake, don't do that to me."

Which, of course, made Molly "orangutan" it up even more, laughing hysterically as she bounced around the bed. (It's possible Billy and I might have joined her.)

"All right, be that way," James said, summoning a good huff, which was, of course, belied by the amusement in his eyes. "I'm going to assume apes do not eat waffles for breakfast."

Molly stopped at once. "Waaaiiit. I'm *not* an ape anymore. I want waffles!"

James smiled, and pointed over his shoulder with his thumb. "Well, come on, then. To the kitchen. You don't think I'm going to make them without my sous chef, do you?"

"Hooray!" Molly bounced out of the room on James's heels. "Wait, I have to pee first—I'll be right there."

"Don't forget to wash your hands," James's voice floated after her.

And there Billy and I were, together on the bed where we first—

I jumped up and ran even faster than Molly had, leaving Billy laughing in my wake.

James was gathering the ingredients in his small but cheerful kitchen. "By the way, it's nice to see you, too," I said. "And I do mean that literally. Any more difficulties on the visibility front?"

"Nope. Maintaining complete opaqueness. I don't expect any further problems, either."

"You sure about that? I'd hate to be walking with you in public and suddenly have to explain the empty clothes walking beside me," I kidded.

"I'm sure, but I can outline my scientific reasoning if it'll make you feel better."

Billy came up behind me and laid his hands on my shoulders, massaging lightly. "For God's sake, no. Not before second breakfast."

"Second breakfast? Are you guys hobbits now?" Molly asked as she whizzed by us to grab the eggs from James. "Hey, I get to crack them, right? Billy, your feet might be big enough to be a hobbit, but you're too tall. Ciel, you're short enough, but your feet are too small. When did you have first breakfast, anyway?"

I mumbled something about Billy and Pop-Tarts (perhaps *implying* he had them with him when he arrived at James's earlier, but not outright lying about it) while James took the egg carton back from Molly and held it over her head. That seemed to distract her from questioning my earlier whereabouts.

"Your adding the eggs depends entirely on whether you'll listen to instructions this time," James said. "Crashing two eggs together over the bowl is not proper culinary technique, nor is eggshell an ingredient I appreciate in my waffles."

Molly tried to look contrite. Not having as much practice at it as her brother, she wasn't especially successful, I thought. But James bought it. "I promise. I know how to do it now. Sinead told me," she said, referring to her older sister.

James handed her the eggs and turned to get the butter from the fridge. Molly maneuvered the step stool closer to the counter, stepped up, held an egg high over the bowl, and lopped off one end of it with a butter knife. "Bombs away!" she said as the goo slid from the shell.

James really should have remembered Sinead is the Doyle sister who can't cook.

Later, when we had finished eating and James was speaking to me again (What? Anyone would have laughed—flour flying everywhere is intrinsically hilarious), we drew straws to see who would be the one to deliver Molly back to her mother. James thought it should be Billy because he was, after all, her brother. Billy thought it should be James because the whole orangutan thing happened due to a mishap at his lab. I didn't really care, as long as it wasn't me. I was still trying to live down my postparty encounter with Auntie Mo and the wastebasket.

"Hey, no fair," I said after holding up my piece of the broom next to the others. "You guys cheated somehow."

"Impossible," James said. "Molly held them while we drew. Now, if you want to accuse *her* . . ."

The innocent look on my youngest cousin's face was the same one I'd seen on her brother a thousand times before. Of course she'd cheated. She wanted her girl time.

"Fine," I said. "But just so you know, when Auntie Mo goes off on a rampage about why we didn't tell her about Molly as soon as it happened, I'm throwing you guys under the bus."

Chapter 24

Auntie Mo took the whole thing better than I thought she would. And by "better," I mean I was still alive. My ears would take a while to recover, and Molly might not see the outside of her room this side of thirty, but all things considered it wasn't too bad. I'd be concerned about what Mo said she was going to do to Billy when she saw him again, but, as Molly so eloquently put it in the taxi on the way over, "Billy can get away with anything with Mom. He's a *boy*."

Uncle Liam was a whole 'nother ball of wax, though. I'd like to have a glass against the door when he found out what had happened to his baby girl on Billy's watch. The legendary Doyle charm Billy had inherited from his father didn't work nearly as well when it was directed back at its source. It's tough to charm a charmer.

But I suspected Billy wasn't fretting about it at the moment. He was more concerned with finding out Harvey's part in whatever was going on. He thought there might be a connection between Harvey and Suze—that Suze might even be a spook sent to find out if Brian was an adaptor, the same way Billy feared he himself might be Laura's assignment.

Personally, I was trying hard not to worry about Brian. If Suze *was* a spook, and had the kind of training I knew Mark and Laura did, Brian wouldn't stand a chance against her.

Walking over to a bigger street to catch another cab, I dialed Thomas, hoping not only to find out more about Laura, but also to see if he'd had a chance to question Monica. Billy had, of course, told James that Monica was still alive, which relieved my brother greatly, but we were all still concerned about her involvement in the whole mess. Who had asked her to refer Thelma Parker (if that was even my client's real name) to me?

It went straight to voice mail. *Fuck,* I thought. Or perhaps I left it on his voice mail. Whatever. Maybe he'd return my call sooner.

Next, I tried Brian. Same thing. No answer. I hung up without leaving a similarly pithy message, since he was still recovering from the shock about Suze and all.

My phone vibrated as I was stuffing it back into my pocket. Sure it was Thomas responding to my less-than-ladylike language, I answered fast, without looking to see who it was. Big mistake.

"Ciel Colleen Halligan, you better be on your way home right this instant. I just talked to Mo, and she told me what happened to sweet little Molly. I want to hear *everything.* You can tell me on the way to the photo shoot."

Gaaah! "Mom, I can't work for you today. I'm busy."

"Don't be silly. Of course you can. You're here in town, and I know you don't have a job of your own scheduled until next week."

"Who told you that?" I was going to kill the rat bastard, whoever it was.

"Molly mentioned to Mo that you girls had plans for the day.
And since Molly has now been grounded, I know you're free."

Damn. Back in D.C., I'd promised Molly plenty of girl time
after the party, since I'd had to work while she was there visiting. Cursed by my own kindness. "What about Auntie Mo?
She's your partner. Shouldn't she be working with you?"

"Well, she was *going* to, but now she isn't going to let Molly out
of her sight for the foreseeable future," she said, skipping the usual
filial-duty spiel and heading straight for guilt. There is no good
argument against maternal guilt. Trust me, I've tried them all.

"*Fine.* I'm on my way."

As soon as I disconnected I redialed Brian to remind him of
our bargain. Recovering from heartbreak or not, he owed me.
Besides, it might help take his mind off Suze. When you really
thought about it, it was the nice thing to do.

Only he still didn't pick up. This time I left the pithy comment.

Central Park on a nice day is spectacular. You can see why so
many Manhattan-based photographers choose it as a backdrop.
Well, that and the fact that it's a damn handy outdoor space.
The clock *is* the clock, and paying models by the hour is expensive enough without adding travel time.

Mom was in her element as a tall, willowy black model who
was a dead ringer for Iman in her younger days. (Mom had made
it a point to collect celebrity energy whenever she had the opportunity, going back years.) She always added a few differences

other than the age, of course, so no one would get suspicious. For her "Immie," they were green eyes instead of brown, a slightly larger bust, and a generic American accent instead of an exotic Somali one. But all the charisma was there for the camera, and that's what counted.

I was "Krissie," the Christie Brinkley knockoff aura. Mom thought her Krissie was wholesome, like me. A way taller, immensely curvier, tons more gorgeous wholesome than me (my opinion, not Mom's; she thought I was the prettiest thing ever to grace the earth—moms are deluded like that), but wholesome nonetheless. Krissie's main difference from the real thing was her sherry-colored eyes.

After two hours in the back of the photographer's van I practically jumped out of my seat when the makeup artist released me. My claustrophobia was kicking in, and pit stains on a ten-thousand-dollar designer dress would not make Mom's client happy. Besides, I was in a hurry to get somewhere I could answer the umpteen messages that had vibrated against my thigh while I'd been painted, polished, and poufed. (Seriously, what was with the sixties hair and makeup? It wasn't pretty the first time around.)

Hiding the phone had been necessary—Mom didn't allow personal cell phones along on her jobs. She wanted everyone to stay on task.

"Daaarling, that's perfect!" *Crap.* Waylaid by the photographer as soon as I stepped out onto the street. "*You're* perfect! The *day* is perfect! And *I* am going to improve upon that perfection!" He was tall (half a head taller than model-me in heels, which was saying something), lightning-rod thin, and humming with creative energy. Dressed in black from beret to wingtip ankle boots, he was flanked by two (short, nondescript) assistants, each yoked with three cameras, ready to anticipate his every photographic need.

We'd worked together on a shoot the previous summer—and no telling how many more when I hadn't been the one called into service as Krissie—so I suppose I should have remembered his name, but apparently I'd blocked it from my mind. Something Frenchified. Andre? Phillipe? No, wait . . . Lumière. Like the candlestick in *Beauty and the Beast*. Somebody had illusions of lighting up the world of fashion photography.

"Oh you!" I said, playfully batting my fake lashes at him. "You're always such a flatterer."

"Every word is true. You mark my words: After this job, demand for your services is going to skyrocket! You won't be able to breathe for the attention, I promise. I'm probably shooting myself in the foot by giving you this kind of exposure. Why, I won't be able to afford you myself!"

I demurred, as expected, and was spared from any more gushing by my mother's exit from the van. Lumière and his bookends dropped me like yesterday's gossip and hurried to the true star of the shoot.

"Immie! Daaaarling . . ."

While Mom soaked up their adulation (if only they knew how she laughed about it at the end of the day, imitating them to perfection for Dad), I wandered down the street a bit (under the watchful eye of yet another of the photographer's assistants), and tried to sneak my phone out from under the dress.

"Can I help you with that?" a familiar fuck-me voice said, making me wince. I lifted my head to look straight into Devon Spencer's violet eyes.

"What are you doing here?" I asked without thinking.

"Same thing you are," he said with a lazy grin. Those pouty lips were definitely model material.

I bit back the urge to ask if James knew what he did for a living. How could I explain knowing James?

"Um, yeah. Duh. Silly me." I shrugged it off, hoping he'd take it for dumb-blonde ditziness.

"It's been a while," he said.

Okay, so he must have worked with Krissie before, when either Mom or Auntie Mo was using the aura. "Yeah, it has," I said, and then jumped as my phone vibrated again.

"You okay?"

"Sure. I'm fine—" *Bzzz!* "—really. Just a little, um—" *Bzzz!* "—you know . . ."

He cocked his head in a very attractive manner. I was sure he'd practiced it in front of a mirror. "Listen, if you need something . . ." he said casually, with just the slightest emphasis on "something." What the fuck? Was he offering me drugs? Mom sure as hell wouldn't tolerate that.

"No! I don't need a thing. Well, except a . . . a ladies' room." Preferably one with a private stall. "You know how it is. Drinking all that vitaminwater for the glowing complexion . . ." I shrugged, keeping it casual. Just two models talking shop.

He nodded sympathetically, and my thigh buzzed again. I shook my leg surreptitiously—it was tickling the hell out of me—and my garter slipped. I grabbed for my phone. Too late. It hit the sidewalk faceup, displaying a picture of James.

Devon, playing the gentleman, reached down and picked it up for me before I could get to it. And, of course, immediately recognized my brother's face. *Crap.*

"Well, well. It seems we have an acquaintance in common," he said, narrowing his eyes and holding on to my phone.

"Um, yeah. He's . . . he's just a guy my, um, sister is trying to fix me up with. He's the TA in one of her classes. She's in college. She's the brainy one. . . ." I trailed off into a weak laugh.

"Is that a fact?" He still didn't seem inclined to hand over the phone.

"Yeah. But he doesn't seem all that interested, you know? I thought he'd be a nice change from photographers and male models . . ." Oops. "Er, not that there aren't some very nice male models. It's just that so many of them are . . ." *Crap!*

"Gay?" he supplied helpfully.

I felt my cheeks blaze. "Look, just give me back my fucking phone, okay?" I grabbed it from him and stalked away.

The shoot went pretty much without incident, except for Devon looking at me curiously whenever he wasn't obeying the photographer's orders to make love to the camera (which he was really good at—I suspected he practiced that in front of a mirror, too). He and "Immie" got along very well. They'd obviously worked together before.

We'd been to several locations in the park, each time driven there by a hired stretch limo (the van being used for equipment and props), which disappeared when it wasn't needed to transport us. Can't just leave vehicles parked anywhere. The park police frown on that sort of thing.

The makeup artist touched us up every few minutes, blotting shine or adding glow as necessary, per the photographer's orders. What the difference between "shine" (bad) and "glow" (good) was, I hadn't a clue, but I bore with it, reminding myself that at least my bank account would be substantially healthier at the end of the day.

We wound up at the Conservatory Garden, next to the Untermyer Fountain, where Devon, Mom, and I held hands and danced like the three maidens in the statue.

"Now for the money shot!" Lumière yelled.

Devon seemed to know what he meant, and started twirling faster, his customary sexy pout replaced with a wide smile. When he had us sufficiently disoriented, and situated in just the right spot, he let go of our hands. Mom and I tumbled backward into the fountain pool.

I came up sputtering. "Shit on a shingle! Why the hell did you do that?" I yelled.

"Keep going!" the photographer shouted, switching cameras with one of his lackeys, and shooting away.

Mom, who'd looked every bit as surprised as I had been, recovered quickly and got into the playful Zen of the moment. She beckoned to Devon, who, to his credit, stepped right into the water and held out his hands to resume our warped game of Ring Around the Rosie. I, of course, took the first opportunity to trip him.

"Fantastic! Beautiful! *Perfect!*" Lumière proclaimed.

Well, yeah. I thought so. But I resisted the urge to bow.

Lumière's directions continued, loud and fast. "Stand up, Devon. Shake your head. Good . . . now, all of you hug! That's right. Now look at me. Make *love* to the camera!"

It's hard to be sultry when your dripping-wet beehive is straggling around your face, but for Mom's sake I tried. Think I managed pretty well, too, until Devon, his mouth close to my ear, whispered, "Which Halligan are you?"

What the fuck? He knew? My mouth fell open.

"Perfect!"

While Mom was in the back of the van changing, I dragged Devon aside. "Just what did you mean by that?"

"Scrappy. You must be Ciel."

Crap. "Look, I don't know what you think you know, but you're not making any sense. Have you been taking something?"

"Nice try, but I don't use. My body is a temple, and all that." He said it with an ironic twist of his lovely lips, but I suspected he meant it. You don't maintain looks like his without a certain reverence for the flesh.

"Maybe somebody slipped something into your wheat germ smoothie when you weren't looking," I tried.

"Give it up, Ciel. I know who you are and what you can do."

I was about to panic when it hit me. "Billy?"

He laughed. "Took you long enough, cuz."

I slugged his arm. He yelped.

"Hey, don't blame me. It was *your* mother who called me in a tizzy because she couldn't find Devon anywhere."

"Why would Mom call you about Devon?"

"She didn't. She called me to find out if I knew why James wasn't answering his cell phone. When I told her I hadn't a clue, she begged me to track down Devon using whatever nefarious means I had at my disposal—what on Earth does she think I do, anyway?—and haul his ass to the shoot. When I couldn't find him, I did the generous thing and took his place. It was the least I could do for my dear aunt."

"Whoa. Mom said 'ass'?"

"Of course not. She asked me to 'escort him firmly.' I was paraphrasing."

"So why didn't you tell me who you were sooner?"

"Because, my darling twit, at first I thought you were my mother. I do *not* want Mommo to know I did this for Ro. God knows, I don't need either one of them thinking I'm available for this sort of thing in the future."

Okay. I could buy that. "But after you saw my cell phone?" I pressed.

His violet eyes glinted with a suspiciously Doyle-like shine. "Well, after that it was just fun."

I wound up for another slug, which he easily blocked, taking me in his arms and pinning me for a kiss. After a token resistance, I joined in. It *was* Billy, after all, and if I was honest, I *had* been curious. The luscious mouth might have been Devon's, but that thing he did . . . well, that was pure Billy. And it got me every freaking time.

Chapter 25

"Never again, Mom."

We were back at the parental homestead, Immie and Krissie dropped as soon as we were through the door. We'd each had a hot shower, and I was curled up next to her on the deep, over-stuffed, red velvet sofa, my head on her lap as she stroked my damp hair.

While in the bathroom, I'd returned James's call. Fortunately, after Devon—or rather, Billy—had discovered my phone at the shoot, I'd stowed it with my street clothes, so it hadn't been dunked along with me. All James had wanted was to find out how it had gone with Auntie Mo, and to ask if Molly's aura was holding. I reassured him that Mo hadn't killed me and that Molly hadn't resprouted any fur, and hung up without going into Devon's lack of job responsibility. That wasn't James's problem.

On the limo ride home I'd asked Mom about Devon. "Oh, he's one of your brother's friends," she'd said, and explained how she'd met him one day when she was delivering a calamari casserole (with sweet cream drizzle—urk!) to James's apartment. She'd been blown away by his beauty, and had given him one of her business cards. They'd worked together several times since, though he was under the impression she just owned and operated the agency, and didn't realize most of the models he worked with were her.

She was a little afraid he might not prove to be reliable, since she'd had to send Billy to find him this morning. But she supposed that was just his artistic temperament, and he *had* apologized sweetly for his tardiness (must have been when I was getting sewn into my dress), so she guessed she could make allowances. Especially since he was such a good friend to James.

She hadn't gone into what kind of friend, and apparently didn't know about the breakup (and possible subsequent makeup), so I hadn't, either. Time enough for all that when things settled down.

"I mean it this time. No more photo shoots," I stated. Firmly.

It was part of the ritual we went through after every job I worked with her. I complained; she listened. She'd think something was seriously wrong with me if I didn't whine about it.

"Yes, dear," she said, and patted my cheek.

"No, really. I'm *not* putting on one of your model auras ever again. Something always goes wrong."

"Whatever you say."

"You can't make me if I don't want to, you know," I said, and snuggled closer, stifling a giggle. It hadn't been that bad. She knew it, I knew it, and she knew I knew it.

She tucked one of Auntie Mo's ugly afghans around me. "Of course not."

"If Dad doesn't have to, I shouldn't, either. It's only fair."

"I couldn't agree more, sweetie," she said, her voice soothing, like when I was a little girl and upset about something. Usually Billy teasing me, or one of my brothers not letting me tag along with him wherever he was going.

"So you won't ask me to do it again?" It was always worth a shot.

"Not unless there's an emergency, dear."

I sighed. "You're still going to expect me to help out, aren't you?"

"Well, it pays very well. And you do need the money."

There *was* that about it. "So, do I get extra for the dunking? Like hazard pay or something?" She expected that, too. I *always* asked for more money. I keep hoping she'll get tired of giving it to me and stop asking me to help. Hasn't worked so far.

"I'll see what I can do, dear."

"Mom?"

"Yes, dear?"

"I love you."

"I love you, too, sweetie."

When I woke up I was alone on the sofa, ugly afghan still tucked around me. Mom had replaced her lap with a pillow, and had gone on to the next item on her agenda, whatever that might have been. Probably cooking dinner. I just hoped like hell it wasn't calamari casserole.

Billy was supposed to call me after he tracked down the real Devon. No word yet, so I assumed Pretty Boy was still AWOL.

I yawned and stretched until my bones creaked. I still hadn't heard if Brian had found Suze, either. Mark was supposed to be on that. Maybe I should call him and ask.

He picked up on the first ring. "Are you okay?" were the first words out of his mouth.

"Yeah, of course," I said. "What's going on? Did you find Brian? Did he have Suze? Where are you?" (I liked to get in as many questions as possible before he started not answering them.)

"Where are *you*?" he said, ignoring my questions. (Huge surprise.)

"At home. I did a job with Mom today."

"Good. Stay there." *Click.*

I stuck my tongue out at the phone screen. "Mom?" I hollered. "I'm going out. Don't keep dinner for me!" I was through the front door before she could answer.

Two blocks away, the Volvo shot past me on the other side of the street, screeched through a U-turn, and pulled up next to me. "Get in, Howdy."

Mark looked only mildly annoyed as I buckled my seat belt. "Didn't I tell you to stay where you were? I could have missed you."

"Yeah, well, you might have mentioned you were coming to get me. I thought you were telling me to stay put while you went about your merry business," I said, a little grumpily. It's not like it was an unreasonable assumption.

"Like I'd think that would work without handcuffs."

I decided to take that as a compliment. "So, what's going on? Did Brian find Suze?"

"Nope. He found a good-bye note, and her stuff gone. She must have cleared out when you guys were performing."

"Why, that bitch! What a sneak. Do you think she knew we were on to her?"

He shrugged. "It's possible."

"Is Brian still . . ." I tried to think of the right word. "Angry" didn't seem to cover the transformation I'd seen in him. ". . . *not* Brian?"

"He relaxed a little after we found out Monica wasn't dead. I think he felt responsible for that somehow."

"But that's just stupid—it wasn't his fault at all. How was he supposed to know Suze was a killer?"

"Monica isn't dead," he reminded me.

"I know that. But . . . hell, what's going on with that, anyway? Did Suze only pretend to kill her? Why would she do that? And Monica *must* have been in on it—she's the one who had to play dead."

"Good questions. I'm getting closer to the answers, but for now . . ." He paused and gave me one of his rare soft looks. "Ciel, I want something from you."

Eep! I swallowed. "Mark, you know Billy and I are . . . um, well, we're . . ."

His smile turned rueful. "Yeah, Howdy, I'm aware." Something in his tone told me he still wasn't entirely happy with the situation. Is it bad that it gave me a little thrill to realize that? It's tough to let go of a decadelong crush all at once.

"What, then?" I asked, proud of myself for not agreeing before I'd even heard his request, like I would have before. Guess I really was learning to let go, if a little slowly.

He didn't speak for a moment, negotiating through traffic

with some maneuvers that left me breathless while he kept a close eye on the rearview mirror. After he settled on a street a few blocks away, he said, "I'm taking you somewhere—"

"Your place?" I'd been there only once, with Thomas, ages ago. It was a tiny apartment in a crap neighborhood, but that was deceptive. It was like a geode—ugly on the outside, a total jewel on the inside. Every luxury and high-tech amenity you can imagine was crammed into a twelve-by-twenty efficiency unit.

He gave me a sidelong glance. "Would you come to my place?"

My cheeks warmed and my heart sped up. I cleared my throat. "Probably not a good idea."

"Yeah. Probably not. So I'm taking you somewhere else, and I'd like you to stay there—"

"Uh-uh, no way are you locking me away somewhere out of some misguided—"

"Calm down, Howdy. I'm not going to lock you away anywhere. I'm asking you—nicely—to lay low for a short time, that's all." He paused. "Please."

I set my chin stubbornly. "There's no reason—"

"There could be. Listen, Howdy . . ." I could tell he was struggling with himself over how much to tell me. "I've moved Laura to another safe house, here in Manhattan. Earlier today, I put Molly there, too. With Mo's permission, of course." He gave me a sidelong glance. "*She* didn't give me any shit about it."

"Molly? Why would you do that? Is she okay? She hasn't—"

"Molly is fine. I just want to make sure she stays that way."

"Okay, I'm not following you here, Mark. Why did you move Laura if she was already in a safe house? And what about Monica? Wasn't she there, too?"

"I had to leave Monica where she was—they were sitting on her too tight, afraid she'd get scared and bolt. I didn't even have a chance to question her. As for Laura—frankly, I wanted her away from all of them until I'm sure about what's going on. So I moved her someplace that nobody knows about."

"Nobody?"

"Only me. It's my own special bolt-hole."

Okay, now I was really starting to get concerned. "Why is this necessary?"

"Look, not everybody where I work can be trusted. Let's just say there are some factions within factions that might not have the adaptor community's best interests at heart. I thought I'd insulated us pretty well, but even the best firewalls can be breached."

"Who? Is it Harvey? Thomas doesn't seem to like him at all," I said.

Mark tensed. "No. Harvey and I have an understanding."

"Who then?"

"Your client."

"Thelma? *Thelma* is CIA?"

"Upper echelon, on a par with Harvey. Big-picture stuff. Doesn't usually involve herself in the day-to-day operations. Until, I think, now."

"Why now?"

"Could be as simple as professional jealousy. She doesn't like it that Harvey has me in his camp. She'd like nothing better than to have her own pet adaptor. The deal Harvey made with me has always annoyed the hell out of her."

"So she's trying to, what, kidnap one of her own?"

"No, I suspect she's trying to *make* one of her own." There was a grim set to his mouth when he said it.

"Huh? But that's ridiculous. Adaptors are born, not made."

"Yeah, that's how it's always been. But after James made his breakthrough with the adaptor genome and came up with that handy formula, who knows how it could be applied?"

"Jesus. That's just . . . frightening."

"Oh, that's not the half of it, Howdy. The worst part is, I'm starting to wonder if Thelma might be considering selling adaptor technology to the highest bidder."

Holy shit. "But that's treason."

Mark smiled. "Hate to disillusion you, Howdy, but it happens."

"Wait a second . . . Suze works for her. So Suze really is CIA, like Billy thought?"

"Billy has good instincts. I just wish he'd come to me with his speculations."

"I think *he* thinks Suze works for Harvey. He didn't figure you'd be, um, receptive to hearing anything negative about your mentor."

Mark's mouth twisted into a wry smile. "Like I said, he has good instincts."

"So why do you want to stash *me* away?"

"Call it an abundance of caution."

"Not good enough," I said. "Listen, Mark, believe it or not, I can be cautious without being confined. I might even be able to help you, if you'd just give me a chance."

"This *will* help me. I told Mo you'd stay with Molly—it was the only way I could convince her to let me take Molly without coming along herself. That wasn't feasible."

"Why not? Seems like that would be best all around." Especially if I didn't have to be locked up with them, because hello? Claustrophobic here.

"A, it's Mo, and Mo is . . . well, Mo. Would you want to be cooped up indoors with her for any length of time? Think of Laura. B, Molly is the one they're after. I need the rest of the Doyle clan to maintain life as usual, at least until I can figure out a safe way to take down a very powerful woman. Nobody watching will be suspicious if you're out of the picture for a while—you're all over the place all the time, so it wouldn't be seen as unusual."

"But—"

"Ciel, Molly needs you." The dove-soft eyes were back. "And I need to know you're safe with her."

I couldn't argue with that. "Cheap shot, Fielding," I said, and he knew he had me.

Molly was happily watching *America's Next Top Model* reruns in the cramped living room of the high-rise apartment in the Bronx when we got there, sitting next to an efficient-looking woman. (And by "efficient" I mean large, with well-defined muscles.) Mark had explained in the car that there was a nurse for Laura—a nurse with extreme bodyguard skills.

The woman acknowledged us with a nod as Molly ran to me for a hug. Her grip around my midsection made me wonder if she hadn't retained a little orangutan strength, but that was probably my imagination.

"Hey, monkey girl. How are you holding up?" I said.

"Great! I can watch TV here. Don't tell Mom, okay?"

"Are you kidding? Of course not. I don't want her to ground me, too."

Molly ran back to her spot in front of the TV (the commercial now over), and Mark led me back to one of the bedrooms.

Laura looked so much better than the last time I'd seen her that it was almost worth getting shunted to the sidelines just to see her for myself. She was propped up by a bunch of pillows, still a little on the pale side, but awake and alert, and even smiling.

Her happy expression might have had something to do with Thomas, who was sitting on the edge of her bed, holding her hand and looking at her with such a soft expression I barely recognized him as my hard-ass lawyer brother. They both seemed happy to see me once they took their eyes off each other long enough to notice I was there.

"You didn't tell me Thomas was here. Molly's cool with him—why do you need me to stay?" I said to Mark after greeting them both.

"Because I'm leaving with Mark," Thomas said. "I have to get Laura's video statement to the judge first thing in the morning if I want to keep Billy out of jail. *If.*"

I knew he didn't really mean that last part. No matter how annoyed he got with Billy, he loved him as much as the rest of us did.

"You can do that?" I asked.

"It's not admissible, but it will do until it's safe to bring Laura down to the precinct to give her sworn deposition."

I looked to Laura. "So it really wasn't Billy? Why'd you let everyone think it was?"

She looked at Mark, her eyes masking something. "That's a little complicated, hon. Maybe we'd better discuss it later."

"But—"

Mark gave her a nod. "It's okay. Ciel, Laura has been officially read in about the rest of you now. Not that she didn't already suspect about Billy."

"Well, I would've had to have been an idiot not to, Mark, as much as he's worked with you," she said. "You were a surprise, though, Ciel. I thought Mark was so overprotective of you because you *weren't* an adaptor."

I cut Mark a look. "No, I think that's just something he absorbed from Thomas when they were roommates. So, you know about my big bro, huh?"

"Oh, I've known about *him* for a while. How could I not when he offered to finish law school for me rather than let me drop out to join the Agency? I had a hell of a time convincing him I really didn't want to be a lawyer. I'd only tried it out just to please my father."

"You were so close to being there," Thomas said. "I still say you should have let me finish for you. Then at least you'd always have a law degree to fall back on."

"You know it's not in my nature to work with a safety net, Tom." Laura sighed. They'd obviously been through it all many times before. My respect for her went up another notch. If she could hold out against my stubborn brother, she must have a titanium backbone.

He leaned over and kissed her, right on the mouth, but only a peck. "We'll discuss it more when you're better."

She pulled his head back and gave him a real kiss, bordering on passionate. "Yeah, and I'll still win, Halligan," she said afterward, a sparkle in her eye.

My brother looked at me and shrugged. "I'll let her think so for now."

"Hee-heee!" I chortled. "You are so whipped. I love it." (What? It was a day I never thought I'd see. I had to enjoy it.)

Even my gloating couldn't wipe the pleasant expression off

his face. Man, he had it bad. He bear-hugged me, scrubbing the top of my head with one palm. "Look after this one for me, Laura. She's trouble."

"Hey! I thought I was here to look after everyone else. I'm the uninjured one."

"Yeah, but even injured, Laura could still kick your ass. So you better behave and listen to her, shortcake." I warmed, hearing his old nickname for me. He rarely used it now that he was a high-powered lawyer—probably figured it was beneath his dignity. Guess he really was relaxed. Whatever he and Laura had worked out between them, I was happy for them both.

After he and Mark left, I asked Laura about Billy again.

She shrugged. "I didn't recognize the man who shot me. I thought he was someone who had come to kill Billy—that Billy had somehow been exposed—and the shooter was just getting me out of the way first. I figured jail was the safest place for Billy until we knew who was after him."

"So, you were really just trying to protect him?"

"I was. It might not have been the smartest plan I've ever come up with, but bear in mind I'd lost a lot of blood. It was the only thing I could think to do at the time."

Okay. I could make allowances for that, as long as her heart was in the right place. I changed the subject. "So, about my brother . . . Are we going to be sisters or what? I always wanted a sister."

She laughed, hugging a small pillow to her side as she did. Oops. Forgot about that bullet wound. "Oh, Ciel. You are price-less. But, no. I love your brother too much to do that to him."

I settled in the place vacated by Thomas. "Aw, come on. He's tough. He can take it. Besides, he needs someone like you to keep him in line."

"And off your back?" Her eyes had a knowing sparkle.

"Well, hell, what are sisters for?" I said.

After Laura was comfortably settled for the night, I heated up a frozen pizza, which Molly, the nurse, and I devoured while watching more episodes of *America's Next Top Model*. Can't say I was thrilled with Molly's viewing selection, my experience with the industry being what it was, but at least it kept her happy. Nurse Kickass seemed strangely taken with it, too.

When bedtime could be put off no longer, I tucked Molly away in the smaller bedroom. She fell asleep easily enough, knowing I'd be there in the apartment when she woke. (Okay, so I bribed her with the promise of doughnuts for breakfast. Sue me. It worked.)

The nurse retired to Laura's room, where she would be sleeping on a cot for easy access to her patient.

Hallelujah, peace at last! I thought, turning the volume way down and flipping through the stations until I found a marathon of *Firefly*. I was halfway through the second episode, drooling over Captain Tight Pants, when my phone buzzed. I checked the number—it was Billy.

"Hey there, sweet cheeks," I said. (What? He was the one who'd called me out on my previous telephone greeting. I was trying to be accommodating.)

There was an appreciative chuckle, followed by, "Listen, I need to come get you. I don't think you're safe."

"Ha. Mark is a step ahead of you. Don't worry, I've already been stowed away."

"What? Why would he—never mind. We can talk when I get there. Where are you?"

"Geez, Billy, you know I can't tell you that."

"Right . . . right. Okay, you'll have to meet me somewhere."

"No can do. I'm watching Molly."

"Molly's with you? What the—never mind. Bring her along. If she's with you, she's not safe, either."

"Are you nuts? I can't do that. Mark would kill me. Besides, I can't just run out on Laura."

"Laura?"

"Yeah, she's holed up here, too. With a nurse who could probably take out Godzilla single-handedly, so really, no need to worry about us."

I heard him exhale. "Ciel, I need you to listen to me very carefully. And once you hear what I say, you'll have to move fast because I'm not sure who else may be listening. Understand?"

"Not really," I said, getting a tad nervous. "But go on."

"Mark thinks he knows Harvey, but he doesn't. He thinks he's put you someplace safe, but you're not. I found out some things . . . Listen, I'm not sure Laura can be trusted. You need to take Molly and get out of there. *Now.*"

My brain started spinning in overdrive. Can't trust Laura? "I think I better call Mark—"

"Ciel, he'll just tell you to stay where you are—he's not going to believe Harvey could possibly go bad, not without proof. Which I'm gathering."

"Good. Great. Whatever. But it doesn't really matter right

now, because Mark said *nobody* knows about this place, not even Harvey—".

"Harvey knows if Laura told him after she got there. I'm not comfortable taking that chance. Not with you, not with Molly. Now, where do you want to meet?"

Gaaah. What if he was right about Harvey and Laura? I'd seen how close the two of them were at the hospital. On the other hand, what if this wasn't even Billy I was talking to? If there was an adaptor out there pretending to be him—

"Ciel? We don't have a lot of time here," he said, his frustration leaking through.

Okay. No time to play Twenty Questions with him. I'd just tell him someplace only the real Billy would know. Problem solved. "Give me a sec, I'm thinking . . . all right, got it. The *first* location of our job this morning."

"Our job?" he asked.

"Yeah, Pretty Boy," I said, hoping the reference to Devon would remind him. "Our *job*."

"Oh, right. Clever you. See you there. And Ciel . . . be careful."

Crap. Bye-bye, Captain Tight Pants.

Chapter 26

They were waiting on the bridge over the pond, the first spot Lumière had selected for our photo shoot that morning. The second guy looked a lot like Billy. Even standing right next to the real thing, the resemblance was remarkable.

But not adaptor close.

The night had turned foggy. The damp trapped the smells of the city close to the ground while seeming to muffle the sounds. Central Park at night could be eerie enough, in spite of the lights, but the swirl of misty air certainly heightened the effect. I held Molly close to me as we walked toward them, one arm over her shoulders.

It hadn't been hard to sneak out of the apartment. Molly had been more than willing to tag along on another adventure, as quiet as the proverbial mouse (with only a few excited squeaks) when I told her we were going to meet her brother. The tough part was wrapping my mind around not trusting Laura. Could my instincts about her really be that far off? On the other hand, how well did I really know her? And I *did* trust Billy, so there really wasn't a choice. We had to go.

I held Molly back when she would have run to her brother. "What's going on, Billy?" I asked, keeping a wary eye on his near twin. If this was the guy I'd seen kissing Monica, no wonder I'd been mistaken. From the distance I'd been standing at, and, okay, as impaired as my focus had been, there's no way I could have reasonably discerned any distinction. So, really, that whole car thing wasn't my fault. Not entirely, anyway.

"I ran across my doppelgänger. Thought you might like to meet him. Seems our worries about a rogue"—he glanced at the guy next to him—"member of our special club were needless. He's just a regular guy who happens to have the good fortune of resembling me. Somebody hired him to crash the party and kiss Monica in order to frame me for her murder."

The guy held up both hands in denial. "Hey, man, I didn't know about any frame job." His voice was much higher pitched than Billy's. Kind of squeaky, like his larynx had stalled halfway through puberty. "All I was told was that I'd get five hundred dollars if I climbed into the backyard of the house having the big party and kissed a really hot, exotic-looking girl wearing a white dress, with a purple flower in her hair, inside that little cave thing. I thought it was a practical joke, man."

"And so it was," Billy said to him, and peeled several hundred dollar bills off a wad he'd taken from his pocket. "The joke was on me. Here you go. Thanks for your trouble. I'll be in touch if I need you."

"Wait," I said to the guy. "At the party you were wearing Billy's shirt—where did you get it?"

"A package of clothes came in the mail. I put them on and

did the job. That's all. Thanks for the cash." The guy walked off, happy, disappearing into the mist.

Huh. Funny how that had never occurred to me. But who sent the clothes?

Molly pulled her hand from my grip, ran to her brother, and hugged him. (Yeah, she pretty much hugged him every time she saw him. She's a huggy girl.) I resisted the impulse to follow suit, figuring I wouldn't want to stop at hugging, and why torture myself?

"Should you let him go like that?" I said. "Don't you think Mark might want to talk to him?"

"The guy is harmless. He doesn't even know who hired him—he was contacted anonymously over the phone."

"You're sure he's harmless? What if he's the one who shot Laura? Maybe he's not as dumb as he looks."

"Hey!"

I shrugged. "Sorry. It's his expression. And his voice."

Molly laughed. "Yeah. He sounded like that guy on *The Simpsons*."

"Whatever," Billy said, but he still looked disgruntled. "I can assure you that he's every bit as dumb as he *sounds*. There's no way he could have shot Laura—even Laura admits the person who shot her looked nothing like me."

"When did you talk to Laura about that? I thought you could only play fly-on-the-wall at the safe house."

"I called her—it was after talking with her that I started to wonder if I could really trust her. Look, come on. We'd better go."

Taking Molly by one hand and me by the other, he led us off the bridge toward East Street. He kept up a good pace, making conversation all but impossible—Molly and I practically had to jog to keep up with him.

"What's the rush?" I said, pulling back.

He slowed, but not by much. "We're meeting someone. Well, technically, you've already met her."

"Who?"

He stopped. A woman walked toward us from out of the shadows beneath a tree with low-hanging branches. "Her."

When she stepped into the cold glow of an LED streetlight I got a better look at her. "Thelma Parker?" I said, shocked, and stared up at Billy. "But she's the one who hired Suze, and Suze is the one who—"

Billy expelled an exasperated breath. "Nobody killed Monica," he said. "And Thelma—Thelma-*not*-Parker—is employed by the same outfit that Mark is, only much higher up the ladder."

"I know," I said, feeling defensive all of a sudden. This was the woman who, according to Mark, was out to get her own pet adaptor. Could Mark be wrong? Was that even possible? Frankly, it wasn't something I'd ever considered seriously before.

"Ms. Halligan," Thelma said, extending her hand. "It's so nice to see you again."

Her grip was much firmer than the last time I'd shaken her hand, when I was gathering pre-job info from her. Almost painful, actually. It was hard not to let myself release first, but I managed. She dropped my hand a fraction of a second before our little game would have become ridiculous.

"Likewise, I'm sure," I said, keeping my voice cool. "So, what did you tell the FONZ board of directors? I'm assuming you're no longer interested in a position?"

She laughed, a brittle sound at odds with her soft face. "My secretary has informed them that a family crisis has come up, and I won't be able to sit on the board after all. They were quite understanding about it . . . once they received my generous donation to their Giant Panda Conservation fund, of course."

"Of course," I said. "And Sir Pantsalot? Was he for real, or just a plant?"

A look of distaste spread over her features. "Oh, he's real enough, the odious toad. He pulled the same routine on a friend of mine who wanted to be a board member. By the way, thank you for dealing with him so creatively."

"You're welcome," I said wryly. "So, not to be crass or anything, but will the check Thelma 'Parker' gave me clear? Or did I donate my services to Uncle Sam on that one?"

"It will clear," she said with another dry chuckle. "If you come along with me now, you may even get a bonus. I know your time is money."

"I don't understand. If you weren't interested in the board position, why go through that charade?"

"Think of it as a kind of interview, my dear."

"What? You want me to work for you at the Agency?"

"Yes, actually. I do want that. But we'll discus it later. Now, come along. It's time we were off."

I was about to object—vociferously—to the idea of going anywhere with her when Billy interrupted me. "Ciel, she's here to help. She's going to take you and Molly someplace safe until after this mess is straightened out and Harvey is no longer a threat to anyone."

"You know what? I think I'd better run this by Mark first," I said, and reached for my phone. Billy snatched it from me.

"What the fu—" I darted a glance at Molly. "—uuudge are you doing? Give that back!"

He held it out of reach while Thelma explained. "It wouldn't be a good idea to contact Mark right now. He's in too deep with Harvey Smith. No disrespect intended, Ciel, but he's been entirely hoodwinked by Smith."

"Oh, so we're back on a first-name basis now? Well, thank you for your concern, Thel, but I think I'd still like to discuss the matter with Mark first. If you don't mind." Yeah. Maybe a tad disrespectful, but something about the woman really got my dander up. I liked her a lot better when she was meek and mousy.

"*I* mind, Ciel," Billy said. "I won't let you risk yourself—or my little sister—out of some misguided loyalty to Mark."

Molly, who had been uncharacteristically quiet during this whole interchange, spoke up. "I think we'd better do what Billy says, Ciel." It was the shadow of fear in her eyes that made me agree.

"Are you coming with us?" I asked Billy.

"I can't. Now that you're safe I have to find Mark and convince him Harvey's the one who's been after more adaptors, and that Laura might be helping him. That won't be easy—you know how stubborn Mark can be."

I sighed. He was that. It wasn't tough to imagine him being blinded by loyalty, either, much as I hated to think of it. But Laura . . . God, what would Thomas do? He'd seemed so damn happy. Then again, so had she. "I just can't see Laura involved in this. For God's sake, Billy, she was working with you. And she was *shot*." Seemed like that would convince anyone of her innocence.

Billy looked thoughtful. "Yeah, she was. But, as it turns out, not fatally. And then she tried to implicate *me*."

I screwed up my brow. "You're not saying she let herself get shot on purpose, are you? That's ridiculous—nobody is that big an idiot."

"Maybe she didn't know about that part. Maybe Harvey surprised her. Or, hell, maybe it was an accident. I don't know. All I know is, she let the cops think it was me behind the gun."

"She told me that was to protect you."

"Oh, sure. Because nothing says 'protection' like sending a guy to jail."

Crap. He had a point. When I'd been with Laura, I'd totally believed her, but what if I was wrong? Maybe I was deluding myself because of Thomas. He'd already been hurt by her once before. If things went south this time, no telling how long it would be before he'd trust another woman. And not to get all selfish about it, I was kind of counting on his being involved with Laura to deflect his overdeveloped protective instincts from me.

Thelma had been carefully assessing me this whole time, her eyes full of speculation. I *hate* being carefully assessed. It made me want to stick my tongue out at her, but I didn't. That wouldn't set a good example for Molly. "What?" I said to her, testy, not liking the smell of this whole thing.

She smiled benignly, trying to look like a trustworthy grandmother, I was sure. "I know this is hard for you, Ciel. You're a good person, and you want to believe only the best of your friends. But I'm afraid you can't trust your gut on this one. It isn't safe for you *or* Molly. So trust Billy."

Billy stared at me intently, his inky blue eyes begging me to agree, tugging at my heart, and maybe a few other places. Then I looked at Molly, who was holding tightly to his hand, confused and scared. Once again, I didn't see a choice. I sighed. "Okay. We'll go with you."

Billy's mouth lifted at the corners; he was satisfied.

As was Thelma. "That's fine, then. If you'll just come along with me." She turned and raised a hand. A man—a big one, young, buzz-cut, dressed in a suit that was a tight fit across his shoulders—emerged from the dark beneath the nearby trees. I must have looked concerned, because Thelma was quick to introduce him as her driver.

"Right," I said. "Just give us a second to say good-bye, okay?"

"Fine." She nodded pleasantly, and went to stand by her driver, tactfully turning her back.

Billy leaned over to hug Molly. "So long, squirt. Behave for Ciel." Molly nodded, and got out of the way, looking from me to her brother with undisguised fascination.

I cleared my throat. Aggressively. Molly reluctantly stepped a few yards farther away and turned her back.

Billy pulled me into his arms and tilted my face up for a kiss. I felt the thrill of anticipation I always did when Billy was near. He leaned down, touched his lips to mine, and kissed me deeply.

I froze. *Fuck!*

Chapter 27

I tore my mouth away from his and stared up into his familiar dark blue eyes, not liking what I saw there one bit.

He acknowledged my shock with a fuck-me curve of his lips and a lazy chuckle. Devon. I'd been wearing James's aura the last time he'd kissed me, but the technique was unmistakable. "What gave me away?" he said.

"Hate to break it to you, Devon, but Billy's a better kisser than you are."

"Guess I'll just have to find out for myself one day, won't I? Maybe as *you*. That could be fun."

Anger flashed through me. I acted without thinking, lifting my knee with great force and an instinctive aim. If I'd been taller, I might have spared the world any future little Devons or Devonettes. Still, I'd managed to surprise him into releasing me, doubling him over.

"Billy!" Molly shouted, shocked out of her ten-year-old mind to see me do that. She ran to help, but I intercepted her.

"Molly, *stop*. Listen to me. That is *not* your brother."

As if to verify my statement, the Billy aura started wavering.

I didn't wait for it to sink in—I just grabbed Molly's hand and took off in the opposite direction from Thelma, heading for the cover of the trees, praying we had enough of a head start on her and the Hulk. I was pretty sure Devon wouldn't be running anywhere for a while.

A quick look back over my shoulder revealed the Billy aura totally gone, replaced by . . . geez, was that *Monica*? What the fuck? But I guess it made sense for Devon to call up a female aura—one that didn't have the injured appendage. Not that he wouldn't still feel some pain—you can't get rid of that entirely—but it wouldn't be as bad once its epicenter was gone. And it would allow him to run without adding further injury.

Which is exactly what he, along with Thelma's driver, was doing. Thelma herself was apparently too high up the food chain to be bothered. *Or else she's back there phoning for reinforcements,* I thought, and then really wished that hadn't occurred to me.

Molly kept up amazingly well for someone with legs even shorter than mine, but neither one of us was going to stay very far ahead in the long haul. We needed to find some transportation, and fast.

Through the trees, I veered onto the pedestrian path that skirted the pond, and headed south toward 59th, grateful for the fog that provided at least a little cover. There *had* to be a taxi there. *Please, please, please . . .*

Gaaah. Only there wasn't. Not one. (There's a reason New Yorkers complain they can never get a cab when they really need one.)

The only transportation in sight was of the equine variety—two horse-drawn carriages. Their drivers were standing together away from the horses, sucking down cigarettes while they waited for the late-night passengers who had reserved them to make up their minds who was going to ride in which carriage with whom. The debate was lively; the drivers looked bored.

Molly was flagging. An energetic child she might have been, but she was still a kid, and a pretty small one. She couldn't keep up the pace forever, and frankly, neither could I. The way I saw it, there was only one thing to do.

I lifted Molly into the first carriage. Jumped in behind her, grabbing the reins and releasing the brake at the same time. "Hyah!" I said.

The horse twisted its head back, with an are-you-kidding-me look in its eye.

"Go, horse! Go, go, *go*!" I yelled, flapping my arms at it.

The drivers ditched their cigarettes and ran toward us. They were joined by Monica-Devon and the Hulk, and the debating carriage patrons, everyone screaming and hollering at Molly and me. That was all it took—the horse shot off like someone had tossed a firecracker under its tail, the momentum almost throwing me from the carriage.

I glanced over my shoulder to see if Molly was still with me. She was, and, judging by the look on her face, having the time of her life.

"Go, Ciel!" she yelled, bouncing up and down on the seat.

"Hold on to something!" I hollered back. "I'm not sure how to steer this thing!"

The horse knew its route and stuck to it, turning into the park at the designated spot. Didn't slow down one iota, either. I can't swear we took the corner on two wheels, but it sure felt close.

"Hey, Molls," I said—loudly—hoping like hell my words

wouldn't get sucked up by the wind, because I didn't want to take my eyes off the road. Or the horse. Not that it was paying a lot of attention to anything I was doing, direction-wise. "Do you have a cell phone?" Maybe she could call Mark.

"No! Mom says I'm too young—bet she'll be sorry now, huh?" she said, equally loud.

Crap. "Can you see behind us? Are they still coming?" I hollered.

"I think I see them—yeah, I do! They're in the other carriage—their horse is speeding up. Faster, Ciel!"

Double crap. It wasn't safe as it was, going the speed we already were.

"How close are they? Do we have time to stop and get away from the carriage?" Not that I was sure I *could* stop the damn thing. But it seemed prudent to try, both for our sake and the horse's.

"I dunno. Maybe?"

Gaaah. I pulled up on the reins. Getting away from Monica-Devon and the Hulk wouldn't mean squat if I killed us in the process. Surprisingly, the horse decided to cooperate with me, slowing first to a trot, then to a walk, and finally stopping altogether. I dropped the reins and jumped out. Molly hopped into my arms, and I swung her down to my side.

"Okay, let's go." I took hold of her hand and started to cross the road, toward the bright yellow police call box. Looked behind me and changed my mind—the second carriage was moving too fast. They'd get to us before I could lift the receiver.

Instead, I pulled Molly around to the other side of the carriage. We were going to have to make another run for it—on foot—and hope we could find somebody to help us. Or, better, a good hiding place. Because, really, what could anybody else do for us? Even if we were lucky enough to run into a cop, all Thelma's driver had to do was run up behind us, show some fancy CIA credentials, and we'd be handed over without a blink.

Before we took off, I briefly morphed into the biggest aura I could within the constraints of my clothing—a female wrestler I'd once gotten out of a sticky love triangle—and, ignoring the pain where my jeans cut into me, waved my arms wildly, freaking the horse out. It took off running again. With a little luck, it would keep going for a while and lead the other carriage away from us.

I dropped the aura at once, praying I hadn't done irreparable damage to my spleen. Molly stuck to my side as we ran to the trees. They wouldn't offer much cover from anyone looking our direction, but I was hoping our pursuers would be keeping their eyes on our runaway carriage. I risked another peek over my shoulder to see if our horse was doing its job.

It had gone maybe fifty feet before it stopped cold, and was blithely taking a dump right there in the middle of the road. *Geez, Ciel, you had to go and scare the shit out of it.*

Molly and I kept moving, now dodging from tree to tree. Next peek I dared was even worse. The second carriage had stopped right behind ours. As soon as Monica—no, it was Devon again—and the Hulk saw we weren't there, they turned our way and started running full out. *Damn it!*

We weren't far from one of the park's visitor centers—the Dairy. For lack of a better plan, I headed there. It wouldn't be open, of course, but maybe we could find someplace to hide near the building.

The breezeway might have been charming and picturesque during the day, when there were plenty of people milling around, but at night, in the crazy thick fog, when we were being chased by two men (one of them a freaking giant), it was damned creepy.

But the lovely landscaping did include a low stone wall, and on the other side of it, bushes. Bushes were good. Molly and I hunkered down between the wall and the bushiest bush we could find, squeezed ourselves together (careful to make sure none of our appendages stuck out), and tried to control our breathing. Wasn't easy, as winded as we were.

I closed my eyes and offered up a brief prayer that there were no spiders hiding with us. If there was one thing that could make this night worse, it would be spiders.

"Ciel?" Molly whispered.

"Shhh, sweetie. We have to be extra quiet now."

I felt her nod. "This isn't fun anymore," she said. Maybe. I could barely hear her above my own heartbeat.

"I know." I almost added that I was as scared as she was but figured she didn't really need to know that. "It's going to be all right. We'll get out of this mess, I promise."

I heard steps pounding along the breezeway.

"You try that way. I'll check over here." *Crap.* Devon's voice, way too close for comfort. If we stayed here, he'd find us within minutes. If we ran again, he'd see us for sure. We were screwed either way.

"Molly," I said super softly. "How good are you at climbing trees?"

"Not very," Molly whispered back. "It's hard to reach the branches. Billy says I'll get better at it when I'm bigger."

The footsteps in the breezeway were getting closer.

Shit. Think, Ciel. Think! "Look, honey, we can't keep outrunning them. They're too fast. And"—I swallowed—"one of them is about to find us. Our only chance is to get someplace they can't reach us. Like up that big tree over there. You see it?"

She was shaking. "Y-yeah."

I hugged her tighter. "We have to try, okay, sweetie?" *Because if they catch us, I have an awful feeling we'll be lost in the system for good.* "And here's the deal, banana peel . . ." She huffed a little whisper-giggle at that; good. "If I can't make it up that tree behind you"—she clutched me, and I patted her back—"if I can't, then you have to keep going. Later, when the coast is clear, you have to get a message to Mark. Don't go home—they'll have somebody watching your house. Go to one of your friends' houses."

"Not Jordy's, right?" she asked.

Monica's brother. "No, not Jordy's. Anybody else's. Even a nonadaptor. In fact, that may be better. And then call Mark and tell him what happened, okay?"

The footsteps were fading—Devon was walking to the other end of the breezeway. This might be the only chance we had. I hung my small purse—really more of a wallet on a strap—over her neck. "Here's money for a taxi. Or the bus. Now, follow me," I said, crawling out of the bushes. I stayed low, keeping to the darker spots where the light from the breezeway didn't penetrate the fog as brightly. Molly did likewise.

I'd chosen a tree in the middle distance. It was slightly riskier staying out in the open that much longer, but being farther away meant there was less chance we'd be spotted as we climbed. We situated ourselves on the side opposite the breezeway, for all the good it did us. The tree trunk wasn't huge, but maybe the fog would help. At least I could easily tilt my head and keep track of Devon.

Linking my fingers together to make a step for Molly, I said, "Come on, kiddo. You were climbing like gangbusters just a few days ago. Just remember what you did then, and go for it."

She laughed nervously, and put her foot in my hands. "Too bad I'm not still an orangutan, huh? This would be a lot easier."

I smiled in agreement, trying to keep things light as I cautiously lifted her higher. Anything to distract her from the fear that would only sabotage her effort. She was one solid little girl—my fingers were straining under her weight.

"Okay, now," I said, once I'd boosted her as far as possible, "can you grab on to that limb?"

She reached for it, wobbly-kneed and quaking. "I—I don't think so." She gave up and hugged the tree. I leaned to one side to check on Devon's progress. *Crap.* He was over the low stone wall and kicking his way through the bushes where we'd been minutes before.

"Molly, we have to hurry now. Let's try it again, okay? Remember, I'm right behind you." I morphed into the lady wrestler again, to gain some added height and strength, pushing her as far as I could. The riveted button on the waistband of my jeans popped, and the zipper crawled open.

Molly stretched, and bounced in my hands, kicking off. She fell short of the limb, tumbling to the ground with a cry. I pulled her back behind the tree quickly, resuming my own aura as I did, but not before Devon's attention had been caught by the sound. He scanned the foggy grounds, running from side to side, checking everywhere between him and us. He'd be here in less than a minute at this rate.

Damn it. There was no way I was going to escape now, but Molly still had one shot. *If* she would take it. I leaned over and spoke softly—voices carry—into her ear.

Her eyes got big. "But what if I get stu—"

"It's a risk, Molls," I acknowledged, cutting her off. We didn't have time to weigh the pros and cons. *But getting caught by Devon is way more dangerous,* I thought but didn't say. If she couldn't, she couldn't, and I didn't want to panic her any more than necessary.

The Doyle determination molded her features. She nodded once, took a deep breath . . . and sprouted fur.

"Good girl," I said, watching her shrink. Her shorts and cropped T-shirt were suddenly a lot bigger on her, but they stayed put, as did my wallet-purse. "Now, up as high as you can go, and wait until the coast is clear to come back down. You know what to do."

Reaching the previously impossible limb with ridiculous ease, she was halfway up the tree in seconds, and going strong. I rezipped (the brass button was a goner) and took off in the direction of the Fifth Avenue skyline, being as obvious as I could. I had to buy Molly time to climb high enough not only to be out of reach but also hidden. If they couldn't see her, they couldn't catch her.

It was still just Devon after me—the Hulk must have been on the other side of the building—and now that he'd seen me he was closing fast. It was possible I'd make it out of the park before he caught me (yeah, and pigs could fly), but I wouldn't lay odds on it.

"Stop or I'll shoot!" *Shit.* Devon's voice was too close. I stopped.

"Seriously, Devon? 'Stop or I'll shoot'?" I wheezed, leaning over to rest my hands on my knees. Sucked to be caught, but at least I got to stop running before my lungs burst. "Exactly how much bad TV did you watch as a kid?"

"Turn around." He didn't sound amused.

I complied, straightening myself into what I hoped was an assertive stance. Seeing the gun made it tougher. "So," I said.

The corners of that sultry mouth lifted. "So."

"Well, Dev, I must say I'm disappointed. I was really rooting for you with James. Can't see you explaining away this one, though."

"Oh, I think I'll manage. He'll need someone to comfort him, after all. Losing a sister is hard. Especially to another senseless mugging in Central Park."

My stomach tightened convulsively. *Stall. Keep him talking.* "How did you know where to meet me? That was Billy on the job with me, not you."

"You said 'Pretty Boy' on the phone. Perhaps I'm egotistical, but I assumed you meant me. It wasn't difficult to figure out Billy must have worked as me on the job I missed."

Well, crap. Guess I wasn't as clever as I thought.

He'd been walking closer as he talked, keeping the gun aimed steadily at my chest. When it connected, just above my left breast, he said, "Now, where did you leave Molly?"

"Geez, Devon, how stupid are you? You already said you're going to kill me. Why should I tell you anything? I'm dead either way."

His lovely eyes widened a notch (Liz Taylor at her dewiest). Then they narrowed. He moved the gun to the fleshy part of my shoulder . . . and fired. *Not much sound* was the first thing that registered with me. *Must have a silencer.* And then the pain hit, like Thor's fucking hammer, and I looked down to see the bloody groove that had been gouged through my skin.

I sucked in a breath, and would have fallen if he hadn't caught me by my other arm, twisting viciously. "Because I can make it hurt an awful lot *before* I kill you, that's why."

"Nice try," I gasped. "But—" I bit my lip for a fraction of a second to steady my voice. I'd broken my arm once, back in elementary school. At the time, I'd been certain that was the worst pain I'd ever feel. Turned out I was wrong. This felt like every nerve ending in my shoulder had been exposed, doused with gasoline, and set on fire. "But . . . no . . . dice."

He lowered the gun to my thigh. "You sure about that?"

No! I thought, but swallowed it, stiffening and waiting for another burst of pain.

"What the hell are you doing?"

Never thought I'd be so happy to see the Hulk. He knocked the gun away from my leg and removed me from Devon's grasp.

Devon pouted. "I wasn't going to kill her. I was just convincing her to tell me where Molly is."

The Hulk took the gun, maintaining a grip on my good arm. I leaned against him and passed out.

Chapter 28

I came to in the Hulk's arms. He was cradling me close to his chest, careful of my injured arm as he trekked back along the path I'd taken. Perhaps he wasn't a total asshole, even if he was employed by the wicked witch of the CIA. Just another working stiff doing his job.

He deposited me in the backseat of the black SUV I'd seen earlier. My arm was still screaming in the background. Maybe the pain would go away if I ignored it. The witch was already there, patiently working a crossword puzzle in the comfort of the customized interior. Thelma not-Parker, mild-mannered lover of word games. Yeah, right.

Devon crawled in and seated himself beside her, across from me. They faced forward; I faced the rear, so I'd be traveling backward. (There was probably something symbolic there, but I didn't want to think about it.)

I raised an eyebrow at Thelma. "Gee, government work must pay better than I thought."

She smiled warmly. "Not really. But the perks are nice."

Okay, so poking *her* was no fun. I turned to Devon. "Don't pout, Pretty Boy. You'll get wrinkles."

Better. If he'd still had the gun, I'd already be dead. Speaking of which . . . I went ahead and looked at my shoulder, since ignoring it wasn't working. Swallowed hard, and bit the inside of my cheek to stifle the pain. Somebody had wrapped it—tightly—with a strip of white jersey. Wonder who sacrificed his T-shirt for me? I glanced at the Hulk, who was now up front behind the wheel. Must have been him. Wasn't likely Devon would have made the gesture.

"Are you quite all right, Ciel?" Thelma inquired as the vehicle started to move. There was so much tender solicitude in her voice it made me want to barf.

"Well, now that you mention it, my arm hurts like a son of a bitch. Thanks for asking." I showed her my teeth. (What? It was almost a smile.)

"We'll give you something for the pain as soon as we get to where we're going—"

"And where would that be?" I asked.

She ignored my interruption. "But for now, if you would be so kind as to tell us where Molly is, I would appreciate it greatly."

"You're kidding, right? Listen, lady, if I didn't tell what's-his-fuck there after he shot me, what makes you think I'll tell you?" She didn't answer, only smiled that annoyingly warm smile.

"I can have fifty of my people scouring the area within fifteen minutes. That might frighten a little girl. It would be so much easier on her if we just picked her up now. She could be with you. I'm sure she'd rather do that than be grabbed and hauled in like some sort of criminal, don't you think?"

I stared her down. "Nope," I said, leaving it at that.

Her crepey-lidded, grandmotherly eyes iced over. "Fine, dear. If that's the way it has to be." She pulled out her cell and shot off a text.

Crap. I hoped like hell Molly got herself out of the park before Thelma's "people" got there. And that she could, you know, manage to turn herself back into a human being again.

I looked at Devon. Anything to take my eyes off my erstwhile client's face. "Who the hell are you really?"

He turned to Thelma. "Is it all right to drop this aura for a while? This stupid penis hurts like hell, and I think the stuff is wearing off anyway."

"Of course, my dear. Ciel won't be sharing your little secret with anyone."

Well, *that* didn't sound promising. But fear of my impending death stopped abruptly when I saw who was beneath Devon's aura. It almost made me stop thinking about my arm.

"Monica? But you're not an adaptor." It had been Monica, not Devon, all along? Then it hit me. "Holy crap. You got hold of James's adaptor juice, didn't you? How'd you manage that?"

She smiled, looking exotic and beautiful and totally insane. "It's more like a perfume. Just breathe in that lovely spray, and before long your birthright is unleashed. Sure, you catch a cold along with it—at first—but what are a few sneezes compared to being able to do what we can do?"

"But how did you . . . James would *never* give it to you. He told us he argued with you about it—that you wanted to be a test subject, but he wouldn't let you."

"No, he wouldn't. Pure and noble James. He knew how much I wanted to be an adaptor. *Knew* it, and still he wouldn't help.

But only because he was too worried about me. So I had to take it while he was distracted with Molly. It's too bad Molly played with it before I got to it—think of the worry I could have spared you all."

"Yeah, right. Shame about that," I said. Of course, then we would have never figured out what was going on with *you,* I thought. "So, how long have you been impersonating Devon? Are you the one who wrote Devon's number on James's arm?" *And swabbed my tonsils when I was him, while you were at it.*

She smiled brightly. "He told you about that? Yes, that was me."

"Um, you didn't happen to stop by James's apartment when I was there, did you?" *With Billy. In bed. Naked.*

Her pretty brow wrinkled. "No. Why, did Devon show up? Damn it, he's supposed to be gone."

Whew. (Maybe. Not sure if it was better that the real Devon had seen my lady parts or not, but I was glad the guy I'd had a talk with afterward was authentic, anyway. For James's sake.)

Thelma was watching us avidly, enjoying our interaction. I gestured toward the big boss with my chin. "Why drag her into it? You obviously got what you wanted."

"That was Suze's idea," Monica said. "Why shouldn't I make some quick and easy money? All the rest of you adaptors do."

"But how did you know Suze?"

Monica shrugged. "She came to my parents' restaurant one day. Introduced herself, and after my shift was over, we went for coffee. Let's just say I liked her ideas. I agreed to introduce her to Brian—she was looking for an in with your family—and she agreed my bank account could use some upholstering. I was damn sick of being a waitress."

"I don't understand—your parents are well-off. You went to college. You don't have to wait tables for a living."

"My parents suffer under the delusion that it's healthy to work for a living, and that restaurant owners should learn the business from the ground up. The restaurant was supposed to be my nest egg, since I didn't inherit the family talent and all, and apparently supporting oneself is good for the self-esteem." The last was said with enough disgust to let me know where she came down on the matter.

"Fine. I understand about the money—you're a greedy bitch." Her lips tightened in a gratifying manner. I hurried on. "I get that now. But why risk using an untested formula on yourself? Geez, you're stunning. If I had to be stuck with just one aura, I sure wouldn't mind yours."

"Why, thank you, Ciel. What a lovely compliment." Apparently it distracted her from the "greedy bitch" thing I'd let slip— gotta love a limited attention span. "But what good is a female aura, no matter how beautiful, if you're in love with a gay man?"

"What? James? You love my brother?" Holy crap. How had none of us ever realized? "But you could have any man. Why . . . ?"

"Why James? Oh, maybe because he's gorgeous and brilliant, and totally understands how it feels not to be the one thing you really want to be. He's always so nice to me. He *gets* me. How could I not love him?" Tears glistened in her eyes.

"God, Monica. I'm . . . sorry." And I really was, at least a little bit. It's hard for me not to identify with unrequited love. "But someday you'll meet the right—"

The tears dried at once, leaving her eyes hard-set with more of the crazy. "There *is* no one else for me. If James can't love this . . . this female *thing* that I am, then I'll be someone he *can* love." And slowly, the effort showing, she became Devon once more.

I looked at Thelma sharply. Her face had gone from phony warm to calculating. "See?" she said. "There's no reason we can't all benefit from some sort of arrangement." Holy shit. She was as loony as Monica. I had a bad feeling about this.

"Monica," I said carefully, "where's the real Devon? You had to pick up his aura somewhere—it's too good to be cardboard."

She puffed up, pleased with herself. "He won't be a problem. We gave him some money and sent him off to Hollywood to find fame and fortune. After I got his cell phone with all that handy information, naturally. That was Thelma's idea." She glanced at the older woman, making good use of Devon's fuck-me smile. "Of course, he won't make it all the way there. He's so pretty he'd probably become a huge celebrity, and wouldn't *that* be awkward. But don't worry, I'll be so much better for James than he ever was. Loyal. I'd never cheat on him with a woman the way Devon did."

Okay, this was really freaking me out. The car was moving too fast for the moment, but next stoplight . . .

Thelma casually pulled a small gun from her understated Coach bag and laid it on her lap, leaving her hand wrapped loosely around the grip. What was she, a mind reader? Better keep talking to Monica.

"How do you know Devon cheated on James?" I asked.

"Who do you think was the woman he cheated with?" she said, her Devon voice laced with pride.

"Geez, Monica, and that makes you better than Devon how, exactly?" I blurted.

"Don't be silly," she explained patiently. "I didn't *want* to cheat. I only did it to show James that Devon couldn't be trusted. Too bad that didn't seem to matter—he'd still rather have Devon. But James never blamed me. Our friendship meant more to him than that."

"Meant?"

"Well, yes. Because I'm dead now, don't you see? You should—you found my body. If I'm going to be Devon from now on, I couldn't very well keep up with being *her,* could I? It's hard enough to keep track of one life."

Um, yeah. Back in Crazy Town. I almost told her that James knew she wasn't really dead—that he was onto the whole fake-her-own-death thing—but then I thought better of it. Hell, the woman had just shot me. No telling what she'd try if she thought her plans weren't going to work out.

"Wow. You know what, Monica? That's really kind of brilliant. I'm glad my brother is going to be with someone who obviously loves him so much." Yeah, I know. It didn't sound sincere to me, either. But I had to try.

Oddly, Monica swallowed it whole. Thelma, on the other hand, wasn't buying it. "You'll see it's the best thing for all concerned, Ciel," she said. "Besides, you'd like working with your new lover, wouldn't you?"

That made me sit up straight. *Ouch.* Stupid gunshot wound. "You have Billy?"

"Not precisely. But I'm quite sure he'll be happy to work for me, after the police finish investigating Monica's disappearance."

"Billy didn't kill anyone. You can't blackmail him with that."

"Well, no, he didn't. But you weren't the only one to see him in an intimate embrace with Monica—several party guests did, too."

"His clothes—you sent that guy Billy's clothes. How'd you get them?" I asked.

"Oh, that was easy," Monica said. "I just grabbed them when I was picking up Molly to take her to James's lab for our little field trip. A big handbag, a quick trip to the 'bathroom' upstairs while Mo was busy with Molly, and voilà! The authentic touch."

Thelma nodded. "And now traces of poor, missing Monica's blood are all over your parents' grotto—"

"How? She wasn't really shot, or stabbed, or whatever you set up," I said.

"Drawn ahead of time, and spread by Monica when no one was looking. And it's so difficult to remove blood entirely, you know. Also, I'm afraid you were witnessed violently attacking your lover's car. We have pictures. Susan Hatcher is handy with a telephoto lens."

So Suze *had* been there. All of a sudden I was freezing. *Great. Fucking fantastic.* "What makes you think Billy is my lover?"

"Please. After what you did to his car? Such a temper you have!" Thelma chided. "The little something Susan added to your Manhattan might have loosened your inhibitions, but there had to be a basis for it to work with. It won't be difficult for the police to put two and two together, and convict you of Monica's murder."

"You *drugged* me?" I was outraged, of course, but part of me was kind of relieved that what I did to Billy's car wasn't my fault. "How?"

"Quite easily. Susan had some doctored cherries with her, and slipped them into your glass while you were distracted. You always order Manhattans, don't you, dear? We'll have to teach you not to be quite so predictable."

"But there's no body," I said, ignoring the implication that I'd be working for her. I was pretty sure you had to have a body to make a murder conviction stick.

"No, but there are pictures of a body, which can easily be sent to the police by an 'anonymous' source. Those, coupled with the blood evidence, and the proof of your violent temper . . . Well, it could get very messy for you indeed. Unless, of course, Billy decides to cooperate."

"How could you know about Billy and me ahead of time—that the drug would make me bash up the Chevy?" I swallowed hard, still feeling somewhat guilty in spite of the extenuating circumstances. Mom's saying kept creeping into the back of my head. *God punishes . . . Damn.* I knew the thing with Billy's car would come back and bite me on the ass somehow. I'd just thought it would be Billy doing the biting.

"Oh, we didn't," Thelma said pleasantly. "That was just a fortunate turn of events. Before we knew you and Billy were involved—you really should be more discreet about kissing in doorways, my dear; you never know who might be watching—we'd been planning to set up Billy for Monica's murder. A lover's quarrel gone bad, that sort of thing. We thought we were very clever, killing two birds with one stone—making Monica disappear, as she wanted, and getting leverage over Billy. But when this opportunity presented itself, we couldn't resist. This way we get you, too. You're like a bonus. The third bird, so to speak."

"Well, isn't that nice?" I said with just a trace of a Southern drawl. A former client had once told me any woman south of the Mason-Dixon Line knew that particular phrase, when delivered with the right amount of saccharine, meant "fuck you." Thelma's smile froze, so I guessed she had some confederates in her ancestry.

"It is for me," she said, shaking off my little zing. (It *had* been kind of pathetic.) "Don't you worry, dear. You're going to love working for me. I understand you at one time planned your own career with our agency and were sidetracked by Mark?"

Where the fuck was she getting her information?

She answered my unspoken question. "Yes, I've been following your life for some time. Your whole family, in fact. Once I learned about Mark, his connection to you made you all quite interesting."

"Peachy," I said.

"Look at it this way—now you'll be able to fulfill your dream. And Billy . . . well, he practically works for us as it is. It won't be that big a change for him, other than reporting to me instead of Mark."

"But why do you need us at all? Monica got you the fucking formula. Why not just make your own adaptors out of some gung-ho Agency sheep?"

"You know the answer to that. It won't work on just anyone, will it? You have to have a latent adaptor gene, and that's a rare thing. Besides"—she glanced warily at Monica—"who knows what side effects might emerge. It will require further study."

"Hey, Monica . . . or Devon—whoever the fuck you want to be—how does it feel to be Thelma's guinea pig?" I said. Why should I be the only uncomfortable person in the car?

The Devon aura wavered, the violet eyes shifting to deep, dark brown. "I don't mind a bit—I'd do anything for James."

"Never mind that, Ciel," Thelma said, sounding peeved. "That's between Monica and myself. Just as the agreement I come to with Billy is between me and him. I'm sure he'll jump at the opportunity to keep his sister safe."

I leaned toward her. "If you hurt Molly in any way, I'll—"

She lifted the gun from her lap. I edged back.

"Calm down, my dear. You'll jostle your wound. I have no intention of harming that wonderful child. We'll study her, of course. Her . . . fluke, shall we say? . . . is fascinating. I'm sure Billy will be happy to convince his parents of the wisdom of sending her to a special school I have in mind for her."

"Lady, you are so far off base you're not even in the ballpark," I said, shaking my head slowly. "Billy will *never* do that."

"Hey, why are we at the hospital?" Monica-Devon said.

Shit. I looked up. Something told me I wasn't going to like helicopters any more than I liked planes.

Chapter 29

"How very considerate of you, Thelma," I said after the Hulk helped first her, then me, out of the car. Guess Monica in Devon form didn't rate gentlemanly treatment. "I really should have this arm looked at. Wouldn't want to risk an infection."

Thelma's smile was gone. "If you're wise you'll come along quietly, Ciel. Remember, I know where your family lives. Your kind are good at fading into society and leaving your problems behind, but one text from me could have someone at your parents' house before they have a chance to get away."

"Geez, you are one cold bitch, aren't you?"

"Not really. I have a Company doctor waiting for you on the helicopter. He'll give you something for the pain. Morphine, maybe. Perhaps I should have him come down here and administer it before we walk through the hospital. Will that be necessary, Ciel?"

Shit. "No need for that, Thel. I'm not going to say or do anything that will put my family at risk."

"I knew you were a smart one. We're going to work together very well."

The elevator ride was tons of fun, sandwiched between Monica-Devon and the Hulk, with the cardigan from Thelma's beige twinset draped over my shoulders to hide the bloody strip of T-shirt, and her gun, hidden under an artfully draped scarf, jabbing my waist. If this was karma for Billy's car, payback was an unfair bitch.

Monica was starting to sweat, the Devon aura wobbling more. *Crap,* I thought, suddenly hit with a new worry. What if Molly was having the same problem? What if she was still up the tree when she lost her orangutan climbing abilities? *Shit, shit, shit.* What had I done?

The helicopter was landing as we got there. My, how synchronized of everyone. Wasn't that just peachy? Thelma gave me a shove in its direction but stopped abruptly when Harvey stepped out of it. He signaled to the pilot, who shut down the engine, leaving us in relative quiet.

"Intercepting my communications, Harvey? Tsk, tsk. And here I thought we trusted each other," Thelma said. She didn't sound particularly worried, which kind of worried *me.*

Harvey tilted his head and lifted one shoulder in a half shrug. "You know what they say. Trust but verify." He paused, his eyes surprisingly sympathetic. "It's not going to work, Thelma."

She set her shoulders back. "It already has. Give it up, Harvey. You have Fielding, and now I have my own 'special' agents. Let's just try to work together on this and keep the collateral damage to a minimum."

"Can't do that, Thelma. You know I gave my word—and, by

extension, the Company's—to Mark. We're not going back on that. None of us."

"Well, aren't you the king of ethics all of a sudden? Ironic, considering how you've kept Fielding dancing at the end of your string with this asinine promise to leave the rest of them alone. If that's not subtle blackmail, I don't know what is."

Harvey shook his head sadly. "You still don't get it, do you? Mark approached *me*. It was his idea. After I made a ham-fisted attempt to recruit his best friend—and failed—I almost lost Mark. I never made that mistake again."

"Label it what you will. I never agreed to let you speak for me—*I* made no promises. Now, if you'll excuse us, the pilot is waiting."

"You can go, Thelma—in fact, I insist you do—but the others are staying with me," Harvey said. For the first time I noticed two men in black suits in the back of the helicopter. They were watching us all closely. I was beginning to suspect they might be Harvey's, not Thelma's.

Looked like the same thought occurred to Thelma. "This is *my* operation, Harvey. Stay out of it, or you might find yourself taking early retirement. I still have some pull with your boss, you know."

I snorted. That was her threat? Early retirement? Ooooh, scary!

She jabbed me in the ribs with the muzzle of her gun. Okay, *that* was scary. I couldn't even tell if Harvey knew she was armed—the small gun was still covered with the scarf, and the stylish handbag hooked over her wrist was an excellent excuse to hold her arm at that angle. He might not think anything of it.

His eyes were still full of pity. Only now he seemed to be enjoying it. "Nah, I think I'll be staying around for a while longer.

Not quite ready to give up the game yet. You, on the other hand, might want to consider bowing out while your pension is still intact."

Thelma's turn to laugh. "Now, why would I worry about my pension when I'm just doing my job, recruiting valuable assets? Ask any of them—they're with me every bit as voluntarily as Mark is with you."

"Oh, I don't know about that." He signaled the Hulk, who pulled a small device out of his pocket and pushed a button. The words were a little muffled, but recognizably Thelma's.

". . . we'd been planning to set up Billy for Monica's murder. A lover's quarrel gone bad, that sort of thing. We thought we were very clever, killing two birds with one stone—making Monica disappear, as she wanted, and getting leverage over Billy. But when this opportunity presented itself, we couldn't resist. This way we get you, too. You're like a bonus. The third bird, so to speak."

"That doesn't sound voluntary to me. Be a shame if it made the press. The Company really doesn't much care for that kind of PR," Harvey said, his easygoing delivery belied by the hardness of his eyes.

Thelma was staring at the Hulk, uncomprehending at first, then furious. "You disloyal piece of shit. I *made* you."

"Aw, don't be too mad at your driver, Thelma. I'm sure he's just as loyal to you as ever. Wherever he is," Harvey said as the Hulk's stony face was replaced by Billy's charming countenance.

"You," Thelma said at the time that I said, "Billy!" I'm guessing I sounded much happier than she did.

"The original," Billy said, flashing his dimples. "Accept no substitutes."

I wanted to run to him so badly, but there was still the small problem of the gun muzzle in my ribs. Having already been shot once that evening (which still hurt like seven levels of hell in spite of my elation at Billy's unexpected appearance), I had no wish for an encore.

Monica, more and more of her own brand of exotic beauty showing through, started inching back toward the door. Billy blocked her, pulling out the gun he'd taken from her after she'd shot me. Deflated, she dropped the rest of the Devon aura and seemed to shrink in on herself. I had a feeling there was lots of therapy in her future.

"Ciel, why don't you come over here to me," Harvey said in that sweet, avuncular way he had. Honestly, I could see why Laura liked him so much. I wanted to hug him myself.

"I don't think so," Thelma said, and pulled the scarf from her gun, making it plain she still had me covered. I shrugged and smiled weakly at Harvey.

"Thelma, don't be ridiculous," Harvey said, not quite as relaxed now. "You can't win this. It's over."

"Maybe I can't win, Harvey, but I can sure as hell make you lose." She lifted the gun, bringing it level with my temple.

Without a nanosecond's pause, Harvey said loudly, "Take it."

It sounded like a couple of monster mosquitoes whizzing by my ear, one immediately after the other. I felt Thelma stiffen, then drop. When I looked down, I saw two small holes had appeared on her forehead.

Okay, I admit it. I passed out again.

I was in Billy's arms when I came to, only this time it was better because I knew it was him. We were on the ground, right where

I'd fallen, so I guessed I couldn't have been out for long. He smiled down at me, his eyes full of concern. "Twice in one night, cuz. You gonna make a habit of this? Do I need to start carrying smelling salts?"

"Give me a break," I said wryly. "Let me shoot you, and we'll see how long you stay conscious."

Harvey swam into my field of vision, lowering his large frame next to us with an amazing amount of grace. "Let's get her downstairs to the ER," he said. Behind him, one of the men in suits from the helicopter held on to Monica and the other squatted next to Thelma's body, carefully removing the gun from her grip with a gloved hand.

"Hey, wait," I said, my head clearing somewhat. "Molly's still out there—she was up a tree by the Dairy. And she's"—I glanced at Harvey, unsure how much he was privy to about Molly's "fluke," as Thelma had so eloquently put it—"um, you know, not really herself. *Upset,* as you can imagine." Not to mention orange and hairy.

Harvey chuckled, his chins wobbling. "Nice, Ciel. Very subtle. Can't imagine why Mark didn't think you were cut out for the life." He patted my hot cheek. "Don't worry about Molly. She's at a police station, waiting for her 'daddy,' Mark, to come get her. She found a cop after she climbed down from the tree. Told him she was a runaway having second thoughts."

Whew! That meant she was able to drop the orangutan aura without any problems this time. Even better, she was smart enough to call Mark instead of her parents, so now maybe I had a shot at seeing my next birthday. Because if Auntie Mo ever found out what happened tonight—how I'd dragged Molly with me away from the safe house where Mark had stashed us—she would skin me alive. Or, you know, give me a *talk*, which would be worse.

Of course, I still had to answer to Mark, which wasn't going to be any picnic.

Billy stood, lifting me with him. "Hey," I said, preferring not to think about any upcoming conversations with the spook, "don't let them stick me, okay? You know I don't do needles."

"Sorry. Can't make any promises."

"All right," I said, feeling woozy already, just in anticipation of getting jabbed. "But you better be there when I go down for the third time."

"Always, sweetheart. Always."

Chapter 30

Laura and I lounged in low lawn chairs, watching the guys—Billy, Thomas, Brian, and James—play Nerf football with Molly on the wide expanse of grass in the Sheep Meadow area of Central Park. I probably would have been fine joining in—my arm wasn't that sore anymore—but Laura was still recovering and I wanted to keep her company. She'd made it through the Children's Zoo earlier with no difficulty, but she still tired easily.

It had been Molly's idea to come back to Central Park. She said she wanted to "reclaim" it as a fun spot. She was one brave little girl, and I was proud to be her honorary relation.

It was a parent-free picnic (trust me, none of the parents in question were complaining) because that's what Molly wanted. The other Doyle sisters were off at college, dreaming up their own ways to make Billy's life as a big brother miserable. I kind of enjoyed that. (What? Relationships can't turn on a dime, you know.)

I'd been more than a little nervous about our foray into the petting section of the zoo, though James had assured us Molly was totally un-juiced now. Besides, he was almost a hundred percent certain she'd been able to project the orangutan aura only because its primate genome was so similar to a human being's. As long as Molly stayed away from apes, she should be fine.

Still, most of us held our breath the first time she reached out and touched a goat. When she pulled her hand back without sprouting horns or a goatee, we all let out a collective sigh of relief.

She hadn't shown any more signs of precocious adaptor-hood, which kind of disappointed her, but, as she philosophically pointed out, at least it delayed her stint in isolation.

Laura and I had been having a great time getting to know each other better as we convalesced together. We'd spent a few weeks up at my lakeside client hideaway, letting Hilda, my faithful doer of everything, fuss over us while we healed. She loved it and so did we. My injury wasn't nearly as bad as Laura's, but I was not above milking it for as many of Hilda's special desserts as I could get.

Thomas spent a lot of time there with us, too. Wouldn't surprise me if there were wedding bells in his and Laura's future. I sure hoped so, anyway. Not only would I gain a sister, but I'd lose a nanny. Win-win.

Brian, as near as any of us could tell, hadn't replaced Suze with a new girlfriend yet, so I thought maybe he was maturing. Turned out Suze wasn't really *all* bad, merely unduly influenced by Thelma. When she'd found out Thelma had given the go-ahead to use deadly force in the "recovery" of orangutan-Molly, resulting in fellow agent Laura getting shot, Suze had come around and filled Harvey in on Thelma's plans. So she'd been reassigned overseas rather than arrested. Still, she *had* drugged me, so I can't say I didn't enjoy the idea of her freezing her ass off during those long winters in Moscow.

James had pleaded with Mark to find a place for Monica where she could get some much-needed treatment. He felt responsible for her slide over to the dark side, and still wanted to help her, in spite of her trying to have his former boyfriend offed.

Devon had been located, unharmed. He'd actually never even set out for Hollywood—turned out he really was in love with James. Guess he'd been honest with me during our little heart-to-heart after he walked in on Billy and me. James was continuing to be cautious with him but seemed happier lately, so I had hopes that things might yet work out between them.

Mark was off on yet another assignment—God knew where—which was too bad, because I did love watching that man play football. Especially when it was warm enough for him to take off his shirt. (What? Sure, Billy and I were officially an item now, but that didn't mean I'd gone blind.)

Once the doctors were done patching me up, and Mark knew I was going to be all right, he'd lit into me, hitting me with the steel-hard eyes and letting me know exactly how dumb it had been not to call him immediately after I'd gotten the call from the fake Billy. I'd taken it meekly (because, yeah, he had a point), even though "meek" goes against my grain under any circumstances. As soon as I'd said the magic words ("you're right"), he'd dropped the steel, donned the dove, and gathered me close in a careful hug.

"Jesus, Ciel, you have to stop doing this to me," he'd whispered, his words squeezing my heart. I wasn't sure if he meant scaring him, or possibly something else. Honestly? I was afraid to ask.

Laura handed me another can of iced tea. "He loves you, you know," she said.

Startled, I almost dropped the can. Had she been reading my thoughts? "What? Who . . . ?" I said.

"Billy," she said. "Oh, Mark does, too, of course, but he's married to his job. Clichéd, but true."

I felt my cheeks redden. That didn't stop her from continuing. "But Billy—you can see it erupt from his eyes when he looks at you. That's special, Ciel." She was looking at Thomas as she said that last part, and added, in her soft Southern drawl, "Don't fuck it up, sugar."

Good advice, I figured, from one who knew whereof she spoke.

Billy had, of course, forgiven me for bashing up his car even before he knew I'd been drugged—which spoke volumes about how much he cared for me—but I felt better about our chances for a successful relationship now that we both knew I wasn't batshit crazy.

The game was winding down. After one last throw to Molly, they all trooped over to the blankets spread out in front of us, Thomas sitting beside Laura and Billy dropping down next to me. Everyone grabbed a drink, and all the guys wiped the sweat from their faces with their shirts. I handed Molly a napkin before she followed suit. Somebody had to be a good role model for her.

"What did you guys pack for us to eat?" Billy asked, digging into one of the picnic baskets Laura and I had provided for the whole gang. "I'm starving." The rest of the guys joined in, each claiming to be more ravenous than the next, sending Molly into fits of giggles with their hyperbole.

When Billy got to the fresh, late-season raspberries he must have added when I wasn't watching, he gave me a knowing look, the devil peeking out from behind those lush lashes as he opened the bag.

But I was ready for him. From the basket closest to me, I pulled out a big jar of kosher dills—slowly—giving him my sweetest smile. And then I licked my lips.

He started throwing raspberries at me, a huge grin on his face.

"Hey, don't waste those—I want some!" Thomas said, which of course sent me into gales of laughter as I tried hard not to look at Laura's chest.

"You should definitely try some," Billy said, tossing a few his way. "I highly recommend them."

"Food fight!" Molly yelled, ripping open a bag of chips and flinging them randomly at everyone.

The lid of the pickle jar was stuck, so I shoved it at Brian while dodging more flying berries. "Here—open this. Fast!" He gave it a quick twist and handed it back to me. I dug in, and held one high. "Aha! I gotcha now," I cried, pointing it at Billy.

"What?" James said, looking perplexed. "Pickles trump berries?"

Billy raised a brow, winking at me before answering him. "Well, I suppose you might think so."

I was laughing so much I could barely catch my breath. "Stuhhhhop. Please. Just stop." I sat hard on the blanket, then fell over backward. Damn, it felt great to let loose. Laughing that hard is almost as good as sex, with the added benefit that you usually won't get arrested for doing it in public.

Billy plopped down beside me, leaned over, and kissed me lightly. Thomas didn't even flinch—another benefit of his relationship with Laura. When I'd finally told him about Billy and me, all he'd done was take Billy aside and explain seventeen different ways he could legally kill him if he ever hurt me.

Molly looked on in glee. "Mom and Auntie Ro are going to be so excited when they find out about you guys!"

I shuddered. God, I was *so* not ready to have my new relationship exposed to *that* double whammy of maternal scrutiny. I liked things just fine the way they were. "Mol-ly . . . remember your promise. Billy and I get to decide when to tell them, nobody else." I included the rest of them in my stern look.

"I have no problem with that," Thomas said, taking Laura's hand.

"Ha! Of course you don't. You still haven't told them about Laura yet, you big chicken," I said. (I know. But it's okay—my brothers are used to my hypocrisy. I'm sure they think of it as a charming quirk.)

"It's purely out of concern for Laura. I think she should be stronger before she's subjected to more of my relatives. Why, one of Mom's casseroles alone could set her recovery back by weeks."

"And if Mommo felt compelled to crochet her an afghan . . ." Billy started, and the rest of us finished with a groan.

"Hey," Laura said, verbally elbowing her way into the conversation, "I happen to adore your mother's afghans. Ciel told me one of them saved my life."

We all sobered at the memory of how close we came to losing her.

Thomas kissed her hand. "For that reason alone they'll be forever beautiful to me."

Brian sprang to his feet. "Later, gators. I'm outta here." He took off at a jog.

"Wait a minute," I hollered after him. "Where are you going?"

"To find a girl!"

I smiled. "Heeee's baaack."

* * *

We ran all the way up the stairs to Billy's place, in a hurry to further explore raspberry and pickle possibilities now that we were alone. Thomas had whisked Laura off to the hotel that was her temporary residence until she was able to return to work. (*If* she returned to work. Thomas could be persuasive. And persistent. On the other hand, Laura had that *Steel Magnolias* backbone. I'd have to give them even odds.)

James had promised Molly a carousel ride after lunch, and would drop her off at home afterward. Billy and I were still chortling about our narrow escape from the park—if James had forgotten about Molly's propensity for motion sickness, he would likely be reminded of it soon. Really, you'd think such a brilliant man would have a better memory.

Billy took the last few steps backward, hauling me up with him. At the top, he swung me around and set me on the floor in front of him. Smiling, I tilted my face up for a kiss—I couldn't get enough of his kisses—and was knocked out of the moment by the look on his face.

I turned to see what could stop Billy in his tracks like that, expecting, at the least, obscene graffiti spray painted on his door. Or maybe more crime-scene tape. Possibly another body.

Turned out to be worse.

"Sweethearts!" Mom said at the same time that Auntie Mo sang out "Darlings!"

They reached down and lifted a giant basket between them. "We brought champagne and caviar," Auntie Mo said. "Let's celebrate!"

I threw a panicked look at Billy. The shock in his eyes was retreating, replaced by rapidly advancing amusement.

"Who's the rat?" he said, a lot more calmly than I felt. "Wait, let me guess. Molly?"

Auntie Mo shrugged.

"How'd you get her to spill?" he asked. I couldn't seem to find my voice.

"I'm her mother. I asked. She answered."

Billy raised one eyebrow and quirked his mouth, wordlessly expressing his skepticism.

Auntie Mo's eyes crinkled at the edges in a gotcha smile she didn't allow to reach her lips. "I ungrounded her. And bought her a Wii."

Mom smiled brightly. "And *I* gave her something called 'Rock Band'—don't look at me like that, Mo. It was for a good cause."

"Yes, but did you really have to include the drum set with it?"

Okay, chalk one up for maternal ingenuity. Molly could hardly be expected to hold out against bribery like that. And it *was* impressive how well she'd kept her lapse contained during our picnic. Still, I was going to have a little talk with her about generational loyalty. I mean, she hadn't even given us the opportunity to outbid them.

"Never mind that," Mom said, her eyes alight. "Now, let's go in and *plan*."

Auntie Mo nodded, a matching determined gleam in her own eyes.

Oh, God. Oh, no. No, no, no . . . I definitely wasn't ready for this. I snaked my hand into the front pocket of Billy's jeans and grabbed his keys. Turned and raced back down the stairs, Billy hot on my heels.

"Ciel Colleen Halligan, you march yourself right back here!" my mother yelled down the stairwell.

"That goes for you, too, William Seamus Declan Doyle!" Auntie Mo hollered. Huh. Both middle names—she meant business.

Billy grinned when he caught up with me just outside the building. Grabbed my hand, and said, "Come on. I know a place they'll never find us."

I smiled back, grateful he understood. Maybe I really could fall in love with this guy.

Acknowledgments

This is where I get to blame everyone I interacted with while writing this book for anything that's wrong with it, right?

Wait, that's probably not nice. Downright rude, really, and definitely not fair. I mean, most of them had no idea I was using them as research material, so they can hardly be held responsible for what I pilfered from their existence and threw into my book.

By the way, if you think you—yes, I mean *you*—recognize yourself in this book, you're wrong. Wrong, wrong, wrong. That's *not* you. (Okay, maybe *parts* of it are you—only the good parts, I swear!—but it's all mixed up with a lot of parts from other people, too. It's like . . . *Franken*-you! And no, I won't say which one of you is the ass.)

Well, *that* was an awkward start. Maybe I'd better begin again.

Ahem. I'd like to thank my brothers for providing insight into sibling relationships, as well as years of practical experience in that arena. If Ciel's interactions with her brothers come across as authentic, it's because I know brothers.

(Not that my brothers are anything like Ciel's, let me hasten to add. While it's possible that *some* of my brothers have a *few* of the characteristics of her brothers, those characteristics are all shuffled up and in no way reflect any one real person. Well, except the "good-looking" part, of course. That applies to all my brothers. But, as far as I know, none of them are adaptors.)

I'd also like to thank the rest of my family, blood relatives and in-laws, for their support of my writing, and for being all-around good people. Plus, they don't expect me to cook much. I like that about them.

My critique partners and beta readers deserve way more than a mere mention in the acknowledgments, both for their genuinely helpful feedback and for putting up with my writing-related neuroticism. But for what it's worth, here goes: Susan Adrian, Tawna Fenske, Emily Hainsworth, Julie Kentner, Kris Reekie, Elise Skidmore, and Tiffany Schmidt, you guys rock!

A big thank-you goes to my editor, Melissa Frain, for her special brand of magic. She has a knack for recognizing what a manuscript needs most and conveying it intelligently. A good editor's contributions are largely invisible to the reading public (or should be), yet so very indispensable.

To Michelle Wolfson, agent extraordinaire and leader of the howlingly fun Wolf Pack, I give my continued gratitude . . . and my apologies for those e-mails that started with "Ack!" Thanks for keeping me sane throughout this whole crazy publishing process.

Finally, to my husband, Bob, I give my unending love. Couldn't do it without you, sweet cheeks.